Also by Victoria Wilder

The Bourbon Boys
Bourbon & Lies
Bourbon & Secrets
Bourbon & Proof

BOURBON & SECRETS

VICTORIA WILDER

Bloom *books*

Copyright © 2024, 2026 by Victoria Wilder
Cover and internal design © 2024, 2026 by Sourcebooks
Cover design © Echo Grayce at Wildheart Graphics
Cover art © Whiskey Ginger Studios

Sourcebooks, Bloom Books, and the colophon are
registered trademarks of Sourcebooks.

All rights reserved. No part of this book may be reproduced in any form or by
any electronic or mechanical means including information storage and retrieval
systems—except in the case of brief quotations embodied in critical articles
or reviews—without permission in writing from its publisher, Sourcebooks.

No part of this book may be used or reproduced in any manner for the
purpose of training artificial intelligence technologies or systems.

The characters and events portrayed in this book are fictitious
or are used fictitiously. Any similarity to real persons, living or
dead, is purely coincidental and not intended by the author.

All brand names and product names used in this book are trademarks,
registered trademarks, or trade names of their respective holders.
Sourcebooks is not associated with any product or vendor in this book.

Published by Bloom Books, an imprint of Sourcebooks
1935 Brookdale RD, Naperville, IL 60563-2773
(630) 961-3900
sourcebooks.com

Originally self-published in 2024 by Victoria Wilder.

Cataloging-in-Publication data is on file with the Library of Congress.

Printed and bound in the United States of America.
LSC 10 9 8 7 6 5 4 3 2 1

To discovering that you're allowed to fall in love as many times as possible in your lifetime. Whether it's with a new lover or an old friend. Whether it's with the same person, but new versions of each other as you grow. Fucking fall. Do it loudly. Do it at your own pace. Rush. Ease in. Enjoy an instant lust, a slow burn, or a happy for now. Rebound. Fall again. And if you're craving a little something extra…

Lincoln Foxx has a few creative suggestions during your discovery. They may include some bourbon…

A note about *Bourbon & Secrets*

While this story is a work of fiction, there are some heavy subject matters that you should be aware of before diving in.

The following is a list of potential triggers that are not meant to be spoilers or tropes, but rather a warning of what's inside if you need it:

Violence and death on page, descriptive gore, violence toward women, discussion of deceased parents and family, scenes inside of a hospital, discussion of animal death and cruelty (not on page), main characters dealing with PTSD, vulgar language, spit-play, and multiple descriptive open-door sex scenes.

Playlist

The Rules of Bourbon

Every bourbon is whiskey, but not every whiskey is bourbon. There are rules for bourbon to be called bourbon.
1. It must be made in the United States
2. The mash must be at least 51% corn
3. It must be aged for at least two years in a new, charred, oak barrel
4. The whiskey cannot enter the barrel higher than 125 proof
5. Nothing can be added but water, and only to lessen the proof when necessary

In Fiasco, Kentucky, there's one more rule that loosely relates to the bourbon that's made there: **Never fall for a Foxx brother.**

Chapter 1

Lincoln

I had gotten it all wrong.

I slam on my brakes so hard that mud flares up and bathes the side of my best friend's bright-purple muscle car. Throwing the truck into park, I lean back in my seat, still fuming. Pain radiates through my hand and up my forearm on the fifth or sixth time I smack my palm against the steering wheel.

"Fuck, fuck, fuck!"

Sucking in air through my nose, I fill my chest, holding it for a three-count. Adrenaline courses through my veins with the need to get as far away as I can. I zone out, staring at the flat landscape and the paddocks peppered with horses running around in the last of the day's light. Fleetwood Mac keeps echoing the same words over and over about listening to the wind and not loving someone now. *The fucking irony.* As I squeeze my fist, the sting of my busted, bloody knuckles makes me wince. My elbow aches, probably bruised from the repeated strikes.

She tipped her chin up, and with watery eyes, delivered the final blow. "This is broken. We're broken, Lincoln," she gritted out.

Before she could say another word, I stormed out the side door. All I could think was now I was exactly that. Broken. I'd never felt more damaged and fucking broken. My fist hit the side of my truck with a heavy groan. On the second punch, I left a dent. On the third, my knuckles burned, and then I followed it up with an elbow like it was a heavy bag and not metal. The girls were already asleep inside and upstairs, thank god.

I didn't have a game plan. I wasn't prepared for this. "Fuck!"

I shut off the truck and slam the door behind me, ignoring the dent along the side panel. I'm not doing well with emotions right now. I can't go back.

The pungent smell of horse stalls being raked permeates the air. Mixed with the thickness of today's humidity, it overpowers the usual sweetness of a Fiasco summer. This late in the evening, the only folks still at the racetrack and in the stables are trainers and owners. I look around for the dark curls piled high, and sure enough, I see my best friend's hands moving enthusiastically as she's telling a story at the far end of the stables. "Hads!" I call out.

She whips around and greets me with her typical welcoming smile. "Linc, what are you doing here?"

But her smile quickly fades as I get closer. She can read me better than most people. Even better than Olivia sometimes. Her eyes cut to my fists balled up at my sides. I clear my throat. "I need a minute."

She doesn't ask anything in follow-up. She simply watches me as I say it, turning over internal questions and trying to figure out what's wrong. "I need a minute" acts as a code. A few simple words that tell the other something is off and we need a place to sort it out. Friendship for us meant making the other laugh when nothing was funny, celebrating the small moments, and knowing when the other required space more than words of wisdom.

Hadley may have started as Olivia's friend, but for some reason, she and I ended up closer. She'd hung around our home since she was in middle school, like the long-lost sister nobody wanted. So that's what she was now—my best friend who felt more like a sister.

"Lady Brittany Christina Pink is still saddled. You can take her." She nods behind me at the stall with one of her newest horses.

Its lighter brown mane and tail make her a helluva good-looking animal. "I'm not calling a horse that," I tell her as I admire the dark horse for a moment. She'll ride fast, which is perfect. I need something that isn't bourbon or fighting.

Hadley flips me off. "She's the ultimate trifecta. That'll make her a Triple Crown winner. I can feel it." She digs her pointer finger into my chest with a poke. "You will call her by her goddess-given name."

I crack a smile. "You're ridiculous, you know that, right?"

"And yet, here you are, calling me your bestie and asking for my help."

I pull at the horse's saddle. "I don't call you that."

Rolling her eyes, she waves me off. "Doesn't make it any less true." She checks the billet straps and runs her hands along the side of the horse's neck. "She's fast." She squeezes my forearm. "Ride smart. Let me get you a bag."

"Thank you," I say as I run my hands through my hair. I look back toward the few guys she had been talking with. "Hads, you okay here with these guys?"

Head tilted, she tosses a glance over her shoulder. "Oh please, they're more scared of me than my father. So, yeah, I'm good." She gives me a reassuring smile. "Take this." She tosses me her bright-yellow backpack. "You need a cover story? Or have I not seen you?"

I hoist the bag onto my shoulder and step toward Lady. "Never saw me."

She grabs my forearm again, only this time she pulls me into a hug. After giving me a good squeeze, she lets go, and her eyes meet mine. "Do I want to know?"

I give her a quick shake of my head, then get settled on the horse without another word. She doesn't want to know this. The truth is, I don't want to know it either. It's a secret. Another one. And at the end of the day, it feels like my fault.

As the warm wind whips across my face, I take notice of the sun dropping lower, finally meeting the horizon line on what's been a fuck of a day. I ride without stopping. The last of daylight reaches across the flat landscape of Kentucky's bluegrass. Not much of it is usually in this part of the state, but for the next two miles, it's tall and thick as it brushes against my boots propped in the stirrups. The humidity has lifted just enough as I ride, turning what was a sticky afternoon into the kind of evening where I can finally breathe.

I could have easily gone to my brother's place and taken one of the horses from the stables since my family owns and boards plenty. But then I would need to explain what I was doing there. Grant would have asked if I was okay, even if he's barely surviving himself. My baby brother is a shell of who he used to be. Ace would have told me about something that needed to be handled. He plays the oldest brother role so well that he forgets sometimes how to be a friend. And Griz would have seen through the mask I would need to wear. My grandfather figures everything out as if he has the ability to tell the future. I don't want to deal with any of it. Not until I sort this out for myself.

There are plenty of hiking and horse trails that lead to the caves and hot springs in Fiasco, and at sunset, there will be plenty of people enjoying them, so I keep riding. I've been in enough fights in my life to know that a swift punch or kick to the stomach doesn't hurt the most, but it takes the most air from your lungs and leaves you remembering never to be in that position again. *How did I end up in this position at all?* With a tight chest, I grip the reins tighter and dig my heels in to move faster.

The air up here near the fall's caverns has a different smell. While Fiasco carries the scent of a never-ending bakery, up here, it's more like salt and moss. Something earthier that makes things seem raw and untouched.

Bringing the horse to a stop, I jump down and tie her to the old oak tree that looks like it's seen better days. With craggy bark manipulated and twisted in a way that doesn't seem natural, it looks charred, as if it had been struck by lightning and then was never the same. It's how I feel—*I'll never be the same.* The only thing I have control over is what I do next. Tilting my head back, I suck in a breath, my butt hitting the tall grass along the bank on an exhale. I cough out whatever is left and drape my arms over my bent knees.

People always say that marriage takes work—that it's just as hard to stay as it is to leave. And I've never been a quitter.

I feel sick. My hands are clammy as I rub my chest with a closed fist and hit it once, twice, and a third time before my eyes well up with tears. I haven't been a good husband. I know I'm a good dad, a great one some days. But a husband… I close my eyes tight. Dragging my hands through my hair, I keep my fingers braced along my neck. I suck in another deep breath, digging the heels of my hands into my eyes. "FUUUCK YOUUUU!" I yell into the night air, as loud and long as my breath allows.

Fuck it. I let my tears fall. Staring out at the clusters of lights that make up my small town below, I work to steady my breathing. It's the only place I've ever known as home. Where I grew up and where my daughters are growing too. As I gaze over the flat land, from the lavender fields to my family's distillery, I wait. I wait until my body relaxes from my anger, my tears dry on their own, and my mind becomes clearer. Clear enough to make a plan for what comes next—the conversations that'll have to happen, the small hearts I'll have to break. It feels like minutes, but the full moon hangs low and bathes the sky in a pink hue. It's the only indication that I've been here for hours. In the grand scheme of things, it's not long at all to decide that the life you had was going to be different tomorrow.

Before I get back on the horse, I send out a text.

LINCOLN:
I'll bring Lady to the stables in the morning.

HADLEY:
Lady Brittany Christina Pink is a thoroughbred. If anything happens to her, I will kick you in the dick.

Sighing, I run my hands along Lady's coarse mane. "How did I get here, girl?" The sniff she lets out is probably her way of saying, *Fuck if I know*. The static sounds from the falls in the distance, along with the deep bellowing of bullfrogs and the intermittent chirp of crickets, is my soundtrack. It's the part of Fiasco that calms me more than any family night or hours in a chemistry lab ever has. It's the one thing people never assume about me. I love it here. I have no desire to be anywhere else.

The only time you'll find Fiasco bustling at this hour is if there's a festival or party that promises bourbon and fireworks. But tonight, it's quiet, as it often is. I likely wouldn't run into anyone on the main road to my house, but I decide to skip downtown, cutting through the woods on horseback and through the cornfields that hug the length of my property. In the distance, I can see the outside light illuminating my back porch. And as I ride closer, I already know it'll stop feeling like home as soon as I cross the threshold.

The clattering of metal has me whipping my head to the left. There's no reason for anyone to be out here. The old barn straddling my property line and our neighbor's is on its last leg. One more tornado or hurricane and it'll come down easily. Hell, it might not even take that much. Along the far side of the dilapidated structure is the small brook where Lark likes to search for tadpoles. It's as secluded as it can get.

Squinting into the dark, I pull on Lady's reins to slow her down, spotting movement by the small stream of water.

"You literal motherfucker!" being shouted breaks the quiet. A woman who sounds more than frustrated and a lot pissed off. The follow-up of a "fuck you" in a lower tone is laced with venom and has me biting back my smile.

I swing my leg over the saddle, and my boots hit the soggy ground with a squelch. Swear words and splashes of water being thrown up her arms make it so she doesn't hear me approach.

The movement stops when I clear my throat. "Everything okay over there?" I call out from less than twenty feet away.

She's frozen in place with her back to me for what must be at least ten seconds of silence.

"You're trespassing on private property," I say as I move closer, trying to make sense of why someone would be out here at this time of night. My eyes have more than adjusted to the lack of light, especially with the size of tonight's moon. But it's when she stands and turns that I realize she's not trespassing at all.

Faye Calloway. The oldest daughter. Her family owns everything from the edge of the cornfield to the other side of their farmhouse. I'm the one trespassing.

"I'm pretty sure you're the one who doesn't belong here," she says with enough of a bite that there's no trace of neighborly camaraderie.

Pieces of her blond hair wildly escape the messy knot on top of her head, her face streaked with something dark. Makeup from crying? Or mud? As my gaze travels lower, I take in her soaked arms and tank top, dripping with water that tracks down her legs. She doesn't look like the buttoned-up police academy graduate that I saw on the local news just last week. There's no trace of that person before me. This version rubs her hands down the front of her shorts, pushes her chest out, and tilts her chin up. She's trying to hide the fact that I caught her off guard, and whatever she's doing, it doesn't include an audience.

Crossing my arms over my chest, I wait for her to say something.

But she stays quiet and watches as I move closer.

"What are you doing out here this late?" We may technically be neighbors, but I've only ever seen Faye randomly around town near holidays, or either coming or leaving town during summers and school breaks. We moved in next door shortly after she left for school. I didn't know her. But that doesn't matter. I know people. And something looks off. When she doesn't respond, I ask, "Are you hurt?"

Putting her hands on her hips, she tips her head back and looks at the sky as she laughs to herself. "Why? Are you in the habit of wandering around at night looking for women to rescue?"

Her mocking tone has me holding back a smile. "It wasn't on my to-do list tonight, so no." I blow out a breath as I swipe at my phone and flip on the flashlight, pointing it at her. I'm a bit surprised at what I see all over her, but it doesn't shake me like it would most people. "There's blood and mud all along your legs," I say matter-of-factly as I tip the light higher.

Her mouth purses as she tries to sort out how to explain exactly what's going on.

I move the light up and down pointedly. "You missed some blood along your neck." I tap my face to show her where. "And your cheek."

She raises her hand to block the light from her eyes. Crouching back down along the small stream, she wets her hands, rubbing away the red streaks.

My brother Grant was a cop not too long ago. He respects the rules and the people who make them, but I like to bend them when needed. Sometimes that makes things dirty and, other times, bloody. I don't care to judge anyone who might do the same, but this isn't someone I'd expect to find out in the dark, up to something clearly sketchy.

I lower the light, but I keep my focus on her. "I'm assuming this isn't part of your interview process for joining the Fiasco PD?"

She shifts with a wince. Her chin dips down, like the observation physically hurts to hear. The question is, is she in trouble? Or is she the source of it—covered in blood and mud along the edge of a cornfield?

"You going to ask how it got there? Or are you just planning on staring at me?" she asks as she shifts her weight and reaches for the hem of her shirt, smirking. I raise an eyebrow in challenge. She's going to try for a distraction, but I'm not interested in playing into whatever she's up to.

I sniff out a small laugh before I stupidly step closer. With just a few feet between us, my eyes wander down her legs toward her muddy pink Converse sneakers and up again. It's hard picturing her as a cop right now. "Nah. Don't really care," I say nonchalantly. I look down her body and then meet her glare. "And believe me, I'm not looking."

She shifts closer, her proximity raising goose bumps along my forearms. Despite the way she's trying really fucking hard to harden herself with her shoulders back, standing tall, and an air of false bravado, she worries her lip.

I blink away all the small things I'm noticing about a woman I barely know. I don't look at women—I'm not the kind of man to break a promise. *But what if that promise was already broken?* Stepping back, I hold up my left hand as I say, "Married."

"You sure about that?" she bites back.

A simple jab like that is enough to make me react. *No, I'm not sure about that.* I take only a few more steps before I'm in her space, crowding her.

A clipped yelp leaves her throat, not expecting me to move so quickly. But she doesn't pull back. In fact, she leans forward slightly, as if to welcome my anger. She's shorter than me, but she isn't dainty or fragile. She'd pack a punch if she knew how to throw one correctly.

But as I look down, I realize my mistake immediately. With us almost toe to toe, her arm brushes mine as she clears her throat. I shouldn't have gotten this close to her. There's enough light for me to focus on the small beauty mark that sits on the apple of her cheek. And to notice the way her eyes bounce between mine and then drop down to my mouth. *Fucking hell.* Anger and chaotic emotions have me looking at someone I'd never planned on seeing.

"Did I hit a nerve with that one?" she taunts in a quiet voice. *Too close.*

"Don't," I warn. Tonight's not the night to push me. "Go home."

Whatever she's gotten herself into, I don't need it anywhere near me. I need to get out of here. Away from her and this fucking shit show of a situation.

I turn my back to her, moving toward the horse.

"Your back pocket," she calls out. I stop in my tracks, turning just as she whips off her muddy tank top, leaving her in a sheer bra that, even in a dark field, leaves nothing to my imagination. I'm caught off guard, and like a fucking pervert, it feels impossible not to scan the curve of her body and the swell of her tits. I feel into the back pocket of my jeans and pull out the heavy metal piece, the size of my palm, rubbing my thumb along the grooves of it. I know it's a folded switchblade, but I ask anyway. "What's this?" Because it sure as fuck isn't mine.

What she does next happens too fast for me to prevent it. She drapes her tank in her hand like a glove and snatches back the knife. "If anyone comes asking, you never saw me." She raises her eyebrow, expecting me to agree.

I'm not in the mood for this shit. It's almost comical how quickly this night keeps getting worse. But I'm not laughing.

"Or what?" I clap back, very aware that I just put my fingerprints all over what I can only gather is a weapon that fucked someone up tonight. The question is, how much? Threat? Assault? Murder?

The knife was heavy when I held it. I should have felt her slip it into my pocket. I played right into her hand and just became her perfect alibi.

She takes a step back and away from me, but it's not far or fast enough.

Too bad for her, I've had too many years of wrestling with my brothers. That and relieving stress via sparring partners has honed my reflexes. It only takes a step and a half to reach her again and seconds to wrap my arms around her middle and yank her against my body. A gasp escapes her mouth as her chest collides with mine. A move I should have thought through first because, in a blink, I forget what I'm doing. The reason I'm out this late and why I'm pissed off at the way my life looks like something I no longer recognize. I stare down at this practical stranger pressed against me, and an exhale rushes out. Her chest heaves, moving as rapidly as mine.

"I don't do well with people threatening me," I say, voice low as I speak inches away from her face.

She leans in closer, staring at my mouth in a way that makes me hold my breath. In an instant, her lips are pressed to mine. I don't expect it. But I don't pull away; I part them for her. Her tongue brushes mine teasingly and she sways into me. For a fraction of a minute, I forget everything else as I kiss her back. All of it. Lost in the unpredictability, I allow everything that's wrong about this to roll closer and settle around us like fog.

The loud snap of thunder echoes in the distance, and like a starting bell, she pushes away and stumbles back, like she wasn't the one who made the move in the first place. Her fingers move to her lips, as if she'll find the marks that mine left.

Faye looks down at her right hand, still draped with her tank and clenched around the switchblade I stupidly held.

"You never saw me." Lightning illuminates the horizon in brief flashes. A warning. The storm isn't coming, it's here. Looming over us.

"You never saw me," she repeats. "And as long as that's your story, then this will never need to be found." She holds up the knife.

I shove down any attraction that may have crested. The anger that had been coursing through me surfaces as I step forward, reaching her quickly as I cuff my hand around her neck nice and tight. If she wants to play, then we're going to play. But now, it's by my rules.

She struggles to keep her confidence intact. I don't want to know the details of what she did before I showed up. I have no interest in guessing what she might have gone through to be in this position or if she's just some deranged level of sociopath. I care about one thing: my family. What's left of it, at least.

As she tries to move my fingers away from her neck, I squeeze tighter. Raindrops begin to fall as if to punctuate the moment.

"I don't want any of what you're involved in near *my* family." So I make a demand: "Leave town. And don't come back."

Her widening eyes search mine as she struggles to get her words out. "I can't just leave—"

Thunder rumbles above.

I grit my teeth and squeeze my fingers again, relishing the feel of her racing pulse. The proof that she's scared enough now to take me seriously.

"You can and you will. Or I will get every fucking cop I know in this town asking questions. My brother may have left Fiasco PD, but he was a K-9 unit. He and his dog still know how to find things, especially if they know where to look. Do you want them to start looking?"

A tear streaks down her cheek and gets lost in the rain that saturates us in the next moment. The severity of my threat plays out in her mind as I watch her eyebrows pinch.

"Let go, Foxx," she says with her jaw clenched, fingers pulling at mine to release her.

I glare down at her. "People assume I'm the nice one. The family man. But I'm very good at letting people believe what I want them to." I lean in and whisper, just loud enough to drown out the wind whipping through the rows of corn, bending the structure that barely stands behind us. "So believe me when I say this...I don't like to be fucked with. I don't want you or whatever you just did coming back around. So you will leave. And I will keep your secret. I never saw you. I don't know you, nor do I ever want to. Do I make myself clear?"

"Crystal," she growls back as she yanks out of my grip.

Watching her walk away, I drag my hands through my hair. I swallow down the lump rising in my throat as my mind snaps back to why I'd run away earlier. Sleep won't come easily, I already know that as the weight of reality settles on my shoulders. Rain pelts my face on the ride to my house. The overhang along the back of the house will keep the horse dry for now. As I tie her up, remove her saddle, and fill up the garden basin with fresh water, my mind keeps replaying everything that just happened. This day needs to end, and tomorrow I'll be thinking more clearly. I stare at the back door. Olivia and I can talk about what comes next in the morning. Shuffling up the stairs, I take a steadying breath.

My stomach twists when I notice the kitchen lights are still on. *Shit.* I don't want to see my wife.

But as I step over the threshold, it's the tangy and sour smell of Liv's wine and then a crunch under my boot from a shattered glass that have me pausing. Those are the last two things my mind registers before I see her legs splayed out on the wooden floor.

"Liv? Liv!" I shout as I race over to her slumped body, heart in my throat. With her wine spilled around her, I slip on it, and my knees hit the hardwood. She's not moving. I look around, as if something will tell me what the fuck is going on.

There's no blood. No sign of a weapon. No pills or bottles. Something made her fall.

I lift her shoulders up and pull her body into mine. "Livvy, c'mon." Her long limbs are limp and her head lulls to the right. Pushing wine-soaked strands of her hair away from her face, I speak shakily. "Livvy. C'mon, talk to me."

My face is wet, nose stuffed, so I can only breathe through my mouth as I call an ambulance. Tears blur my vision as I focus on her. Her eyes are open. They stare blankly, void of any recognition or movement. She's not blinking. She's not looking at me or hearing anything I'm saying to her. *She's so heavy right now.*

I suck in a breath, trying to fill my lungs with air so I can keep telling her to wake up. "Talk to me, Liv. Don't do this." Hands trembling, I look for a pulse. Dizzy with panic, I feel around her neck, but there's nothing. Not one beat to count. *This isn't happening.*

"Liv, c'mon. You can't leave them. We'll figure this out. You can't leave them…"

5 YEARS LATER...

Chapter 2

Faye

Pink is absolutely my color. Add in the shimmering lace, the black wig, exaggerated cat eyeliner, the deep-red lip, and I'm the fantasy. The distraction. A show. And I'm itching to put on a good one tonight. Everyone loves a glam, Gatsby-styled pinup girl this time of year. Tonight's audience is rowdier than usual, but it's expected for New Year's Eve burlesque. Every single person, from prude to promiscuous, in this audience is here to be entertained.

The Gin Fizz hosts a cabaret-style burlesque show. It's dinner, cocktails, and some heavy teasing on the menu. And while the cabaret laws in Nashville have been enforced heavily over the last handful of years, it's still a sexy night out. Pasties are a must, underboob has to be covered up, and that perfect crescent where my ass meets my thigh can only peek out "by accident."

Deep and quiet, the drumbeat starts, growing louder just

as the trumpet kicks in. A punctuation before it quiets. Its bluesy, teasing sounds from the saxophone and trumpet make everyone pay attention. I like numbers like this one. It leaves the audience eager for more.

I tilt my chin and flirtatiously smile at the front row. The bulkier man in the navy-blue suit pants and white dress shirt is wearing as much of a costume as I am. The facade of someone who's only here to be entertained but has plenty to hide. His square jawline and the symmetry of his face make him nice to look at, but there isn't anything memorable about his features. If I had to guess, I would say mid-fifties, but I already know his age. His date of birth puts him at forty-nine. He's a Gemini. Enjoys a shot of lemon juice and turmeric to start his day and a glass of brandy to end it. Most people wouldn't know any of this with only a few glances, but I'm not most people. And as it turns out, neither is Mr. Brock Blackstone.

Months of surveillance and orchestrated casual run-ins brought him to the Gin Fizz tonight—a wrong coffee order, the witnessing of a parking ticket disagreement, and my favorite of the damsel-in-distress setups, the "I'm so lost, do you know where I can find…" All of it had him coming in here as a regular. Then asking for my number and then getting more and more bold with his "requests." And tonight, on New Year's Eve, Blackstone smiles at me as if I'll be the one to kiss him at midnight. He's overeager, and that's exactly where I want him. It'll be an incredible coincidence when I'll be performing in the same town as his upcoming business trip.

I take on jobs that feel right. Anything from assisting local police to helping a wife catch her husband in a lie or in someone else's bed. Private investigating means digging in and doing research. Focusing on the details that don't connect. Asking questions and trying to find the inconsistencies in answers. Every once in a while, I'll get called into something that has some meat on it.

Blackstone has depth, and I've been working all the angles, from undercover activity to interaction and technology that make it easier to do the job. It's a hefty budget, but when the FBI wants a guy, the avenues in which to get him nailed down are endless.

Flirting makes people vulnerable. It has the capability to knock people off course and can be the kind of high that far surpasses one found in a bottle or a pill. Though I smile at everyone in the front row, it's Mr. Blackstone who will get my specialized attention. Because he keeps coming back for the high I give him.

The chorus kicks in, and I slowly turn in time with the other four dancers—the bump and grind is the easiest move to master. If it's done right, and you add a few props with some eye contact, you'll be unforgettable.

I undo the corset one hook at a time until it detaches, and I'm left in a pair of high-cut, satin shorts and a sequined balconette bra. I'm more than comfortable being naked—a switch that had flipped when I leaned into burlesque. Confidence like I'd never known billowed around me like a fucking halo. There's something about the tease that has people panting and sitting taller. Talking more and loosening up. And I like the power in that. It serves me well.

The audience hoots and hollers at the peeling and plucking of lace and satin. Three of the five of us are still covered, but two wear a cupless bra and nothing more than the letter X in black taped across each nipple. Our host for the evening says, "Looks like X marks the spot tonight. Who's up for a little treasure hunt?"

I loop my feather boa around Blackstone's neck, kicking my leg up and over his shoulder. The back of my knee leans there as my thigh rests along his chest. "Hello again," I say in a low, coy voice.

Burlesque is meant to be campy and sometimes comedic, but always sexy. The spotlight hasn't made its way to me yet, which makes it the perfect time to set a plan into play.

"Hello there," he says slowly, relying heavily on what he believes is a charming Southern drawl. Out of the corner of my eye, his colleague smiles and sits back, taking me in. A shiver works its way down my spine as he watches, and Blackstone glides his hand higher than anyone respectable would normally dare.

"I'm so glad you came tonight." I fake it and smile wide as I lean closer. "It's my last show here for a little while." Kicking up my leg again, I turn with a wiggle, taking a seat on his lap. "If you're planning to hit the bourbon trail in the next month or so, I'll be up in Kentucky."

He stares at me closely as his hand lingers along my thigh, his pointer finger drawing a small circle right above my stocking where the garter clips. If this wasn't a performance, and if I hadn't been playing a part, then a man like this would never get close enough to touch me, never mind linger. But on stage and in lights, I'm Rosie Gold. And tonight, Rosie Gold needs Blackstone to pay attention so he knows where she's headed next.

When the spotlight moves to me, I bend with sensual movement, elongating the lines of my body without breaking eye contact until my neck tips far enough back. If he keeps his eyes on me, Blackstone's getting a helluva view of my body. I'm hoping for that. I reach for the floor and plant my hands, arching into a slow and smooth back walkover.

This is the only time on a job when I don't have some kind of weapon hidden on me.

In time with the beat, each dancer pulls out the confetti poppers strapped to our thighs and sets them off as the drummer hits his first cymbal. The audience loses it right on cue. Loud whistles, clapping, and catcalls ring out just as the song comes to a close. Tassels swing in time with applause, the host announcing each of our stage names in succession.

"Let's give these beautiful women one final round of applause. And an extra special holler for Rosie Gold, who'll be up in Fiasco for a residency at Midnight Proof."

I smile and wave at the crowd. And *that* is how you end an evening.

The DJ takes over as I hustle back to the greenroom and change. I have no intention of meeting Blackstone after the show. I need him to be hungry for more, all the way to Fiasco. I exhale slowly, trying not to overthink any of it. *Fiasco*—a place I've done my best to leave behind.

It takes only twenty minutes after my performance to be walking through the door of my apartment. And while it isn't technically mine, it's convenient. The five-hundred-square-foot studio is cramped, but the rent is palatable for this Nashville neighborhood. I don't like being stuck in any city for too long, so subletting is just fine with me. It seems irresponsible to settle. The only place that I've ever considered home hasn't been that for a little more than five years now.

When we first moved to Fiasco, Kentucky, it felt like we exchanged cattle for corn and horses. All of it seemed like a downgrade from living in Wyoming when we first arrived. But Mom inherited the farm at a time in her life when she realized she could use a fresh start.

My eyes blur with tears when I think about her and all the things I wish I could have said.

She was a barrel racer and then a horse trainer, touring with the rodeo circuit until she got too pregnant. When you're twenty-two and have the whole world ahead of you, getting pregnant isn't a concern. Until it is. She didn't have anyone claiming her or me as theirs, so she started over somewhere new. That time, her fresh start landed her in Wyoming, where she met my sister's father. He gave my mother a ring and told me to call him Dad. We were happy there for a while. Except, he already had that with another woman in the next county. A wife and two other kids who called him Dad too.

She never had great instincts about the men she fell in love with.

Knocking the memories from me, my phone buzzes.

> BLACKSTONE:
> Where'd you run off to, Rosie?

I know what he wants—men aren't all that difficult to figure out. Instead of sending a text response, I filter through the images in my saved folder for this specific situation. I choose one that I took in the dressing room at a department store. Trying on lingerie for my costumes was the perfect time to snap a few for this exact scenario. I didn't have the black wig on that day, so I crop the image starting from my lips and ending it just below my waist. I'm flashing a bright smile and plenty of cleavage. *Perfect*.

I toss the phone aside and take in what still needs to be done. Most of my things have been packed. I've gotten good at curating a capsule wardrobe for each season, keeping clothes limited because I never stay anywhere for too long. I like efficiency when it comes to my life—it's something I can control and simplify. My equipment for surveillance along with my costumes and burlesque props are always stored in the covered bed of my truck. I toss my makeup and jewelry into the last duffel bag.

Looking around, I am painfully aware of how easy it was to pack up my life. Less than a couple of hours and it appears as if I was never here. The buzzing of my phone pulls me out of my head once again. Loneliness is funny like that; it hits you at the strangest times. Mostly when I'm alone but surrounded by people who don't know me, or at times like this, when I'm ready to move and realize I didn't make a single memorable mark while I was here. The phone's chaotic vibrating keeps going—it's a call, not a text.

I smile, answering. Del would be one of a small handful of people happy to see me when I'm back in Fiasco. "Del, on a scale from one to ten, how pissed off is Marla going to be when she sees me?"

He lets out a clipped laugh. "How are ya, kid?"

"I'm alright," I answer as I glance at the time on the microwave. "It's late, everything okay?"

The long pause erases my smile. "Ah…Faye, there's no good way to tell you this, but you need to come home."

I hop up onto the small counter space. "I'll be there as planned—"

A fact that he's already aware of since it's his connection with the FBI that pulled me into this Blackstone case.

"Maggie's been arrested." Before I can ask what the hell my sister has done this time, he adds, "She's been beaten up pretty badly."

"What?" I slide off the counter. "Who was it?" Guilt and anger swirl around my chest as I hunch over and listen.

"She was picked up on a 'drunk and disorderly' this time. But she doesn't look good. She won't say who did it." He exhales loudly. "She refused medical attention and finally passed out."

"Is she seeing anyone right now?" I swallow the dryness in my throat. "Anyone who might've done that?"

"I don't think so. At least not anyone she would have brought around. But you know her; she's not all that forthcoming with details."

Actually, I don't know. The truth is, I don't know my sister anymore. The same way she doesn't know me. And both of us resent each other for it. When I left Fiasco, my explanation to her was weak at best. Mom told me to do whatever I needed to. She knew what I gave up. What I had done. But Maggie didn't.

She won't be happy to see me. She barely spoke to me at our mom's memorial service, and that was almost three years ago now. But being back in Fiasco isn't about Maggie or me or our feelings. And it isn't for healing old wounds or reminiscing.

I look around the almost empty room. "If I hit the road in a little while, then I'll be there by morning." I bite at my lip, even more anxious now. "Thanks for the heads-up, Del."

"See you soon, kid," he says, sounding relieved.

I feel everything but relief. We're gambling with my return to Fiasco, and Del and I both know it. I would be there for long enough to run into people. For gossip to make its rounds. To see *him* again. I shake away the nerves. I need to stay focused. I'm not going to let a change in plans fracture the confidence of who I've become or what I've built. I'll be there for a job, and as soon as that job's done, I'll be off to somewhere new.

Chapter 3

Faye

I ROLL DOWN THE WINDOW of my truck and let in the cold air as a familiar smell settles into my throat and skin. I'd been to places all over the United States, from the mountains and coastlines to cities and suburbs, but there's something different about small towns in Kentucky. Fiasco, in particular, feels big and suffocating all at once, with the flat land, the quiet, the memories I'd rather forget. Coming home has nerves and hunger pangs at war in my stomach that I have no choice but to stifle.

The red neon sign outside of a gas station that doubles as a restaurant still glows nice and bright, even as the sun brightens the morning without peeking over the horizon just yet. Black iron light posts that line the street look new. And signs that read "Celebrating 100 years of Bourbon & Horses" hung from each light. A familiar logo—a fox head wrapped around an *F*—is lit at the center of the town green.

I've missed the way the air lingers around your fingers, even in the winter. And when the wind kicks in from the northwest, the air smells like just-baked, flakey croissants with hints of cocoa. That's when it hits me. A reminder as to why Fiasco carries those delicious scents. Bourbon. Specifically, Foxx bourbon.

I take a deep breath, remembering that spring and summer carried hints of fresh whipped cream and it mingled with whatever herbs lined the flower beds along the front of the house. While right now, in the heart of winter, when neighbors burn leaves left over from the fall and remains of Christmas trees in firepits, the scent shifts slightly, making the wind smell of burned sugar and a nostalgia of when life felt less complicated.

"We can't bake a cake and eat it for dinner," I said, giving my sister a glare. "Mom put me in charge while she's at the stables tonight."

Maggie hopped up onto the counter. "Do you think the foal will be all white like the mare?"

I gave her a shrug. My sister and my mom had the same level of love for horses. They could talk for hours about horses that Mom trained and how she gained their trust. I opened the refrigerator and stared at the leftovers. The chicken looked gray, and the noodles were over-inflated. "Let's do peanut butter and jelly," I suggested with a sigh.

Mom had been working late this entire week, which meant dinner was whatever we could figure out on our own.

"Peanut butter and jelly both have sugar. There's bread, which is just like cake anyway. Let's just make a cake and have that for dinner," Maggie said as she pulled out the box mix.

She had great ideas—even at eleven years old.

"Fine, but I'm pulling the 'oldest card' and making chocolate." Laughing to myself, I took out the eggs and butter.

"Yessss!" She thrusted her fist in the air. "With vanilla frosting. And if I forget to tell you later, it was the best dinner ever."

I couldn't help but smile as I pointed at her. "You're cleaning up the mess."

With a beaming smile, she saluted me. "I'm all over it. Dishwashers get two slices anyway."

Mom didn't even get mad, having a piece for breakfast that next morning and dancing in her seat as she enjoyed every bite. I swallow down the thickness in my throat at memories that feel so far removed from my current reality; I wonder if they even happened sometimes.

Daylight and half a decade later, Fiasco's more charming than I remember. The landscaping and attention to detail make it feel less like a small forgotten town and more like a destination.

When I finally pull in to the police station, the morning light is bright enough to highlight all the ways the place has changed. Before I left, it was a few blocks back and half the size. The Fiasco Police Department has gotten an upgrade. I imagine it's more than just taxes paying for this. We had two of the biggest businesses housed right here in Fiasco—bourbon and horse racing. The men who ran both, I'm sure, had some hand in making this place look the way it did. This building used to be the old post office, but now it's a state-of-the-art facility that houses the police department, 911 dispatchers, and even an FBI field office, according to the signs that hang just above the entryway. It looks like a smaller version of Grand Central Station during that quiet slip of time between the last train and the first.

"Excuse me, I'm here to bail out my sister. Maggie Calloway," I say to the front desk officer. There's nothing friendly about the way he doesn't respond, glaring and judging instead. His mutton chops are the only part of his demeanor that appears lighthearted; they match the coiffed hair that's been combed and styled. Putting a toothpick in his mouth, he turns back to his computer, typing away.

"Are my eyes deceiving me?" a familiar voice calls out from behind the front desk. "Faye Calloway walking into *my* station. Are you finally here to say yes to that date?"

I know exactly who it is before I look up.

"Cortez." I take in his kind eyes and bright smile. He's only gotten more handsome since I last saw him. "Still looking like a snack," I say with a smile. We were both always great at flirting.

Alex Cortez charmed his way into my pants when we were in the police academy together. You never forget your first. *And the only*. But flirting didn't equal chemistry, and I realized that quickly.

"Hey, baby girl," he says, coming around the front desk and wrapping his thick arms around me. That nickname isn't one I expected. "You look incredible."

I glance at his chest and notice there's no badge and that he's not wearing the full khaki uniform like the other officer who's eyeing us from behind the counter. "Are you working or…?"

"Decided to move up and was able to stay local." His smile takes over his whole face with that response. "You're looking at one-fourth of the FBI unit for Montgomery County. They wanted to open a field office, and since Fiasco PD had the space for it, my change from plain clothes to FBI had me moving from the cubicle pit to an office."

I raise my eyebrows at that. Del had folded me into the surveillance for Blackstone, so I know what I've been doing has been filtering to the FBI. I just didn't think about who my contact would be while I'm here. "So you're working with Del?" I ask.

With a wink, he confirms, "Yes, ma'am. Well, more like Del did me a favor by suggesting a private investigator when we were grasping at straws for this case. Then he mentioned your name. He shared your surveillance. Your work is pretty damn impressive."

I try to mask the smile that compliment pulled from me.

"Always hoped we'd end up working together," Cortez says with a lightness to his voice. Giving my arm a squeeze, his brow furrows. "You're here early." He searches my face before he asks, "Maggie?"

I nod, lips pursed. "Del called and said she was picked up last night. What kind of shape is she in?"

He moves back around the counter and types something into his computer. I toss my license, the bail bond, and my social security in front of him.

"She was sober by the middle of third shift. She was her usual sunshine self when I told her I couldn't give her anything for her hangover," he tells me.

Huffing a laugh at his sarcasm, I take in the man in front of me. Someone familiar but different. A friend. Maybe more at one point. But a stranger from a life I haven't participated in for years. There's no ring on his left finger.

"I'm not married, if that's what you were looking at."

I smile and find his brown eyes studying me right back.

He clears his throat, and the humor that was there a moment ago lifts when he says, "I heard when she came in it was pretty bad. But I don't think she was drunk until *after* she had gotten shoved around."

Maggie's the Calloway sister everyone knows, the one who

stepped up and took over the farm when Mom passed. The daughter who stayed and took care of a woman who needed therapy and not just a bunch of cornfields and farm animals to heal. The folks of Fiasco respected that, and I became the villain for leaving. They have no idea what transpired—the deals I made. The things I did to make things okay. But right now, my sister isn't okay at all.

Violence is easier to digest when it doesn't touch you personally. I have to ask, "Any idea who might be responsible?"

He makes a few notes and then steps away for a moment. I watch as he moves toward the back of the precinct and gives some of the papers I had to sign to one of the other officers. When he comes back, he doesn't return to the computer, instead he walks around the desk and signals for me to follow him. When we move past the waiting room and down the hall, he clears his throat. "Listen, Faye." The small sigh that follows has me bracing for whatever he's about to say. "Your sister is trouble. You're not going to find many people in Fiasco who'll think otherwise. And trouble has a tendency to find trouble."

I don't agree and that doesn't answer my question. "Trouble can mean a lot of things, Cortez. Don't forget what I've been hired to do. *That* feels an awful lot like trouble."

"Fair enough. Wrong thing to say," he says, backing off.

"Let me handle things with my sister and get settled before my first performance." I lean in closer and pull out my phone to make this interaction feel casual. There isn't anyone within earshot, but anything regarding Blackstone isn't public knowledge. "We should plan a place to meet that isn't here, obviously."

He smiles, taking a few seconds to respond. "You asking me out for drinks, Faye?"

I ignore him, because as much as I like flirting, Cortez is a colleague now. Granted, a colleague who has seen me naked, but much like everything else familiar around here, that's in the past. This is business, and I intend for him to stay in that category.

The door buzzes open. My sister leans against the wall, looking like someone I wouldn't have recognized if I walked by her on the street. It takes almost everything in me not to rush to her and a single second to confirm that my plans may not have changed, but now they need to be adjusted. There's no way I can leave her by herself if she's in any kind of danger. Her hair is either wet or greasy, and her black sweater has been stretched out at the neck and hangs from her shoulder. She has one gold hoop in her left ear, the other one missing. Her tight light blue jeans have a large rip in the knee that's dirty and a little bloody. And yet the mess of it all is eclipsed by the fact that her right eye is almost swollen shut, accompanied by a nasty ombre of purples and blues, and her split lip that's puffed and angry. Streaks of red run down the front of her neck and disappear into the collar of the sweater. It's like someone clawed at her front. I bite down hard to keep my emotions in check.

"Jesus, Maggie," I say on an exhale.

"I didn't call her," Maggie says, looking at the officer unlocking her handcuffs. "Who called her? Because I sure as hell didn't."

She may not have, but I still came running.

"That'd be me, kid," Del cuts in from behind me. I turn around smiling, gliding into his open arms for a hug that feels long overdue. It feels good to hug someone—it's been a while.

"Faye," he hums, giving me an extra squeeze. As we pull back, he taps my chin with his knuckle. "It's been too long, kid." He looks over my shoulder at Maggie. Her arms are crossed like this entire exchange is torturous to endure. "You've been remanded into Faye's custody on bail. You are obligated to appear in court at the end of January. Please, for the love of all things sacred, don't get arrested between now and then."

Cortez tries to hide his smile by looking down.

"Cortez, you're still an asshole," Maggie bites back. "You're only happy to see her because you're still obsessed with her." Her eyes flick down to his crotch. "Get over it, man, you popped her cherry. She's moved on."

Fucking Maggie.

He points at her. "Watch it. How about you don't end up back in cuffs before you even step out of here."

"You're so boring. Maybe that's why you fell into the friend zone," she says, sending him a smile that says she thinks she won this round. She walks down the hall from where we came and over her shoulder, she shouts, "Faye, you can go home now."

It's almost funny how fast she needs to get away from me. Laughing and calling her an asshole under my breath is easier than thinking about how those words sting. Del and I follow her out toward the front of the building.

"Do I need to know anything?" Del asks quietly. "Between you and pretty boy FBI here?"

"Just some history. It's not going to be a problem." I glance again at Cortez as I walk through the station and give him a wave.

"Good to see you, Faye," he calls out. With an audience now, albeit small at this hour in a police station, it's still too many people who don't need to know that I'm here to help.

Just as I push through the doors, leaving the station, my phone vibrates in my hand.

UNKNOWN:
I'll be in touch.

I glance back inside and watch as Cortez types away on his phone.

FAYE:
You never asked for my number.

UNKNOWN:
FBI remember?

When I look up from my phone, Maggie's gone. "Dammit, where the hell did she go?"

Del sniffs out a laugh as he stands next to me on the landing of the concrete steps. "Probably for breakfast. Her car is in the impound. Figured it would be good to make sure she didn't wrap it around any trees or telephone poles while she was working through whatever brought her in."

I didn't plan on being my sister's keeper while I was here. In fact, I didn't have a plan for Maggie and me when I found out I was being sent to Fiasco. I couldn't allow myself to even consider it—she hated me for leaving, and I couldn't forgive her for that.

"She's been running with the wrong crowd for a while. Misdemeanors at first. But now..." He shakes his head. "Now, I know for a fact she's involved in something she can't get away from. Not without getting hurt. So no matter what she tells you, she needs your help."

"Yeah, I gathered that it wasn't going to be something easy. Not with a beating like that," I say, running my fingers along my wrist.

He clears his throat before saying, "There's a lot of pieces in play here. Are you ready for this, kid?"

He's referring to my involvement with Blackstone, but I'm merely a piece of it. Private investigators only have a fraction of the story, not the full view. But for my part, I'm ready.

"As long as people believe the lie, and that gossip doesn't catch up to Blackstone before we get what's needed, then it'll be smooth."

"Be smart. If something doesn't feel right, you wait."

I give him a curt nod. Del lost his daughter in the line of duty. She followed a lead, didn't have the backup she needed, and he found her bleeding out on scene. A year later, I left town, but he made sure I knew what was happening. Who was arrested, who died, the chaos that came to Fiasco resulting in rickhouse fires and I'm sure even more. I had quit my plans to join the PD, but somehow Del made sure I didn't lose sight of what I had been good at and trained in.

I opened an email with the subject line: Ways to be a cop without being a cop.

> *Faye, here are a couple of names down in Louisiana who are always looking for private investigators. Their departments are too small for some of the shit they're dealing with. Might as well put what you've learned to some use. Your mom mentioned you were working in a coffee shop. You serve a mean cup of coffee and a slice of pie. Marla would be proud. But for what it's worth, I know you pay attention. More than most. We both know that the devil was always in the details :) Talk soon, kid.*
>
> *—Del*

I release a heavy breath and scan the sidewalks on both sides of the road. It takes me a couple of minutes to find her down the block in front of a sidewalk sale.

"Maggie!" I shout as I hustle closer.

She grabs a trucker hat from the turntable and keeps walking. *Seriously?*

"I never asked anyone to call you," she calls out. "I don't want you here."

I speed walk in her wake. "That's nice. But I don't need an invite to be here."

She stops short, which has me stumbling into her back. When she turns, she looks at me with pure annoyance. "Go home, Faye."

I didn't come back here to word spar with her. "This is home. For a little while, at least."

She blinks at me, almost like, out of all the things she thought I was going to say, that was the absolute last one. As she tips her hat back, I see it again, the bruise that takes up the whole right side of her face, not just around the eye. That's more than just a punch or a slap. That's a beating.

Quietly, I ask, "Who hurt you?" I've seen plenty of beat-up faces over the years. Hell, I've contributed to making some of them myself when necessary, but it's different when it's your family.

"Don't you mean, 'What did you do, Maggie?'" she says, hardening the words.

"No. I don't think a woman could do anything that warrants this."

The outer edges of her eyes are more blue than green. Same as Mom's. Everyone used to tell her how beautiful her eyes were. I shake off the memory.

I have no business asking for details, but I do anyway. "What are you involved in?"

Maggie shoves her hands into the pockets of her puffy jacket and looks at me for just a second. I can't help but search her face for some kind of tell or softening that'll remind me of my sister.

More quietly she asks, "Why do you care all of a sudden?"

If I had blinked, I would have missed the way her eyes glass over. Or how her shoulders slouch as she exhales. It's not lost on me that she doesn't have anyone to ask her. It's the only thing we still have in common. We both have no one.

But a car horn from a minivan knocks us both back into the reality of our situation and it has her widening her eyes and swiping at her watch. "Wait, what's today?" she rushes out.

The shift in conversation feels abrupt, but I answer. "Monday."

"Peaches and cream stuffed French toast," she says, looking over my shoulder one second and then brushing past me the next.

I know exactly where she's heading.

At the end of the block and after passing two gas kiosks, the bell on the door chimes as it opens. A bell that sounds like it had been rusted and is pissed it is still being rung. The floor-to-ceiling wood paneling makes Hooch's feel vintage. It has me feeling nostalgic, the same way Christmas music does every year. It's welcoming, familiar, and my lips twitch into an easy smile. The vinyl of the booths has been updated from the russet orange I remember to a deep cranberry. Awards and newspaper write-ups from decades of sponsored baseball teams and local festivals still decorate the walls. The tables have been upgraded and the layout changed, but the long counter is exactly the same. Oak barrel wood rims the mustard-colored Corian running the length of Fiasco's gas station restaurant.

Heads turn as we make our way to the woman standing with a coffee carafe in one hand and the other on her hip. Marla Hooch doesn't like very many people. Tourists, out of towners, even seasonal visitors aren't greeted with open arms at Hooch's. You have to be a townie for that. Walking in here isn't about to be any type of welcome wagon.

"What'll it be, honey?" Marla asks Maggie.

Without lifting the brim of her stolen hat, she says, "Coffee and the special."

"Hi, Marla." I smile. "I'll have the same." I had to shoot my shot.

Marla's resting bitch face is top-notch. It always had been. She gives me a side-eye, barely acknowledging me—it stings a little. I spent a lot of time at this counter growing up, and if anyone was going to hold a grudge for me not visiting, it was going to be Marla Hooch. She held grudges over shitty tips and people who forgot to turn off their phones at supper.

Maggie laughs to herself. "You really think she's going to bring you breakfast?"

I turn my head to look at my sister. She isn't the same person I grew up with, but she also is in some ways. She's a little taller than me, thinner too. Her blond is darker than mine. It's clear she takes the time to get highlights, but it's been a while with her roots growing out. The brim of her hat is low enough to keep a shadow on her face, but I'm surprised that not even Marla asked what happened.

Marla backs through the swinging kitchen door with a tray of food in one hand and a single mug in the other. Sliding the mug in front of Maggie, she pours her a hot cup of what smells like hazelnut coffee. When she returns the carafe to the hot plate behind her, she moves around the counter and toward the tables. It's the corner booth that gives me an unsettled feeling. Usually, it would be retired fire and police department guys playing poker, sometimes it would be a packed-in group of high schoolers, but today it's Wheeler Finch and Waz King.

Finch & King is the most celebrated brand in horse racing. It has a hand in every facet of the industry, from breeding and training to racing and gambling. Wheeler Finch is respected. Maybe even more than that. He's revered. And it isn't just that he has an obscene amount of money. Or the fact that he makes sure everyone knows it too. It's the simple fact that he helps make other people wealthy.

Every piece of the horse business has some touchpoint to Wheeler Finch. And the day that the King brothers came to Fiasco was when that started. Tullis and Waz King were horse trainers who helped deliver Triple Crown winners—horse training, jockeys, and teams that delivered year after year. The King brothers provided horses, while Wheeler Finch tied it together with sponsors, off-track betting, and any other piece that had the ability to cash out. There have always been rumors about how Wheeler conducted business and how the Kings manipulated other trainers. Finch & King Racing is a powerhouse.

The only piece of it that ever mattered to me is that Tullis King took one look at my mother and decided she was what he wanted. And our lives were never the same.

I watch as Marla drops off two plates to their table without a smile. I know she isn't a fan, but in Fiasco, there are some people you just don't cross. Finch and King are those people.

When she comes back, she puts a small empty glass in front of me and then, for the first time since I stepped foot in here, looks me in the eye as she pours water from the sweating pitcher.

I let out a sigh before I ask, "How've you been, Marla?"

"Sounds like a question for someone who wants something and not like a question from a person who really wants to know the answer." She raises an eyebrow.

For fuck's sake. "Okay, then. May I have a coffee?"

"We have water," she says, turning back toward the kitchen.

I sniff out a laugh. *This fucking town.*

"Told ya," Maggie says with too much amusement.

If they both only knew *why* I left to begin with, maybe they wouldn't be such dicks about it. I glance over to the corner booth again before I lean into my sister's space, hovering right near her ear. "I'm here for a month."

Maggie glances at me without much reaction.

I had planned to keep my distance—headline at Midnight Proof and do what I was hired to do in regard to Blackstone. But that was before. So I continue. "I had plans to stay in a little apartment while I was here, but not anymore. Until you tell me what you're involved with, I'm moving back into the house."

Maggie barks out a laugh just as Marla slides a plate of steaming French toast doused in bourbon-soaked peaches and topped with whipped cream onto the counter.

"I don't think so," she mumbles.

My mouth waters and stomach grumbles just smelling that breakfast. I had a bag of almonds on my drive here overnight and nothing since. I'm a naturally thicker girl, but I follow macros and eat every three hours so I can manage exactly where I want my curves to remain. Overindulging is one thing, but forgetting to eat, that's entirely out of character for me.

I'm not going to argue with her here. "See you at home, Maggie," I say as I shove away from the counter. I purposely avoid making eye contact with anyone, especially the two powerful men in the corner booth. My pocket vibrates with a text as I'm leaving.

"Your room is a gym now," Maggie calls out over her shoulder. She's such a *dick*.

I ignore the heads turning in my direction, shrugging off the way it feels not to be welcomed here, and pull out my phone.

> BLACKSTONE:
> Rosie Gold, looks like I'll be seeing you at Midnight Proof this weekend. How about a little something to hold me over...

Chapter 4

Lincoln

"Not many people find fractions and chemistry sexy, but what ends up in those barrels over there is called 'the heart' for a reason. It's what remains after a variation in temperatures can condense and vaporize what came from that massive container of mash and yeast." I point to the side of the room we had just come from. Fuck, I get a semi just talking about this shit.

The photographer smiles at me, and I know just by that one look I've got her undivided attention. And it has nothing to do with the way bourbon is made. But when I focus back on her colleague, a sour expression on *The New York Times* reporter's face has me worried. "Mr. Foxx, that's all well and good—"

"Lincoln," I interrupt and hold my hand over my chest.

His mouth forms a thin line, like he's not interested in personal stories about how we make our brand. "Lincoln. I've heard all about the science behind bourbon. The math, the percentages of corn and wheats or whatever else sets a mash bill apart.

There's nothing new you're going to tell me that I haven't already heard from a number of other master distillers or found with a few web searches." Turning off his phone that he's been using as a recorder, he pockets it. "This is a feature about distilleries popping up all along the East Coast, and to be quite frank, the angle I'm working with is that great bourbon *doesn't* have to be made in Kentucky."

I take a shallow breath, because now I want to flick this guy in the face. It's as condescending of a move as his words. I shift a glance at my older brother, who's been standing just off to the side. There are plenty of reasons why *The New York Times* would be sniffing around Fiasco—we've been known to attract trouble. But today it's about the heart of what my family has done for decades: bourbon. And specifically, how Foxx Bourbon does it best. Not just different from anyone else, but how the sum of it is only as incredible as its parts. Those parts are my family. It's our legacy.

I break it down in a way that I know he'll connect to as I tell him, "You're right, great bourbon can be made anywhere in the U.S., just like great pizza can be made anywhere. Or bagels, for that matter."

From how his brow creases, I think he knows exactly where I'm going to go with this. But I'm on a roll to make a point, so I continue.

"If you've grown up in the Pacific Northwest or the mountains of Colorado, you'll probably be able to call out the pizza joints that have the best slice. You're comparing where you've been." I point my finger up with a wiggle. "But there's a caveat. New York and New Haven, hell, even Boston, will change what anyone considers great pizza. That includes bagels that are worth a damn. You have to have tried the best in order to make a proper comparison of what the actual best might be. And maybe you're a person who wants to boast the talent of your local city or restaurant, but if you're going to be honest with yourself, you know that pizza, whether it's wood-fired or hand tossed, is the best"—I tip my head to the reporter, then the photographer—"where you're from."

I walk farther down the line of aging barrels and grab the long copper whiskey thief. Dipping it into the opened barrel, I pull out a serving to taste. "Just like our bourbon." I pass two glasses, each with a small sample, to both the reporter and photographer. As I tip my glass up to the light, I admire the deeper tones of this special reserve. I noticed when they showed up that he had a handful of gold caramel wrappers he tossed in the trash, which might mean he prefers that easier sweet finish of a double barrel. I won't be condescending and tell him to let it coat his tongue before swallowing, but if he does, it'll taste as rich as the caramel that made those candies. "It's the water. And more than anything, it's the chemistry of what bourbon does inside those barrels *in* Kentucky that makes Kentucky-made bourbon the best."

"Not just Foxx Bourbon?"

I love dancing around this question. I smile at him. "Everyone has a different palate. Most people, if they've had a bottle of ours, will want more. To try more and experience the versatility." I sip what's in my glass and savor it for just a moment. We make great fucking bourbon. I know that, and he knows that, but I can be pragmatic. "There's a lot of old blood in bourbon—there are plenty of brands not too far from here who like to talk about how they were here long before Foxx Bourbon. But they're operating with old beliefs and struggle to change with new consumers and connoisseurs." I shift a glance at Ace because he likes to play it safe, just like those old brands. But we're only as great as the next evolution of our brand. When I shift back to Murray, I make sure he can quote me as I answer his question directly. "But we've grown, evolved, yet still, Foxx Bourbon is the best."

I wink at the photographer just as she takes the rest of her shot.

"In Kentucky," he clarifies, pulling his phone out of his pocket again and tapping away at the screen.

"Kentucky makes the best bourbon. And Foxx makes the best in Kentucky," I say pointedly, just as the photographer takes my picture.

Again, I glance back to where Ace stands. The amusement he's trying to bite back has my mouth kicking up on the side. He was anxious about where this conversation would go, but what my big brother forgets sometimes is that I can handle it. I might not have the same approach to business as he does, but we always have the same goals: Protect the family and build the brand. And in that order.

"Would you mind if we take some photos of this space?" the reporter asks, still typing on his phone.

"Not at all." My gaze shifts to the photographer, her long dark hair pushed to one side as her camera bag drapes on the other. I take in how she leans against the wall, changing position to gain the right shot. She studies the camera screen after a succession of shutters, and I catalog the sexy way she confidently moves around the space.

I'm just arrogant enough to know that if I talked her up a little more and asked about her profession, it would be easy to ask her for a drink tonight. Getting a woman's attention has never been the problem. The issue is keeping mine. I chase thankless moments with strangers, finding pockets of pleasure where I can while trying to remember myself as someone other than a father. Or a husband. Or widower.

"Do places around Fiasco stock any other bourbons besides Foxx?"

I smile at the way she asks me that question quietly as she moves closer. Her camera clicks away, focusing on the bourbon barrels stacked along the back of the space.

"There's plenty of bourbon brands on shelves. Some have more specialty bottles."

Murray clears his throat, trying to get my attention back.

I think it's a good time to seal up this article, so I start moving toward some of our oldest bottles. "How about I break out a few of my favorite years and we do a proper tasting?"

Two hours later, I've learned that Murray Ackroyd had spent a total of twenty-four hours as a police officer in New York City before he listened to his gut and decided to quit. A fact I wouldn't have known had my brother, Grant, not been at the cooperage late today. Toasted barrels are still part of Grant's end-of-week workload. He may have delivered some of the best, most sought-after bourbon we sold this past year, but my brother still enjoys his routines. Finishing the week in the cooperage with the rest of the crew is part of it.

"Hey, cowboy," Laney shouts as she walks by with their dog, Julep.

Grant turns to her with a full-blown smile. "Be right there, honey." He shakes the reporter's hand. "My boss is ready to call it a night," he says, signaling toward Laney.

Murray lets out a laugh and nods. "Pleasure, Grant."

With a clap on my shoulder, my brother says, "I'm going to hang out with my little flowers tonight, right? They wanted to spend some time with Julep, so maybe I'll bring her along with me. Lily told Laney that she needs to learn how to be a dog mom."

"I don't want to know what the hell that means." I shake my head with a smile, slinging my hands into my back pockets. My girls like to take on projects—building a bird sanctuary, selling wildflowers on the side of the road, and the last one was creating an inventory of friendship bracelets for every person who lived in Fiasco. But if I listen to my gut here, something tells me that they're going to want to open the discussion of getting a dog again. "Whatever you want is fine with me. Come over around 7 p.m."

I don't have specific plans, just that I need a night out. My family's great about offering to take the girls here and there. It gives me a chance to do something on my own, which is practically impossible as a single parent.

I glance over at the photographer again. She's exactly my type—beautiful, easy, and eager. It's the only type of interaction I want—surface level. Take a night to flirt, fuck around, and then get back to my life.

"Most write-ups or social posts I've seen have assumed that your Cowboy Edition was a nod to the hardworking men in this country, but I think I just discovered the real reason behind that one," Murray says with a small smile.

If anyone was going to charm them that wasn't me, it would be my sister-in-law, Laney. "Isn't it usually a woman who ends up being behind the best things? I've got two little ones at home who bring out just about the best there is in me."

Nodding fondly, he smiles in agreement. "If I can convince my editor to adjust the tone of this article, then a fact-checker will follow up shortly before we go to print." He folds his arms over his slender chest. "It usually takes a lot for me to be convinced, Lincoln. But I appreciate the history. The stories that fuel the reasons why." Tilting his head toward the mash bins, he adds, "Even more than the science behind what you're doing here."

I know a favor or request is coming just by his body language alone.

"Your brother, Grant, used to be Fiasco PD," he says as I wait for the question. "He wouldn't happen to have someone still on the force who I could talk to about all the chaos happening on the Tennessee and Kentucky border, would he?"

It isn't the kind of conversation you bring up on a whim. It's clear Murray has an ulterior motive. A small piece of Fiasco ran along the southeastern border of Kentucky, hugging the Tennessee state line nice and tight.

"There's been a lot of commotion along that line lately. Reports of horses missing and then their remains being found dispersed," he says, pocketing his phone again. "Real disturbing stuff. Especially in horse country."

And while I am protective of our small town, I steer away from things that don't have anything to do with me or Foxx Bourbon. This is one of those things.

"I grew up in Fiasco, Murray. Everyone knows everyone. And there's plenty of gossip that travels about who left an unhappy marriage or went missing. You might want to try Teasers for some information. You'll get a helluva lot more out of that crew than you will the Fiasco PD. My brother, especially." Grant wouldn't talk to this guy, not a fucking chance.

"Fair enough," he says, holding up his hands with a laugh.

The photographer smiles to herself, overhearing the conversation.

"There's a speakeasy in town, Midnight Proof. They have

some of the best Foxx bourbon on hand. It also happens to be my best friend's place. Interested?" My invitation is meant for whomever wants to join me.

"I'm on deadline," Murray declines. "But thank you for your time, Lincoln." He shakes my hand and starts requesting specific shots from the photographer.

She nods at his directive and then starts clicking away. I watch as she smiles at the screen of her camera just before she glances back my way. And in that look, I know I read the entire thing right. Beautiful, easy, eager, and most importantly, only here for the night.

Chapter 5

Faye

"Rosie motherfucking Gold," she says with a warm laugh and clap of her hands. It's impossible not to smile at Hadley Finch. She isn't a friend. An acquaintance at best, someone who went to the same school, lived in the same town, but that's where the commonalities end. Everyone in Fiasco knows who she is. And everyone who's ever watched a horse race knows her last name—Finch. Two things people in Kentucky—Fiasco, especially—took seriously: horses and bourbon. Hadley's folded into both worlds.

"Hadley, thanks for working with me," I say with a bright smile, moving down the back stairs of Midnight Proof. The truth is, I've been eager to start. A few days of getting settled and watching as my sister actively tried to either avoid me or blatantly ignore me stopped being entertaining after my first night here.

"Faye, are you joking?" She talks more loudly as we walk

farther into the building. The sounds of a trumpet and saxophone croon over the melody of piano keys. "You're going to bring me so much business. I looked you up online when Cortez pitched this favor. And damn, I might have started crushing on you right then and there."

I chuckle at her enthusiasm. I hadn't remembered much of Hadley, mostly what gossip fueled and the randomness of being strangers. But she seemed fun to be around and had that easy, comforting energy that was always so refreshing to find. I glance down the hall toward the crowded speakeasy. Glasses clinking and a nice hum of chatter kicks up my anticipatory nerves.

"I have a spot for you to use as a dressing room." Waving for me to follow, she moves down the long hallway, past the restrooms and what looks like a space she uses as an office. "It's small, but the only talent I've had to accommodate are my jazz band and the occasional singer."

I look into the small space, and it's not much smaller than my last apartment. "It's perfect. I usually come mostly ready to go. Just a few costume additions and I'll be set."

"Feel free to keep your costumes here and any props." She nods at my arms draped with two garment bags and my makeup case. As she leans against the doorway, I hang my things and shed my jacket. "Cortez has assured me that you're simply working someone for information for him. That there is no chance of something dangerous transpiring here." That's a bold claim. There's always the possibility that things could go wrong. I know to be prepared for that. But I understood why he would have said it—to ease her mind. This was a big ask. She searches for a response, but before I can give it, she adds, "This place is important to me. It's separate from what's normally associated with the last name. And I'd like to keep it that way."

I give her a nod in understanding. Reaching around to the thigh strap that holds one of my knives, I make sure the slit in my skirt doesn't ride too high for her to see it. There's also a palm-sized stun gun in my bag and a switchblade tucked into the makeup case that she just moved to the vanity. Safety means being prepared.

"I'm helping a friend. And the only thing you or anyone else will ever see is that I'm here to entertain." It's not a lie, just not the entire truth. I can't ever promise anyone that something won't go wrong. I know that better than anyone.

"Great. The jazz band will start your set in about an hour. Come take a look once you get settled—water, drinks, whatever you might need. The bartenders know you're part of the staff. It's a packed house tonight. Plenty of people in town for the next few weeks; seasonal depression hits hard this time of year and people want nothing more than to escape and explore bourbon country as well as its recreational benefits." She hesitates for a second. "I'm not anticipating too many locals on a Thursday night, but people are going to catch wind that you're performing here." I know what she's getting at, but I let her say it. "People are going to talk. They're going to come out to see you."

"That's the hope, isn't it?" I say with a confident smile, easing the little bit of worry her thoughts just dredged up. "You can ignore how you hired me—forget about the request from Cortez and treat me just like another paid employee. And I will do a damn good job." I look around the room first, taking in the size and how perfect it is for a show. I say to her, "I don't owe anyone an explanation, Hadley. But if you're curious whether I'll be able to do this when Mr. Dugan from the hardware store, Prue the librarian, or even if a Foxx comes in here—"

"Mr. Dugan would never be seen here." I don't miss how she didn't say anything about a Foxx brother, however.

I tip my chin up just a fraction of an inch. "It's irrelevant who sees me because I'm more than confident in what I do, how I dance, what people will see when they watch me. I'm not the same person I was when I left Fiasco, and I have no problem with letting people recognize that. And as far as you're concerned, I'm purely your new entertainment."

She smiles wide. "Well, all-fucking-right." With a single clap, she spins away from the little room, calling out from down the hall, "Look out, Fiasco, Rosie Gold is ready to turn heads and bulge pants tonight!"

I'm back in a town that I used to love, but one that's filled with people who still have no idea why I left, who had forced me to barely look back. I carried it everywhere I went. Everywhere *except* when I was Rosie Gold. I was different when I danced burlesque. Dancing had only ever been a hobby. Being thrust into adulthood meant earning a living over the tinkering of hobbies, so I planned to leave dancing behind and join the police force. Start a life. But then life turned on its axis, and there were no longer expectations of getting married or settling down to have kids. There was no pressure to choose stability over exploration. I needed to earn a paycheck, and that was it. And suddenly, the possibilities felt endless.

It's easy to play a part and lean into Rosie—the confident fantasy of a woman who's unapologetic about using her body to tease, entertain and get what she wants.

I lean against the bar, taking in the space, trying to figure out my path of choreography. The bartender pours me a club soda that I sip on as I map Midnight Proof. The chandeliers hanging in the center of the main space are warmly lit and bathe everything in just enough light. It's the perfect air of sophistication, while the red velvet drapes make it feel more like a theater than just a speakeasy. It's exactly the kind of Gatsby-era vibe you'd expect in a speakeasy. Mix it with the leather couches and wrought iron metal accents, it's masculine yet really fucking pretty. The lounge-style room means that I can easily work with the audience and have a little more fun.

"Drinking on the job?" Cortez says as he leans next to me.

I tilt the club soda toward him. "Considering it." My eyes flick down to see what he's wearing. Jeans that fit tight in the thighs, brown boots, and a white collared shirt tucked in beneath his sports coat. Even if he took some time to get ready, he still looks exactly like an off-duty cop. "Didn't realize you'd be here tonight," I say with a curious lift of my eyebrow.

"I need eyes on this guy, but more importantly, I need to know exactly who he's shaking hands with," he explains. I watch as two women give Cortez an interested glance as they pass by. "In a perfect world, you get on the invite list for that event, Faye." My surveillance determined that Blackstone is running his private auction this month—something that piqued the FBI's attention immediately. The estate he rented to host this private affair is smack dab along the county border.

Cortez's gaze flitters away, and he hums, like he just realized something.

"What?" I ask, curious if he'll share more with me.

"Ace Foxx wasn't who I thought I'd see rubbing elbows with him," Cortez says as he stands tall. "I can't say I'm all that surprised. This just got a helluva lot more juicy. Do you remember any calls or emails between them?"

On the coattails of Atticus Foxx is another man I don't

recognize, and behind him is the person I'd watched too closely for far longer than anyone ever should.

Brock Blackstone is nothing more than a swindler. A man who runs one of the largest auction house businesses in the U.S. He's a curator, having developed a knack for getting people what they needed. The same way Christie's or Sotheby's auction things, like antiquities and priceless jewelry to fine art and historical landmarks, Blackstone Auctions does the same. But I discovered quickly that it's Blackstone's *private* auctions that are worth a little more attention.

I shake my head. "I would've flagged it."

If I thought it through, Foxx Bourbon is the most sought-after brand of bourbon around the world. It isn't surprising to see the head of that brand with someone like Blackstone. I just hadn't prepared for it. That's a problem. I should have. Their bourbon is auction worthy. The reselling of rare bourbon ranges anywhere from a few hundred dollars over label pricing to somewhere north of ten, even twenty thousand. Blackstone Auctions holds auctions all over the world, but it's the figurehead's private auctions that are in the FBI's crosshairs. What he procures for these auctions, and for whom, is what I'm supposed to find out. Cortez is tight-lipped about exactly what they're looking for, just that they need any and all intel.

"If there had been any sign of a Foxx involved, Cortez, I wouldn't be involved in this." I push away from the bar and move farther away from where Blackstone and his small party have settled in. As much as it pissed me off, I'd made a deal. I needed to stay clear of the Foxx family if I was going to be back in Fiasco for any length of time. We had an agreement, and I was bending it by being here.

"What do you mean, you're leaving?" Maggie asked in disbelief.

It had only been a few weeks since I came back from the police academy over in Frankfort. Before then, I was away for my undergrad. I only traveled back home during breaks. It felt good to stretch my legs and have my own life away from home. But I missed being here. I knew she missed me, too, but she was busy with school now. The university kept her living at home, but she went out with friends when she wasn't in class or studying. She would be okay without me here.

"I'm having second thoughts about what I really want to be doing, and I need to clear my head. I found an apartment, and I'm going to get some space from here." *I folded up the clothes in the laundry basket, trying to control my trembling hands. I felt sick having to lie to her. I didn't want to go anywhere. I wanted to keep my plans, but that wasn't possible anymore. If I wanted everything to stay buried, and for Lincoln Foxx to keep his end of the agreement, then I needed to leave. I fucking hated him for making me leave like this.*

"Faye," *Maggie said quietly. Her eyes watered as she watched me move around my room. If I stopped moving, I'd start crying, and I couldn't do that right now.* "Mom's upset. She didn't get out of bed for work, and I'm worried... I think—"

But I cut her off. "I can't—" *I correct myself.* "I'm allowed to change my mind, Maggie, about what I want to do for the rest of my life. And becoming a police officer sounded better than the reality of it." *I swallow down the way it hurt to say any of this.* "Mom understands. Why can't you?"

She widened her stance. "That's what you're sticking with then? You changed your mind about a career you've been talking about for the past decade of your life? Are you sure you have nothing else to tell me?"

I had made a choice, and I'd make it all over again if it meant protecting the people I love. And if that also meant I had to lie to my sister about it, then I would.

Chapter 6

Lincoln

I SPIN MY GOLD BAND around my finger. I only wore it when I was around my girls. It hasn't meant what it was supposed to for a long time—a promise to love someone. It's a promise I hadn't realized had been broken. And I couldn't even be mad about it. I mourned someone I was so angry with, so many words left unspoken between us. A family curse, a tragedy, whatever anyone would call what happened to Olivia, it doesn't matter. I lived through it all, knowing what she'd done to break us. And it feels like it left me that way too.

"I have no desire to fix it. I stopped loving you a long time ago." She said it not like she was sorry, but like I should have known that she had kept secrets so well that it never crossed my mind that she'd had any in the first place.

So now, the ring came off when I'm not playing any of the roles I've been given—lonely widower, single parent, loving father, or Kentucky's most sought-after master distiller. When

I need to be someone other than the easygoing Foxx brother and take what I want instead of following pleasantries or rules.

> GRIZ:
> You planning to talk about your batch any time soon?

My grandfather is pushy when he's excited about something. Hell, he's pushy about most things. He just delivers it in a way that makes it seem like your idea. And when it comes to bourbon, he's always excited. Ever since my baby brother released his special edition of bourbon, Griz expected both Ace and me to do the same. Exceeding expectations is Ace's department. I'm expected to put out great bourbon every day, and now I need to do something exemplary. I'm not excited or inspired by that. If anything, I'm annoyed.

I have an idea about what I could do, but it isn't going to go over well. My grandfather is open-minded, but Ace is adamant about following the rules. He doesn't want to put out anything other than bourbon. No bourbon finished in specialty barrels or anything that could steer away from the core of what Foxx Bourbon delivers. I can't find the right time to pitch my idea because of that, so I've been ignoring Griz's question any time he asks.

Clearing my throat, I stare in the mirror, wiping the condensation from the shower with one swipe. More lines around my eyes than I remember. Still plenty of hair on my head. It's one asset the Foxx men have in our favor. Even Griz still has a thick head of hair. Though his is almost stark white now, matching his thick mustache. At one time, he and I looked the most alike. Our hair was darker brown than both my brothers', and wavy when it was long enough. Maybe it's time for a new look.

I clean up around my neck with the razor, but instead of a clean shave, I leave my five-o'clock shadow. It's the middle of winter, and the weather is cold anyway.

"Dad, are you almost done? I need to get my robe." Lily knocks, then again, louder, not even a few seconds later. "Can you hear me? Are you staring at yourself in the mirror again?"

Jesus, this kid.

Chuckling, I wrap the towel around my waist and open the door. "Why is your robe in my bathroom?"

She rolls her eyes. She's gotten really good at being nine. "You have the better bathtub, duh."

I smile at her. "Bought you some new bath bombs."

Her eyes light up as they meet mine in the mirror. "You did? Where?!"

"Just added them to the shelf." I nod to the corner. It's not hard for me to lean into being a girl dad. If bath bombs get me smiles like that, then I'll gladly buy as many as they want until they move on to the next obsession. My girls have had enough tears and felt enough sadness in their short lifetime. They deserve better than what they've been given.

I make my way into my walk-in closet and pluck a pair of jeans for tonight.

"Cozy vanilla cream and sparkling razzleberry. Dad, razzleberry isn't an actual fruit, right?"

I'm fingering through my shirts when she finds me.

"Don't think so, Lil," I shout from the closet.

"It doesn't say it's a real fruit." She holds up my phone to show me the search. "Oh, you got a text. Uncle Ace says he's drinking with a few assholes at Midnight Proof." Her eyes widen, lips rolling inward, realizing what she just said. "I'm just the messenger."

With a quirked eyebrow, I hold out my hand for my phone. "Don't read my texts, please. You should owe the curse purse."

"Technically, Uncle Ace owes."

I put my glasses on and look at the screen. "Lily, my phone has a passcode."

With a nod, she smiles up at me. "I know my birthdate, Dad."

How am I not supposed to laugh and applaud that? But I keep my dad hat on for a couple more minutes. "How did you know it was your birthday and not Lark's?"

She walks to the back of the closet and stands on the small stool, reaching for the row of darker dress shirts. "You use Lark's birthday for your computer password. And your birthday for the passcode on all the doors."

"Seriously?" I deadpan.

"Here! Wear this one." She hands me a black dress shirt, then hops off the stool. "You look the most handsome when you wear this one."

"Stay off my electronics, kiddo," I call out after her.

When I come down the stairs, Lark is sprawled out on the couch, roaming through Netflix. I do a double take because my eleven-year-old looks more like a teenager every day—braids and dresses exchanged for sports T-shirts, high socks, and lip gloss. It honestly makes the center of my chest ache.

"Lark, you're going to hate the next few words out of my mouth, but I'm going to say them, anyway." I look at the clock. Grant will be here any minute. "You need to watch something that your sister is going to like too."

"C'mon, Daaad," she groans. "Why do I have to? Lily isn't even in here right now." Sitting up quickly, she glares at me as I move toward the kitchen.

I take out the ice cream tub and two bowls as my oldest gives me a look of death. I thought this wasn't coming for another few years, but Lark is on the cusp of turning twelve, and my sweet girl is quickly turning into a fire-breathing dragon of chaotic emotions. She also refuses to laugh at any of my jokes anymore. It's an eye roll, or a huff, or, my favorite, being ignored.

"So did you decide what you want to do for your birthday this year?" I hold my breath, waiting and hoping she just says hanging out with a couple of friends.

"Spa party sleepover, just with some of the girls from my softball team, and maybe a few from my class last year. A few from this year, too. Maybe."

Thank fucking goodness. A few friends I can handle. "Okay, who's planning this spa party sleepover?"

She smiles at me, but it's one of mischief. One that tells me I don't know what I'm in for before she even responds. "Maybe Auntie Hadley can help you?"

Shit. I give her the side-eye and grab two spoons and hold one out for her. Raising my eyebrows, I make circles in the air with it. "What does that mean, 'help me'? You're going to have to break down what this is going to look like. And how many people are we talking about?"

"Like, fifteen or so." She glances up at the look of sheer horror I'm trying to mask.

But I'm already shaking my head.

She follows it up with, "That's not that many, Dad. And we probably won't even sleep. And maybe things like doing face masks and making our own lip balm."

"Lark, that's the *entire* softball team. Not a few friends," I say as calmly as my brain will allow. "Can you pick two?"

She exhales heavily and tilts her head like the question is ridiculous. "Dad…"

Clearly the wrong question—leave it to a preteen to have you second-guessing the kind of parent you actually are.

"My softball friends are really my best friends, but if I invite some of them, then I have to invite all of them. So that would be somewhere around twenty-ish."

"This is not winning me over. What happened to fifteen? I liked that number better."

She rolls her eyes, but instead of letting her fall down the rabbit hole of catching an attitude from this my-dad-is-so-lame moment, I open the top of the ice cream tub and try to throw her off her game.

"Come, tell me if this is poison before I try it. You're younger, you're more likely to survive."

A small smile cracks out.

Got her.

She digs into the new container, taking out a massive hunk of the chocolate peanut butter swirl.

Almost exactly as the ice cream hits Lark's mouth, Lily runs into the kitchen, sliding a solid three feet in her fuzzy socks until she ricochets an arm length from the counter. "Dad, please, please, please, can I have ice cream?"

"You have an Oreo in your hand."

She plops it in her mouth and then holds up her now empty hands. With her cheeks filled while she chews, she gives me a double thumbs up. I stifle a laugh because it's exactly what I would have done at her age.

Lark digs in for another spoonful and says, "Then fifteen for the party is okay?"

I'm being hustled by my own kid. "You swindled me, didn't you?"

Over a mouthful of ice cream, she smiles. "I learned from the best."

"Mm-hmm, I see how it is." Licking my spoon, I drop it in the sink. "Bedtime tonight is nine o'clock," I tell them while I grab the sprinkles from the top cabinet. "You both had a busy week. I don't want to come home and you're still awake."

"When are you coming home?" Lark asks as she clinks spoons with her sister.

"Late. And definitely after nine."

"Are you going on a date?" Lily pipes up. The question has me pausing, because they've never asked me that before. I'll get an occasional update about a friend's mom asking if I'm still single, but they make barf faces and never really say much else.

I clear my throat. "Nope, just meeting a new friend."

And that's the truth. I haven't been interested in dating. Flirting, drinks, and some casual encounters are the extent. I'd already had the parts of life that allowed for more. The falling in love, marrying, kids, and then slowly falling out of love. And even after that, it didn't end well. Hell, anyone who knows my last name doesn't want that either. It's foolish, but it feels too real to ignore the fact that just about any woman who fell in love with a Foxx ended up dying. With the exception of my new sister-in-law, Laney, who barely escaped a massive fire, a rickhouse explosion, and a serial killer. My hope is that she paid her penance to carry our last name and avoid the curse.

My girls don't need to know why there won't be anyone coming into their lives. It just isn't something I want.

"What new friend?" Grant asks as he walks through the living room and toward the kitchen.

"Uncle Grant!" Lily shouts and jumps up on the couch, catapulting herself onto his back.

"Never gets old," he says with a smile as Lark gives him a high-five and knuckles.

"I'm assuming you're heading to Midnight Proof at some point?"

I look around for my other boot. "Yeah, why?"

"Hadley roped Laney into bartending with her tonight." He gives me a look that I know very well—he's not thrilled about it. "Keep an eye on my wife, please."

My brother has always been possessive of the people in his life, but he took that up a notch after Laney came waltzing into his world. It feels good to see my kid brother in love and happy again. I wasn't sure that I'd ever get to witness it. We'd had a handful of tough years—the Foxx family. It messed Grant up in a way I understood, because I was experiencing it too.

"I got her," I tell him as I kiss Lily on the head. "Laney can also handle her own, you know that." I point at Lark. "We'll talk about the party later. Be nice to your sister for me?"

She smiles and squeezes my shoulder. A sentiment of the Foxx men. We aren't huggers, but when one of us is proud or happy to see the other, it's always a firm shoulder squeeze. Lark pays attention. I still get hugs from her, but I love a good shoulder squeeze all the same.

"Did you want to come up for a drink?" the photographer asks me. A pretty brunette whose name I've been purposely ignoring for this very reason.

I have no interest in allowing this to go any further—something felt off, and this woman was tied to a huge publication. Local gossip is one thing, but I'm smart enough to know that her affiliation with *The New York Times* is a red flag. There are plenty of ways for her to influence Murray's story. She's beautiful, but a night of fun isn't worth the potential complications.

"I have an early day tomorrow, and I need to talk to my friend behind the bar before I head out." While that's mostly true, I'm not ready to go home yet. "But thank you for indulging me and keeping me company tonight."

I can tell by the tight-lipped smile and nod that she wasn't planning to be dismissed so easily. She wanted to have a drink at the hotel bar, which meant she really had no interest in leaving and seeing Fiasco or the speakeasy I had mentioned earlier today. It would be effortless to take her upstairs and fool around. Suck, fuck, rinse, repeat. I struggle to remember the last time I felt anything that resembled genuine heat, never mind the kind of chemistry that doesn't allow room for thinking, just reacting and leading. That dance that wipes away common sense and leaves two people breathless and wanting for more. Yeah, none of that's happening tonight. I give her a kiss on the cheek, pay the tab, and thank her for the beautiful company.

Less than twenty minutes later, I walk down the stairs and through the double oak doors of Midnight Proof. I'm greeted by the warm, dimmed lighting from the chandeliers and the sound of the jazz trio kicking off their set. The sultry crowd and familiar faces wipe away any lingering thoughts about my evening with the photographer. Going home would have been the smarter choice, but Ace has texted me twice more complaining about the company he's keeping tonight. I'm always better at charming the people who grate on Ace's nerves.

I catch my best friend giving me a wide-eyed smile as I head toward the bar. "What are you doing here?" She glances at Ace across the room. "Figured it'd be past both your bedtimes by now."

I flip her off. "He can't hear you making fun of his age from all the way over there."

The speakeasy is packed tonight, with a variety of people in town to talk about bourbon and horses. Business in a relaxed setting always makes for better deals.

I glance down the length of the bar toward my sister-in-law. "Whatcha making down there?"

She does a double take. "Linc! Did my husband send you to check on me?"

I smile at her. "Never!"

Laughing, she finishes her drink order.

Hadley stares at me knowingly. "Crap date?"

"Not a date. Just a distraction." I shrug a shoulder.

She gives me a deadpan glare, wanting more details. When she realizes that's all I'm going to say, she gives me an understanding smile. "Here, you get a Manhattan tonight," she says, sliding the cocktail to me. "Can you let Brady at the door know that the show is starting in five?"

I tap my knuckles on the bar. "On it." By the time I make it to the double doors, the lights are dimming. I lean into Brady, the bouncer. "Hadley says the show's about to start, so let's hold out on any more entries."

He gives me a nod and does what he has to do.

I linger there just as the jazz band gets a little louder, playing something I recognize but could never name. In a low riff, the bass starts, and the trumpet chimes in a few moments later. Leaning my back against the brick wall draped in black velvet curtains, I look around, watching couples and friends peppered throughout the high top tables and lounges, all sipping on something in coupe, rocks, or champagne glasses. I notice my brother entertaining another suit just as the room grows quiet.

It's the type of silence that feels predictive of a winter storm. A storm you know is coming, but it just hasn't broken through the clouds yet.

Hushed voices whisper and wait for the singer and the elusive burlesque performance to begin. I forgot that's what tonight's entertainment would be. It explains the above-normal packed house on a weeknight. It's been months now since Hadley mentioned the "smokeshow burlesque dancer" she had hired. Tonight was the first show.

I sip on my Manhattan—the rye whiskey is a nice switch from my usual bourbon neat. When I come to Midnight Proof, I let Hadley, or whichever bartender is pouring for the night, choose my drink for me.

The vermouth coats my tongue, and the rye eases down nicely. Dim lighting mixed with the music prelude and my drink have my body relaxing. But then a trumpet pitching loud and abruptly ending has me snapping to attention. In the center of the room, a single spotlight flips on, and underneath it, a woman stands in a black trench coat. Her dark hair is pinned up to one side with some kind of netting and pink gems that reflect the light. The dramatic sounds and lighting amplify everything. I'm fixated on her silhouette, eager to know the way it curves and dips beneath that coat.

I adjust my glasses and take another sip of my drink. But when she turns, the feeling of contentment that I had momentarily is ripped out from under me.

Green eyes I had once mistaken for blue are framed by smudged dark makeup that tips up to points along each side. A small beauty mark, one that sits slightly to the right, just above the curve of her cheek, is more confirmation. I know that mark. The same way I know that her hair is naturally blond, not black.

Faye *fucking* Calloway.

Anger flares inside me, the same way a match would ignite when dragged along red phosphorus. It's a chemical reaction that changes one element into another in a millisecond. The powerful emotion catches fire along my limbs, down my back, making my cock tingle and every inch of my skin overheat.

I grit my teeth so hard that my jaw hurts. What the fuck is she doing back in Fiasco? I flex my hand at my side, remembering the night, along the edge of the cornfield next door to my house, being blackmailed with a fucking murder weapon moments after a kiss that never should have happened. It should have felt like payback, our kiss in that field, after everything that my wife had admitted to me that night. But it hadn't felt anything like payback—and *that* pissed me off.

The music evolves into an old tone that dips off, and then the band's singer draws out the opening chorus. This entire room must be sharing the sentiment of her lyrics, that she's *feeling gooooood*...because the echoes of hoots and whistles ring out just as Faye unties the belt to the coat. Each end of the belt hangs on their respective sides, swaying because of the dramatic way she flicked her wrists. Her fingers cloaked in satin gloves grip the long coat together, keeping it closed for a moment longer. Seconds later, the music gets louder, higher, and she sheds her coat in a way that's so effortless and seductive I can't look away. She's left in nothing more than a blur of dusty pink lace and satin. It's sheer and shimmering as the spotlight follows her movements.

Fucking hell. I shift, fully aware that my body's reacting to her. With my dick hardening and my face flushing, I'm fucking livid that she's here. And then it clicks—she's not visiting. She's fucking working here.

I glance down the length of her, salivating as I watch her hips and thick thighs sway. And how her waist dips in like an hourglass. It's impossible to look at anything or anyone else as she moves through the crowd, her hips ticking back and forth in time with the drumbeat. When I finally swallow, I look around to see the entire room focused on every detail of her. She's an entirely new kind of focal point. The kind that turns heads and bodies on. There isn't a single person paying attention to anything or anyone else other than her, including me.

Faye stands in front of where Ace and his party sit. The three men casually watch on, each of them with a glass of bourbon in one hand. Their eyes glide down the length of her body, and I'm sure a roster of thoughts about her run through their minds. Plenty are running through mine.

She perches herself on the table in front of them, eyes locked on one of the assholes my brother spoke of earlier, as she raises one gloved arm above her head. Taking her time, she drags the satin glove down to her elbow and then, with one finger in her mouth, uses her teeth to pull it off the rest of the way.

"What do you say, boys?" Faye says to the band, loud enough for the audience to hear, cutting into the sultry song. "Are we feeling good?" Some hoots and whistles echo off the walls, and I'm smiling like a goddamn idiot. She smiles in that sexy way that she's perfected. Every facial expression and movement are for a purpose.

Her hands meet her hips, chest out, and she pulls some string on the already barely there dress, removing the outer layer of sheer pink. She's left in a pink satin bra and shorts set. Beneath the reflection of the chandeliers and spotlight, her skin shimmers. Two rows of crystals hug her neck, and as if they are droplets of water, they splash down from her collarbone, loosely dripping down to her chest, framing each mouthwatering breast.

A loud whistle from the bar has me clearing my throat and blinking. I feel like I've just been slapped across the face. I should leave. I should go home and deal with these feelings in the morning. But I don't move from my spot. I can't.

I track her movements across the room. Faye smiles and takes a seat on one of the men Ace was rubbing elbows with. Some asshole who owns auction houses who had been on a private tour of the distillery earlier today. His meaty hand rests on her lower back, fingers splayed lower than what I would consider a respectable way to touch a stranger.

She leans closer and whispers something to him. Smiling, she cranes her neck away from him as her head dips back, leaving her sprawled across his lap. But it's when her head is tipped fully back that she locks eyes with me. It's brief, but her body tenses, and the carefree, flirtatious expression falls as she keeps her attention on me for a few beats more.

"You're not supposed to be here, and you know it," I mumble to myself. I can't figure out what pisses me off more: the fact that she's back in my town or that I can't stop watching her. My dick twitches as she drags her hands up the center of her body, and then, with the change in tempo, she stands up and moves along the open space between chairs and the stage. She's teasing the entire room, and I'd put money on the fact that not a single seat in the house is dry or soft.

Crossing my arms over my chest, my eyes roam down her body once more. Her shoulders thrust back, accentuating the shape of her full tits that strain to escape the pink satin propping them so perfectly. My thumb finds its way to my mouth, and I drag it across my lips, wondering what hers would feel like—urgent, plush, an appetizer. The smooth skin creased between her bottoms and where the curve of her ass ends as she turns looks like the perfect place to drag fingers and graze teeth.

What the fuck am I thinking?

The singer kicks into the chorus again and the room echoes with more whistles as Faye unbuckles her right garter belt first and then covers her mouth as if to say, "Oops!" When she flicks the other side open, her eyes meet mine with a smirk this time. That's when she starts moving toward me. *Don't you fucking dare.*

I hear Brady, the bouncer next to me, say, "Holy shit, she's coming this way—" He nudges my chest with the back of his hand.

Walking right up to me, she winks—*she fucking winks*. And then her attention veers to Brady. The fucking guy who looks like a linebacker and is a good six inches shorter than me. He swallows and stares at Faye. *Jesus, she's rendered him stupid.*

"Hi, handsome," she says in a sweet, projected voice, her Kentucky twang loud and proud. "Would you mind helping me?"

But I don't let him answer. "Is there a zipper, or will I need a knife?" I interject. My voice is deep and loud enough so that I know she hears me.

Her eyes shift and anchor to mine. The exchange between us is simple. *He's not going to fucking touch you, so you better ask me for that favor.*

She looks over her shoulder at the crowd. The spotlights throughout the room highlight various tables, making it just bright enough for everyone to see who she's planning to play with. *Me.* With a smile dancing along her lips, she turns back and slides her hand along my forearm and clasps her fingers around mine, guiding me back toward the bar where a vacant stool waits. When we get there, she presses herself close, runs her fingers down the center of my shirt, and then gives me a little shove onto the stool just as the trumpet tips up in a high note. The crowd isn't as loud, but the move encourages a few whistles and hoots. Stepping back, she raises her leg slowly, the ball of her heeled foot hitting right above my belt. I don't move my hands when she leans forward, her foot pushing into me as she asks, "A little help, Foxx."

It's impossible to ignore where we are, but my body buzzes with the anticipation of touching her. The jazz band plays just the instrumental interlude as I do. Her heels don't have a buckle. The feathery pouf that rests along the top of her shoe is a nice touch—she's a goddamn pinup girl from head to toe. I slip the back off first and then the front, tossing it to the side. I hear a few people shout out my name and Hadley or Laney—one of the two—whistles again from behind the bar.

Starting from her ankle, I glide my fingers and the palms of both hands up her calf and to her knee, where the ninety-degree angle forces my fingers to her thigh. I let my palms run underneath instead of up the sides of her leg slowly pulling at the light pink fishnet stocking. Rolling it down her leg, my fingers brush along her smooth skin, leaving goosebumps in their wake. Touching her like this shouldn't feel so good. And people watching should make me think twice, but it doesn't.

She switches legs and signals for me to do the other. As I repeat the same movement, I can't help but look at her face this time, focusing on the plump bottom lip painted in the same color pink as the netting I'm gliding down her leg. When I move my attention upward, having no problem looking someone in the eye, she swallows, and the playful hint on her lips struggles to stay in place. My heart races as my fingers linger against her skin. And my breath catches as I catalog the beauty mark on her upper cheek, the way her throat works to swallow, and how her chest expands as she watches me.

The second my fingers pull away, the trance between the two of us is broken, and she snaps back into character. Now even shorter without her heels, she keeps eye contact with me for an extra beat and then flicks her eyes back toward the small circular stage. She drapes the stockings around her neck, each resting against her tits. The trumpet, bass, and singer end the song on a long drag of the words "feeling good" as she tosses the satin bra to the side, revealing only the valley of skin between her tits. The fishnet stockings hang strategically over her as she struts away, the lights cutting out, leaving behind the echo of applause. I rub my thumb along the pads of my fingers. I feel like I've just been fucked. And the satisfaction isn't lingering.

It's a very distinct feeling, the same one I experienced the night I stumbled into her on the edge of a dark cornfield. Only now, she's exchanged dirt and blood for satin and fishnets. Time hasn't changed a fucking thing—she's still dangerous.

It was easy to figure out what she had been doing in that field, especially after discovering who had been considered missing shortly after, and why she would need an alibi. Whatever her angle is for being back now, I'm going to figure it out. But not tonight.

"Lincoln." Ace's deep voice cuts in as he waves me over. I clear my throat, my head still reeling over a woman.

I smile as I walk past the bar, and Hadley asks, "What'd you think about the show?"

Giving her an unimpressed glance, I focus back on my brother. Anything that would pull my focus away from who I just watched peel off her clothes so publicly, so seductively, is what I need right now. *Goddamnit.*

"I'd like to introduce you to Brock Blackstone," Ace says as I step closer.

I extend my hand to shake his as I recall the name and how his business supports ours.

"Yes, that's right. Blackstone Auctions. I've heard some remarkable things are auctioned and sold through your business."

As he shakes my hand, I try not to think about how they're the same fingers that were splayed across *her* back. The same hand that glided along her skin. "So much more than what you would expect," Blackstone answers. "My private auction, specifically, might interest the both of you. I've acquired…" He pauses curiously. "Very beautiful things. And many more that are useful to businessmen in multiple arenas."

He looks around the room. "Speaking of, where did that gorgeous thing flitter off to? Will you excuse me?"

I toss back the rest of my Manhattan and watch as he meanders toward the bar. Ace stands next to me, drinking his bourbon. "Interesting crowd here tonight, don't you think?"

I give him the side-eye. "The entertainment included?"

He lets out a laugh and takes another sip. "She looks… different."

And just like I had done a handful of years ago, I lie to my brother again about the same person when I say, "I didn't notice."

Chapter 7

Faye

A PASSING WIND CHILLS MY arms and legs like I left a window open or fell asleep outside. *Shit.* The whispering of quiet voices is what wakes me. I'm immediately assaulted by the sizzle of Pop Rocks and the smell of sugary cherries. Before I squint an eye open, I listen. My neck is stiff and crooked sideways, while my head barely holds on to the throw pillow I stuffed under it.

"She has diamonds on the corners of her eyes," I hear in a shouted whisper. "Lark, how did she get diamonds on her face like that? It must be glue, right?"

It's been a handful of days since that first night at Midnight Proof. I've done two more shows since and find comfort in the late nights that I've gotten used to keeping. Luckily, there haven't been more surprise appearances from anyone with the last name Foxx. But I can't figure out why I'm not more relieved.

The porch swing sways and dips as the saccharine smell gets closer. *Damn, it's cold.* Even on the enclosed porch. I didn't plan to sleep out here, but I sat down, needing to clear my head after last night's show. I'd been thinking too hard about seeing Lincoln Foxx again—I don't know why I had assumed it wouldn't matter. I took his threat all those years ago seriously, and it had left me angry. But if I'm being honest with myself, it was an out. I don't know how I could have stayed and pretended like everything was fine after what happened that night. How would I have stuck to my plans and built a life where my perfect blueprints had become so diluted and smudged?

So, I was reeling about all that mess that is my life, why I cared that he hadn't come to another show, and then fell asleep. Now I shiver as the crisp morning air licks at my skin, goosebumps raising along my bare arms. *Where's the blanket I had wrapped around me?*

"She has tattoos on her arm. Almost all the way up to her shoulder," a quiet voice says. I feel the lightest touch of a finger tracing the vine and flowers that wrap around my arm. "So pretty," she whispers to herself. Then she whisper-shouts, "LARK!"

I open my eyes to look at the human alarm clock. Her head is turned toward the front of the house, so she doesn't see me watching her. Her dirty-blond curly hair is a stark contrast to the color of her father's. I hadn't realized that time would make them older too, but it isn't hard to recognize her as the youngest of Lincoln's girls. "Lark, come see the diamonds."

"They're rhinestones," I say, sounding groggier than expected.

She yelps and the packet of Pop Rocks explodes over the both of us as the porch swing sways haphazardly. Gripping onto my arms, she keeps herself from falling butt first onto the porch floor. "Crocs and rocks, lady. You scared the sparkle right out of me."

It's well past sunrise, but it's cold. Kentucky seasons like to play in the extremes. Summers are humid and balmy, while winters love to lay a shock to the system. This morning has a bite to it.

My voice sounds like I swallowed gravel when I ask, "Good. Who are you? And what are you doing on my porch?"

She stands up, and her bright pink puffy coat practically blinds me. "My name is Lily Bernice Foxx," she says with all the attitude she can conjure.

It's not bad enough that he lives across the street, but his spawn is nosy. I forgot that Fiasco's like this—minimal personal boundaries disguised as warm welcomes.

"And this is Maggie's porch."

A suctioning empty sound echoes around the porch, coming from the cup that looks an awful lot like mine gripped in the other blond's hands. "Did you just drink my water?"

The girl smiles, and instead of saying anything in response, she looks at the front door and walks right into the house.

I glance back at Lily, who's looking at a palmful of small rocks. "You two realize this isn't your house, right?"

Lark comes back out, the screen door opening wide and slamming shut behind her, before she hands me a new glass of water.

Lily perches on the railing. "You're Maggie's sister."

"Faye Rose Calloway," I answer with my full name, just like she did. Stretching my arms up above my head, I try to break free from the haze of sleep. It isn't the first time I've fallen asleep on the porch swing since I've been here, but it's the first time I didn't wake up and go inside. This spot had been one of my mom's favorite places—Maggie and I would doze with her out here on lazy Sundays in the summers when it was just the three of us. That feels like a lifetime ago now.

Lily gasps and whispers my middle name to herself. "Rose."

"I remember you," Lark says while side-eyeing her sister. Perched on the porch railing, the girl emanates all the Foxx features—blue eyes, confident stature, a small divot on her chin, and a scowl that looks eerily familiar. Her hair color and paler skin must be from her mother's side. I follow her line of sight out into the rows of corn. "Cool T-shirt, by the way," she says.

I look down at my tank top, not remembering what I'm wearing. And then I say, "I remember you too. You must have good taste. This is one of my favorites." I pluck at my shirt. "Freddie Mercury was fabulous."

I glance at Lily, who's focused on a collection of rocks in her palm. "Did you find those or buy them?"

Nodding, she holds each one up. "Agate, calcite, and I've been trying to find celestite." She holds up a larger one. "Geodes are my favorite. I found this one in a gem shop."

"Beautiful," I say as she hands it to me. I turn it over in my hand. The craggy inside of purple crystals is sharp, but the outside is smooth, brown, and gray.

"That one helps keep away negative energy. Mrs. Davis, my science teacher, says that rocks don't have that kind of power. That they're the product of 'pressure and time,' but I really just think she needs one of these in her pocket." She smiles, waving her hands. "Too much negative energy."

I can't help but smile back.

Lily nods to the one I'm holding. "My mom gave me that one."

Lark mumbles out, "Lots of good that did for her."

A small pink rock gets tossed her way. "Hey, captain of the attitude team, hold that one and give it a rub."

She throws it back to Lily, but instead of either of them getting mad or dwelling on any of it, they both laugh lightly, and Lily puts it back in her pouch. I remember when it was easy like that with my sister. Get mad, fight it out, move on. It was so simple back then.

Lark asks, "Did you ever see that movie about the guy who built the baseball field in his cornfield?"

The question throws me off. I glance at my phone—just after ten in the morning means I've gotten less than five hours of sleep. But I know exactly what she's talking about. Kevin Costner, before he was a rancher, was a farmer in Iowa building a baseball field, believing that if he did, the greatest baseball player of all time might show up and play on it.

"I have. A few times, actually. Seems like a bit of an old movie for you." I study the way she stares into that field, resting her chin on her knees. "Did you like it?"

"Parts of it," she says. "That if you believe in something, listen to your gut, it'll work out in the end."

I feel those words—*listen to your gut*. It's not often I'm in the presence of kids to have these kinds of conversations. I don't lead the kind of life where I've been around very many of them, and I definitely wouldn't expect for one to say something that hit as hard as that.

"My mom used to say that to me." I peek over at her. "To do what feels right and that it'll all work out." It's not lost on me how ironic that is, considering how things unraveled for her. For us.

"I liked your mom. Shelby," she says with a smile as she plays with the ends of her sleeve. "The horses always listened to her, and she made Griz laugh so hard that he would turn red."

Maggie leans against the screen door and interrupts, "Hey, little Foxx ladies, want a smoothie?"

They both dart their attention to each other and then glance at me before Lily hides her face and makes a barfing sound.

"What kind of smoothie?" I ask curiously, chuckling at her reaction.

Maggie barks out a laugh and says, "Fuck off, Faye." She takes a sip of her smoothie and then mumbles, "The offer wasn't meant for you."

That's the most words I've gotten out of Maggie since I dropped my bag inside the front door and she realized I was serious about staying here. She's doubled down, really leaning into being an asshole. Maybe the silent treatment was better.

Lily clears her throat. "That's five dollars, Maggie," she says without even looking up.

Lark whispers to me, "You don't want the smoothie. It's green and smells like feet."

Maggie huffs, walking away from the screen, and I can't help but crack another smile. A woman in her mid-twenties having temper tantrums is nothing if not entertaining.

"Aren't the two of you supposed to be in school," she yells from inside.

I look between them.

Before I can ask any more about it, the loud slamming of a truck door has the three of our heads whipping toward the driveway. "Lark and Lily Foxx. You've got to be kidding me. I watched both of you get on the bus for school thirty minutes ago. And then I catch sight of two girls about the same age as my two girls over here. One of them has a pink puffy jacket, and I say to myself, 'That can't be Lily Bernice Foxx. She's in school right now. Who could the other, older and more mature one next to her be? Definitely not her sister, Lark. That would be impossible.'"

His sarcastic tone has me biting back a smile and my stomach swooping as if I'm in trouble too. It's the same feeling I had when I saw him the other night.

Lark mumbles, "We're in so much trouble."

Lily shouts, "Dad, *youuu* said sometimes you have to make your own rules. So that's what we're doing."

He barely glances at me, but with his attention on his daughters, I take advantage and my eyes wander. In the broad light of day, Lincoln Foxx is beyond handsome. A full head of dark hair, which is a luxury for most men dancing around forty. I always remembered him as more clean-shaven, but now his sideburns blend into stubble. Everyone who has a pulse feels his confidence and more than recognizes that he's the prettiest Foxx. And somehow, he's improved. Light blue eyes behind dark-framed glasses make me want his attention even more. Why I didn't tell him to fuck off the other night is beside me. But right now, in dad-mode and pissed off, he's disturbingly sexy. It would be so much more convenient for him to be aging poorly.

I've done plenty of questionable things and made some morally gray decisions throughout my life. I knew someday I'd have to answer for them. I hadn't realized that karma would be dressed in Wranglers and a crisp black shirt and dark wool coat, ignoring my presence.

A chill works its way down my arms and around my legs, reminding me that I'm outside and not dressed for the winter weather.

The default emotion whenever I think too long about Lincoln Foxx is a combination of hate and annoyance. We both painted each other into corners. I hate that he was there that night. I hate what that night made me. I hate that he saw it, accepted it, and kept it a secret. I hate that at the core of it—of all the shit people I'd come across—the person I chose to hold a grudge against was probably the most honorable. It's annoyingly inconvenient.

His gaze shifts to me for a brief moment, and oh yeah, hate and annoyance are mirrored right back to me. "Why are you here?"

I look around the porch. "This is technically still my house. Well, half of it, at least. Why are you here?"

Letting out a sarcastic laugh, he rubs his hand behind his neck as he repeats the question to himself more quietly. "Why am I here?" He looks at both of his girls. "Let's go," he bites out from the bottom of the porch steps.

But Lark chimes in, "Dad, please can we just take the day?" Her hands clasp together in prayer. "We all need mental health days."

I try to mask my amusement. She's right. We all did, but I don't think her dad's buying it. Especially not after seeing me here talking with them.

"I don't know what you're smiling at." My eyes connect with his when I realize he's talking to me.

I raise my eyebrows.

"When I'm done handling this," he says, pointing at his girls, "you and I are going to have a little chat."

I shake my head no with a smile at the audacity. "I don't think so, Foxx—"

His dimples pinch as he smirks right back, like my words were meant to be funny. Looking down at the porch floor, his hands glide into his jacket pockets. "Lily and Lark, get in the car."

One of them starts up again. "Oh, c'mo—"

"Now," he clips back in a tone firm enough that it makes me sit just a few centimeters taller. The girls hustle down the stairs, but Lily stops and turns, hustling back up the steps.

Quietly, she says, "Here. This one is supposed to give you courage. Don't lose it, okay?" She tosses the gray rock next to me. When it bounces and flips over, the ragged purple crystals land face up.

I clamp my lips together, trying to keep the amusement off my face as she walks away, but as I shift my attention, I meet her father's glare of disapproval.

"Do not go anywhere," he says, pointing at me.

"You're trespassing," I clap back. They're the same words I said to him five years ago in that cornfield. He doesn't miss it by the narrowing of his eyes.

Shaking his head, his hands meet his hips. "You're a fucking peach," he mumbles.

Why does it feel so satisfying to piss this man off? "I'm not a fan of pet names, Foxx." I scrunch my nose at him. "Sorry."

His deep voice pitches an octave lower. "I want you gone."

I stand up, letting the blanket that had fallen in my lap drop to the floor. The cropped Queen tank hits just above my navel, but below is nothing more than a pair of tiny sleep shorts. Lower than that is a pair of fuzzy socks hiked to my knees, but I don't think he gets that far. His gaze snaps to everywhere there's bare skin—my arms, then my waist, and to my thighs. *So predictable.*

"You sure about that, Foxx?" I glance at his legs and up toward his belt, letting my gaze linger just to irritate him further.

Swallowing roughly, he looks over his shoulder at the Jeep. But instead of walking that way, he charges up the stairs, stopping right in front of me. "Those two little girls are my entire world. A decent set of tits and perky ass doesn't mean I'll forget that you're not the kind of person I want anywhere near them." He looks down the front of me and back up, meeting my eyes and searing me to the spot. "So yeah, I'm sure."

I wish his words didn't sting as much as they did.

"You have no idea what kind of person I am," I say on less than sturdy footing as I brush past him and through the front door, kicking it closed behind me.

I huff out a breath as I lean against the door. Frustrated, angry, and...hurt. Dammit, I loathe feeling hurt more than anything.

Trying to shake it off, I take the stairs two at a time and head right into the bathroom. With blurry eyes, I turn on the shower, whip off my clothes, and bat away a tear that falls unwantedly. When I step into the low-pressure spray, I let the hot water seep in and drown out his words—*you're not the kind of person I want anywhere near them.* Jesus, what did I expect? I blackmailed him, and he told me to never come back.

Jolting me from my spiraling, Maggie pounds on the bathroom door, shouting, "Don't use all the hot water!"

I pinch the bridge of my nose and suck in a deep, grounding breath. What the hell was I thinking coming back here?

Chapter 8

Lincoln

Society will tell me it's too early for bourbon, but I'm about to shove two middle fingers enthusiastically in the air and spin on my boots in a 360-degree *fuck you* to the universe. Not a single *fucking* thing about today is going my way.

"Dad, this isn't the way to school," Lily states warily from the back seat, her head turning as we drive by Hooch's and toward the distillery.

"Well, you two wanted to kick off the week by breaking the law, so I figure there's only one person who would be able to talk some sense into you."

Pulling onto the long gravel road, I already see Julep waiting patiently for our arrival. Grant must have told her the girls were coming. That dog considers Lark and Lily part of her pack.

"We didn't break the law," Lily claps back.

"It's the law that you go to school, and the two of you were planning not to do that today... So"—I shrug my shoulders—"now you can take it up with Uncle Grant."

That quiets her quickly. Grant might be a retired cop, but he can still pull out the intimidating follow-the-rules speech when needed. He still does it to me.

Skipping school is something my brothers and I did all the time as kids. We'd get on the bus, and as soon as the bus opened its doors, we'd find a way to distract the teacher on bus duty and hoof it to the edge of the woods that line the school's property. When our parents were still alive, we'd usually stop at our grandfather's house first. He would always leave a few Ale-8s in the cooler behind his shed and a key for the distillery hanging on a hook.

"I like her," Lark says, knocking the memory from me. I glance back in the rearview mirror. "Her name is pretty."

"Who?" I ask without registering what she's talking about.

"Faye. It's pretty," Lily says, picking at her newly polished nails.

"You just got those done, don't pick." I clear my throat. "And you can't just like someone because of their name."

"Why not?" Lily rushes out, at the same time as Lark interrupts, "Plus, I like how she talks to us."

"What?" I laugh out.

Lily carries on like her sister hadn't interjected. "She was really pretty too."

"Pretty..." I say on an exhale. "There are more words I could think of to describe that—"

Lark cuts in, "Her nails looked like daggers."

"Probably uses them as weapons too," I mutter under my breath. I glance in the rearview at Lark, who's staring at her nails. Fucking hell, I feel like I should reevaluate the way I've been parenting if my girls are so easily won over by a pretty woman. "You can't like a person just because you like how they look."

As soon as I say it, I know what's going to follow. Lark squints at me in a way that screams, *you're an idiot*. Then she scrolls through her device that's currently only being used as her source of music. "She had on a cool Queen T-shirt. It said 'Killer Queen.'"

"Fitting," I mumble.

"She has a matching beauty mark." Lily points to the right apple of her cheek. "It's like we're soulmates."

Jesus Christ.

"Plenty of people have beauty marks on their face, Lily."

I slow the Jeep as Julep runs next to us. Lark rolls down her back window so she can greet Julep. "Julep, you get to hang out with two more of your favorite people today."

Lark leans back in and looks at me through the rearview. "Dad, she seemed nice."

"She's not."

Lily claps back this time. "How do you know?"

I don't plan on telling her the exhaustive list about how Faye is not the "nice" person my girls believe her to be.

"I just know."

"People don't talk to us like that. It's either sad eyes about Mom or fancy voices about you," Lily says. My stomach lurches at how I know exactly what they mean. "I heard the moms from Girl Scouts talking about what the curse means for us." Hearing *that* pisses me off. Fiasco loves its gossip, but the people in this town wanted to pin a reason on why our family had to deal with so much tragedy and loss. It was a ridiculous thing to say: *Every woman a Foxx loved ended up dying.* But bringing it up around my kids wasn't going to go unanswered.

Lark gazes out the side window, looking sad and contemplative, and the only thing I want to do is make sure she's okay. If I don't pull out some kind of motivational moment here, I'm going to regret it.

"Hey," I say, trying to get her to look at me through the rearview mirror. "Lark."

She gives me a side-eye that reminds me so much of her mother it has me swallowing the lump in my throat.

"Listen to me right now." I turn off the radio and step on the brake. "You're Foxx girls." Raising my eyebrows, I sit taller. "That's strength, darlin'. There isn't a single soul in this town or the next who's as strong, and smart, and beautiful as the two of you."

Lark's chin wobbles at that affirmation, and it takes everything in me to keep my shit together too. We talk about their mom often. The good things. The things that made Olivia lovable and kind. The things I hope they somehow get from her, because those things aren't me. They'll get strong and loyal, smart and aware, but the parts that had made me fall in love with my wife are the things I hope my girls somehow absorbed.

Lark gives me one nod, as Lily throws both arms up high, fingers out as she repeats those words. "We're Foxx girls."

Lark cracks a smile. "Fine. We're Foxx girls."

I pull up the rest of the way in my brother's driveway, throw it into park, and turn in my seat. "Alright, Foxx girls." I look between the two of them. "No more skipping school, even if it's to see the pretty new neighbor."

"See? You just called her pretty," Lily retorts with a giggle.

Dammit.

Grant opens the front door to his place. There are only three things that make my baby brother smile like that: my sister-in-law, making barrels, and *my* girls.

"Are my little flowers turning into weeds? Why'd we skip school today?" he yells out, with a little too much amusement.

"That doesn't sound even a little bit like tough love," I tell him.

He crosses his arms as Lily rushes out of the Jeep telling him all about her newest rocks and gems. "Alright, Uncle Grant, pick your favorite."

My brother points to a small opaque white crystal.

Lily palms it and says as I walk closer, "Dad, how long are we going to be here today?"

Grant falls for the ploy to look away. That's when my daughter pockets the rock and I play along.

"Later this afternoon." I glance at Grant for confirmation. "That okay?"

He nods. "Fine with me. I'm all yours today, my little flowers."

She smiles wide as he turns his attention back to her. With her closed fists still held out, she says, "Okay, now. Pick a hand."

It takes him a second to choose her right hand. The same one she initially closed the rock in, but when she opens it, it's gone.

He barks out a laugh. "Lil, how'd you do that?!"

"Alright." Smiling, I clap. "Now, where's my new favorite Foxx?" The easiest way to rile him up is to flirt with my sister-in-law, Laney.

"She's helping Hadley again today. I would have thought you'd know that since you three are all up each other's asses."

"Is that new territory for you, baby brother?" I lower my

voice so my girls won't hear. "You having trouble being up your wife's ass? Need me to step in for some pointers?"

He punches me hard in the arm and follows it up with a shoulder squeeze. The menacing kind that's going to round out with a punch to the gut. *I know, I deserve it.* I let out a gasped breath as he does as predicted—anchoring a nice tight fist right under my ribs. "You know you deserved that one, right?"

I bend at the waist, hands on each knee, as I take a minute to catch my breath. A few seconds later, I follow it up with a "yep" and a nod.

Blowing out one more breath, I stretch my torso. *Fuck, that hurt.* "I'll text you after lunch. I should have been at the distillery two hours ago. Ace's cranky ass said he wanted to see me, and I'm still not there."

I turn my phone around to show Grant our oldest brother's demanding wall of texts.

ACE:
Need you here ASAP.

ACE:
It's not optional, get your ass here.

LINCOLN:
Why? Hadley giving you shit again?

ACE:
I'd like to see Maggie too. Please pick her up on the way. She's not answering.

"Who fucked up?" Grant asks after reading.

"Fuck if I know."

"Heard that Faye Calloway is the new burlesque girl at Midnight Proof. Still surprised she didn't end up a cop, if I'm being honest. Del used to talk about her like she was one to watch."

She's one to watch, alright—it's fucking hell trying not to. What the fuck was she wearing on a goddamn porch in the middle of winter?

"You catch her when you were there the other night?" My brother's asking for a reason. Grant's never passively curious. "Laney said she was incredible. Or rather, her words were, 'She's a total smokeshow, I have a girl crush, and Hadley said Faye gave her lady boner.'"

Rubbing my hand across my mouth, I hide my smile. "Jesus Christ, those two." I clear my throat before I lie. "I hadn't really thought about it, but yeah, I saw her when I was there."

His eyes narrow at me, and then he crosses his arms. "Hmm, that's interesting. Is she next door staying with Maggie?"

I try to be cavalier. "Why are you asking me?"

"You live next door, first of all. And second, you're being weird."

"I'm being weird?" I say, pointing to myself.

"Yeah, it's weird you didn't mention it. You always have something to say about beautiful women around here. Fuck, you're still being an asshole about Laney every chance you get." He swats at me.

"You and your wife need more exciting things to talk about." I turn back toward my car. "I'm leaving. Lark, Lily, I'll see you a little later," I call out over my shoulder.

"You realize I know when you're lying, Linc?"

I don't respond, instead flipping him off with a big smile as I get into my car.

Lily's eyes widen as she catches my middle finger waving in plain sight. *Shit.* I flick on my podcast so I don't hear her, but I watch in my rearview as she rubs her thumb and pointer finger together up high and mouths out, *Middle fingers are ten bucks, Dad!*

I should have never agreed to a curse purse.

Blaring music is the first thing that hits me when I stomp up the Calloway's front porch. After knocking and waiting, it was easier to just let myself in. I told Faye I was coming back, but the more important thing now is to bring Maggie into the distillery to talk business with Ace.

With a mouth full of cereal, Faye turns down the hallway and stops dead in her tracks when she sees me. I had expected a screech or scream, but instead, she cocks her head to the side and yells, "Couldn't stay away, Foxx?"

It takes a lot of willpower not to laugh at that. After everything I said to her before I left—and I know it was harsh—she claps back with sarcasm. I don't know why I like that, but it throws me off guard. *Again.*

One hand holds the bowl while she drops the other from holding the spoon. The cereal milk splashes as she glides her now free hand into the pocket of her brightly colored tapestry robe. The movement loosens the belt, and it gapes open just enough to see the valley of smooth skin that runs from her neck to her navel. A mere slip of skin and something in me thrums to life. The same way it had at Midnight Proof. The same way it had for the briefest moment in that cornfield. *Fuck, I forgot what the hell I'm doing here.*

I clear my throat and meet her gaze. The smirk playing along her lips tells me she knows exactly where I was looking. She thumbs the screen of her phone, and the music cuts out. "You want to tell me again how uninterested you are?"

She shifts her weight, just as another song comes on. Her movement gives me a better view of her robe, which might be covered in richly colored florals, but the material is practically sheer. I can see just enough that it takes everything in me not to catalog every detail.

The same tone of music that played the night I watched her at Midnight Proof comes over the speakers placed throughout the room, a trumpet kicking high and then the sultry voice of Nina Simone crooning about putting a spell on someone. I smirk at the song choice because she's really fucking good at tweaking my attention. Looking down, I spot something wrapped around her thigh. "Is that a knife strapped to your leg?"

She quirks an eyebrow. "Did you just think I was happy to see you, Foxx?"

"Fucking hell," I mutter. The handful of minutes I've spent with this woman doesn't matter, because every damn time she says or does something, it throws me off-center. It pisses me off almost as much as it turns me on.

I push my glasses up the bridge of my nose and wipe my hand along my jaw and across my mouth. "Where's Maggie?" I ask, changing the subject.

Over the music, she yells, "You realize you can't just walk into someone's house and demand things—"

But that's where she's entirely wrong. It takes no more than a few quick strides until I'm inches away from her. I flick my eyes down, taking in the tint of her skin and the smell of her body this close to mine—warm, smoky vanilla. Her chest rises and falls with the smallest hitch.

"You don't know the first thing about me," I tell her, my voice coming out gruffer than I'd like. Her chin tips back as my attention flicks to her pursed lips, lingering there. "Because if you did, you would know that I don't ask. I don't take well to threats. And I don't forget." I tilt my head to the side to see if she has anything to say back to that. But I'm met with silence. "And I'm the furthest thing from happy to see you." Leaning in closer, my mouth hovers over hers. "So I'll say it again, Peach. I don't want you here."

She sways slightly as I take a step back. It's a more satisfying reaction than it should be.

"Maggie," I shout, my eyes still trained on Faye. "If you're here, you need to come with me. Ace wants to see you."

Maggie jogs down the stairs just a few seconds later. "I'm right here. What's up, Linc?"

At the same time that Faye says, "*Linc?*" I can't help but react to the purples and greens peppered all over Maggie's face. A scab runs vertically across her upper lip and more bruises look like they're almost healed in the yellowed tint along her forearms.

Jesus. "What the hell happened?" I rush out.

She glances at her sister, who's watching the exchange. "I advertised to the wrong people." Her eyes water as she stares at my chest, zoning out. "I've been doing really well. It's been one of my best streaks."

Maggie has problems with gambling. My brothers and I know that, but as long as it doesn't touch our business, who are we to get involved?

"Did this have anything to do with—?"

She cuts me off. "No. Nothing like that."

But by the way Faye studies her sister, I'm not sure she believes much of what she's saying. If this was a result of what she's been doing for us, then I plan to make it right.

Maggie wraps her arms around my waist and rests her forehead against my chest. It's not typical behavior. I don't usually hug Maggie Calloway, but she's been folded into my family for the last few years, not to mention she's been good to my girls, so it doesn't feel totally unnatural to show her some comfort. "When did this happen?" I ask as I watch Faye.

Her arms are crossed, looking pretty fucking angry. "Go ahead, tell Linc. We both know you're not telling me a damn thing about what or who you're involved with."

But instead of acknowledging her sister, Maggie pulls back, face damp as she asks, "Ace wants to see me?"

I give her a nod and a tight-lipped smile.

"Maggie. You don't need to go anywhere," Faye says in a huff as her sister pushes through the front door. With a confused look, she asks me, "What did you and your family get my sister into?"

"I don't think that's something I should be talking to you about." I tip my head to the door. "If she wanted you to know, then my guess is that she would have told you."

The roar of an engine pulls our attention, and Faye rushes to the window. "Did she just take my truck?"

I let out a laugh. "Yup." I flip my key ring around my fingers. "Your sister is a bit of a loose cannon sometimes, case in point."

She stares at the dirt and dust that's kicking up from the tire tread, then her eyes snap to mine, full of fire.

"Are you sleeping with her?"

My head rears back. "What?"

"You heard me, Foxx. Are. You. Fucking. My. Sister?"

She can't be serious. "You can't be serious?"

I know what kind of reputation I've accumulated over the past handful of years. And it's never once bothered me. Until right now. I can't tell if she's asking because she's feeling protective of Maggie, or if she's been here long enough to listen to the gossip that swarms around me, or if she just wants to piss me off.

I stare at her for a moment, admiring that beauty mark on her cheek that my girls noticed too. A small gasp of air escapes her lips when the tips of my fingers brush along the edge of her hand. "You're really serious?" But she must be, because she doesn't blink as she waits for a response.

When I don't give her what she's looking for, she clears her throat. Licking her bottom lip, she says, "Answer the question, Foxx."

"Would it matter if I were?" I ask tauntingly.

Her eyes drop to my mouth before she corrects herself, realizing what she just did. The simple move makes me want more.

"Y-yes," she stutters out as her eyes meet mine.

Fuck. That isn't the answer I anticipated. It stirs something low in my gut, arousal definitely, but something else full of heat and curiosity. I can't tell anymore if this is still her way of gaining the upper hand. It feels vulnerable. As I step back, she leans forward, her hands gripping my shirt. I don't think she planned to do it as her eyes snap to where her fists are balling the material.

"Don't," I grit out, my voice low.

My tone snaps her out of whatever this is. And I instantly hate myself for it as her hands loosen their grip. She turns around, pausing for a moment before she heads straight for the stairs.

Without looking back, she calls out, "If you want me gone, then I need to talk to your brother. And since Maggie just stole my truck, you're going to give me a ride."

And for some reason, I wait for her. Ten minutes later, she's glaring at me as I open the door to my Jeep for her. Instead of a thank-you as I close it behind her, she continues to type away on her phone, only pausing to flip me off.

As we pull into the private road to Foxx Bourbon, she says, "I haven't been here in a long time." She takes everything in as we approach the distillery. The property has always been large, but we've grown to multiple buildings, from the distillery and offices, to the rickhouses and exterior patios and entertaining spaces.

"A lot of changes since you've been…" I search for the right word. "Away." From the sound of the crunching gravel underneath my tires along the main drive to the pride I feel every time I see one of our bottles on a shelf or being enjoyed, one thing remains the same. I love everything about what we do here.

She looks out her side window, past the rickhouses and toward the flat quiet landscape of our hometown. "What would you do if you didn't do this?"

The question surprises me, but I have no problem answering her truthfully. "I never imagined doing anything else. That's the one thing that my brothers never understood. How I couldn't want more than what I'd always known." I glance at her. Her attention stays fixated on each part of the property that we pass. "At one point, they both did something else for a little while. Eventually, they came back. But I'm the exception. I've always known what I wanted. Always knew that I'd spend every day here until my last. Even when things are…" I let the thought linger for a moment. I don't want to think about all the days I come here at war with how I'm feeling versus how I should act. "Coming here always makes me feel good."

When she finally shifts her gaze to me, I struggle to meet her attention. I didn't mean to share that much. And while none of it's a secret, it still feels that way. Something private and vulnerable that I haven't ever shared with anyone. I don't know why it seems natural to share it with her.

"I've had that feeling too," she says quietly. And just when I think she might say something else, she opens the door and hustles out.

I catch up with her to cut off her stride.

She stops and turns toward me with a sigh. "I already know what you're going to say."

This attraction I feel is irrelevant. We had an agreement. I let it slide when her mother passed and she came home for the memorial—a part of me felt like a monster for making her leave in the first place, but she pushed and we made a deal. I expect people to keep their promises.

"I want you gone, Faye. Like I said, in case you forgot, you blackmailed me. I don't know what went on in your life, the same way you don't know what went on in mine. But I don't want your brand of crazy anywhere near the people I care about."

I watch as she tries to harden herself to what I'm saying. Her eyes search mine, but before she says anything, her attention is caught when she looks over my shoulder. I turn and spot Griz perched in his golf cart, talking with her sister.

The affection between my grandfather and Maggie doesn't go unnoticed—it was an instant camaraderie between the two of them. And it's stayed that way even after Maggie and Faye's mom passed.

"Is that Faye Calloway back in Fiasco?" Griz calls out from his golf cart, interrupting his conversation.

She smiles at the old man as she walks toward him. "Griz, how have you been?" She says it with much more warmth than she's given me.

He wraps her up in a hug and then lifts her arm to give her a twirl in true Griz fashion. When she's done with her forced twirl, he says, "You look just like Shelby."

I watch what that compliment does to her. Her shoulders relax, and she smiles easily; it's like she needed to hear something kind from someone familiar. And I don't know why that makes me feel shitty.

Griz glances at me. "And by the look on his face, it seems like you're tipping worlds and taking names, just like she did."

Chapter 9

Faye

The dynamic between my sister and the Foxx men is curious and unexpected at best. Troubling, if I focused too hard on it. They aren't the kind of family that you just fall into. They're Kentucky royalty. Businessmen who have a stronghold on one of the most lucrative markets in the U.S. They should only be acquaintances, connected by the fact that we're from the same town and are neighbors to Lincoln Foxx. They attended my mother's memorial, but so did most of the town. I barely remember the people I spoke to that day.

As I watch Griz turn over Maggie's arms, examining her bruises with tenderness, I have to wonder: *Why does he care?* He squeezes her hand while he whispers something that forces her eyes to the ground, looking apologetic. It isn't just familiar; it feels familial. And we were never part of their family when I was around.

"Faye," Griz calls out to me, looking up. "I want you and

Maggie to come to dinner tonight. I need to hear what you've been doing with yourself all these years."

"Griz, that's really nice of you, but I have plans tonight."

His mustache twitches, maybe his version of a smile. "Alright. Sometime soon then?" he says with a wink.

Lincoln cuts in. "Faye was just telling me how she'll be leaving soon."

I clear my throat, refraining from rolling my eyes. "Must have misunderstood me, Foxx. My residency at Midnight Proof is at least until the end of January." I punctuate it with a sarcastic smile. "I'll be here for a little while."

Griz glances behind me at Lincoln and then at Maggie. The tension here is thick, for layers of reasons that I can't figure out how to unpack. "I'm guessing you're not here to do a tasting?"

Lincoln shakes his head, asking, "Is Ace in his office?"

"The lounge," Griz tells him, tipping his head toward the door. I haven't kept tabs about what has been happening, but if I dug a little, I'd find that even if Griz isn't in the day-to-day business of Foxx Bourbon, he still knows everything that goes on around here. The old man squeezes Lincoln's shoulder. "Make sure you bring a good bottle for dinner later, yeah?"

Lincoln gives him a nod and a clap back on the shoulder as Maggie walks off toward the building.

"Faye, this isn't a group meeting. I'll make sure Ace comes to find you when we're done," Lincoln says as he steps up next to me. I don't look at him or acknowledge the statement. I'm uninterested in what he or his brother *need*. What I am interested in is why Ace Foxx is employing my sister *and* rubbing elbows with a man like Blackstone.

"Faye has a hard time accepting when she's not wanted

somewhere," Maggie says over her shoulder and then takes the stairs two at a time, putting plenty of space between us.

Her words burn. She doesn't want me here and neither does Lincoln, but I'm not here to make either of them feel more comfortable. I'm here to do a job and, whether she likes it or not, to make sure she's going to be okay when I leave again.

I push through the group of people coming down the main staircase of the tasting room, and it would be impossible not to appreciate the opulence of this place as I look around. From the wrought iron light fixtures that resemble the Foxx Bourbon logo to the smell of bourbon that wafts throughout the massive space. When I reach the top floor, the office area is empty. It gives me a second to look around and get my bearings.

"What part of 'this isn't a group meeting' didn't you understand?"

For as long as his legs are, I'm still a good ten feet ahead of Lincoln as I ignore him and look around the private floor. The walls are embossed with a collage of photographs that lay out the story of Foxx Bourbon. Four generations of Foxx men who turned backyard moonshine into one of the most sought-after bourbon brands in the world.

"Ignoring me won't get you what you want," he says in a resigned tone behind me.

Coming to a stop at the end of the hall, I look to my right at the empty corner office. Lincoln stands in front of me with an annoying smirk on his face.

"There are plenty of ways to get what I want, Foxx." I step closer to him, biting my lip. "Should we consider all the ways men can be easily manipulated? Or would you prefer I demonstrate?" I run my fingers along my collarbone, thrusting out my chest just enough to garner his attention.

"Does this work for you?" he asks, unimpressed.

I look down at his crotch first and then back up to his face with a hinting smile. "You tell me. Feeling a little intrigued about—" I cut off my words when I look at the large black iron *F* intertwined with the outline of a fox hanging in the center of the wall, seeming like an odd placement.

"I said it's a closed meeting," he says again.

But I move around him and tilt the logo up. The wall slides open. *Jackpot.* Just as I walk through, I hear Maggie say, "You asked me to find more buyers. So that's what I did. There were no parameters to that request, Ace."

Lincoln is at my back as I waltz into the room, interrupting their discussion as I try my best not to seem too impressed by the clandestine grandeur of this hidden space. I hate that this surprises me. It shouldn't. The Foxx family is known for their impeccable taste and the richness in what they deliver. That's felt throughout the entire expanse of property and simply elevated in here. The dark walls, a quad of leather chairs, and a couch hug the farthest wall. There's some kind of carnival machine in the far corner across from a poker table, and behind that, a fireplace that's as tall as it is wide.

Ace stands eerily still, waiting for someone to say something about what exactly it is that I'm doing here. Anyone who lives in or has passed through Fiasco knows Atticus Foxx isn't someone you cross, let alone threaten. He's the oldest brother and the one in charge, but they are each commanding and intimidating in their own ways.

"Faye Calloway," he says calmly as he glances at his brother. "It's been a while."

I stand taller and keep my attention focused on him, mimicking his cadence and tone. "It has."

The way he's wearing almost a full suit, while the rest of the people here are in jeans and polos or T-shirts, is a conscious decision. There's nothing casual about Ace, which means I need to approach things differently with him than I have with Lincoln.

He smiles, looks down, and then surprises me when he says, "Quite a show you put on the other night. You went a different way for a career than I expected."

I smile at the condescending remark. Whether he means it that way or not, I have no problem in setting the record straight. "See, Ace, I never thought I'd need to explain this to grown-ass men. But you and that one over there"—I nod to Lincoln, who crosses his arms and glares at me—"should know that most women nowadays don't lead their lives based on the expectations of men. Maybe if you realized that, then you might walk around less surprised by our choices and more aware of yours."

He folds his hands together and answers that with a brief smile before he moves on. "You have quite a fan base."

I watch him, because I know he's referring to Blackstone. I can only hope that he didn't run his mouth and tell Blackstone all about how he knows my real name, or worse, how much of a departure my current career path is from the one I had trained for.

I see Lincoln allow a half smile escape, matching his brother's smugness.

"I didn't realize you two knew each other," Ace says, shifting his attention to Lincoln. "You and Blackstone, that is," he says glancing back at me.

"Brock Blackstone and I are..." I pause and smirk. "Friends."

Lincoln lets out a clipped laugh.

I glance at him, his arms crossed over his chest as he leans against the poker table. I tilt my head to the side. "Something you want to say, Foxx?"

"How did you end up working at Midnight Proof?" he asks in response, trying to figure out what the hell I'm doing, playing in the same circle as him and his brother.

"I had a multi-show agreement set with Hadley through my agent," I lie. "But I moved up my arrival when I got a call that my sister had been arrested—"

"Yeah, that wasn't from me," Maggie grumbles, like an in-trouble teen. "I never called her."

Ace looks at her. "Did this have anything to do with…?"

I look between the two of them. "With what, exactly? What is she involved in that you would even need to ask her that question?"

Maggie flicks her attention to me. "Not your business, Faye."

But Lincoln chimes in, his fingers rubbing together like he's trying to distract himself. "Your farmland is leased by Foxx Bourbon." He looks at me and adds, "The corn that's grown and harvested is a part of our business now. We lease that land from your sister. All of it above the line, and she's well compensated. Your cornfield helps make our bourbon."

I know that's not all. "That's nice." Brow pinched, I look at my sister. "Interesting how you're signing leasing agreements without my consent, but we can cover that another time."

She flips me off, her middle finger thrust up like it's an actual answer.

I ignore her. "What else?"

Ace smiles and picks off a piece of lint from the forearm of his shirt that I doubt is even there. "That's the only part you get to know."

"Ace," Lincoln interjects. It surprises me that he'd push his brother here. Fine by me.

He doesn't know this, but I'll eventually find out anyway.

Ace sits down in the brown leather club chair, his leg spread wide. Both arms drape across the sides, his wrists hanging over the ends. He isn't married; no ring on his left hand as his fingers lightly grip the rim of his bourbon glass. It wasn't hard to recognize that he's married to this business. They all are.

The way he manspreads in his chair isn't intimidating; instead, I find it rather amusing. Some men need to take up space in order to feel bigger. Especially when they feel threatened. He lets out an exhale just as his mouth tips up in a confident half smile.

"Your sister has been using her talents to find buyers of rare bourbon that we sell on the secondary market. Maggie is exceptional at what she's been able to do for us." My sister being exceptional at something she puts her mind to isn't a stretch. Maggie's always been smart.

I glance at my sister as she smiles to herself. She looks proud, and until right now, I hadn't realized how rewarding it is to see when someone feels good about what they've done.

"With how Maggie operates behind a computer screen, there's no way anyone would be able to tie her to Foxx Bourbon. Let alone any kind of exchange that would result in violent activity."

"Even if some of the people you associate with tend to be violent?" I fire back.

Maggie interrupts, "Oh, come on. Faye, are you serious right now?"

Calmly, Ace says, "Maggie spends time at the tracks—and even more money. Thinking that might explain her bruises." When my sister looks back at him, he continues. "It might be a good time to transition our agreement, considering your recent arrest."

Maggie barely lets Ace finish, her pride evaporating. "What kind of transition?"

But it's Lincoln who answers this time. "The one where you're not getting into trouble, Maggie. The kind of transition that won't bring your sister back to Fiasco and violence too close to my front door."

Ace doesn't so much as glance at her again. Instead, he keeps his attention on me. "Faye, we should discuss my associate. I'm interested in knowing how you might be involved with someone like him."

"Another time," I answer. I've already said too much.

My phone buzzes in my back pocket, distracting me from the conversation. *Speak of the devil.*

> BLACKSTONE:
> I'm hosting a private gathering at the end of the month that I think you might enjoy, Rosie.

This was what Cortez had been banking on happening. An invitation that will allow access to Blackstone, but beyond that, I'm not privy to the details of what the FBI is hoping to gain.

> ROSIE GOLD:
> Would I be performing, or is this a personal invite?

> BLACKSTONE:
> Is there a difference, Rosie?

A shiver works down my spine at what a private event would entail. When I look up, Lincoln's jaw is tight, one arm holding his phone while the other braces on the pool table. But he's the least of my concerns now. Blackstone is the focal point, and I want to keep it that way.

I've already sent half-naked photos and teased a somewhat dangerous man in an effort to obtain access and information. And now, I'll be walking right into the fire.

"Excuse me," I say, brushing past Lincoln, through the long corridor and out the way we came. I send a text as soon as I hit the stairs.

> FAYE:
> Got the invite.

Cortez doesn't even text back. My phone starts ringing. "We need to discuss our next steps," he says before I even say hello.

"More like I need to understand what I'm looking for while I'm there."

He clears his throat, speaking more quietly. "Meet me for a drink at Bottom of the Barrel tonight. I can't tell you all of it, but this is good, Faye. Dammit, it's really good."

When I turn around, Maggie is standing in front of me with her arms crossed.

"Alright, I'll see you there around eight then."

She raises her eyebrows as I end the call. "Making plans? That must be nice for you."

"Don't get pissed off at me. You had every chance to talk to me this past week, but you decided to act like a child and pretend I wasn't there. So no, I don't feel bad for you getting into trouble with"—I search for the right words for what she's been doing—"your *employer* or whatever the Foxx family is to you. I'm not digging you out of whatever hole you've dug for yourself."

She pauses and then smiles at me, like I should have chosen my words more carefully. "You know a thing or two about digging holes. Don't you, Faye?"

My eyes dart to Lincoln, who's walking closer now, looking right at me.

"Fuck off," I bite out as I snatch my keys hanging from her back pocket.

"That would be easier for you, wouldn't it? Bury shit, leave, tell everyone to fuck off so you can just do whatever you want with your life," she calls after me.

I stop in my tracks and turn back to her. "Shut your fucking mouth, Maggie."

"Why? Did I hit a nerve?" She sniffs a laugh. "Well, our mom cried for months." Shaking her head, she grits her teeth. "Months. And you didn't visit her. You barely called. And then it was like you never existed. So yeah, maybe everyone else around here is so enamored with the fact that you've come back, to what? Save your poor, fucked-up sister? Strip off your clothes so people will pay attention to you again—"

"That's enough," Lincoln says from behind me, standing close enough for me to feel his warmth. I don't expect it. And I hate that I like it.

She rolls her eyes. "Nice." Her gaze flicks to Lincoln and then back to me. "You're here less than a week and already under a man. Maybe you're more like Mom after all."

Chapter 10

Faye

Five years ago ...

"Mom, put the knife down," I rush out. I can't inhale a full breath into my lungs, so I swallow down the lump in my throat. Ignoring everything else, I stifle the wave of emotions that instantly drenched me when I walked into the kitchen. Instincts kicked in immediately.

Dark red blood drips over her hands and tracks down her wrists in rivulets, getting lighter the longer the air has a chance to greet it. It trickles and then disappears over the body lumped awkwardly on the linoleum floor. I may have hated the man, but I never pictured this. This can't be undone.

I hold up my hands, showing I'm not a threat. I may not have a badge yet, but I know she needs to see I'm here to help. Tears stream down her face, her eyebrows pinched in anger and maybe confusion. Her chest rises and falls with every exaggerated breath, matching mine.

There isn't time to process any of this. She may be shit at loving the right men, but my mother is kind and loves with her eyes and arms wide open. She's always told me to follow my instincts and find a path that would make my soul happy. But this version of her, angry and shaken, is one I've never seen. I don't want the rose-colored glasses removed or to know this version of her. But I catalog every detail without even realizing it. The low whistle from the wind outside, the glasses in the sink, the bourbon on the counter, the back screened door unlatched, the way she isn't sad but scared and in shock. I'm taking mental snapshots that'll make it impossible to forget.

"Mom, look at me," I say firmly.

She glances back up at me, slightly dazed. There's a smear of blood along her lip from where it split. Pieces of hair stick to her neck. Shelby Calloway is a lot of things, but a murderer isn't going to be one of them. I love her too much for that to be true.

I walk closer and hit the hot water valve with force. She doesn't move, only stares into the stream of water beginning to steam.

I move around the body and tell her, "I'm going to call for some help—"

"No!" *she snaps, breaking her trance as she points at me. Her black mascara streaks down her face as if the darkness around this moment is bleeding into her.*

She held her own with Tullis, but it never looked like love. When I was home, it felt more like "benefits." Arguments and gaslighting disguised as passion. The horses she trains are more loyal than her live-in partner—people know he fucks around on her. I wonder if she does too. But she loves her job, training thoroughbreds for Finch & Kings Racing. If she broke up with Tullis King, she would find herself without a job. It isn't right, but most of what men got away with in this town wasn't. Everyone knows not to piss off Wheeler Finch and the King brothers, Waz and Tullis. And now one of them was on our farmhouse floor, choking on his blood.

Fuck, he's still alive.

The glasses piled in the sink clatter as water fills them. Mom drops the knife in and leans forward, her weight on her arms as she hovers over the farm sink with her eyes closed. "This isn't... He's dangerous, Faye."

I pull my phone from my back pocket. "Mom, I need to call for help or else he's going to bleed out."

"You think the police are going to take my word here? You think those men aren't on Finch & Kings's payroll?" She laughs, but it's one of panic. "I promise you I will not walk out of that police station if you call for help," she says, shaking her head.

I want to be a part of the Fiasco Police Department, but she's right; Tullis has friends, he and his brother have too much influence. There are too many people in higher places who would be able to spin this differently. She doesn't deserve what would become of her.

I glance at Tullis again, his chest barely rising as his body awkwardly lies there.

I watch as the arm that's tucked under his torso remains motionless. His fingers curve upward, as if he's holding a baseball. "A mishap of training," he'd said. A horse stepping on a hand and the bones that hadn't been set right. I hated his stories. They always seemed like half-truths.

I've always been good at thinking too many steps ahead, and every minute that ticked by would be studied and scrutinized by detectives and the district attorney. The longer we wait to call for help, the story changes from accident or self-defense to calculated and premeditated.

I turn it over in my head, heart racing and sweat beading along my hairline, watching her stare off and play over whatever just happened. She's a single mother who had gotten caught up time and time again with trusting and loving the wrong people. It's a cycle that got her here, to this moment. And it needs to stop now. I love her and Maggie more than anything, and I'll protect the people I love over anything else.

I look again at Tullis, who's bleeding out on the floor. There are two slices along each side of his neck, pulsing blood more slowly now. His chest stopped moving.

I clear my throat, making up my mind.

The things needed are in the barn.

My mom's going to need something to calm down.

I'll have to take off his shoes.

Gather his wallet and turn off his phone.

I factor in his weight.

The weight of this…

I can fix it. I have the foresight, training, and knowledge to know what has to be done. And it's ugly. It will change every part of who I thought I was and who I had been planning to become. But I'll deal with all of that later.

I grip onto the top corners of the blue plastic and pull. The sound of it crunches as I gather it tight in each fist, and I hold my breath as I use all of my strength to focus. "Focus on the task and do not fall apart." I keep repeating those words to myself over and over as his body thunks down each step and onto the pavers of our back walkway.

The wet grass makes the tarp easier to drag than I expected.

"Mom, listen to me." But she doesn't even look at me. Endless tears track down her face as she stares ahead. "I'll be back in a little while," I call out.

The air stops moving—the calm before the storm.

I rub the back of my hand along my forehead and sop up the sweat dripping into my eyes. I need a minute. Dropping the shovel, I lean forward, bracing my hands on my knees. At least it was summer, and the ground is wet from the heavy rainfall that still lingers. I need his belongings buried as deep as I can dig. His phone and shoes are piled eye level next to me on the edge of the hole I've been digging. I think through my forensics class and roster out the chemicals I need to clean the kitchen properly. I'll make sure our clothes are burned and our bodies scrubbed thoroughly.

Swallowing the lump in my throat, I look up as emotion builds. The strawberry moon lights the sky in a pink tint. It's supposed to bring a broader sense of responsibility. Summer solstice and a strawberry moon only happened every twenty years. The only thing I can do is huff a laugh—it'd be easier to blame the moon. Its gravity and pull can manipulate tides, but it isn't powerful enough to force will or effect choices. It couldn't undo what she had done. Dammit, this isn't the life I want. I squint my eyes closed and yell again at the dead body. "Fuck you!"

This isn't the life my mother wanted either. She talks about horse training like it's what she always wanted, but the goal for her was always building out a sanctuary—a place for the ones she trained to live out their lives in open fields.

I glance down the dark rows of corn, pull myself out of the muddy hole, and toss the shovel to the side, where Tullis is slumped and bloody. There were good parts of him, I'm sure. My mother fell in love with some piece of him, and she's my compass. My true north. The person who always centers me when I find myself spiraling. But now, I have to be that for her.

I wipe my hand down the front of my shorts, pushing away the mud and sweat caked along my wrist and fingers. A blister on each palm already forms right where my heart line splits. I wonder if they'll leave scars. The sky rumbles in the distance, making the night feel even more volatile, reminding me that there's so much more to do. I wedge the shovel under Tullis's hip and use it as leverage to roll his body into the ditch. I'm not sure I'll ever forget the sound—a thud and squelch as he meets the mud.

Tossing on three cinder blocks, I close my eyes each time they hit him. I don't need wet earth rejecting him and him rising from the dead. This isn't Practical Magic—*my sister won't come to the rescue with spells, and a sheriff won't ride up on horseback to help me bury the truth. My mother and sister are the dreamers in our family, and I'm the realist. If anyone were to find Tullis King along the edge of this cornfield, there wouldn't be anything charming or enchanting about it.*

Two hours later, soaked from the rain and reeling from the way my life has spun out so quickly, I return to my mom still sitting on those steps. I don't tell her about Lincoln Foxx or the blackmail and ultimatum. But I just buried a body along with the life I had planned for myself with it.

"I have to leave. After tonight," I tell her, swallowing roughly as my eyes glaze over. "I'll take his phone and make it seem like he left. You need to withdraw a chunk of money and make it look like he did."

"Faye…" She covers her mouth. "This isn't—"

But I cut her off and finish her words. "No, Mom, this isn't okay. None of what happened here will ever be okay…" I stop talking and rest my head on her shoulder for the briefest moment. "Maggie won't understand why I'm leaving. But you're going to need to make it okay. Promise me that you're both going to be okay." And I know she can't, even as I plead with her. After tonight, there's no promising anything, but I need to hear it anyway.

Her voice cracks when she says, "I promise."

Chapter 11

Lincoln

The firewood cracks loudly as it splits and fully catches fire. Leaning into the chair, I let the warmth from the fire pit seep into my boots that are kicked up along its edge.

I knew this conversation was going to be a fight, which is why we're having it after dinner at the house and not at the distillery. Rubbing my thumb across my bottom lip, I glance at Ace, and it's obvious he doesn't like it. That fucker doesn't like much when it comes to pushing our brand forward.

"I'm not going to do a finished double barrel," Ace barks out, loud enough to get me to focus on this discussion. "The answer is a no from me."

I shift in my seat without saying anything and glance at Grant.

He speaks up first. "Why the hell not, Ace?"

"Because that's not who we are. Foxx Bourbon is known for

our bourbon. Real fucking bourbon and not the bullshit craft that's churning out all over the place."

I sit up and lean my elbows on my knees, trying to tamp down my frustration. "Everyone has done a double barrel variation. It's still bourbon."

Ace stares into the flames for a minute before he answers. "It bends the rules."

"Exactly." I point at him. "Bends, not breaks." I've had enough of hearing how shitty my ideas are lately.

"You wanted to pitch your concept. Now that you have, I'm telling you no." He stands and walks to the bar cart and pours two fingers of the Cowboy Edition bourbon that Grant developed.

"I don't think that's your call, Ace," Grant says.

"Really, Grant? You've been doing this job for, what, a year now? And you have all the answers?"

Grant gives me a tight-lipped smile, and I know what's coming next. He has the luxury of leaving. The luxury of being the one who can check out and say he's not going to engage. I've never had that luxury. Ever.

"Fine. You two figure it out." He stands from his seat around the fire, looking inside at the rest of our family laughing in the living room. Turning back, he locks eyes with me before he opens the slider to move inside. "I know my opinion might not matter here, not as much as his"—he nods to Ace—"but it's a smart idea. We don't have any blends finished in anything other than our oak. If we don't try new things, then we're not getting any better. You and I both know it's not living if things stay the same all the time. You have my vote, Linc."

I take a taste of the burned sugar old-fashioned that Hadley whipped up. It's sweeter than what I usually like, but it's warm and comforting during a cold night and even colder discussion.

"You can do better," Ace says, interrupting my thoughts. "You can do so much better than what any of us can do, Lincoln. You're making great bourbon. You've perfected combinations of grains. Don't take the easy way out and make it all about the ending."

I exhale and try not to feel instantly annoyed at where this conversation might lead with my older brother.

Ace hands me a tasting pour of the Cowboy Edition. "That is what good bourbon tastes like," he says.

As it coats my palate, I can taste the small adjustment of barley instead of rye that Grant chose in our newest bestselling blend. Where his barrels were aged made the wood expand differently. The sugars had broken down in a way where it really tasted beautifully original. Grant had time to work through loss on his own, figuring out what would make his life have meaning again. This bourbon helped him do that. I didn't have that same kind of space.

Hadley throws open the slider. "I can't do it anymore," she says dramatically. "I might actually die." Releasing the loudest, most exaggerated sigh, she drops into the oversize chair that Grant just left.

After a few beats of silence, Ace asks her hesitantly, "You alright?"

She turns her head to him and smiles. "Yeah, Daddy, just fine."

"Jesus Christ," he huffs out and stands up. "Quit it with that shit."

I lean back and give my best friend a look that she knows pretty damn well.

"What?" She laughs. "Don't give me that look."

"You're even more over-the-top tonight," I tell her. She's always the one to make all of us laugh and lighten up. "Everything going okay?"

She twists a curl of her dark chestnut hair and stares at what's going on inside. "Midnight Proof is great. The biggest headache lately, as usual, has more to do with my father." Hadley's dad, Wheeler Finch, went ahead and made himself a very rich and very famous man when it comes to thoroughbreds and racing. If there's a princess of the racing world, it's Hadley Jean Finch. Between her love of horses and her father's penchant for finding the best, from jockeys and trainers to mares and stallions, the Finch family is Kentucky's version of power. An industry that's grown to intense levels of influence, with horse racing raking in billions.

"What's he asking you to do?"

She crosses her arms and speaks softly, only for me to hear. She knows that if Grant catches wind of it, he'll step up on his proverbial high horse and start talking about it with his old cop buddies. It's one of the many negatives about having someone from law enforcement in the family. Even though he quit, his moral high ground is stories higher than where the rest of us play.

"My horses are my horses. That's always been the case. Now he's telling me that whatever I own is rightfully his. And that he'll help himself to it whenever he damn well pleases."

"I'm sure that went over really well."

"Yeah, well, I cried." She gives me a side-eye. "The disappointment billowed off of him when I told him that I bought, housed, and cared for my horses the same way I do Midnight Proof." She puffs her cheeks and blows out air. "He wants to cash in on the breeding potential that my horses have. He wants to stifle anything that I remotely consider mine. It's not fucking fair."

I agree. "No, it's not fair. He has no fucking right."

The door slides open and Lily spills outside with Lark on her heels. "Dad, that's going to round today at twenty-five."

Hadley wipes the corner of her eye and brushes away the lingering conversation about her father to focus on Lily, who decides to sit on her lap. "Twenty-five what?"

"Dollars," Lily answers.

"You're still paying into the… What do you girls call it?" Hadley asks.

Lark chimes in. "The curse purse."

Lily reminds her while looking at me, "Five dollars for every curse word. Dad had to start capping it at twenty-five per day instead of easing up on his word choices."

"I have one flaw," I clap back playfully, throwing my hands up.

The three of them look at me with annoying smiles, but it's Hadley that digs in. "Just one?"

I push my glasses up the bridge of my nose with my middle finger, making sure she sees it.

"Dad, we know what the middle finger means," Lark says matter-of-factly. "You do it to Uncle Grant all the time, and you know it's ten bucks."

"I have no idea what you're talking about." I smile into my glass as I finish my drink.

Julep follows Laney outside, stopping at Lily's side first for a pet and then moving over to Lark.

"Dad, did you know that all puppies are born deaf?" Lark asks.

I smile at the randomness of some of the things that come out of her mouth. "I did not know that."

"Do you think that's why dogs like people so much? Because we talk to them?" Lily asks no one in particular.

"It would make sense," I say, watching Lark. And I can almost tell what might be coming next. I'm just wondering which one is going to ask this time.

"Highland cows actually form the same kind of bonds with humans as dogs tend to do, which isn't typical for most cows," Lark says as she folds her legs under where she's perched on the arm of my chair. "Maggie said that she and Faye used to live in Wyoming before they moved to Kentucky, and they had cows everywhere."

Hadley smiles at me as I say, "Cattle. They probably would have called them cattle in Wyoming, and I doubt they were highland cows."

Lily swats at the air. "I think dogs are cuter than cows, Lark."

"Well, nobody asked you, Lily."

I clear my throat. "Be nice," I say to Lark before I look to Lily so she knows I mean both of them.

"I'm with Lily," Hadley says as the last log finally cracks and catches the flame. "I prefer horses, but if I had to pick, I'd pick a dog over a cow any day."

"Me too," Laney says as she pets Julep's head.

Lark looks to me to weigh in, and I narrow my eyes.

"What am I missing here? Why is this a conversation?" I try to shift the topic. "Laney, please tell me you brought dessert."

"I brought dessert," she says with a laugh as she tips back her glass of bourbon, then looks at me for a beat. "Chocolate mousse bombs. They might pair nicely with one of the bourbons you've been working on, yeah?"

I send her a grateful smile. "Maybe."

"Keep pushing for what you want, Linc," she says as she hands Hadley her glass to take a sip from. "You know bourbon better than anyone. I might be the new kid here, but I know *that*." It feels good to hear that from someone who hasn't been here for years.

Lark picks at her mostly chipped nail polish and says, "Dad, if you had to pick. Which one would you choose?"

Before I can answer, Lily says, "Hypothetically, of course."

This doesn't feel hypothetical. "Of course," I repeat, giving both of them a look that says I'm on to them. I know my girls. I'm going to get their birthday wish lists this year with both a cow and a dog scribbled across the top, just like their Christmas lists, with pictures and hyperlinks included. They're going to wear me down. I did the same to Griz countless times growing up. I know exactly where their tenacity comes from.

"Highland cows seem like oversized outdoor dogs. And if it's a dog like Julep, then I'd have to say both. I couldn't choose."

"Seriously?" Lark says, eyes lighting up, genuinely surprised.

The sliding door opens, and Griz peers out. "I just ate three of those chocolate mousse things. I suggest you all get in here before I polish off the rest."

Lark and Lily don't need to be told twice as they rush past Griz.

Hadley barks out a laugh before she asks, "Both?"

"What? It's hypothetical. I'm not getting them a dog or a cow."

Laney and Hadley share a look, a quiet exchange where I'm

clearly the topic of their raised eyebrows and whatever other facial expression I might have missed.

"Lark has slept with a stuffed highland cow since she was a toddler. I'm not surprised she'd want a real-life Dottie."

Hadley says, "Oh my gosh, I remember when Liv bought her that stuffed cow."

I remember too. "She still sleeps with Dottie. But don't tell her I told you that." If my girls want to think about animals and all the ways a dog or cow could make them feel like our family wasn't broken, then I'll indulge them. The truth is, I couldn't bear to see them lose an animal, which is why I haven't given in yet. Dogs have maybe ten to fifteen years if we're lucky, and then a cow, who the fuck knows. Watching them mourn Olivia was, and still is, enough sadness to witness for a lifetime. I wouldn't give them something else to love and lose. "We're good. Just the three of us."

Chapter 12

Faye

Penny drafts and country music are what brings most people from around the county to Bottom of the Barrel, but it's the way I know these Southern boys could move a person around the barrel wood dance floor that had me anxious to come here on a Saturday night.

The weatherman's promise of a good dusting of snow throughout the entire county didn't keep anyone from driving here tonight. The place is packed and overflowing all the way into the church's lot across the street. I stomp off my boots when I hit the landing and smile at the bouncer. Even though he's easily ten years younger than me, I flash him my ID, then head straight for the bar.

It only took me a few minutes to shower and find something to wear. My clothes were thrown around my makeshift bedroom, but I had organized it into a system of sorts. Tonight called for a flirty skirt with some movement and my favorite pair of purple suede cowgirl boots. Any combination of those two things is like a uniform when coming to a place like this. And I wanted to fit in.

I haven't seen Maggie since I left Foxx Bourbon Distillery, which is fine by me. I'm not interested in running into her again today. We both said enough to each other. As far as I'm concerned, she didn't deserve any sort of asshole beating her up, but if she wants to keep playing whatever games she has been and dancing in the same circles that had gotten her into trouble, I'm sure as hell not going to stop her.

I lean up against the oak bar and smile at the bartender. Her pretty tattoos cover both arms and wrap around her neck in a way that screams confidence. I love women who have no problem showing off the parts they're proud of—clean skin or decorated in ink. Anybody who works in a bar or club would tell you that the more skin on display, the better the tips, and people who balk at that clearly haven't done that kind of work before.

"Hey there, what're you having?" she asks me.

"Just water for now."

She nods and pulls a glass, filling it with water and propping a lemon on the rim.

My phone buzzes. *Another* text from Blackstone.

> **BLACKSTONE:**
> To my disappointment, Rosie Gold isn't at Midnight Proof tonight. I thought you liked me, but I'm not feeling very special lately.

I send him a picture of the outfit I'm wearing. Maybe that'll hold him off. But a few seconds later, he responds.

BLACKSTONE:

> Pretty. But I'm getting tired of just pictures, Rosie...

Dammit. Dirty pictures and suggestive text messages are only going to satisfy someone for so long, and now he's getting impatient. Blackstone might have every aspect of the creep factor, but I need to deliver more.

"You're going to be a cheap date, I see," Cortez says as he slides in beside me.

"This is business, Cortez. You know that." I give him a flirtatious smile, thinking about how at one time I wouldn't have minded if he'd called this a date.

He leans in, looking at the text exchange. "Looks like someone is getting demanding."

"I can handle keeping him occupied if you tell me what the endgame looks like."

Cortez just looks at me for a minute without giving me an answer. "Alright. Let's talk then." He nods toward the crowd. "Come on, I've got a high top closer to the dance floor."

The bartender cracks a fresh Corona for him in exchange for his empty bottle before he lifts my drink as well and carries it to the massive dance floor that's flowing with people all lined up and moving in time with some combination of a two-step shuffle.

"They made the dance floor bigger," I say as he pulls out my chair for me and holds my hand as I hop up.

Cortez points at the far back as he tells me, "They bought the movie theater next door, blew out the back side of this place, doubling its size. Maybe even more than double."

I look at the left side of the room that's buzzing with the

energy of a full band playing. At the back of the dance floor, there are industrial-sized garage doors opened. Despite the cooler air outside, with this many bodies moving in here, it's plenty warm. Shrugging off my jacket as I glance around, I catch a Foxx with my eyes, sans glasses as he moves a curvy little brunette around the floor. It's like I can't escape him. And who the hell is that? My stomach swoops and sinks like I'm on a damn roller coaster ride. I really don't need a Foxx-sized distraction right now.

"Shit," I whisper.

Cortez follows what just caught my eye. I know the minute he sees Lincoln. Without looking back at me, he says, "There's not something going on between you and Foxx, is there?"

My eyebrow quirks as he meets my gaze. "Wouldn't need to know that information even if there was, would you, Cortez?"

He smiles against the mouth of his beer and then takes a swig. "You can see how I might be concerned about you rubbing elbows"—he glances down at the cleavage I know is peeking out of my jean vest—"or *other things* with one of the Foxx brothers."

I raise my eyebrows. Ballsy thing to say, but I try to school my reaction to it. He can think whatever he'd like. I'm more interested in doing this job and coming out of it in one piece. "You know I'm going to need more details if you think I plan on setting foot inside of that private event."

Nodding, he leans in a bit closer so he doesn't have to yell over the band. The music shifts from something bluegrass to a cover of Dolly's "9 to 5."

"We knew that Blackstone was heading to Fiasco, but the fact that he's got some kind of connection to Foxx Bourbon... Let's just say, that isn't the businessman I had expected him to be dealing with while he's here. I can't give you everything on this one, Faye. You can know what we need you to, but beyond that, my hands are tied."

My phone buzzes next to me just as Cortez signals the waitress.

UNKNOWN:
> Are you on a date?

For some reason, instead of nerves, a whirl in my chest has me looking toward the dance floor where Lincoln was just dancing. He's not there any longer. Where did he go? I scan the space. Instead, he's off to the side, leaning on the railing and staring right back at me with a curious smile.

FAYE:
> Wrong number.

I look back up and give him a tight-lipped sarcastic smile.

UNKNOWN:
> Interesting choice. Cortez. FBI. Seems dangerous considering the little secret I know about you.

FAYE:
> Like I said...wrong number.

UNKNOWN:

> Unless that's not really a date.
> Want to tell me what you're really doing back in Fiasco, Peach?

I swallow my nerves and try to think on my feet about what I could possibly say that'll keep Lincoln from running with that thought.

"I'll have two shots of tequila with two limes and a club soda," I say to the waitress just before she's out of earshot.

Cortez chuckles. "Do I want to know what just changed from *I'll just have water* to a bachelorette-party level order?"

My saccharine smile masks what I'm saying for anyone who might be looking. "I don't think you do. But I am going to be very clear with you."

We have a standoff of silence until the waitress comes back with our drink order. I don't waste any time taking the first shot and then squeezing the lime into the club soda. Taking a sip, I let the bubbles coat my tongue. I hate that I'm rattled. The tart lime levels out the bite of the tequila, and I pocket my phone, trying to play off that whoever was on the other end of my messages didn't just drive me to take out my aggression with a side of tequila.

Cortez leans back in his chair and takes a sip of his beer as he watches me.

"I'm not going to be some expendable pawn in this case with Blackstone." I kick back the second shot. "And respectfully, fuck you for thinking I'm going to walk into a situation where I don't know the entire story. Your hands are tied?"

"Faye, that's not the agreement we have. You—"

"If you want me to keep Blackstone interested so I can walk into his private event, then you'll amend our agreement."

He rests his head on his hand, looking at me for a beat too long. "Please tell me you're not single, or I'm seriously going to try to marry the shit out of you, Faye Calloway."

Rolling my eyes, I shift my attention for a brief second back to Lincoln, who has moved on from watching me to spinning Hadley around their section of the dance floor.

"You're deflecting. My relationship status is not up for discussion, Cortez. And the only thing I want from you is answers." I glance back at him with a tilt of my head. "And a dance."

Chapter 13

Lincoln

"This wouldn't have been my first choice for a night out," I say to Hadley as I raise her arm and lead her through a short spin.

"Yeah, well, sometimes you just need to shimmy to a shitty Morgan Wallen cover." She laughs, breaking from our coupled movement and joining the line dance that's been moving in unison around us.

She follows my line of sight that's locked onto Faye and Cortez as he guides her from their high top to the already crowded dance floor. Faye doesn't waste a minute leading them into a dance—she looks like she wouldn't know how to let someone else lead. Before Hadley even opens her mouth, I cut her off and change the subject.

"Griz told me an interesting little bit of gossip from his last book club."

She wiggles her eyebrows. "Oh yeah? I'm assuming it's about me."

I smile at my best friend, holding out my hand for her and bringing it around the back of me until she's front and center. "They love talking about the 'wild' Hadley Jean Finch."

"I'm *wildly* single, Linc. And you know, as well as anyone, that creeping into your mid-30s single means a person is actually *obligated* to explore." She leans her head on my shoulder as the chorus slows. "You been doing a lot of 'exploring' lately?"

I don't consciously do it, but I find Faye in the crowd again, just a handful of feet away. She's trying really fucking hard not to glance back at me. I clear my throat, tamping down thoughts of the short blond who has all but barreled her way back into my mind. "It's been a little bit."

"Getting bored with your dip-and-slip routine?"

I can't help but smile at Hadley's special brand of interrogation. She shifts her attention to the hand that's holding hers and leading her through another turn.

"The girls won't remember their mother any less if you stop wearing that all the time, you know."

I glance at my empty ring finger. "I'm not wearing it now."

"Alright. Then it's a good night for you to explore with someone who is not even remotely boring." Then she mumbles, "You can kill me later," as she pulls me farther into the crowd. The song changes and everyone gets rowdier when the distinct plucking of guitar strings intros the cover of "Shivers." It's not even a country song, but somehow the band throws twang onto an Ed Sheeran song, and all of a sudden, the floor's mobbed. "She's a professional, Linc. Better show off a little," Hadley says, letting me lead her in a series of spins and pass-throughs.

"Cortez!" Hadley shouts, throwing herself right at Faye and Cortez, who've somehow ended up a few feet from us. "Come dance with me, you sexy son of a bitch." My best friend just made tonight a helluva lot more entertaining.

I finally get a full view of Faye. She looks too fucking good in a short-as-hell skirt that reminds me of the flowers tattooed on her arm. Add in the jean vest that's framing mouthwatering cleavage, and I want to watch her peel each piece off in a show that's just for me.

Faye smiles at Hadley as my best friend manages to tell this side of the room, "I need a sample of your date tonight, Faye. You're welcome to mine."

When Faye looks at me, I swear her neck takes on a pink hue that works its way quickly up to her cheeks. She immediately shuts that idea down with a "no thanks." She brushes right past me, and it has me biting back a smile.

Hadley's head is thrown back, laughing at whatever Cortez is saying to her, so I follow Faye's path through the crowd. She pulls her phone from her boot and heads toward the narrow hallway that leads to the bathroom.

The bartender steps over to me as I lean against the bar. "What'll you have?"

"Bourbon. Neat."

"Any preference?" she asks with a sweet smile.

"Dealer's choice," I tell her as my phone buzzes. I sit on the bar stool as I look at who it's from. I stop paying attention to what the bartender is going to pour and instead open Faye's text.

> PEACH:
> This should hold you over until I get to play with you.

This should be good. There's no way that message was meant for me, but it's the video message that's attached that has my interest piqued. When I click it open, my screen is a zoomed-in image of Faye's cleavage, the phone propped just right as she steps back and smiles into the picture, then she turns around and bends at the waist just enough so I have a view of two perfect fucking creases right where the tops of her thighs meet her ass. *Fuck. Me.* My mouth waters and I rub my hand across my jaw and over my mouth. This better not be for *fucking* Cortez.

She lifts the sides of her skirt—the same one she's wearing tonight. *Is she doing this in the bathroom?* Then she rolls down the string she had on for panties. Every part of me is screaming, *Hell yes.* My cock jabs me in the thigh, making sure I'm seeing this too. I look to my left to make sure no one else is watching, but instead of someone peering over my shoulder, Faye's striding down the corridor to the bar, glancing around furiously for someone. Pretty sure that someone is me, and I'm instantly lit up with amusement. She knows she just sent this to the wrong person. She does a double take and stalks over when she sees me already looking at her. *Fuck, she's beautiful.*

"Give me your phone," she demands, holding out her hand.

Tilting my head to the side as I look at her, I slip my phone into my back pocket and then take a sip of my bourbon. "Why would I give you my phone?"

She shuffles closer to me, wedging herself in between my spread legs. I'd be lying if I said her body this close doesn't do things to me. Maybe it's the little teaser I just watched, or maybe it's just her, but I'm annoyingly turned on. She moves in closer. Her cheek brushes mine as her lips linger right next to my ear, my pulse ticking up in response. "Give. Me. Your. Phone."

I sniff out a laugh, which has her pulling back. She's furious. "Not going to happen," I say as I sip on my bourbon to keep from letting another smile escape. "Did you send something to me you weren't supposed to? Is that it?"

Now she's glaring. "You already watched it?" And before waiting for me to answer, she sarcastically croons, "So eager, Foxx." Her attention dips to my lap as she quips, "Can't say I'm surprised."

Fucking hell, this woman. I look back at the dance floor and see Cortez laughing with Hadley and another few people. "I'm more interested in who that was meant for." I nod in the direction of Cortez. "It wasn't for him. That's just business, right?"

I loop my finger into the waistband of her skirt and yank her closer. Her eyes widen and her lips part, letting a gasp escape. She hadn't expected it, and I'm finding far too much enjoyment in surprising her. Pushing her. "Who are you teasing with a video like that?"

The question comes out sounding more possessive than I wanted.

Eyes on mine, she pouts. I've never craved to bite something more than I do that bottom lip. "Oh, what's the matter, Foxx? Are you jealous? Or are you more of a prude than everyone thinks?"

Why am I turned on by the mouth she's got on her? She's not far off, but she doesn't get to know that. "Nah, Peach. I'm not jealous." I lean into her ear, the same way she had done to me moments ago. "You and I both know that if I wanted you, you'd let me have you." With my finger hooked in her skirt, she's not able to pull away. I run the knuckle of my finger back and forth along the slip of skin under the waistband. "Wouldn't you?"

A slow smile curves her mouth, her tongue peeking out to wet that plush bottom lip. Waving to the bartender, she lifts my hand from her waist. She stands on her tiptoes as the bartender approaches, then leans over to say something. But it's when she turns back, smiling at me, a wicked gleam in her eyes, that I realize she didn't just order a drink or close out a tab.

"Faye, what did you—"

I get cut off as the bartender pulls out a silver triangle and starts hitting it with a piece of metal. *Fucking hell.* Everyone within earshot knows that means a round of drinks has been paid for.

She calls out, "This round is on Lincoln Foxx!" The crowd around me and the entire length of the bar start whistling and clapping.

When I glance to my right where Faye had just been, I realize she's gone and already halfway to the door. "Hey!" I shout.

She stops, looks over her shoulder and then turns her full body, flips me off, and walks backward toward the door while holding up *my* fucking phone.

I throw down my credit card. "Cap it at five hundred," I tell the bartender, and then I'm moving through the crowd and out the front door. I look around for a second, trying to see if she went toward the parking lot to the left of the building or across the street, but when the door to the bar closes behind me, it's quiet. Which means I should have no problem finding her. The line that was here when we arrived is already through the door and the only other people out here are a smoker and a bouncer. A few seconds later, I hear a woman's laugh and turn toward the small alley between the bar and the building. Cloudy plumes of warm breath billow from the same direction. *There you are.*

"I thought you might have liked that," she says in a low, sexy tone just as I round the corner. "Of course. I already said I would be there."

My boots scuff the pavement as I round the corner to interrupt.

Her head jerks up and eyes widen when she sees me. But then whoever she's talking to makes her laugh. *Who the fuck is she talking to?* She hums right before she says, "But teasing is the best part."

My entire body feels those words like a caress, especially with her eyes on me. The way she drags her bottom lip between her teeth, making it wet and reddened, makes me second-guess if that was meant for me. She starts to pull the phone away from her ear so I can hear the deep voice talking on the other end.

I hold up my hand and say, "Don't hang up."

I wasn't going to, she mouths. I take it as a challenge.

I take a step closer and raise my finger to my lips, signaling for her to be quiet.

She clears her throat. "Yes. I'm still here."

I don't know, nor do I care, who she's lying to on that call. It's not my problem. My problem is the five-foot-something blond in front of me. I haven't been able to stop thinking about her, maybe for even longer than I care to admit. I should walk away and keep my focus on my own life. But the lines that feel so thin between us make it difficult to tell if it's attraction, anger, or just an unexplainable primal need drawing us together.

I move closer, forcing her to keep moving until her back hits the brick wall behind her. When I look down at her hand, her fingers are still wrapped around my phone.

It's what she says next that removes any common sense that should have me ending this game right now. "Then you'll have to tell me what you'd want me to do," she says seductively into her phone.

With those green eyes locked on mine, I glide my hand down her forearm to her wrist until I wrap my fingers around my phone. I try prying it from her, but she grips tighter. Stepping back, I pull her with me until I move the phone behind my waist and slide it into my back pocket.

When she finally lets go, she turns her back to me with a flick of her hand, like that was the only thing I wanted from her. *Fuck.* It should be. I got my phone back. I can go back to the bar and find my friend. But it's not. I scrub my hand across the stubble on my chin and over my mouth as my gaze travels over her again, now that she's paying me no attention. There are a thousand reasons why walking away is the logical choice. But I've done logical and expected, cavalier and thankless. Right now, I just want her.

Fuck it.

Reaching out, I wrap my arm around her body and pull her to me. She sucks in a breath as her back connects with my front. Any sense is thrown entirely away as I keep my body pressed to hers and move my mouth to the opposite side from where she's holding her phone.

My lips ghost along her neck, and in response, she grinds her ass back into my cock. I hold her tighter against me as a couple walking by at the end of the alley laughs. *Fucking hell, this is reckless.*

"Tell me to stop," I whisper as my fingers toy with the top button of her vest.

"Keep going," she tells me in a quiet, breathy tone.

I flick open the button and my fingers slide along the smooth warmth of her skin. Her breath catches. My palm and fingers grasp as much of her full chest in my hand as I can. She leans back, dropping her head along my shoulder, my lips brushing her cheek as my fingers play and pluck at her nipple, rolling it with the pads of my fingers. Her mouth opens and tilts into a half smile as she rubs her ass from side to side, grazing my cock with each sway of her hips.

She releases a small moan just before she says, "Keep going." Her breath catches as she whispers, "Please, don't stop."

"Those panties still off?" I ask along her skin.

She nods and lets out a hum in anticipation.

I shift my weight, moving us closer to the wall and into the shadows between these two buildings. I drag my hand down the back of her thigh to lift the back of her skirt. My fingers only find her warm, smooth skin. "Tell me this is okay, Peach."

"Don't you fucking stop," she says on an exhale. I don't hear any muffled voice or see the light of her phone anymore, but she still has it pressed to the other ear. I don't care who hears her. The only thing I care about is knowing that I'm the one about to make her come.

My cock is so hard I can feel it dampening my jeans with every roll of my hips. I run my fingers along the exact place I wanted to touch so badly when she shed her coat during her "date." That strip of skin, the crease of her ass, that perfect spot where it meets the top of her thigh. *Fuck.* Her skin is soft, but the cold has it pebbling as my fingertips move closer to her pussy.

She widens her stance and leans her weight into me. I grip a pinch of her ass before I glide two fingers right between her legs and along the entire length of her pussy. She's fucking soaked already, and I have to hold back a groan at the feeling. She hums as I slip two fingers back and forth through her pussy lips and up to her clit. I haven't even fucked my fingers into her and she's already shaking in my arms.

"You like this, don't you?" I nip at the skin below her ear. "I think you more than like it. I think you want me to give you more. Do you want more?" I taunt, drawing circles around her clit as my wrist rubs against her slit. "Beg me for my fingers, Peach."

"No," she bites out.

My cock twitches as I grind against her. I pinch her clit and her nipple to draw out the truth.

"Oh fuck. Fine, please," she whines, arching back.

"Please what?" I say along her neck.

"Fuck you, Foxx. You know what."

I rotate my hand for a better angle and let my middle finger sink into her. And *holy fuck*, do I feel it once I do, reveling in her shuddering gasp.

"*More*," she says on an exhale as her body sinks into me.

My low laugh has her cursing me again. "More, what?"

"You're an asshole," she says.

I add another finger and sink it in deeper. She melts into the pleasure I'm allowing, leaning against me and letting out a small, quiet sound that I need to hear more loudly. "You're not being very nice," I say teasingly.

She huffs as I keep the same slow and deep pace without increasing my speed. "You don't want a nice girl right now, Foxx."

"What do I want, then, hmm?"

A small moan crawls up her throat as she says, "You want someone to tell you to be a good boy and do what you're told."

I slow down as punishment. "Is that what you think? That I need your praise and for you to be in control?" I push my fingers in and move the tips of them just enough to hit that spot just right. She's full and eager for more as she squirms for me to give her what she wants.

When I thrust harder, just once, she sucks in a breath. "Please, oh fuck. Please, give me more, or I'm going to do it myself." Her free hand grabs at my forearm and she digs her nails into my sleeve.

Chuckling, I rest my cheek against hers before I tell her exactly how much I don't like that idea with my actions instead. I slide my fingers out, kick her stance wider, and bend her forward just enough to slap her pussy from behind. She yelps at the fast slap and lets out a small giggle before I'm pulling her back up. I turn her body, moving her a few feet toward the wall until her back is pressed against it and her eyes are on mine. One arm loops around the back of my neck while her hand grips onto my forearm. She drags her teeth across that beautiful lower lip.

"You're not allowed to touch yourself right now. That's what you just begged me to do." Leaning in, I run my nose along her neck. "So you'll take what I give you."

She watches me, lust and need as visible as our warm breath hitting the cold air. I hike up her leg and drape it over the crook of my elbow, and with my other hand, I suck two fingers into my mouth and then lick the pad of my thumb. Rubbing circles around her clit, I let my fingers play.

"Fucking tease," she bites out with a smile and the tiniest moan.

"Unless you want an audience or to be arrested, I suggest you keep quiet when you drench my fingers."

She doesn't say anything else after that. Instead, she enjoys the hell out of my fingers fucking her. Her grip along the back of my neck tightens, but I'm not ready for her to be done just yet. I pull them out and rub along her clit just enough, edging her so closely, to the point where she's writhing against my touch. Let's see how wet she can make this.

Her words come out gasping, "Foxx, stop, I need—"

"I know what you need." A third finger fucks into her dripping pussy. The lewd sounds are going to have me coming in my fucking pants right along with her. Mixed with the way she says my name on whispered breaths, I'm barely hanging on. The only thing I can smell is her, and it's so fucking good. She's overtaking every one of my senses.

I shift into her, hiking her leg higher, and the angle hits exactly where I want as I fuck my fingers into her, feeling the pressure of what I want to happen.

"Lincoln—" Her breath hitches. Mouth dropping open, her back arches away from the wall, her pussy pulses, and she saturates my hand. My cock wants to reap the warm-up and slide right into what I've just prepared as she unravels because of me.

But that's not happening. Not in an alleyway outside of a bar. I suck on the skin right below her ear, drag my teeth along her neck as her pulse beats dangerously fast. And because I can't help myself, I whisper against her wet skin, "You sound so pretty when you're pissed off and moaning for me."

I can feel her smile before I see it.

Pulling back, I look at how perfectly ravaged she is, leaning against the wall, hair messy, neck red from my nibbling, skirt hiked up, vest half unbuttoned and chest heaving, teasing the deep set of her cleavage. I can't hold back moaning at the sight of her. Bringing my fingers that were just inside her to my mouth, I lick them clean and then give them a good smell as she watches with a dazed expression.

Voices echo as they walk by the alley, snapping us both out of this bubble of desire we've found ourselves in. More than a few people come pouring out of the bar, and as much as I want her hand wrapped around my cock, I'm going to settle for my own.

"Let's go." I hold out my hand as she rights herself. I'm not going to leave her like this at this time of night. No fucking way.

She follows behind, my hand holding hers as my mind reels at what the hell I'm supposed to do when we reach her vehicle. If I kiss her, this isn't ending here. And it needs to.

But as we get closer to her truck, she lets go of my hand and makes the decision for me. "I'll take it from here." She walks ahead, turning her head to the side before she calls out, "You're pretty when you're pissed off too, Foxx. Too bad I couldn't get you to moan for me this time."

Sighing, I drag my hand through the front of my hair and remove my glasses from my coat pocket, taking a second to watch her pull out of her space and peel out of the lot. I laugh to myself and tilt my head back, looking up at the sky. She said "this time." Like there's going to be a next time. My cock twitches at the thought, working against my brain.

What the hell am I doing?

Chapter 14

Faye

The porch swing shakes, interrupting me for the third time in the past fifteen minutes. Maggie storms out of the front door with barely a glance at me, my keys hanging from her fingers. This particular set also happens to have a little tag embedded into the mirror ball keychain that tracks everywhere it goes. She's spending an awful lot of time down by the racetracks, considering it's the offseason, but every time I ask her a question, she answers with, "Isn't it about time you fucked off?" Or at least some version of the same sentiment.

"Where are you going, Maggie?" I shout after her. "You realize that's my truck and not yours, right?"

She just flips me off and keeps walking, ignoring what I've just said.

I close my eyes and try not to let it get to me that she hates me so much and wants me gone. As the sun warms my face, it takes away that sting of cold that January in Fiasco brings. It's not until the engine of my truck fires up that my attention flicks to watch my sister peel out of the driveway. *Asshole.*

Even with plenty more to occupy my mind, my thoughts keep wandering back to that alleyway. Blackstone only heard the opening of all of it. I hung up on him the second Lincoln asked if my panties were still off.

I wasn't thinking clearly. And I sure as hell wasn't focused on Blackstone. And now, once again, I'm replaying the finger bang from the sexy, seemingly irresistible single dad I blackmailed years ago.

My cheeks heat, and it's not from embarrassment. It's satisfaction. It's rather frustrating how hard I came from his fingers and the way he whispered dirty things to me. *I suggest you keep quiet when you drench my fingers.* I haven't come like that in my entire life.

Maybe that was enough. The thirst was quenched. Action completed. And yet, I keep glancing at his house, hoping to see him hustle out with his hand moving through his dark hair and forgetting to take off his glasses. *Jesus, what is it about a man like that in glasses?*

I blow out a breath and slam my eyes shut, shaking off the thoughts, because that entire interaction was merely an unexpected consolation prize for having successfully uploaded a mirroring app that is now running in the background of his phone. I have full access to everything he has open. Lucky for me, that man hasn't closed out a single app or web page for a single day since he bought this phone.

As I scroll through another folder of emails, I'm relieved I haven't found anything glaringly ugly hiding on Lincoln's phone. There's no organization to his app folders, zero social media accounts, and plenty of open articles about the effects of seasonal highs on corn, along with periodic table element letters in formula formats that I don't know the first thing about.

I swipe through an obscene number of photos. Lark and Lily like to steal his phone and use the photo burst feature often. There are thousands of unexpected, face-cropped selfies, pictures from softball games and horseback riding to first days of school and the randomness of a full life together. The ones that I can't help but pause on are the selfies with the three of them crammed into the screen.

There's no faking love like this—seeing it warms me in a way that had nothing to do with the morning sunshine. It either exists or it doesn't. There isn't a gray area with kids. And I know that, feel it, because it isn't something I ever had. With my mom, I did. But a dad who would smile on cue or sit and watch fashion shows or impromptu performances? That never existed for me.

The wind kicks up, and I pull the plush blanket over my lap. What I wouldn't give to have a few minutes sitting on these porch steps with my mom. Tell her I'm mad at her or how I just wish I'd known how bad things had gotten before she thought she didn't have another choice. Plucking out my headphones, I put on a winter hat I found stuffed into the closet of my old room, getting myself more comfortable to continue my search through Lincoln's phone.

A high-pitched cry has me stopping just as I'm placing my headphones on. I sit quietly for a moment and wait to see if I'll hear it again. The wind whips against the glass windowpanes of the farmhouse, making a familiar rattle that has a shiver running down the length of my arms and leaving goosebumps in its wake. Unnerved, I uncross my legs and stand. It could have easily been the wind bending along the house. Everything might look new inside, but the bones of this place are the same. The creak on the second step still groans, no matter where my foot falls. But if it wasn't...

I watched Maggie leave, so it wasn't her. Another faint yelp clips out, only this time I can pinpoint it's coming from the newly constructed barn.

When I hear the sound again, I'm hoping it's an animal and not *someone*. The hairs along my arms stand tall as I make my way down the porch stairs and along the gravel driveway.

With my Taser tucked into my waistband at my back, I pick up a small hand shovel that sits along the planting bench outside of the barn. There's so much more here now. This time, it's a yelping bark that sounds as I slide open the barn door. Its well-greased track makes it the quiet entrance I was hoping for, but that doesn't stop the two small bodies huddled right in the center of the room from turning their heads at the same time to look at me, both letting out a clipped scream.

"Shits and glitter, Faye," Lily says, holding her hand to her chest.

Lark breathes out a relieved laugh. "You're lucky Dad didn't hear you just say that, Lil."

"We're lucky this isn't Dad, you mean," she snaps back.

The smell of hay and mud permeates the space. When I left, Mom had three horses. It smells like that's still the case, but I know there aren't any here anymore. One of the many things that Maggie changed about the place.

"Why would your dad be mad?" I follow it up with the obvious that they probably don't even know. "Aside from hanging out with me?"

The question turns rhetorical when I step closer and look at what they're huddled over.

"Can we keep her here?" Lily asks, lifting the puppy in her

arms. Its light-brown color is splashed with patches of black on her head, making her look like a little masked bandit. "Please, please, Faye?" Her words tumble over as she continues. "She was the last dog at the adoption drive. They were going to bring her back after all her friends had been taken. They shouldn't have pet adoption drives on cold days. She's going to associate the cold weather with being left behind. It was a form of animal cruelty if we didn't take her home."

What the actual hell am I supposed to say to that? "Um, well…I don't think—" But my words cut out as I glance at Lark's hopeful expression first, then at her little sister's.

Lily's eyes water as she says, "I was supposed to find her. I just know it." She kisses her head as the puppy tries to squirm out of her hold. Her body wiggles and thrashes, and she escapes, flopping over and hustling toward my feet. Whatever kind of dog it is, she'll be big. "She has her shots. We have food and water. She needs a little extra, so she gets a dropper of something. I already have mama instincts, see?" She pets the dog's head as it leans into her body, knocking her off balance with a giggle.

I look at Lark, and she must know what I'm thinking, because she crosses her arms and lets out an annoyed sigh before I've even asked "Why do you want to keep her here?"

"Dad says it's a phase," Lark says. "That we'll move on to something else, but—" Her eyes water this time, but she catches the tears before they can trail down her cheeks.

The dog fops onto her belly and starts chewing on the laces of my boots.

"But that's not true. She's here now, right?" I say as she wipes the corner of her eyes.

They both look at me and wait for what I'm going to say

next. And while I must be out of my mind to agree to this for a roster of reasons, I ask, "What's her name?"

Lily stares at her sister for a beat before she says, "Kit."

Two days later and nearly two hundred dollars' worth of dog supplies, I clip the leash to Kit's harness. With trying to puppy train to the best of my ability, planning for my next performance at Midnight Proof, and continuing surveillance on Blackstone, I'm happy to get out of the house for a bit. It feels like a reward to stretch my legs and enjoy what's left of daylight as we walk down the sidewalk of Main Street. The wind from this morning has eased up, and the sun has been bright, keeping it warm even in the late winter afternoon.

We hadn't worked out the details about how long I'd look after Kit. My time in Fiasco would eventually end, and then the girls would take over. If not sooner. While I hadn't planned on staying for more than a month or so, I also hadn't thought about where I was going. I should feel anxious about it, not knowing. I always know my next steps. But I'm not thinking past Fiasco; I can't for some reason.

Kit lets out a bark and slows her steps, like she already knows where we're headed.

"My roots are looking a little dark, aren't they?" I say to her as we come to a stop in front of Teasers. I peer through the big picture window. The name of the place sounds more like a strip club than a beauty parlor, but it's the only spot in the county where people come to get everything done from a blowout to a manicure.

The bowl of water and small bucket of treats next to the

front double doors has me tying Kit's leash to the iron loop connected to the building.

"Stay here, pretty girl." I give her a stern look. "And behave yourself. I'll let you have one of those yummy bones we bought if you take a nap for me." The sidewalk is dry, and the sunshine must have warmed it, because the moment I step away, she lies down and rolls onto her back, making me chuckle.

The twangy echo of Dolly Parton laying down her laws, along with blow-dryers whirring, overpower the bell on the door when I walk into Teasers. The smells of burning hair and acetone are faint, but the environment knocks me right back to plenty of haircuts and one horrific perm from when I was eleven.

"Holy fiddle shits, Romey, are you seein' what I'm seein'?"

I smile at the familiar face adorned with a thick cat eye and a front bump that would put any 1950s pinup to shame. I couldn't tell you how old Maeve was, just that she's looked the same as the day I met her.

Romey's mouth opens mid-bite of something that looks like ambrosia.

"Maeve, hi—" I barely get the words out when she holds my hands, arms extended, and twirls me around like a damn show pony.

"Ladies!" she squeals, and the busy shop quiets. "Look at what the winter winds dragged in…"

I give a tight-lipped smile at her quirked eyebrow. If that face doesn't say it all—*where the fuck have you been, so nice of you to grace us with your presence*, and all of that. I knew I'd surprise a few people and that the welcome was going to be dicey, so I might as well lean into it now that I'm getting some more positive reception. Stepping inside Teasers was like ripping off the Band-Aid.

"Hi, it's nice to see all of you." I take a deep breath. All eyes on me and working a crowd is my strong suit. However, I usually have music, feathers, and sequins to help.

"I would ask what you're doing in here, but those roots are looking a bit longer than what I would consider natural," Maeve says as she fingers through my hair. "I'm thinking some thick highlights, a glaze, maybe help out with that little bit of fuzz above your lip. Unless you're only here to ask if we've seen Maggie." She raises her eyebrows and puts her hands on her hips in the best Wonder Woman stance I've seen in a long time. Only this one's wearing Carhartt pants, cowgirl boots, and a crop top that reads *Kentucky's Finest* across the chest. She's tiny, but her attitude makes up for it.

"The shop looks really great, Maeve. And if you have time, I'd love a refresh," I say with a warm smile.

I look around the place as it busies up again after the screeching record stop from when I came in.

"Alright, Faye, would you like a mimosa, bloody, or just some sparkling water?"

I blink at Romey, who's nudging me to follow her to the back of the shop, where a nice little bar setup awaits next to four floral wingback chairs. A couple of younger hairdressers ignore the little show and keep working, but I take note of the other people here.

Some familiar faces—a smiling and waving Prue, Fiasco's librarian; Tonya and Darla, both secretaries to the town council; and Mary, who worked as a lunch aide at Fiasco Elementary. All semiretired by now, I would imagine, and not too far from how old my mom would be. They were her friends.

The salon has been upgraded with plenty of new equipment since the last time I was here. Modern with a country flair.

Whitewash with some pretty florals and black wrought iron worked in where necessary—the mirrors, sconces on walls, and around the coffee and bar station. It's a far cry from the small-town salon I remember.

"No bourbon?" I tsk. "Breaking the cardinal rule of Fiasco, Romey."

She smiles at me. "What do you know about Fiasco anymore, darlin'?" The jab isn't unexpected. She eyes the leather straps that wrap around my shoulders and torso, a typical place that someone would hold a gun, but I like it for the pure contrast of something edgy paired with a simple white thermal shirt and well-fitted jeans. She doesn't need to know that I have a small blade stuffed into the side of my boot, pepper spray with marker ink, and a small stun gun in the secret pocket of my bag.

Romey clears her throat after she looks at something over my shoulder—likely her sister telling her to quit the shit. "The mimosa can also be dirty with a little shot of bourbon, a splash of orange, and topped with prosecco." She winks as she pulls a mason jar glass.

The best way to get people to answer questions is to get them to start talking about themselves or gossip. It's not a tactic, rather a little piece of common sense I had picked up long before I ever left Fiasco.

I clear my throat. "I'm guessing you heard about Maggie?"

"Oh, honey, your sister has been playing with the wrong crowds for a while now. That's nothing new." I hate hearing this again from someone else.

Everything's unsettled when it comes to my sister. *If I hadn't left...*

Maeve comes up behind me and loops her arm around mine. "You've been gone a while, sweetheart." Taking a pause, she hands me the thin black wrap to drape around me as I take a seat in her chair. "Maggie is not—" She sniffs out a breath. "Your sister has a gambling problem. And the company she keeps… Well, I'm not surprised…"

Maggie is dead set on me knowing I'm not welcome, but it doesn't matter in the grand scheme of things. She's been hurt, and I won't let something like that happen again.

I brace myself when I ask, "Who?"

Prue cuts in. "Waz King, for starters. Saw them having an argument a couple weeks ago." Hearing his name soured my stomach. I didn't trust anyone with the last name King, never mind when it was associated with my sister.

Why would she be involved with him in any way? I buried his brother Tullis in a cornfield five years ago. There should be no reason why my sister is hanging around with, never mind arguing with, Waz King.

Dammit, Maggie.

Romey adds, "Your sister doesn't go anywhere without that damn laptop of hers. And it's surprising, considering I thought she wanted to be a trainer just like Shelby…"

Maeve mixes up the purple-tinted cream with the painting brush and gets to work as she starts sectioning off my hair. "I don't think she's been on a real date in years. Your sister is a beauty, but holy hell, she doesn't pick any winners. There was one from the rodeo a few years back. I think he did a number on her. I know that Jimmy Duggan has asked her out a few times, but he's too good for her and what she's up to. Even though that boy—"

Romey cuts her sister off. "He's a man, Maeve. He's in his twenties now."

She cocks her hip and gives her sister a glare. "Anyone who isn't well into their forties, in my opinion, is still a kid."

Romey grins at me. "Enough about Maggie. I'm more interested in the chatter I've been hearing about this burlesque woman. Rosie Gold, is it?"

I smile, not meeting her attention in the mirror.

"Might need to take in a performance at Midnight Proof. See what all the buzz is about," she says with a teasing tone.

A while later, my hair is refreshed, looking even better than it has in a long time. "Maeve, it looks incredible. Thank you for squeezing me in."

She sprays an overly excessive amount of hairspray over the top of my head just as an echo of loud barks sound from outside, pulling all our attention.

"Your dog is basking in some lovin' out there," Romeo says.

The shop carries on a quiet buzz, the sound of hair dryers and "Jolene" mingled with gossip about the latest plans for next month's Valentine's Day celebrations and who had been rumored to be cheating on whom. But the chatter stops abruptly, and my guess is that they're watching exactly who I am. Through the front main window, Lincoln Foxx, with his dark wool coat and perfect smile, casually stands with his hands slung into his pockets as he watches his girls being licked by a very overeager puppy.

I have no say in it, but my body remembers everything his fingers are capable of doing as if he's touching me again. My face and neck feel hot. Taking a breath, I stand from the chair, trying to mentally gather myself.

"I swear that man gets better looking every year," Romey tuts next to me.

Maeve swats at her hand. "He isn't even forty yet." She leans in close to me. "A lot of rumors about that one. And it's nothing bad, in my opinion. A shame he's doing life on his own right now."

I give her a tight-lipped smile.

"He's single," Romey says, popping a Modjeska in her mouth. "But he's not alone. He's got those sweet girls."

"Widowed," Maeve corrects.

Romey looks at her with annoyance and then to me. "One doesn't make the other one untrue." She tilts her head to the side with a shrug.

"I'm not—" Shaking my head, I clear my throat. "That's not on the agenda."

"They usually never are, dear," Romey says.

The funny part is, I want to believe my own words. Since I left Fiasco, each decision I've made has had a purpose—a well thought-out plan and path to either complete a job or preserve a sliver of calculated enjoyment in my life. But a handful of days back here and plans suddenly feel incomplete and riddled with detours. One very specific one stands a few feet away, with glasses and a devious smile that makes my insides melt and renders me stereotypically stupid. A quiet, buried part of me kicks alive when I'm around him. And the worst part is, I like that feeling.

Maeve smiles at Lark and Lily as they come into the salon. Lark with her EarPods in, wearing a vintage *NSYNC T-shirt, which I'm pretty sure I got at a concert on the original tour. Lily's behind her with a crossbody bag that reads *Hufflepuff State of Mind*. It's hard not to smile at them.

Maeve says, "Girls, I'm going to have you wait just a few minutes. I have to wrap something up over here, and then we can get those manicures started. Maybe Romey can make you both a little mocktail while you're waitin'." She smiles at Lincoln, and holy hell, they're right. That man can steal the oxygen out of just about any room he wants. He's not even smiling, and almost every face in this room is grinning in his direction.

Lincoln asks, "Maeve, it might be a painted toes kind of day too. Do you have time for it?"

She taps his arm and says, "For my favorite Foxxes? Absolutely."

A smile starts to take over his face as Maeve leaves him. He glances at me and that smile gets wider, like he just caught me doing something I'm not supposed to be doing—which, to be clear, I was. I was checking out his ass. My face heats thinking about his confident stride in those damn Wranglers that make him even more delicious, but instead of looking away, I blatantly look down his body and back up again.

"Ohmygosh," Lily rushes out. "Faye, I love her harness."

I smile, feeling good about picking one she approves of.

My eyes dart toward Lincoln, who's watching the exchange. *Shit, he's going to see right through this.*

Lark notices and tries to cover it by adding, "Faye asked us what color harness we should—I mean, *she* should...what harness she should get for Kit."

Lincoln glances at me and stays quiet. When he steps closer, watching his girls ask Maeve about new nail colors, he quietly says one small word. "Peach."

Maybe it's because that's what he's called me a few times now for no good reason, or it's just the proximity of his arrogance, but I ignore the way his jacket brushes along my back and the sound of his voice—quiet and just for me—makes my body tingle. "Forget my name already?"

I step up to the counter and settle the bill with Romey. Her eyes track him as he moves closer to me again. *What the hell is he doing?*

He leans in, his hand ghosting around me and touching my hip as he whispers, "Believe me when I say that I've tried to forget. But those sounds you made… The way you came so beautifully for me…" He lets out a small laugh, and my stomach swoops. "That's not something a man forgets." When he moves a few inches closer, I have to suppress a shiver. "So no, I didn't forget your name. You're making that really fucking hard for me."

I turn to look at him, his blue eyes searching for a reaction. If he could see underneath my clothes, he'd see the response—goosebumps seeking a soothing hand, nipples hard and ready to be plucked, my pussy tingling and leaving a wet spot right in the center of my panties.

I glance back at Maeve and Romey, who are watching the entire exchange with delighted smiles. *Jesus.*

"Thanks, ladies," I tell them both, acting like Lincoln didn't just throw me off-balance once again. "Rosie Gold puts on a helluva show. You should try to catch her while she's in town," I say, smiling and giving them a wink.

Lily waves. "Bye, Faye," she calls out after me.

Lark gives me a wary smile as she looks between her father and me. She saw all of that too. This is getting too messy. He has kids. Kids I actually like being around. The idea of them not hating me is something I care about a lot more than I should. And caring about what they think makes whatever Lincoln and I are doing feel more important. *I can dissect that another time.* I hustle to get my coat on without looking like I'm fleeing the scene.

When I step out of the salon, wind whips at my face, messing up my hair and making it a struggle to unwrap Kit's leash, but the door swings open before I can yank it free.

"You got a dog?" Lincoln asks from behind me. I should have known he'd follow me out.

"I'm fostering her. Just for a little bit while I'm here."

"Fostering?" he says, brow furrowing like he's trying to figure out what would possess me to do this, considering he knows I'm not a permanent fixture in Fiasco.

I let out a huff. "Yes, fostering. Why are you… Go back inside, Foxx."

He smiles at me, but it's taunting. "Are you flustered? Peach, am I flustering you?"

I brush the hair out of my face again. I can't get the leash unclipped. Looking up at him with a pinched brow, I bark out a laugh. "Oh please, Foxx."

He hums. "Yeah, I remember you saying that with a little less sass last time. I liked you sounding so eager and needy."

Just as my thighs clench, the triple beeping of a horn snags both of our attention. Kit barks out wildly too, just as Griz pulls up at an alarming pace in his golf cart.

"Are you able to drive golf carts around town like this?" I say through a laugh as he comes to a stop.

"I'd love to see Fiasco PD try to tell me otherwise," he says. "Faye, I'm glad I caught you. One of my book club girls said you were down here. What do you say to dinner at my place on Friday night?" His eyes shift to Lincoln, who's standing next to me now. "My great-grandbabies in there right now? Or are you hanging around looking for women?"

Lincoln squints at him like that last question was ridiculous. "Post-therapy manicure day," he says to his grandfather.

"Rough one today?" Griz asks him.

"Depends on what they talked about," Lincoln says. I feel like I shouldn't be here for this discussion, but he looks at me and says, "We're a pro-therapy crew."

"It's a good idea. I'm part of that crew too." I realize how that sounds and try to backtrack, stumbling over my words. "I mean, pro-therapy. Not in your crew. I like your crew."

He licks his lower lip and then smiles at me. "It's alright, Peach, I know what you meant." He clears his throat and realizes Griz heard that too.

"That your dog?" Griz asks as he nods down to the puppy sitting as if I trained her to do it.

I glance back up at him with a smile. "Yes, she is. For now, at least."

The golf cart whirls to life again as he tuts, "Huh, Lily drew me something with a dog that looked just like it. What a coincidence. Alright, I'll see you Friday, Faye." And then he's gone as fast as he arrived, without even getting my answer to if I could make it to dinner.

While it would be smart to make the same kind of escape, I can't stop myself from lingering for a few more seconds. Watching as Griz drives off, I smile as I ask, "Is he always like that?"

Without missing a beat, Lincoln says, "Always."

I feel like I knew the answer already. Griz is adored by his family. My sister too, apparently. He reminds me of Lincoln—the arrogant charm with a sense of protectiveness that emanates when it comes to their family. I understand that. It might be the most glaringly obvious thing we have in common.

In the late afternoon light, Lincoln Foxx, with his black-rimmed glasses and nearly perfect features, looks like he's in disguise. A different version of the man I met on the edge of a cornfield and in a dark alley. I clear my throat, trying to knock myself out of this. A little breathing room from this man would be smart. I make a smooching sound to get Kit moving. But as we take a few steps away, I can't help but instigate.

"I know you're watching me walk away," I call out as I turn my head to the side.

"Hard not to when you consider how much I liked watching you come," he says, far too loudly. Before it even registers what he said, I turn around, and he's opening the door, smiling at me as he walks back inside Teasers.

I realize I'm smiling too as I focus back on the sidewalk and toward my truck, but it's the lingering feeling of still being watched that has me looking around and sliding my hand inside my pocket. I feel for my pepper spray and hold it in my palm as a low whistle rings out from across the street.

It's the familiar sound of a race beginning, that recognizable sound that's typically a trumpet or bugle, but right now, it was a slower whistle. The hairs along my arms stand on end, Kit growling just as I catch the tall, thin stature leaning against the lamppost. *Waz King.* My heart picks up pace as he watches while I move to my truck door. When Kit barks, Waz lets out a laugh that makes my skin crawl. She keeps barking as he turns away and walks down the street.

I don't scare easily. My knee-jerk reaction to intimidation is to get angry, but Waz, he's the kind of man any woman should be concerned about. And my mind immediately goes to my sister. Whatever Maggie is doing for Wheeler Finch and Waz King needs to stop.

Chapter 15

Lincoln

"Hey, Hal." I wave as I jog down the porch steps, barefoot, my hair still wet from my shower. Lark and Lily have their arms crossed at the foot of the driveway, watching as Hal jumps down from the cab of his truck.

"Lincoln, how ya doin', man?" He shakes my hand and then moves to the back of his trailer. Hal's family owns some of the farmland that we lease; however, instead of corn and crops, they own livestock.

I'm not sure what he's doing here, but I ask, "How's business these days?"

Unlocking the right side of the trailer first and then moving around to the left, he keeps the small talk brief. "Every year is a little different, but mostly this has been a good one."

I rest my hands on my hips. He didn't stop over for a simple hello. "What's going on? Did you need something?"

Shaking his head, he lowers the back trailer door. "Nope, all good. This one is good natured. I really think she'll take to y'all."

And before I can even form the question, a sandy-colored cow moseys down the trailer bridge. The hair atop its head is longer than the rest, but still short enough to see its big black eyes.

I laugh nervously. "Lark and Lily Foxx, what's happening right now?"

Hal looks between them, shifting his focus back to me. "I'm delivering your highland cow." The look on my face must tell him exactly how much I know about this. "Paid in full. Your girls dropped off the final payment a few days ago."

Eyes wide and chest tight, I turn my head slowly toward my girls. "You bought a cow."

You've got to be fucking kidding me. "I'm sorry, Hal. You're going to have to take her back—"

Lily yells, "No! Dad, c'mon!"

Lark stays quiet as she worries at her lip and plays with the hem of her Spice Girls T-shirt.

"How did you pay for this?" I ask quietly. It's the even tone that tells my girls I'm about to flip my shit.

"Curse purse," they respond in unison.

What. The. Fuck.

Hal smiles to himself and walks over to me with the cow meandering behind him. "It's a great animal to have around, if you can afford to keep her sheltered in these cold weather months and fed with some mix of grass hay and alfalfa. If you need some time to decide if that's something you'd like to do, I can keep her for a little while." He looks behind me at who I would assume are my girls trying to figure out how to explain this to me. "Give me a call in a few days and tell me if you'd rather I find her a new home. My animals need to be somewhere they're wanted and well looked after. And I'm real sorry, Lincoln. I shouldn't have assumed you cleared this."

"We'll love her, Dad," Lark says, looking right at me, eyes pleading. "Please." And it guts me. It hits me in a way that has me realizing that I'm not the kind of man who's going to say no without good reason. And I'm realizing I don't have one.

"Lark, what are you going to do with a cow?"

"Dottie," Hal corrects. "The girls named her when they bought her."

I glare at Hal as Lark follows up by saying, "Doesn't she look like her name should be Dottie?"

Taking a deep breath, I move my hands to my hips. "You realize we don't have a barn or the type of property needed to house a cow, right?"

Lily chimes in with, "Dad, we're Foxxes. We can figure anything out."

Touché.

My eyes close for a moment as I tilt my head back. "Using my own hype words against me should be against the law." I point at her with a quirked eyebrow. When I look between my two girls, all I can think is, *How am I supposed to say no to this?*

Fucking fuck.

I scrub my hand down my face. "Alright. Hal, I'm going to need a little bit of time to figure out how this is going to work." I watch as Lark's eyes water and a big smile takes over Lily's face. "You mind if my girls find their way to your place daily to learn the chores that are needed to take care of her, and then I'll work on making sure we give her a good home in a few weeks."

"I think that would be a great idea, Lincoln," Hal says with a relieved smile.

I clap my hands in front of me. "This is the last time you do something like buy an animal without me knowing." I gesture to the cow being loaded back onto the trailer. "That's a family decision. Something that's living and breathing is not a curse purse purchase."

Lark side-eyes Lily.

"No." I point between the two of them. "Nooo. Nope. What's that look?" I know this look—it means there's more. And my girls are smart; they aren't going to divulge information that might prolong whatever it is they're doing. It's like they're waiting for another shoe to drop. Then it dawns on me—the brown and black puppy. *Kit.* "Dammit, you bought the dog too, didn't you?" I deadpan.

"Kit," Lily says. "Her name is Kit, and we adopted her. We knew you weren't going to say yes right away, so we hid her in the barn next door. But then Faye found us."

Lark chimes in, "And she said she'd look after her until…"

"Until when? Girls, seriously? You're just folding animals into our lives without my knowledge. How did you see this working out?"

But it's Lily who smiles and says with a shrug of her shoulders, "If you build it…"

"No. You talk to me, and then we figure it out. Together."

Lily and Lark slam the truck doors as they hop out and run up the driveway to greet Julep and the elusive puppy named Kit. I breathe in the good of being around my family and then exhale the self-hatred for not paying better attention. *Whose fucking kids buy farm animals or bring home a dog without them knowing?*

I rest my head along the back seat—it would be so much

easier if Liv were here. Doing this parent thing alone is really fucking hard sometimes. It's the first time I've let myself think about having someone who'd do this with me. Laugh after a parenting fail and figure out a way to avoid this happening again. Listen to me freak out about how smart my girls are—they just swindled me, for fuck's sake.

The open space surrounding Ace's house is postcard Kentucky. Between the flat landscape and the wide expanse of paddocks that are peppered throughout the left side of the property, and then the massive white stables that take up space all along the right side, it's clear that my brother has two very distinct passions: bourbon and horses.

Dusk colors the horizon with a splatter of deep oranges and soft purples. *Beautiful.* I exit my Jeep and watch my girls talk a mile a minute to Hadley, who must have just pulled in right before us. Griz sits in his spot on the porch laughing at the same sight. And just cresting the knoll that runs along my line of sight, two people are racing toward us on horseback—it's hard to make out who it might be other than a man and a woman. The sound of hooves hitting the earth is still quiet as I watch on, but it echoes loudly when I really focus on the riders. They are neck and neck, my brother gets closer, and the smile on his face isn't one I see too often.

A few feet behind him is none other than Faye.

My stomach sinks, realizing that she's the one putting that smile on my brother's face. I'm positive she's not going to let up either.

"What the fuck?" Hadley says as she approaches my side, her hands on her hips as we both watch them streak by. They kick up the wind and whatever dirt had been settled along the pathway.

I give my best friend a glance. "Didn't get asked to go for a ride?"

"Not the kind of ride I want."

I bark a laugh and look down at her hair pinned up high with curls spilling all over the place. "You just get here?"

"Hadley Jean Finch, your favorite Foxx needs a squeeze," Griz interrupts, sliding up next to us. She gives him a good hug and the old man eats it up. As Hadley wraps her arms around one of his, all three of us watch Ace and Faye jump down from their horses and laugh about something. *When the fuck did Ace get to be funny?*

Hadley says, "Griz, are you inviting every pretty girl who rolls into town to dinner?"

He chuckles. "Stunning, isn't she? I have a good feeling about her." Looking at me over her, he says, "My grandsons might know a thing or two about bourbon, but they don't seem to know what chemistry looks like…"

Maybe not what it looks like, but I know exactly what it feels like. I haven't been able to shake it since she's been back. He squeezes my shoulder and walks back toward the porch, yelling, "Might want to start going after the things you two want instead of just sitting back and waiting for them to miraculously happen."

"Read the room, Griz," Hadley says under her breath.

I give her a kiss on her head. "Heard you were dating the fire chief."

She looks up at me and smiles. "Define dating."

"Going out for food. Enjoying each other's company…"

She sighs. "Linc, it's like you don't know me at all. I am absolutely *fucking* the fire chief…" Then she lowers her voice. "And his newest recruit."

I raise my eyebrows. "Do they both know that?"

"They know." She nods, grinning. "Oh, believe me, they know."

"Dang, girl," I shout with an added twang. I know there's more to it, and when she wants to share, she will. Because as much as my best friend has a good time and goes wherever the wind takes her, she craves stability. It's why she started spending so much time with us growing up, as wild as me and my brothers were. We've always had family dinners. Griz was there to ask where we'd been and what was coming. Nobody cared about her enough to ask until she ended up at our dinner table.

"Proximity is everything," she goes on. "You know my roof deck has direct access to the fire station across the street…"

I do my best to listen, but I can't stop myself from glancing toward the stables. Ace takes the reins of both horses as Faye follows him. *Smiling, smiling, smiling.* Why is she spending any time with him? I'm still thinking about the way she felt leaning against me. The smell of her that lingered on my fingers later that night. How close I came to storming next door and fucking her like I wanted.

And now she's throwing her head back, laughing at something Ace is saying. He's not that funny. My common sense snaps. "I'll be right back," I interrupt.

"Oh-kay…" Hadley says in response, and I can hear her chuckling as she realizes where I'm headed.

Hands twitching at my sides, I rack my mind with what I'm going to say once I get there, but I come up blank. My boots scuff along the concrete pathway and into the stable's double doors. The only thing I'm certain of is that I don't want my older brother anywhere near her. *Can you be considered unhinged if you know what you're about to do is exactly that? Stupidly unhinged.*

If it wasn't for the cool breeze working through the open doors, you'd never know how many horses were in here. The place is pristine. Faye's voice kicks up in another laugh toward the end stalls, and the sound of it shouldn't do a fucking thing, but it does. The echo of it sneaks under my skin and edges me into a streak of anger I haven't felt in a long time. One that makes me want to take things I have no business taking or wanting. She's wearing an oversized men's shirt she's buttoned only halfway, one that better not fucking be his, and tight black pants that disappear into her tall cowgirl boots—these dirtier and more worn than the purple ones she wore at Bottom of the Barrel.

Ace laughs about something she said, that smile still stuck on his face when he notices me. "Hey, Linc." He lifts the saddle off the horse he was riding.

"Hey," I say with a labored breath, shifting my attention solely to Faye. "I need a minute."

Faye looks at Ace quickly and then back to me.

"Ace, I'll make sure the horses are set before we come inside for dinner." And because he's my brother, he doesn't ask any more questions. He respects that I need a minute alone here. With her. He pauses momentarily, trying to read between the lines. *Yeah, brother, this one is mine.*

"Great ride, Faye," he says as he claps his hand on my shoulder. Then, with a half-tipped smile as he walks by me, he adds, "I'll be here if you're up for another."

Under my breath I mumble, "Fucker." Just loud enough for him to hear.

His shoulders bounce with a clipped laugh as he walks off.

Faye picks up the tack box and sighs before she says, "I'm starving."

Lifting the tack box out of her hand, I put it back on the stool she pulled it from. With just one more step forward, I'm crowding her. "What are you doing here?"

As I keep moving forward, she steps backward. "Pretty obvious I was out with your brother." She lifts her chin in a challenge. "It's been a long time since I've had a good ride." The innuendo is loud and clear.

"No," I grit out, and she searches my face for the meaning of that simple word. "You misunderstood me." As her back reaches the wall, she stops, and I leave just enough space to breathe between us. "I don't like being lied to, so I'm going to ask you again, what are you doing here? In Fiasco. And don't give me some bullshit about headlining at Hadley's place or what Maggie's up to. You two barely look at each other."

I lift my hand and let my fingers push the hair away from her face. I don't know what it is about being near her that feels good. I should ignore it, move on, and forget all about the other night in that dark alley. Erase every moment of that night in the cornfield before my life got even more complicated and confusing. I shouldn't want to be around someone I can't trust. "Of all the places you could dance, why here?"

She tilts her face up, swaying into me as I twirl a piece of her hair. I pull it just slightly, tilting her head back a little farther, just where I want her. With her lips parted, it's like she's trying to decide if she should let me lead. "What makes you think it's any of *your* business knowing what I'm doing here?"

Her eyes focus on my mouth when I say, "It's *my* business when you start working at my best friend's club. It's *my* business when you come to my family's house for dinner. It's my *fucking* business when you have a secret that you keep from me when it's about my girls."

"Dammit," she says on an exhale. "They're very convincing. But then you fold a puppy into it…"

I can't help but let out a small laugh, and it snaps me out of my anger. "Oh, I know." Shaking my head slowly, I release a heavy breath. "Somehow, they've figured out how to skirt around asking me for what they want. They just do it on their own." I don't know why I'm telling her this. "They bought a cow, Dottie. Honestly, I'm more impressed than anything that they did it."

She barks out a laugh. "And now you have a dog named Kit to add to the brood."

Feeling more relaxed, I can't help but laugh with her. "I feel like I should be mad, but I'm—"

She moves her hand to my chest, and my breath catches, cutting me off. Her fingers run along the seam of buttons as she says, "I never really knew my real dad. My mom had a lot of stand-in boyfriends. Maggie's dad was in the picture for a while, but he never made me feel like he was glad I was around. Everyone who came after was interested in my mom, not in her insta-family."

She watches my fingers brush and soothe along the inside of her wrist as she continues. "Your girls are lucky to know what it feels like to be loved by their dad," she says softly. Hearing that from her warms my chest. The idea that my love for them is visible to a practical stranger has me feeling like I'm doing something right.

As I tip her chin up and push away a piece of blond hair that fell in front of her eye, her smile fades. Our eyes stay locked for a moment just before she focuses on my lips. I don't understand how we can so quickly go from anger and frustration to a sweet vulnerability to a heat that we're both too damn smart to ignore. It's reckless.

Yeah, Peach, I want to kiss you too.

I've wanted to kiss her again for longer than I'd care to think about.

"We both know this isn't a good idea," I tell her, but it doesn't sound the least bit convincing.

"You're right. It isn't," she says on an exhale. But her words die off when her fingers curl and she fists my shirt, pulling me into her. She holds on to me like the last thing she wants is to stop or let go.

I clear my throat, trying to remember what has me holding back. I'm coming up short at this proximity. So I give her the only truth that really matters. "I don't trust you."

Her breath hitches as my thumb runs along her jaw toward her mouth. "But you want to," she says, her eyes never leaving my mouth. "Just like I want to hate you."

I run my thumb along her lower lip, whispering, "But you don't."

She moves her head slowly right and then left, signaling no. As her tongue peeks out, wetting her bottom lip, despite all the probable reasons to stop this, the only thing I can think about is how she would feel wrapped around me. How with a few words and enough spitfire from her lips, I'm hard and so fucking ready for her to grant me the permission to have exactly what I want.

"So what are we going to do about it?"

Chapter 16

Faye

I'm enveloped in the smell of him—the warmth of toasted oak and a tartness, like a bourbon-soaked cherry. He clouds my judgment, muddles memories, and practically erases all the reasons I had started to tally about why this shouldn't go any further than what happened in that alley. The grip I have on his shirt is needy, the material fisted in my hands, and it's like I can't control it. The things that we're healing from, hiding from, and equally trying to forget seem to converge when I'm with him. And he feels like a net or a shield. I shouldn't feel safe with someone who's seen the worst of me. The same man who ordered me to leave the only place I ever wanted to call home. But I do. I feel safe. And I don't want to let go.

A shuffle of dirt along the concrete floor has our heads turning toward the main aisle of the stables. It merges with the sound of a horse kicking its stall. A beat after that, my phone buzzes in my back pocket. We're being interrupted every which way.

"Linc? Faye?" Hadley calls out from the front of the stables.

When I try to break away, he holds on to me, still tight against his body, a hair's breadth from his mouth, his hard dick pressing into my belly. I'm practically buzzing with anticipation as he tilts his forehead onto mine.

"I'm going to need an answer to that eventually."

So what are we going to do about it?

Just as I settle into the way he's holding me, his body so close, he steps back. He runs his hand from the front of his hair to the back of his neck. It's the only indication that he's as affected by what just happened as I am. As his eyes meet mine, the smile he gives me is sinful. All that confidence and those dimples, I doubt many women say no to this man.

Swallowing roughly, I pull out my phone. "I need to check this."

CORTEZ:
> How do you feel about a little side job, baby girl?

I don't realize he's looking over my shoulder when I unlock my phone.

"I didn't think you were actually on a date with Cortez the other night."

"It wasn't a date," I respond with a shake of my head. I won't tell him what I was doing with Cortez at the bar. As far as Lincoln is concerned, my job is purely that of a burlesque dancer. "I thought that was clear when it was your fingers I ended up riding," I say with a little sass as I type out a response.

FAYE:

If you want me to do anything else for you, then I'm going to need a fuller picture here.

And before I can say anything more to Lincoln, he's already halfway down the main aisle of the stables. I take a deep breath and push away the last few minutes, focusing on my job, my whole secret reason for being here. One that's getting harder to keep close the more I'm pulled into Lincoln Foxx's orbit.

And while I haven't found anything share worthy on his phone, Ace might be another story.

CORTEZ:

Blackstone is only a piece of the larger puzzle. What are the chances you can plant surveillance on Atticus Foxx?

It's still not clear to me how far the oldest Foxx brother's involvement with Blackstone extends, and more importantly, I only know a fraction of the story since Cortez won't give me more information.

FAYE:

You'll never guess where I am right now.

CORTEZ:

Hooch's?

> **FAYE:**
> No. Marla is still only serving me water.

> **CORTEZ:**
> Not surprised. You're missing out though, she had buttermilk pie last week.

> **FAYE:**
> I hate you.

> **FAYE:**
> And I'm at Foxx's house now. I'll see what I can do.

> **CORTEZ:**
> Make it work.

> **FAYE:**
> We'll see if I'm willing to share.

"I see the appeal."

I slap a hand to my chest and jump as soon as I hear it. I didn't expect anyone to be leaning to the right of the doors, but Hadley's standing there, seemingly waiting for me.

"You scared me," I say with a laugh. "I didn't know anyone was out here."

"Freezing today, isn't it?"

I open my mouth to answer, but she doesn't let me.

"What's going on with you and Lincoln?"

I wish I fucking knew.

"Quite frankly, I have no idea," I say truthfully.

With a sigh, she jokingly says, "I feel that. Down to my toes." It's easy to see how much she cares about him. They both have an ease that makes me feel welcomed and seen. "I'm nosy as fuck when it comes to my people, so you can expect me to be prying later. Maybe some drinks after dinner?"

I smile at her frankness. "Drinks sound nice," I tell her as we walk through the front entrance of the estate.

The floor of the foyer is stamped with a giant letter *F* and the head of a fox hugs tightly around it. If I had forgotten where I was, this house would have quickly reminded me. The masculine colors mingle with the scent of tobacco, charred oak, and bourbon, making it abundantly clear this house is in the heart of Fiasco, Kentucky.

Laney moves around the massive kitchen island, mincing mint leaves as a long piece of red licorice hangs from the side of her mouth.

She glances up, spotting us right away. "Finally! You two took forever." She smiles at me. "I'm so happy to see you again, Faye. Did Hadley convince you to join us at Midnight Proof later? Seasonal cocktails samples!" Glancing around like she's looking for someone, she whisper-shouts, "It's how she wooed me into loving this place."

Grant yells from the next room, "I heard that, honey. And it's not even a little bit true, Faye. Hadley had nothing to do with it. Don't listen to my wife; she's been known to lie."

That has Laney laughing, a guilty-as-charged look on her face.

I glance at Hadley, who's distracted by Kit as she chews on the pom-pom to her boots. "Hadley, how long since you opened Midnight Proof?"

Smiling proudly, she says, "I bought it the year I turned thirty. Best thing I ever did. It took some work renovating the shithole into what it is now. I had to gut the entire building and ended up renting the upper half to the girls from Crescent de Lune."

"Great coffee," I add.

She points at me, oh-so-serious. "Great fucking coffee."

"Amen," Laney says.

"Most of the building is Midnight Proof. And there's a top floor pied-à-terre specifically designed for one-night slams."

"Stands," Laney corrects, just as Ace comes into the kitchen.

Hadley pops a raspberry in her mouth. "Sometimes standing is fun. But"—she sighs—"I prefer a good ol' slam." She winks, and I can't help but laugh.

"Totally appropriate conversations happening in here among the girls," Ace says as he pulls down rocks glasses from one of the cabinets.

Hadley doesn't miss a beat. "You're going to have to do a little more than roll your eyes and grind those teeth if you want to call me your girl, Daddy."

Laney and I look at each other, eyes wide. I keep my facial expression neutral because, as much as I want to laugh, Ace looks unamused, and Hadley looks like she's ready to word spar.

"I said *the* girls, Hadley," he says, walking over to the counter to bring the fruit salad that Laney just finished to the other room.

"You sure about that? Sometimes people in their elder years tend to forget what they've just said." She smiles coyly, head tilted like she's the picture of innocence.

"And sometimes mouthy brats—" He cuts himself off as Laney and I barely bite back our smiles.

Hadley is still standing there, staring at the doorway that he just walked out of, looking like she's in awe for a solid ten-Mississippi seconds. "You heard that, right? Like, my brain didn't short circuit from seeing him in that friggin' pair of Wranglers tonight. WRANGLERS!" she whisper-shouts to Laney. "And he called me a *mouthy* brat. What the actual fuck?"

Chuckling, I glance at Laney for some kind of explanation, but she just shakes her head as she lifts the dish of French toast and brings it out to the three-season patio.

The cool night air hits me as soon as we step into the living space. I find Lincoln immediately, and before I can make any moves, Kit stretches her front paws on my legs. "Hi, pretty girl. Did you enjoy your bone?"

She barks a response I'm assuming is a yes as Lily slides over to us.

"Did she just answer you?" Lily asks.

"She's very smart," I say, rubbing her ears as she leans into it. "Aren't you? You're a very smart lady."

"Faye, can I sit next to you? I want to show you a trick."

Lark doesn't seem to be interested; in fact, she's given me the stink eye since I came in.

I look up and find Lincoln watching me with Lily. Despite what's happened between the two of us, I haven't forgotten what he said about not wanting me anywhere near his family. I understand why he's so protective.

I mouth out, *Is this okay?*

He doesn't answer right away, just watches with a stoic glare for a few extra beats before he gives a nod.

Griz cuts in, "The guest of honor gets to sit next to the oldest man in the room." It throws me off for a second to be so welcomed. He nods to his right, where there's an empty chair waiting. When I sit, he says, "Glad you decided to join us for dinner."

My cheeks heat at the nice words.

Clapping his hands, Griz straightens, reaching for a tall bottle of what I assume is bourbon.

My sister uses that moment to lean in on my other side and dump a cold bucket of water on me when she says, "Don't make yourself comfortable here, Faye. You may have forgotten, but they're not your family."

"Funny," I whisper. "Considering my only family would rather tell me to fuck off than actually talk with me."

"Hurts, doesn't it?" she bites back. I try not to wince at those words.

When I look around, I notice Hadley is paying attention to what's occurring between Maggie and me and mouths, *Asshole*.

I snort a laugh, and Maggie flips me off as she rests her hand on her cheek.

As I glance around the table, I realize that Lily must have noticed it too. Her mouth is dropped open in surprise, looking at me with eyes wide, wordlessly asking, *Did you see what your sister just did?*

Yeah, kid. I did.

Laney starts talking about the private tastings that'll kick off next month at Foxx Bourbon. Grant watches her talk with enthusiasm about the Tennessee whiskey distillers that'll be coming to participate. He smiles at her with so much affection that it's obvious how much he adores her. When he glides his fingers along her back, she tilts her head back toward him, melting into it. I can't stop myself from thinking about how nice that must feel. That affection and care. It's not something I've experienced before.

Griz teases Hadley about the jazz trio she's booked at Midnight Proof. "You call those clowns musicians," he tuts. "You should hire some good old-fashioned country boys to come in there and play."

"It's not the vibe, Griz." Hadley smiles, shrugging a shoulder.

Ace watches on quietly. His eyes connect with mine, and I give him a quick smile, an appreciative exchange for allowing me to be here among his family. He responds with the smallest nod, and it makes me feel like a real jerk for what I'm going to excuse myself to do. It doesn't take a keen sense of intuition or much time with the Foxx family to know there's a lot of love here. Respect. Support. It's comforting to be inside their orbit, even for just a meal.

Lincoln talks to Hadley about something that has him animated with big hand gestures, and it gives me pause, taking in someone like him. He has such a full life; it's so different from mine, but I feel such a connection when I'm with him.

"You have a nice smile," Lily says while chomping on three stacked pieces of bacon while trying to balance a half-dollar coin between two fingers. I can tell she's been practicing moving it between each knuckle. I bite at my lower lip. Until she said that, I hadn't even realized I was smiling.

I glance at Lark, who's staring back at me with a scowl. She definitely caught me staring at her dad.

"Dad always says you can tell a lot about a person when they smile." Lily takes the coin between two fingers. "I can make this coin disappear. Want to see?"

I reach for the syrup, but instead ask her to pass it to me. My nerves are making it so I don't have much of an appetite, but I don't want it to look that way. When I take it from her, I pour a bit over what remains of my French toast and say, "Sure. But what coin?"

Lily looks down, baffled by my question. "Wait, where'd it go?"

When I look across from me, Lincoln's watching. With his focus on me, my mouth goes dry. "Check her right hand, Lily."

Lily looks at me, confused, and then focuses on my right hand.

When I lift my fingers, I roll the clunky gray rock over to its side with the sharp purple crystals.

She looks up at me with a smile. "You have it with you."

"I've needed a little extra courage lately. I keep it in one of my pockets." Then I open my left hand where the silver coin stands slotted between my pointer and middle fingers.

Lily gasps. "How'd you do that? Oh my gosh. Please, Faye. Please, you have to teach me."

"Sure. It's really just practice. And paying attention to the people around you." I look up at her father. "It's all about creating a distraction."

Nerves flutter around my chest as I say it because that's what this dinner turned into tonight. A distraction.

Nothing looks glaringly suspicious. Foxx Bourbon is a big business, and while it would take a team of people to comb through this in detail, there's nothing that's worth sharing with the FBI. I expected Foxx Bourbon was doing well, but the kinds of numbers they have coming in and going out are incredible.

It was easy to slip into Ace's office when I excused myself to use the bathroom. The best time to do it would always be just as dinner's finished being served and everyone was focused on their food. It took less than two minutes to connect to their guest network, then the VPN, and then from there, Ace's phone. The same mirroring app that I've been using on Lincoln's phone I was able to upload through the cloud, and now I have a full view of what the oldest Foxx does on his device. Ace's phone is very organized. There's a system for his files, and his emails are mostly marked read or flagged. The only communication I can see recorded between him and Blackstone is an email regarding bourbon being sold for a rather ridiculous amount of money at auction. I'll review that in more detail later.

I've been straddling my attention between scrolling and listening to Hadley talk about the seasonal drink menu we're sampling at Midnight Proof. It's a quiet night here and not as packed as it usually is during performance nights.

"You don't have to stay in that house if your sister is being a swashbuckling douche," Hadley says matter-of-factly, snagging my attention back to our conversation and drinks. "You're welcome to use the lovely one-night slam apartment upstairs."

I snort a laugh. "Thanks, but I chose to stay at the house. She wasn't happy to see me, but no matter how mad she is at me, someone beat the shit out of my sister, and I'm not about to let her live in that place alone until I know it's not going to happen again."

Hadley sizes me up. "You're kind of scary, Faye." She points her finger at me, dragging it up and down like she's drawing midair. "You look like... Well, you're ridiculously beautiful and in this very delectable package, but I feel like you'd throw down if you needed to."

She's not wrong.

Laney chimes in, "She has a way with compliments, doesn't she?"

"Best one I've gotten in a long time," I say, smiling into my glass.

"It's official. You are the coolest person I know, and I'm in love with you," Hadley laughs out.

Laney shouts, "Hey, what about me?"

"Always and forever, babes. But, c'mon, a burlesque dancer? She's sexier than the Cher movie with one-third of the ultimate trifecta, and she's fun." Hadley looks at me and squeezes my forearm when she says, "Faye, you're a lot of fun."

I furrow my brow. "Ultimate trifecta?"

Laney rolls her eyes. "Christina Aguilera was in that movie. And the trifecta, according to Hadley, is Britney, Christina, Pink."

"Obviously," I say without missing a beat.

Hadley raises her arms with sarcasm. "See!"

I can't help but laugh with Laney.

And for a few minutes tonight, I forget what brought me here and what I still need to accomplish. Tonight is the first time in a long time that I feel good surrounded by people who look an awful lot like new friends. My phone buzzes.

FOXX:
I need to talk to you.

The residual humor from my conversation with the girls bleeds over with my response.

FAYE:
Sounds serious.

I try to school my features, but I don't do it in time because Laney asks, "Who's got you smiling like that, Faye?"

"It's nothing like that—" I say, watching the bubbles bounce, awaiting what kind of response I'll get.

> FOXX:
> Open the door.

Is he at my house?

But it's Hadley who asks, "Does nothing happen to have glasses and a smirk you just want to slap off sometimes?"

> FAYE:
> Can't. Sorry. Not home.

I smile at her words, but follow it up with, "Okay, where did we leave off?"

Putting my phone on *Do Not Disturb*, I slide it into my pocket. I'll deal with him later.

Hadley claps her hands. "Alright. Deflecting. I like it. We'll circle back. How do we feel about an espresso martini, maybe with a pistachio liqueur shooter?" she asks, breaking out the shaker.

Quirking an eyebrow, I look at Laney as I answer, "Sounds like we're going to be drunk after this."

Hadley starts pouring when she corrects me. "Tipsy." She smiles, finger pointed in the air. "To tipsy friends."

Chapter 17

Lincoln

Chemistry has always been my drug of choice. Bourbon, of course, had its place; I'm a Foxx after all. But I get high off the way it feels to solve a problem. To transition parts into a whole and help it evolve into something new. I know the exact combination of grains it takes to tweak a flavor before it goes into a barrel. The science of it, what happens before it ever touches American toasted oak, is what makes me hard. I shift my body—apparently, not as hard as Faye Calloway makes me. *Fuck, what is it about her?*

I'm wound tight from dinner. Usually family dinners ease whatever the week drops on me, but tonight, I watched Faye fold into my family so easily that I couldn't look away. Even the attraction I feel toward her could be dealt with, but watching her make Lily laugh or seeing her leave with Laney and Hadley for a girls' night out, I didn't know what to feel. I wanted to kiss her. I wanted to hear her come again, only this time I wanted it loud and as she rode my cock. I wanted her both in my bed and out of my sight.

My phone buzzes with a message from my brothers.

> ACE:
> Going to need some help tomorrow night.

> GRANT:
> Is this directed at anyone in particular?

> ACE:
> I'm going to need some muscle.

I know what that means. We sometimes play along gray lines to keep our business moving in the right directions. I'm feeling more than amped up lately, so if he needs some muscle, then I'm happy to step up. Grant had been the rule follower, Ace liked to bend them, and I liked to surprise people and come out swinging.

> LINCOLN:
> I'll be there.

It's quiet out tonight, much quieter than my thoughts. The cold air makes my breath visible, but I love being in the dark and the calm I feel when it settles in next to me.

"The fuck am I doing?" I say to myself. But before I make the decision to get up, I hear the slamming of a car door.

"Thanks, Del," Faye singsongs. "Nope, I'm good. Thanks for the ride, big guy."

I lean my elbows on my knees and listen to her humming as she shuffles up the walkway.

"This bra sucks," she says to herself, shifting her top as she kicks off her boots when she makes it to the porch landing.

"Are you drunk?"

She yelps, hand flying to her chest. "Fucking hell, Foxx!" She laughs out nervously. "No, I'm not drunk." Dropping her bag, she steps closer. "Tipsy. But didn't want to risk it, so I called Del for a ride."

Internally, I applaud that small and slightly inconvenient decision. I lost both parents to a drunk driver, so I like that she's smart enough to not risk it no matter how close she was to home.

"You know he's the greatest? Del. He's the only one who's gone out of his way for me. Maybe ever."

I didn't realize she kept in touch with him.

"Is he the one who told you Maggie had been arrested?"

She tilts her head to the side, not answering. "There's so much you don't know." She looks down at my phone. "So much more than I don't know about you…"

"I doubt that," I tell her as she walks closer. I lean my weight on my elbows and look down between my knees.

The girls stayed with Griz tonight, and I found myself drinking too much bourbon and staring at her dark house before I made the decision to come over here and wait for her. *What the hell do I think is going to come out of this?*

Her feet shuffle to a stop between mine, forcing me to tilt my head up and sit back to look at her.

"You do realize what time it is, right?" she asks as I widen my legs, welcoming her to keep moving closer.

She must have changed after dinner because she ditched the

oversized shirt and black pants for a pink sweater and blue jeans. Her loose sweater drapes forward just enough to give way to the best sight of cleavage I've seen in a long time as she bends over, bracing her hands on my thighs. She catches my wandering eyes and gives me a half smile.

"What are you doing in the dark on my porch at this hour, Lincoln Foxx?" Her eyes flit to my groin. The cotton navy-blue pants are fine for sleeping in, but they don't leave much to the imagination. My cock has been semihard since the stables. Now with her hands on me and the way she's biting at that lower lip, it's made a very distinct move that I know she doesn't miss.

"Why come back now?" I ask, hoping to get an honest answer out of her this time.

But she ignores the question, as expected, and instead flips open the button of her jeans. I lean back and drape my arms along the back of the porch swing. If you can call it that. It's more like a daybed suspended by thick ropes to the porch ceiling. She pushes the pants down her legs and steps out of them, her arms moving to my shoulders. Shifting her weight just enough, she straddles her knees on my outer thighs and hovers over my lap. I let out a hum before I say, "It's cold out here. You want to go inside?"

She shakes her head slowly. "I like it out here," she says quietly as she settles down onto my lap, nudging my dick as she gets comfortable.

I grab the blanket that's draped beside me and wrap it along the back of her.

"This house doesn't feel like home anymore. Everything is different." She takes a deep breath. "Maggie remodeled the house and got rid of everything familiar except this swing. I feel like I can take a breath and think out here."

I push her hair away from her face. "What is it you think about?"

She smiles. "I think about that night. In the cornfield. With you. More often than I'd like to, if I'm being honest. How that night changed me in ways I'm still trying to understand." Her eyebrows pinch. "I think about how my sister hates me."

"I don't think she hates you. She's mad at you…" I say as I drag my fingers along hers still braced on my shoulder.

"Oh no," she laughs out, but it sounds sad. "Maggie can't stand that I'm here. She's so mad that I left, but she doesn't want me back in her world. She doesn't know the whole story. And even if she did—" Shaking her head, she cuts off her thoughts. "Maggie is the only family I have, and I don't know her."

A rift that large between my brothers and me would be unmanageable. I wouldn't have survived the last five years without them. And she's been doing it entirely alone.

"Someone beat her up. And she won't talk about it. Nobody in this town, a place that's in everybody's business, has anything to say about it. Something doesn't feel right—the details aren't adding up." She brings her attention back to me, like she's trying to work something out in her head. "I don't know why I'm telling you this," she mutters, moving to slide off me, but I stop her.

"Don't." I clear my throat, my hand on her hip to keep her in place. "I like you here."

"Why?" she asks, her eyelids heavy. "Why does it feel good to be near you like this?"

"I don't know," I answer on an exhale. But I feel it too. I don't understand it, but *fuck*, I feel it too.

She settles her weight forward, grazing my cock. When her eyes meet mine, for the life of me, I can't figure out what she's thinking. She's intriguing, unpredictable, and what's happening between us is dangerous. "I hate you a little."

I can't help but hold back my smile, because as she's saying that, she rolls her hips the slightest bit. "I hate you a little too, Peach."

The smile that danced on her lips a moment ago fades away.

"You call me Peach like I'm sweet, but Foxx, you know better. I'm the furthest thing from sweet."

"See, that's where you're wrong." I yank her hips forward. The move jerks her closer and forces her chest to press into mine. "I've never tasted anything as sweet as what you dripped all over my fingers."

She releases a shaky breath as she studies my mouth. "Seeing you in glasses does something to me," she says with a sexy smile and insinuating tone. She's focused as she reaches with both hands for the edges of my black frames, gently pulling them down the bridge of my nose and away from my face.

I watch as she folds them and reaches forward, shifting her weight to place them on the ledge behind us.

When she's facing me again, closer now, there's a look in her eyes I decipher before she even speaks the words.

"Kiss me," she demands on a whisper. The warm breath escaping her lips mingles with the cold night air, making it so I can see, not just feel, what she's asking for.

Wrapping one arm around her lower back, holding her body to mine, I let myself give in. My other hand cups her jaw, thumb brushing along her lower lip as my fingers weave into her hair. There's no coaxing or hesitation, only a hungry sound that vibrates from my chest as my lips meet hers. She sinks into me easily, moaning sweetly against my mouth as her lips part and her tongue welcomes mine at a seductively slow pace.

I'm lost to the way she touches me, how her nails dig into the back of my neck and her hips roll, the way her lips drag and tease me. I'm a slave to her mouth in this moment, and the only thing I can think is that I'll never want to stop kissing her.

Chapter 18

Faye

My nails graze along his warm skin and my fingers thread through his short hair. I can't help but grip it and pull just enough so he knows I want this. Maybe it's the drinks from tonight or the dance we can't seem to resist between us, but being around him clouds every judgment. It muddles memories and practically erases every and any control I might have had over this. The way he licks at my tongue and holds me tightly against him pulls a needy moan from my throat.

He smiles against my lips in response. "Feel what you're doing to me?" he whispers.

I hum, feeling exactly what I'm doing as I roll my hips again.

He brushes his thumb along my lower lip. "Such a perfect mouth," he says as he releases an audible breath.

I dart my tongue out and wet his finger.

And he doesn't miss a beat. He rubs the wetness around my

lips before he drags it down my chin. My body buzzes at every single small move this man makes.

"Foxx," I breathe out and lean forward, rolling my hips again.

"That's it," he praises. Those two words hit me right in the panties, core fluttering with anticipation.

I fumble with his sweatshirt, trying to pry it off him. Along with it comes his T-shirt, and I'm rewarded with a thick chest with short-trimmed hair and decorated with dark tattoos expanding from his right pec up to his shoulder. A twisting of words along the edge of what looks like three window panes on the inside of his bicep, only two filled in with colored ink. Cursive letters run down his side and disappear into the waistband of his pants. His skin is warm as I drag my fingers across his stomach, dipping them into the waistband. "You're pretty, Foxx."

He snorts. "How drunk are you right now, Peach?"

Meeting his eyes, I smile. "I'm just appreciating the view." I look out beyond where we are. Not a single glow other than from the moon and the dimmed lights near the door. But even in the dark, I know what I'm doing. "If you're looking for consent, you have it."

A small laugh escapes his lips. "Is that so?" He licks his bottom lip as he toys with the hem of my sweater, running his fingers along its edge and leaving goosebumps in his wake. "I've wanted to touch and taste you for so long…" Dragging his fingertips up the curve of my breast, over the sweater, he pulls it down enough to see the cleavage emphasized by my bra. His touch feels like he's cataloging curves and learning what he likes. My chest rises and falls more quickly. Hell, I need more.

I stretch the neckline down and pull at the top of my satin bra, letting my breasts pour out of it.

He rubs his hand down his face and over his mouth. "Fuck, you're beautiful." And the approving words, ones I already know about myself, feel like a drug. I want more. He leans forward, capturing my breast in his mouth. My belly spirals and pussy tingles at the way his mouth works me over. Dragging his tongue along my nipple, he moans as if they're the kind of dessert he's been patiently waiting for.

My mouth opens to plead for more, more, more, but the only thing to escape is a quiet "please."

His approval rumbles deep in his chest.

I grind my hips down onto him, his cock nestled against my center and hitting my clit with satisfying precision. And while dry humping Lincoln Foxx wasn't on my agenda tonight, I roll my hips again.

"Oh, fuck," I exhale. It feels too good.

He sits back, his teeth sink into his lower lip as he watches me work myself over him. I shamelessly pull my pussy back and thrust it forward along the length of his cock, his thin cotton bottoms are the only thing separating us. *Dammit, I want him.* The hiss he sucks in through his teeth is enough of a reaction to urge me to do it again.

"Do you like that?" I lean forward and whisper along his lips.

He nips at my lower lip. "More than you know." He pushes my body against his harder.

I pull my hips back again to repeat the same movement.

Grabbing both of my wrists, he holds my hands behind my back. "Look at you, so needy right now."

I smile at his teasing tone and the way he holds my wrists with one hand behind me, the other on my hip guiding me. I arch my back and work over the thick length of him—back and forth, giving in to the pressure and pace that I'm craving. I let out a gasping moan. The sight of us must be filthy, and I smile thinking of it. If I wasn't on the cusp of an orgasm, I'd want to watch him lick and savor my pebbled skin all over. I roll my hips again. The tingle that runs through my clit has my breath catching and pressure building as the feeling wraps around my limbs. A tiny vibration that starts along my edges, seeping into my skin.

His teeth drag along my neck, sparking another sensation. The sounds of his heavy exhales and the hitch of my breath are the only warnings before I'm moaning so loudly that his hand moves over my mouth, and I come so hard that my thighs quiver against his. My stomach muscles clench, pussy pulsing as my body is rewarded with the most decadent current of warmth. I'm whimpering as I tremble over his lap and wring out the last of my release, until every part of me relaxes in a daze.

I slump against his chest, and his fingers drag away from my mouth and glide along my back, soothing the small tremors that follow. I'm panting. My hair is stuck along my neck and across my forehead, but I'm too wrung out to swipe it away.

"That's twice now," I whisper. "I've come twice with you, and you haven't…"

"I very much enjoy watching you lose control," he says with a hint of a smile in his voice as he runs his fingers down the center of my back. I nuzzle into him. I fit here so nicely that it's hard to want to move. It's far too intimate, but neither of us stops it from happening. Everything feels quiet after that as I sink into this for just a little longer.

It's not until I wake up with the sound of Pop Rocks and arguing whispers that I realize I fell asleep on him. And he's still here.

"I can see his feet. I know he's there," one of the girls says from a foot or two away.

The blanket is pulled up over us, his arms wrapped around me and our legs intertwined. Lincoln shifts back so I can see his face when he whispers, "Maybe they'll leave if we stay very still." He smiles and then closes his eyes.

"I don't have pants on," I say as quietly as possible.

"Are we going to get a peep show if we pull this blanket off you two?" Griz says loudly. Oh god, there's an actual audience out here.

"What's a peep show?" Lily asks him. I'm praying he doesn't answer her.

I hear Lark rush out, "I don't think it's the marshmallow kind, let's put it that way."

"Alright," Lincoln says, sitting up and pulling the plush blanket down to keep me covered up. "No peep show." He glares at Griz. "Just fell asleep out here."

I squint at the brightness of the day and rub my eyes, guaranteeing that the makeup I had on is a blackout mess. Lily stares at us from the floor as she scratches under Kit's neck, while Griz sips on a coffee, smiling and waiting for one of us to say something else. But it's Lark who glares at me first and then says, "We went home, and you weren't there. And then somehow Kit sniffed you out and, well"—she pauses as she crosses her arms—"here you are." *Oh, she's not my biggest fan right now.* I hate that feeling of disappointment.

"Dad, you're not wearing a shirt," Lily says.

Oh god.

But he doesn't even sound nervous when he says, "Fell asleep. Faye runs hot. Ditched my sweatshirt." Reaching for his glasses from the window's ledge, he puts them on like none of this is a big deal.

"Dad, it's winter," Lily says.

"A mild one," he says as he scoots out and stands. "I need some coffee."

"Only brought this one," Griz says, holding up his cup.

"Thoughtful," Lincoln mutters as he stretches his arms above his head.

"Breakfast?" he asks me as he grabs his phone from the ground somewhere and starts typing away. I can't help the surprised look I'm sure I'm giving him. He wants to bring me to breakfast? It's unexpected. Maybe even more so than being woken up by his grandfather and daughters, all studying exactly what it is we were doing out here.

I feel like I'm still asleep. Definitely a bit hungover, but entirely unready to face two kids and the reality of this morning.

The front door swings open. "Are we having a party out here?" Maggie says with an unusually bright demeanor. "Faye, Linc, what are you two doing out here on the porch? I thought I heard the two of you last night, but—"

I cut her off, looking at Lincoln. "I'm okay. Not hungry right now."

He smiles back at me. It's a knowing exchange that feels... good.

I look at Lily, who's still petting Kit who is chewing on her leash. "Thank you for taking care of her last night."

My attention moves to the brown-and-black fluffball making growling sounds. "Kit."

She stops what she's doing and looks up at me, her tongue sticking out as she opens her mouth.

"Were you on your best behavior last night?" I ask her.

Lily answers, "She was very good. She slept on the floor right next to me. And then this morning, she had her puppy vitamins, and we went for a walk to the stables. I think she likes other animals."

Now might be a good time to offer the girls some assistance with this dog situation. I glance at Lincoln before I ask Lily, "Would you want to help me with her? Maybe she can stay with you on the nights I work late?"

Lily's eyes widen, and then she gives me a knowing nod. "What a good idea, Faye," she says, her voice a pinch louder, as if this was a line we practiced. "Dad, can we? I'll make sure she gets walked and fed. It would be like a job, but I only get paid in puppy time?"

He leans into me as he scratches his chin and then smiles. One of those dimples puckers in as he says, "You're good. I'll give you that."

I rest my chin in my hand and try to keep from smiling. He knows exactly what's happened here—he just got swindled.

"Yeah, Lily. We can take her home now. And then you're going to tell me how you managed to adopt a dog without a grown-up."

"Oh my gosh, Dad, really?!" Lark shouts at the same time that Lily squeals. It's all very loud with a lingering hangover headache, but it's hard not to admire and appreciate. The way they are together is endearing.

"Did you hear that, Kit?" Lily says as the dog barks, seeming just as excited as the girls.

"How about you both thank Faye for fostering Kit for you."

Lily singsongs, "Thank you, Faye."

Lark gives me a short smile when she adds, "Thanks."

Lincoln kneels in front of me. "I have something to ask you," he says as he ties his shoe.

My smile falters from the chaos that just erupted about Kit.

Lincoln stands up and asks, "How do you take your coffee?"

"Why?" I ask, curiously watching him.

"Something my brother said to me once. Stuck with me. Wanted to know."

I sit up a little taller, very aware of how his girls are petting Kit, but they're watching our exchange. "Depends. Some days I just want to wake up and have strong black coffee. Other days, I want to sip on something sweet and iced."

He smiles at the answer.

"Are you going to bring me coffee, Foxx?" I smile curiously.

The corner of his mouth ticks up to one side, flashing his dimple, before he says, "Maybe next time."

Oh hell, I want to kiss him again. Feel him again. This isn't what I came to town for late-night hookups and morning flirting with Lincoln *fucking* Foxx. So why does it feel so good? So effortless?

He claps his hands out in the most dad-like move and says, "Alright, let's go, girls. Who wants to get pancakes at Hooch's?"

"Me!" Lily shouts with a little jump that Kit matches. "We already had breakfast, though."

Lincoln smiles, giving her shoulder a squeeze. "Brunch, then?" he asks as they walk down the porch steps and meet Griz at the bottom.

Looking over his shoulder, he gives me a wink before he calls out for Lark. "Lark, come on, kiddo, I'm hungry!"

"I saw you, ya know," Lark says to me, standing at the top step.

My stomach sinks because I have no clue about *where* she might mean.

"In the stables at Uncle Ace's. You were going to kiss my dad."

I swallow, and even though I don't want to, I answer her truthfully. "I was."

"Lark, you coming?" Lincoln calls out from down the driveway.

"He's the greatest dad in the world," she says, tilting her chin up, but I see the way it wobbles just a little. "We don't need anybody else."

It's easy to be swept up in this attraction that I have for him and forget he has a whole life that's centered around these two girls who depend on him. I never had the courage to say this to any of the men who came into my mother's life. But I felt that way too. How threatening it was for them to take any part of her away. So I ignore the way my eyes water the slightest bit and say the only thing I can. "Okay." I nod, hoping she can see I mean it.

She doesn't say anything else as she turns on her heel and walks away.

Releasing a heavy breath, I lift the blanket to stand and am quickly reminded I'm sans pants. *Fuck! It's freezing.*

My phone buzzes from somewhere under the blankets. I feel around for it. Where the hell is it? When I finally find it, I have to push my hair out of my face with a huff.

> FOXX:
> They cramped my style. I wanted to kiss you goodbye.

I'm smiling at the message without even realizing it until I hear, "So you're slamming Lincoln Foxx?" Maggie startles me as she leans against the front doorway.

Fuck my life. I tilt my head back, puff out my cheeks, and groan internally. It's not even worth lying about this. She was clearly home. "Technically, no."

She raises her eyebrows. "Sounded like trash pandas being attacked out here."

I flip her off.

"Slamming? No. Dry humping and making out with? Yes." I leave out the public finger bang. I don't think she needs that little detail.

She barks out a laugh. And I can't help but glance at her and crack a smile from hearing it. "Is it something?" I search for what she might be asking. "With Lincoln. Is it something?"

"Feels like it."

She holds her cup of tea between both hands and looks out to the cornfield, letting what I just admitted linger in the cold for a few beats. "Just be careful. Everyone who falls for one of those men usually ends up…"

"Ends up what, Maggie?" I say with an uncomfortable laugh.

"Just some townie gossip, that's all." She turns back into the house just as she adds, "Never mind, it doesn't apply to tourists."

Chapter 19

Faye

All my hard work and long nights of watching and placating Brock Blackstone led to this event. It was why I came back to Fiasco in the first place. And yet here I was, at 4 p.m. the evening of this private auction, about to waltz into a small-town boutique shop and hope for something that would match what I needed.

Loni's Boutique is nestled right in between Fiasco Flowers and Fiasco Creamery, but when I cross the threshold, I'm pleasantly surprised by the displays of trendy sweaters laid out in an ombre of greens to blues. But it's the dressmaker's bodice to the left side of the room near the lingerie table that's draped in the kind of dress tonight calls for. Sexy, elegant, and meticulously constructed. The soft pink layers of chiffon hug the dress stand as the light picks up the shimmer from each crystal bead sewn intermittently from the bodice and straps down to the thigh-length skirt. Its straps are so thin they almost look nonexistent except for the way the crystals shine. Their length and position allow for the dress to drape low in the front, showing off the perfect amount of décolletage.

"It's beautiful," Lily says, sliding up next to me.

I do a double take, not having noticed she's standing beside me. "Hi—" Looking behind her, I see Laney following, with Grant stuffing his hands in his pockets just as the door closes. "What are you guys doing here?"

"Lark wanted to see if any new band shirts came in since last time," the youngest Foxx says, rolling her eyes. "I like that dress. Are you going to get it?"

I smile at her, and her Aunt Laney gives me a wave as she comes closer. "It's too pretty not to."

The store owner comes over and asks, "If you'd like, I can do some quick alterations."

"That would be amazing."

"Alright, let me move some things around in my dressing room, and then we'll get you all set. I think it'll look perfect on your figure," she says.

"Is that for one of your performances?" Laney asks.

I glance toward Grant, who's watching the both of us. He was always good at intimidation. I remember that from when he had done one of the training sessions at the academy—he was one of the few K-9 officer units in this part of the state when he was with the department. It felt like I was about to get an interrogation from him, or at the very least, the promise of questions sooner rather than later.

It's not a complete lie when I say, "A performance I've been planning, but apparently I forgot the most important piece."

"Laney!" Lily calls out from the back of the shop.

When I look at Grant, I can tell that he's trying to piece

things together about me. I don't think it's possible that Lincoln's left him in the dark completely.

He clears his throat. "You know, Del told me how he kept in touch with you. Helped him out here and there on some work while you were down in, where was it?"

Crossing my arms, I smile at him, answering easily, "Louisiana. They needed someone to talk with a handful of people who had been performing at a club. Jog their memory about things they had seen but maybe hadn't registered as suspicious."

"We never really lose that edge, do we?" he asks. "No matter if we retire or turn to something else, we always have a gut feeling or instinct when something feels off."

He knows there's more to me being here; I just need to hope it won't interfere with tonight. "I suppose that's true."

"Uncle Grant," Lily calls out, saving me from having to answer any more questions. "Can we please get matching slippers? They might have a size big enough for you too?"

He nods as he moves away and approaches his niece and wife.

Out of the corner of my eye, Lark rummages through the T-shirt display. "I went to that tour. I was in Washington, and someone said if I wanted to see Dave Matthews Band live, then the only place would be at the Gorge."

Glancing at me briefly, she goes back to looking through the pile. I think she's dismissing me until she asks, "Well, did you?"

"See them there?" I laugh. "No. Sold out. But I scalped a ticket in Seattle and got to hear a few of my favorites."

She quits looking for her size and then walks away.

Fucking small towns. There's no reason I should be running into any of them here. And as charming as this store is, the last thing I was prepared for was an interrogation and a preteen's wrath. Truthfully, I'm more jilted by the latter. I don't know why it bothers me, wanting her to like me, but it does.

An hour later and I've been perfectly fitted for what might be the prettiest dress I'll ever wear. It almost seems like a waste to wear it for someone like Brock Blackstone. But I don't have any other options. I have just under three hours before I need to be ready for the car service. He didn't ask why I was being picked up at Midnight Proof, but I wasn't about to give him the address for my family's farmhouse. The less he's aware of who I was before Rosie Gold, the better.

"So you make jewelry now too?" Maggie asks as she leans against the doorway in my makeshift bedroom. "Another surprise hidden up those sleeves?"

"Yup," I say, focused on what I'm doing, before her words sink in. "Wait, what the hell is that supposed to mean?"

She looks around the room, taking inventory of what gym equipment I've had to move to make space for my things. I watch her attention flick to the lineup of small weapons laid out on the floor near her elliptical. "Those are *interesting* accessories."

"I'm a single woman who takes her clothes off as entertainment. I'd be careless, borderline stupid, not to have some sort of protection with me."

"I heard about some kind of high-profile event tonight. Is that where you're going?"

It has me pausing. I close my eyes and shake my head, trying to understand her sudden interest. "How would you hear about something like that?"

She crosses her arms over her chest. "Better question—why are you attending?"

We stare at each other for a moment, neither one of us

tipping our hand. But she's the one to crack first when she says, "There's so much you don't know. And somehow, I feel like I'm the one in the dark."

Narrowing my eyes on her, I let out a sigh when I ask, "Then why don't you enlighten me, Maggie? I'm not the bad guy here."

"You sure about that?" she mumbles, and my head rears back.

"What the hell is that supposed to mean?" I shout after her as she steps into the hallway.

But per usual, she doesn't respond to my question. "Nice dress, by the way," she calls out, and then a few moments later, the front door slams shut.

I'm staring off, a bit dumbfounded, trying to make sense of whatever that just was. I know there's more to unpack, but tonight isn't going to be the time to figure it out.

My dress was a jackpot in more ways than just being stunning. It needed to match the jewelry this time around. And the long chain necklace that glitters also has a little extra flare. The 2mm camera was under fifty bucks and fits perfectly into its crystal onyx center. My phone will act as its Wi-Fi hotspot in my clutch bag so that everything from tonight is recorded and stored in the cloud. Tech doesn't need to be complicated to work in my favor—between the mirroring software I had coded and cheap gadgets like this, it makes private investigating far more comprehensive than simple stakeouts and note-taking.

I'm not going to miss a single moment or face. I've spent the past few weeks filtering through countless emails and fulfillment orders from freight companies regarding Blackstone Auctions. Procurement could mean a lot of things. But a private auction that the FBI was sniffing around meant there's more than authentic paintings and Fabergé eggs to be sold. Cortez still hasn't shown his cards, but that doesn't mean I can't figure out other ways to see them. So I dug into the details of exactly what types of things Blackstone had been "acquiring" for tonight. I wasn't going to wait and see. The bill of lading that listed out what was delivered to Blackstone's estate wasn't what I'd expected—multiple quantities and variations of erectile-dysfunction drugs, fertilizers and chemicals, a single line item that just read "snakes," which, again, troubling, but the smuggling of reptiles didn't seem like something Cortez would have been so elusive about. None of that felt like the bigger picture, but simply details.

"The only thing I need from you, Faye, is confirmation on the attendees," Cortez says over my phone. "If the auction happens and you're within earshot, then take note of who is purchasing."

Pulling the straps of my dress on carefully, I slide the zipper up the side of my waist.

I turn to the side and, damn, that's perfect.

As I pick up my phone from the bathroom sink, I make sure he can hear me when I say, "You can tell me exactly who I should be looking at, Cortez. That would make my job here easier."

I toss my lipstick into my glitter handbag that has a special sewn-in compartment that holds my karambit knife. The small blade has a finger hole for easy maneuvering when necessary. I adjust the elastic of my garter belt, functioning to hold up my thigh-high stockings and doubling as a convenient spot to fasten the palm-sized pepper spray. They weren't much, considering I didn't know what Blackstone was capable of, but having weapons makes me feel safer. They always have.

"All I can say is that if anything feels off, or if you need to get out of there, then get out. This isn't a situation where the cavalry is waiting to raid this place. I have some support, but you need to operate here as if you're on your own. I need you to be smart."

I keep playing back Cortez's words—if anything feels off, then get out of there. It's like telling someone to "be safe." It doesn't add value other than the fact they didn't want to see you hurt. Of course I'll pay attention and listen to my instincts—I've been operating solo like this for a while now.

The car ride is quick, but I feel prepared. My makeup and jewelry, along with the weapons and the killer dress, are all a mask as I stroll up the stairs and over the red carpet leading into the estate. When I pass by another few security guards stationed along the main hall, I catch Blackstone's wandering eyes canvassing my body. I shake off the grotesque shiver it pulls from me and smile instead.

"Rosie," Blackstone says as he greets me at the threshold of the main ballroom. "You're the prettiest little thing I've seen in a long time." He kisses along my knuckles, his wet lips slobbering more than is necessary, but I do my best to school my grossed-out reaction. "Is my girl ready for me to taste tonight?" Holding up my arm, he guides me to show him a 360-degree view of what I'm wearing. I've already calmed my mind and made sure I'd be fully settled into my role as Rosie Gold tonight. Had I not, I would have retched all over the Brioni tux that looked a size too small around his neck and arms.

I force a coy smile and step into his embrace. "Brock, I'm always ready."

"Good." He raises his hand and signals a waitress over. "I'll take a whiskey ginger, and please bring a glass of champagne for my beautiful girl." Grabbing my hand, he kisses my knuckles again. *More slobber.* "Come, I want to show you off."

A ballroom like this should be bathed in rich colors and warm lighting, but instead it feels cold, stark, and almost sterile. With its modern design and clean lines, generic grays and cool-toned blacks, it's the opposite of what most people from Fiasco would consider "rich." The people gathered in groups throughout aren't much better. Designer tuxedos on men who are only slightly engaged in their conversations because each one we pass turns their head to either smile or study.

It's not until Blackstone pulls me onto his lap, his fingers digging into my hips, that I realize he meant he *literally* wants to show me off. Every single person who greets him has also been introduced to me—*his* Rosie Gold. Perched on his leg as my pedestal. If I wasn't working to keep a tally of every big name I recognize, repeating their names back to them so that they're properly recorded, then I would have been disgusted by the smell of his breath that lingers along my skin. Or the way he moves his palm down from my hip to the hem of my dress. It takes a great deal of focus not to flinch each time. I purposefully try not to linger on one face or place for too long. My pulse races as I take in the head count and try to remember the items in the shipping documents. Would I be able to place items with people I've been introduced to? I'm too in my head about all the items that need to be remembered here.

It's why I don't notice the small group of men approaching. Not until I see Blackstone raise his arm, signaling the group closer as he says, "Gentlemen. Come and join us."

Chapter 20

Lincoln

Pain radiates through my knuckles as the first two split open, the impact traveling up my forearm and into my elbow. I shake it out at the same time Joel spits blood and a succession of apologies that I've gone numb to at this point. Apologies mean less when you're pummeling someone to make a point.

"Linc, man. I didn't mean to do it—"

I flex my hand and cut off his lie. "You didn't mean to drop a case into your trunk? You didn't mean to use your key card at 3:43 a.m. to come to the distillery and help yourself to a barrel of bourbon?" I rest my hands on my waist as I watch this man, whom I've shared drinks with at picnics, lie to my face that he hasn't been stealing from us for the past six months.

"I needed the extra money, man. I got bills and people I owe."

"Look at me, Joel." I point to my face. "You worked for us. You earned a paycheck and full benefits. But you know that's where it ends." I cock my arm back and give him one last punch to the gut, just below his ribs.

"Alright," Ace says from behind me. "I think he understands. Right, Joel? You understand?"

He coughs and nods his head.

"I'm going to need to hear you say it, Joel."

"I understand," he says.

"Good," Ace says as he types away on his phone. "Linc, we need to get going."

Joel looks at me with a bloodied nose and lip, searching for what I'm going to say next.

"Your job will be waiting for you on Monday," I tell him as I clip off the zip tie that I used to bind his hands around the loading dock railing.

"You're not firing me?"

"Your daddy worked here, Joel. And your uncle." Griz speaks up from the far side of the room. "I don't think they'd feel much pride in knowing their last name was associated with stealing from a brand they've helped build." He clears his throat and the easygoing nature of Griswald Foxx slips away in these moments. Instead it's the man who built this brand with an iron fist. This was always how he did business—we learned by example. "You've been here for just over twenty years now yourself. Why would we fire you, Joel? From where I'm standing, you just tasted what's waitin' if something like this happens again, am I right?"

Swallowing roughly, he nods. "Yeah, Griz."

"Good. Go clean yourself up. I'll see you on Monday—expect unpaid overtime until you can work off what you stole."

A white towel hits me in the face. "Let's go," Ace says.

"I'm driving," I say as I wrap my hand. "Griz, you good to get home?"

He smiles at me. "Golf cart is juiced up. You boys go have some fun."

"Haven't had to do that in a while," I say, rounding the front of my Jeep to leave the distillery. I unbutton my suit jacket to get in. There are two spots of blood on my white shirt, which is fine by me. I have an all black tux dry-cleaned and waiting for me.

As I finish with my cuff links Ace says, "You do realize that this is black-tie, right? Not just all black attire?"

"My last one got ruined. Besides, I'm not going to put on a fucking bow tie to play poker and schmooze some asshole who wants a cut of our sales, Ace."

"The sales from Blackstone Auctions last year alone doubled our net profits. It's a higher scale than what Maggie's been able to accomplish with her secondary market sales. If we want to stay in front of the reselling of our most valued bottles, then we need to have a direct connection to who's curating those sales. Blackstone might be a prick, but he's the kind of man who gets people things. Our bourbon is on the playing field, and if we shake some hands tonight, it'll have been worth the connections alone. Just need to decide how dirty we want to get here."

Twenty minutes later, we're pulling into an estate just outside of Fiasco's town line. It feels a bit ostentatious as we make our way up the long drive. It looks more like a museum than a home. The landscaping is meticulously kept, with the large fountain in the center of the circular driveway and uplighting that disappears into the night sky.

"What else is being auctioned off here?" I ask Ace.

"The only thing that I know is what I've negotiated directly with Blackstone—our rare bottles. I want to see where they land and for how much. Beyond that? No idea."

The valet opens both mine and Ace's door at the same time.

I stand and button my jacket, pocketing my glasses for now. "How much money we spending?"

"We're not," he says as we walk through the double doors. A rolled-out deep-red carpet runs from the threshold to the main ballroom at the end of the long entryway. "We're only here to play the politics on this."

People, mostly men in tuxedos, are peppered throughout the event. The few women who are here are either serving cocktails or are dressed like showpieces. It's evident it's a boys' club.

"Atticus and Lincoln Foxx, what an interesting turn of events," Wheeler Finch greets as he walks closer. And just on his heels is Waz King. Wheeler walks around Fiasco as if he runs the place, while Waz acts as his crony. I fucking hate both of them. Finch & King might be the premiere brand in Kentucky horse racing, but they're self-serving, sleazy hustlers to the core.

I hear Ace mumble, "Goddamnit," just before he signals the cocktail waitress circulating close by.

I'm not surprised to see Wheeler at something like this—if it felt shady before, his attendance confirms it. I'll have to tell Hadley I got to see dear old dad tonight, looking as pretentious as ever in his white suit jacket and black bow tie, rubbing elbows earlier with a circuit court judge and the rumored candidate running for governor next election year.

"Wheeler." Ace nods. "Waz," he says with a glance.

Wheeler tuts, "How's my daughter doing? She's still nannying for you?"

"Your daughter runs one of the most successful spots in Fiasco," I clap back, trying to make him feel like an asshole for the backhanded question. "She spends time with my family. That includes my girls."

Waz pipes in, "She doing *favors* for you too, Ace?"

Just as Ace starts to tell him to shut his mouth, Wheeler cuts in, "Take a walk, Waz. Blackstone wanted to show off something shiny. Maybe go see what it might be."

But it's the sound of laughter behind Wheeler, who's circled by a set of leather club chairs and candlelight, that captures my attention. More than that, it has my heart racing and stomach clenching.

I hadn't talked to Ace about what's happening with Faye, but he shifts closer and quietly asks, "That's who I think it is, isn't it?"

I grit my teeth, grinding down on my back molars so hard that I'm surprised they aren't cracking. "Yeah. It is." I take in every inch of what I'm seeing and still can't process what the hell she might be doing here. She said they were "friends," but that "show-and-tell" game he's playing doesn't look like the kind of friendships I know.

Blackstone raises his meaty hand holding a rocks glass and calls out, "Gentlemen. Come and join us." He snickers to himself like we're not close enough to hear him say, "Two Foxxes and a Finch." But it's where his other hand is gripping that has me fuming. Faye sits perched on his lap, his other hand resting on her thigh, nearly at the fold of where her thigh crease meets her hip. As if she's his. *What the actual fuck?*

I pull in a steadying breath, something to ground me so I don't react and yank her off him. His hand doesn't belong on her. Why is she allowing it? I can feel Ace glance at me as I stare at Blackstone's hand. *Motherfucker.*

The moment we step forward and her green eyes meet mine, I see the panic immediately. She tenses, her bare shoulders lifting slightly as her chest stutters with a subtle gasp. Her dusty pink cocktail dress shimmers in the low lighting, her hair tucked beneath a wig of pastel peach and pink streaked hair right around the same shoulder length as her natural blond.

She doesn't look anywhere else except at me, searching for what I might say or do next. I give her nothing, because as much as I want to rip her off of his lap and into my arms, I know that she's been telling me half-truths since she showed up in Fiasco, and this isn't the place or time for explanations. I expect to get those later, as I'm officially done waiting. For now, I'll play along.

"Gentlemen, I'd like you to meet some of my guests," Blackstone says, starting introductions to the half dozen men peppered around him. But I don't register any of their faces or names. I'm only focused on one. "And this beautiful, shiny thing is my Rosie Gold."

Her eyes stay connected to mine for only a moment longer before she smiles and greets us politely. But it's Wheeler who says, "Rosie Gold. How interesting. You're not what I was expecting. The burlesque dancer at Midnight Proof. Isn't that right?"

Looking up at him, she smiles, but it's one for show. "Mr. Finch, it's very nice to see you. And yes, I've been dancing at Midnight Proof. Your daughter was more than generous, booking a short residential spot at her beautiful speakeasy."

Wheeler watches her for a beat before he taunts, "You remind me of someone, but for the life of me, I thought that person hadn't set foot in Fiasco in years."

"Fortunate coincidence," Blackstone says as he drains his glass. "This lovely girl perched this pretty little ass right on my lap in Nashville, and it ended up being a helluva coincidence that she's performing right here in Kentucky while I take care of some business." He rubs his lips along the curve of her shoulder, as if he's earned the right to touch her like that. It has my fist clenching at my side, something Faye takes notice of as her eyes flick to me again. "I knew she'd make a nice little showpiece for tonight."

I've heard enough. "If you'll excuse me. I'm going to take a look at what your bar has for bourbon."

Ace follows with a nod to the small crowd of people. I won't look at her again. I can't. When we reach the bar, I fix the cuff links that peek out from my black jacket, my mind running through some of the inconsistencies I've noticed with Faye back in town.

I glance at the bartender. "Foxx Bourbon, the Prohibition bottle, neat."

"Make that two," Ace says as he turns to look back at the group we just rushed away from. "She's not just here in Fiasco to dance at Midnight Proof, is she?"

"I had a feeling that something was… I don't know, the timing of her being here felt off. Then she was out with Cortez."

"A date?" Ace asks, brow furrowed as he looks at me.

I smile knowingly, thinking about how that "date" ended with my fingers making her unravel outside of that bar. "It wasn't a date."

"Grant said he was surprised that she hadn't ended up in some part of law enforcement," Ace says as he sips the bourbon just placed in front of him and watches. He nudges my arm to look as she slinks away from the crowd and moves down the hallway, out of sight. "Graduated best in her class, had a job practically lined up at Fiasco PD, and then leaves town and pivots to dancing?"

"If I told you I knew exactly why that happened but I wasn't sure of the details, would you trust me and cut your losses with this business regarding Blackstone?" I say to Ace while I watch as Blackstone follows the same path she just went. "This doesn't feel right."

My brother studies me for a moment before he finishes his glass. He claps my shoulder. "Then it's done." He looks in the direction I just was, but Wheeler Finch cuts in.

"Interesting seeing you here, Atticus. I wasn't expecting another businessman like myself attending this event."

Ace lets out a small sniff, a laugh I know is more annoyance than anything else. "We both know I'm nothing like you."

"Be nice, Foxxy. Let's not forget how much you both enjoy things that belong to me," he says as he smiles at the bartender. I swear I hear my brother practically growl at that comment.

But I answer because my best friend deserves more respect than that. "If you're speaking of your daughter, then I'll kindly ask that you remember Hadley doesn't belong to you."

He ignores me and kicks back his bourbon. *Pretentious asshole.* He looks around toward the group we had just come from. "You recognize the Calloway girl, I assume? Interesting coincidence, her ending up in bed with Blackstone. He's given me quite lurid details about his little *Rosie Gold*."

My chest tightens at the thought. As much as I want to get out of here—I scan the room for her again—there's no way I'm leaving without her.

Chapter 21

Faye

Waz watches me like he can't figure out if he should call me by my real name or try to play this in his favor. The moment I spotted Wheeler Finch strolling in here, I knew I'd have to think on my feet. I feel like I've been thrown into the deep end of something that has far wider reach than I had anticipated. As prepared as I was for tonight, I didn't expect to see Lincoln walking toward me, fully dressed in a black tux. And I was even less prepared for the way my body responded instantly. He barely blinked during the introductions, looking just as shocked to see me. His eyes only left Blackstone's hands on me when I was introduced as *"my Rosie Gold."*

Fuck, this just got far messier. I grip onto my clutch handbag and lean into Blackstone, knowing now's the best time to make my next move. "I'm going to use the ladies', and then I'll get myself a drink. Would you like anything?"

"Rosie," he exhales and then leans into me, his nose running along my neck. I hate hearing my stage name out of this man's mouth. Somehow he makes it sound like a threat. I want only one person close to me like this, craving me in this way, and he hasn't turned to look at me since he moved to the bar. Chills and disgust run down my back, and it takes effort not to pull away from Blackstone's touch. "Go ahead, before the auction begins."

He taps my ass, but instead of flinching or telling him to go fuck himself, I smile and walk calmly toward the long hallway that leads to a bathroom. It also happens to be the same hallway that leads to the master suite and office. If I'm lucky, I have ten, maybe fifteen, minutes at most before he starts wondering where I went. The room is mostly men in tuxes, so the woman in the short pink sequin dress will be noticeably missing if anyone's looking.

There's no door to the office since the architecture of this place has open archways instead of closed doors. I look over my shoulder and make sure security isn't walking past this corridor before I move inside, pulse pounding in my ears. Having already been monitoring Blackstone's digital footprint, I'm hoping to find something, *anything* else that might tell me more than just who of his associates are in attendance. The disorganized desk has an array of handwritten to-do lists that are barely legible. I scan the legal pads without disrupting the way the papers are laid out. But there's nothing more than details I've already noticed from the shipment documents. Huffing to myself, I pull out my hidden knife and try opening the top locked drawer, but it doesn't budge. As I put my knife down, that's when I notice a small sticky note with the word "MONTANA" scribbled across it.

"Have you seen anyone come down this hallway?" I hear in the distance.

Shit, shit, shit. I move to the center of the room and type away on my phone. I don't have time to get out of here, so I'll have to sell the fact that I've wandered in here by accident.

"Ah, there you are, Rosie," Blackstone draws out from the archway.

I hold my hand over my chest and smile as I turn. "Oh my goodness, you scared me."

He strides toward me with the kind of look in his eyes that I've tried hard to avoid seeing—the satisfaction of being alone with something he desires.

"Who are you texting?" he asks, just as his phone buzzes in his pocket. And when he pulls it out, he gives me a nausea-inducing Cheshire cat smile. I texted him:

> ROSIE GOLD:
> Come and find me...

"Rosie, Rosie," he taunts. "You are a naughty girl. I have a room filled with very important people, and you want me to play with you, is that it?"

Fuck. I don't know how I'm getting out of this.

I play the part and offer a coy smile. "I know your auction is just about to start, but I was feeling"—I let out a sigh—"like it might be fun to play." Giving him a teasing look I've mastered, I move to step around him, but he steps in front of me, stopping me.

He draws his finger up my arm as he says, "Did you see all of those men salivating over you out there? Does that turn you on?"

Normally, yes. When I'm on stage and in control. But not while I'm doing this job. Not right now.

"You're mine, aren't you, Rosie?" he says as his hand moves to my waist.

I swallow and nod as his fingers skate up my arm, along my

shoulder, and across my collarbone. My skin crawls everywhere he touches, and I'm mentally preparing myself to either kiss or punch this man if it comes down to it.

"Sir?" one of the security guards interrupts from the doorway.

"Not now," Blackstone calls back as he stares blatantly at my cleavage. Gross.

When I glance at the security guard and look at his perfectly coiffed hair and mutton chops, I pause. It's the same tight-faced scowl that greeted me at the Fiasco police station the morning I bailed out Maggie. A sense of relief watches over me. I didn't think he was FBI.

The "security guard" removes a toothpick from his mouth when he says, "Sir, the auction room is filling up, and I was told your assistance was needed for a misunderstanding on a silent bid."

Blackstone looks at me and tips up my chin. "You stay right here. I'd like to play before the night really begins."

I smile and nod, trying to keep my body from recoiling at the promise.

He turns and brushes past the undercover security officer. "Let's go then. Where exactly am I being requested?"

The security guard glances at me again without saying anything more, before he follows Blackstone down the hall. It looks like Cortez had my back, after all. But I have no interest in waiting for him to return. I need to get out of here. I'll deal with the fallout of this decision later.

I didn't find anything in that office except an almost sexual assault. I'm done. Whatever Blackstone is curating for his clients and these private auctions isn't what the FBI wants. He's not the target, one of his guests is. They're going to use him as a source. Or as a pawn, at the very least, to hit someone more important.

As I turn back down the hall for the double doors that lead to what looks like a terrace, I try to guess how far the valet parking is from here. I don't register the click of a zippo lighter closing and clipped notes of a low whistle until the eerie tune of it catches my attention, and my head whips in that direction.

"You went in an interesting direction, girlie. Burlesque?"

I stop short at the unexpected voice. Its Southern drawl is so similar to one that had tricked my mother into believing he'd loved her. Yet the timbre of Waz King's voice is slightly more grating on my nerves than his brother Tullis's was.

Straightening my shoulders back, I ignore the question and move along the walkway, heading directly to the front of the estate, where the black car service that brought me here awaits. He follows me in a slow shuffle that's as irritating as his sly smile.

"Where ya goin'? Thought you were one of the goodies up for auction tonight."

I shudder at the thought.

"Just need some fresh air," I say as a sweep of cold air pricks at my skin and flutters my already short dress even higher. I hold it down with one hand, the other already full with my small bag and phone. There's no time to stop and get my coat. In the front pocket, there's a small knife disguised as a house key. And with a jolt, I realize my karambit is still on Blackstone's desk. *Fuck.* I feel around the side of my glittered clutch. In its hidden pocket is a palm-sized stun gun with just enough charge. I let out a small breath of relief. It won't do much, but it'll buy me some time to run if I need it.

"Faye, Faye, Faye," he tsks, unrelenting. "This is a very... interesting place to find you." Walking alongside me, he peers behind me to look at my ass.

A shiver of disgust runs through me when I stop mid-step,

and with as much attitude as I can muster, tell him, "I'm simply existing here, Waz. Just like you."

But he ignores my words and drags his eyes down my front. "Heard you were back in town. Maggie mentioned you were dancing at Midnight Proof. I'd wanted to see it for myself, but Hadley doesn't like her father's associates near her place of business. Might need to find a way to sneak in and catch a show…"

"I doubt my sister would be talking about me at all, never mind telling you details about what I'm doing back in Fiasco."

He hums to himself like he's got a secret he's just dying to share. "There's plenty you don't know about your sister. Starting with the fact that she owes me a bit of money…among other things. And I'm expecting her to deliver."

When I left, Waz had been training horses. It was Tullis who had shifted focus from training to overseeing the entire team and logistics for Finch & Kings. They'd apparently dropped the *S* once Tullis was out of the picture. But after hearing this, confirming that he speaks with my sister and she has been working with him, I have a gut-wrenching feeling I'm talking to the person who beat her up before she was arrested. Suppressing a shiver, I clear my throat. "You should take that up with her then. Not me."

"Already have. Made sure she heard me loud and clear."

Motherfucker.

He steps closer, quick to keep me from moving anywhere but back. My heel wobbles on the grass. The ground is hard and frozen this time of year. "You've been gone for a while, Faye. I don't think you recognize how things work around here now." I try to right myself, glancing to the left and right to find my best route to escape.

I'd rather not cause a scene out here right now, but it's

polarizing knowing that it's just the two of us alone. Or so I thought.

A blur of a tall body dressed in black behind Waz snags my attention. The next few seconds happen quickly as hands wrap around Waz's shoulders and throw him off balance. *Lincoln.* It's just long enough that with two broad steps and a half-cocked arm, the charming Foxx brother thrusts two quick jabs to Waz's nose before the asshole can even find his footing. The crack of cartilage on the second punch, coupled with the spray of blood, should make Waz go down, but cockroaches are stronger than they appear.

More than twenty feet from me, Waz's blood-soaked smile is laced with calculating interest as he stands at his full height. "I should have known you'd be in bed with a Foxx. Didn't take Shelby much time to cozy up to them either."

I glance at Lincoln, not understanding the reference.

Lincoln's chest heaves as his fist remains clenched and twitching at his side.

Waz laughs and spits. "Better watch out with this one, Lincoln. She has a habit of murderin' men."

My stomach sinks. It's nothing that Lincoln probably hasn't already thought about, but hearing it out loud makes my throat dry and fingers twitch along the pepper spray that I'm clenching in my hand.

Lincoln doesn't miss a beat when he says, "I know exactly who she is. And I think you might be underestimating her, because if I had to guess, she's got at least one weapon in each hand, ready to call this exactly what it is." He looks over his shoulder at me with a wink and says, "Self-defense."

Waz glares at me, ignoring Lincoln. "Faye, we should have another talk. We'll include Maggie next time. You Calloway women were always such a surprise." He spits out more blood so it hits right in front of Lincoln's foot. "Foxx, those little girls of yours are growing up real fast now—"

I step in front of the Lincoln and pull out the pepper spray, flip off the safety feature, and let it rain, nailing Waz square in the face. I box Lincoln out the best I can, and he grabs my hips, trying to move us away from the remnants of the blinding spray.

"That's for laying a hand on my sister," I grit out.

Waz cries out a series of "fucks" while tripping over his own feet as he moves backward and away. His ass hits the pavement with a thud. "You're so fucking dead, girlie."

I huff a laugh, walking closer to him as he tries to scoot away from me. "You better watch who you threaten, Waz. Like you said, I have a habit of murderin' men."

Being blindsided by tonight's attendees and the fact that he hurt Maggie was more than enough to be the last straw for me. But hearing him even mention Lincoln's girls, I snapped. My hands shake with adrenaline as I cover my nose and mouth, trying to keep from inhaling any of what I just sprayed.

"Faye," Lincoln says in his deep voice. "I said let's go." His hand grabs ahold of mine and interlocks our fingers, pulling me down the alleyway, away from the ugliness.

He laughs out, "That was stupidly badass, Peach."

I let out an exasperated sigh. With my adrenaline pumping, I focus back on what Waz said, that I still didn't understand: *Didn't take Shelby much time to cozy up to them either.* "What did he mean? About my mom?"

Lincoln's brow furrows as we walk. When he turns his head to meet my attention, it registers just as the words leave his lips. "Shelby and Griz were together. It was short—only maybe a few months before she—" He clears his throat. *Before she passed.* "Griz fell hard for Shelby." His voice changes and looks back as we walk. "You didn't know?"

I think through this, concentrating on the new information. *My mom and Griz Foxx?* It clicks why Maggie and Griz had that exchange—the familiarity and closeness I witnessed. He spent time with my mom, meaning so did she. Lincoln takes over for the valet, opening the passenger door of a souped-up Jeep, and ushers me inside. I zone out and stare at the road ahead as he floors the gas pedal. I try to take a deep breath, but I can't seem to do it. *I missed so much.*

After a few minutes, he breaks the silence. "We teased Griz about finding new things to do outside of the distillery. And then one day, Shelby showed up at family dinner. Maggie came with her a few times too. And Griz…" He shifts gears and the Jeep punches forward. "They were happy. It was nice to see him like that again. It'd been so long since we lost my nana." He swallows, and without me saying a word, he keeps talking. "Shelby was the one who got Griz to find more things—got him to go to her book clubs. And bake sales. She was quiet at first, didn't share too much. But they both laughed. Sometimes just a look between the two of them and they'd start cracking up. It would always make Lark and Lily laugh too. I think you would have liked seeing her with him."

My eyes water at the idea of her being happy. I hadn't thought she'd found that. I pictured her the way I left her—broken and sad at what she had to do that night.

"They weren't what anyone expected, but when you saw them together, there was no question that the oldest bourbon boy fell for the rodeo cowgirl."

I bat away the tear that falls as I stare out into the blurred darkness of trees and sky. What I wouldn't have given to see her with someone who made her feel that way.

"It's why the rodeo comes to town. They do their end of season pro-am event here in Fiasco. Foxx Bourbon sponsors the event, and the rest of the money gets donated to local charities. Griz told her it was his gift to her—his rodeo princess."

I suck in a breath. This isn't what I was expecting to learn when coming home. I look up, trying to keep the rest of my tears from trailing down my cheeks. Thank goodness for the dark interior of the car. It's not lost on me that he's talking to me about this so openly, being so kind. Answering my question when I know he has plenty of his own.

"This town has a lot to say about people who fall in love with a Foxx. It's considered a tragedy what happened with my nana. Then my parents were killed a handful of years before that. Then it all went to shit. First Fiona, then Olivia, and then Shelby—" He cuts himself off, and my chest tightens as I look his way. "People find it easier to assign blame for something, so Fiasco named our 'something' the Foxx curse." He lets out a sarcastic laugh before he mumbles, "Fucking feels like it some days."

"You don't honestly believe that?" I tilt my head, waiting for a response that doesn't come as he takes the next turn sharply and punches the gas down the road. He glances at me briefly as I study his profile.

"I could use a drink. How 'bout you?"

"A drink would be good," I say as my body settles into the leather seat. "Have anything other than bourbon?"

The right side of his mouth kicks up and that charming dimple divots low on his cheek, just barely noticeable beneath his facial scruff. "I know you didn't just say that to me."

Chapter 22

Lincoln

"It still smells so good here," she says, tilting her head back, eyes closed as we walk toward the distillery. "There has never been any other place where the air smells like cinnamon, sugar, and bread had the most delicious time together."

I swallow, my mouth watering at the way she describes it. It's a reminder of how special it is here. "It's the sugars breaking down in whatever mash bill we're pushing. Fermentation causes that bread-like smell, and then you add in the wind from whichever season we're in and that's Fiasco." I smile as I flip the metal key to the left, unlocking and pushing through the double oak doors. "Everyone says that it lingers more in the humidity of summer, but I think it's stronger, more distinct, in the cold."

The motion lights illuminate the tasting bar and ignite the gas-powered sconces peppered along the walls of the entryway. A nice little feature that Ace labeled as "extra," but right now, I'm happy I ignored that opinion.

"I have questions," I say as I link her fingers into mine.

"I know."

The tasting bar is made from American white oak, the same that's used in our barrels. It's stained dark to keep the warm aesthetic. I love trailing my hand along the top of it—a random habit I have to do every time I'm here.

She looks around like she's taking inventory. Cataloging every detail. I always feel a sense of pride run through me knowing that I've built and nurtured this place. That it's as much home as it is work. I never thought I'd feel that way about anything else, and then I became a dad.

"There's only bourbon back there..." she says, watching as I study what's displayed and then pull a few bottles from shelves. "Is it against the rules to tell Lincoln Foxx that I don't love bourbon?" She scrunches her nose and finishes it with a smile.

I wrap my fingers around two Glencairns, the small glasses we use specifically for tasting, and put them in front of her. "Bourbon has plenty of rules. In order to call it bourbon, it needs to follow them."

Plucking a bottle from the middle shelf, I give it a quick pour. I tip the glass back, letting the alcohol burn along my tongue. A palate starter.

As she rests her elbows on the bar, she says, "Outside of making bourbon, I think rules can be dangerous."

I lean toward her and take a second to really look, pushing my glasses up the bridge of my nose. I've looked at her in so many different lights and lenses. "Almost as dangerous as secrets."

She smiles as her eyes search mine. "But you and I tend to have some of those, don't we?"

I don't answer right away, instead I let the look we share

linger for just a few beats longer. Pouring a splash of the reserve in one glass and the specialty blend in the other, I lean close to her and lift the glass, studying it in the warm lighting. "I think we have less from each other than from other people." It's true, but it's the first time either of us has acknowledged that.

"This bourbon is the one that I look forward to having. It was a fluke—a mash bill gone wrong. It's still 51% corn, but the wheat and rye had been botched. It had almost broken the rules." I take a sip before I tell her exactly what makes this one special. "I had been distracted, and the lavender that had been hanging in my workstation from Lark fell into my test batch. But I figured, why not? Let's try it. That week had been the worst of my life. I had found out my wife wasn't—" I cut myself off. "I had just been blackmailed by a woman in a cornfield. I figured, 'Fuck it, let's see what comes of this.'"

She holds hers up as well, mimicking my move. "So this is basically my fault."

"Which means you can't hate it now," I say with a smirk as I tilt it to my nose to scent the notes. This one is a higher proof—harsher and stronger, but it'll make the rest feel easy. "What should we toast to? Punches and pepper spray?"

With an unexpected chuckle, she studies the color, swirling the bourbon in her glass. "To bourbon and secrets."

"To bourbon and secrets," I repeat and clink her glass. "You're going to take a small sip, just letting it coat your mouth. And your tongue."

When she really smiles, that beauty mark moves a little higher, her eyes squint, and lips tilt up and out in a way that makes you want to mirror it. She tips the glass back and then squeezes her eyes shut as she swallows. "Yup, still just tastes like burning."

It's not the first time I've heard it, but coming from her, it's cute.

I move down the length of the bar, my fingers skimming across the bottles that have built up our brand—Grant's Cowboy Edition Bourbon, Griz's 1910, and Prohibition Special Reserves. And while both Ace and I produce the bulk of our most sought-after Straight Rye and Single Barrel Bourbon, we don't have a blend that is distinctly ours. This bottle I pull down, however, with the black Foxx logo embossed across it, is one of my favorites, for no other reason than it was bottled the first year that I started here as a master distiller.

Faye leans forward, the pink dress draping just low enough that her tits look fucking edible. "Eyes up here, Foxx." She smiles, her fingertips grazing the rim of the glass. "You didn't have glasses before I left."

I remove the stopper from the bottle. "It was a present for my thirty-eighth birthday—my eyes went to shit. Everything was a little blurry. And, as it turns out, Christmas lights aren't supposed to look like sparklers. But really, the joke is on people without astigmatism."

She barks out a laugh. "Does everybody know that the charming, single-dad Foxx brother is also kind of a nerd?" She holds her hand out in front of her. "And I don't say nerd as a negative. I think exceptionally smart people are highly underappreciated. Nerds got a bad rap in the 80s and never came back from it." Eyes widening, she sucks in an excited gasp. "Have you ever heard of nerdlesque."

I can't help but narrow my eyes on her. "There's no way that's a real thing. And were you even alive in the 80s?"

Pointing at me, she bites back her smile. "Not the point, Foxx. And yes, 'nerdlesque' is a real thing. Some of the costumes..." She purposely bites her lip. "Very delicious. And I'm only saying that I feel like you've allowed me to see glimpses of you that not many people have."

I unclip my cufflinks "Maybe that's true." Taking a moment to let what she just brought up linger, I fold and then roll up each sleeve. "You ready to tell me what you were doing there tonight? It looked like a different kind of performance."

She stays quiet and then drags her small bag across the bar top, feeling around inside of it, and then she removes a long grayish-brown rock and places down on the bar. "I need a little courage right now," she says, flipping it over to the side with jagged purple gems. My chest warms as I swallow, feeling along the rough expanse of the rock that my daughter gave to her.

"They like how you talk to them." I brush my fingers along hers.

"How do I talk to them?" she asks with a tilt of her head.

"I don't know." I smile and joke. "Maybe you can give me some pointers." I watch as she stares off, smiling. "The first day they found you on the porch, they told me afterward that you listen to them. And treat them like you want to know them. Something like that."

"I think your girls are badasses. They have these unique interests and just say what they feel," she says, and I smile, thinking about how fearless they are to let all of it show. "No apologies about who they are—takes some people a lifetime to do that... I think Lark is unsure about me, but I get it. I've been there. Needing to be wildly protective of a parent." When she smiles at me this time, it fucking makes my knees weak.

"Is that what you did?" I ask. I know there's more to that night in the cornfield. And after spending time with her now,

Faye murdering Tullis King in cold blood never felt right. "You were being wildly protective?"

She shifts her weight on the bar stool, crossing her arms against her chest as her finger traces her tattoos.

She's trying to decide if she can trust me. If she should tell me the details. I know more than most, obviously. It didn't take long to figure out whose blood was splashed all over her shirt. Chatter of Tullis King disappearing hadn't surfaced until weeks later. Maybe it was sooner, but I had been too busy managing my own nightmare to focus on anyone else's.

"There wasn't time to process any of it. My mother was kind, and she loved with her eyes and arms wide open. She's the woman who told me to follow my instincts, find a path that would make my soul happy. And the way she loved horses..." Faye smiles fondly, but it quickly fades as she continues. "That night, my mom was scared. Shaken." Taking a deep breath, she stares at the glass in front of her. "So I shoved away anything that looked like a moral compass and took inventory of what we would need to make him go away. If anyone was going to get away with that, it would be me. I had spent the last six years of my life learning how to read a crime scene and develop a case. Forensic science in undergrad, an internship, and then the police academy. I knew what would be looked for and scrutinized. And then a protective instinct kicked in."

Calm, smart, strong. It's all I can think of as she's sharing what she went through that night.

I swipe off the tear that tracks along her cheekbone before it can splash against her beauty mark. "She wouldn't let me call the police. She had a point. We might have had friends, but Tullis King and his brother? They have people in their pockets, on payroll. So I made a choice. Maggie had said she was drinking more than usual lately, but my sister liked to play up the drama of situations. I should have listened and come home sooner.

"Tullis King was a condescending asshole on his best day and a demoralizing pig on his worst. By the time I came back with what I needed to move him, he was dead. My mother was practically catatonic. So I buried it. Everything."

"And then I found you," I say as I move around to her side of the bar.

She lets out a small, sad laugh. "Then you found me. And I panicked."

"You thought on your feet." I tilt my head to the side. "Blackmail was a creative choice. Quick thinking. Not sure I would have thought on my feet like that," I say with a reassuring smile, trying to lighten the heaviness of all of it.

Her shoulders loosen, arms uncross, as she looks into my eyes and then reaches for my shirt, rubbing the material between her fingers. "Do you forgive me? For putting you in an impossible position and—"

"There's nothing to forgive. I would have done the same to protect my family." I have enough of what I need to know. She'd protected someone she loved and there wasn't a single thing I considered wrong about that. At least some portion of the truth would be enough for now. "I have more questions."

She leans away, creating space I don't want between us. "I thought you might—"

"I know there's more to the story of why you're back in Fiasco. That you wouldn't kiss me like that the other night, come for me like you have, and then perch yourself on Blackstone's lap if there hadn't been a damn good explanation."

She opens her mouth to say something, but I hold up the second tasting glass between us for her to try.

"When you're ready to tell me all of them, every last secret you have, Faye Calloway, then I'll listen. But I don't want just parts of your story anymore. Right now, I'd rather have a drink with a very sexy, very beautiful woman."

Those green eyes watch me in a way that makes me feel wanted and maybe even needed.

Instead of reaching to take the glass, she tilts her chin up, parting her lips.

I dip my finger into the handblown glass and then paint her lips with the bourbon that drips off. Her fingers tighten against the front of my shirt as she pulls me closer, widening her legs to make room for me. Her tongue peeks out and licks away the bourbon across her lips.

"Alright, Foxx," she says in a low and soft voice that hits me just right. "Just a drink?"

Threading my fingers into her hair, I kiss her the way I've wanted to since I left her on that porch swing. She hums at the first brush of our lips, and seconds later, she's deepening the kiss like she's been waiting for this too. The way this woman kisses, her entire body participates, and everything outside of us might still exist, but it doesn't fucking matter. The taste of my bourbon along her tongue makes my cock so much harder that I can't help but groan.

She smiles against my lips and then fists my shirt so tightly that I fall into her, erasing the space and any lingering hesitancy about this being exactly what I want.

I move my hands to her hips and nudge her closer to the edge of her chair. Her skirt hikes up past her thighs as they widen more for me, my fingers digging into her as a moan crawls up her throat. I can't help but look down for a second—her body turns me on in a way that I've never felt.

When I move, she holds me tighter, and I'll be honest, it feels fucking good. Needing me for longer. Wanting me closer. Demanding that I stay instead of just accepting or assuming I'll leave. She nips at my lips as I pull back again, only this time, it's not to smile and appreciate the way that it feels to kiss this woman.

I keep my voice low as I look into her dazed eyes, my gaze drifting lower to that puffy lower lip when I tell her to open.

Chapter 23

Faye

Stomach flipping, I run my tongue along my lower lip, the one he's always focusing on. And then I do exactly as he asks. He takes off his glasses, folds them up slowly, and then smiles to himself. His hand moves to my neck, fingers threading into my hair as he tilts my head back to where he wants me.

I open my mouth just as he wraps his lips around the bottle of bourbon. He drinks from it, shifts over my waiting mouth, and then spits. He doesn't let me savor it. He barely lets me swallow before his lips capture mine again. The bourbon dribbles down the sides of my mouth as I wrap my arms around his shoulders, gasping when he pulls me up onto the bar top and my ass settles on the cool, dark oak. He rakes his fingers down my back, pulling me toward the edge of the bar as I run my fingertips along the back of his neck and into his hair, and he lets out a satisfied moan, leaning into it.

"Now, tell me you don't like bourbon," he teases. His mouth

trailing down the side of my neck to kiss away the bourbon that escaped my mouth.

"I don't think I can do that." I smile.

He shifts his mouth lower, pushing down the straps of my top and running his lips along my shoulder. With his lips still on me, he mumbles out, "Tell me what you tasted."

I hum at the game he's playing. It might be the most fun foreplay of my life. "I tasted the smokiness of the wood."

His teeth rake along my skin as he pulls my top farther down, mouth moving over the swell of my breast until he yanks the bra next. The move jerks my body slightly, and I bite down on the smile it pulls from me. When his eyes meet mine, checking that this is okay, my smile and nod of consent unleashes a breathy moan just as he sweeps his tongue against me.

"What else?" he rasps as he wraps his mouth around my nipple and lazily drags his tongue around it, so slowly that I can feel the taste buds mapping my flavor. It sets my insides on fire and unleashes a shivering wave of how much I want this right now.

I throw my head back at the sensation. A delicious pull at my breast and the ache between my legs intensifies. "It was sweeter—" I'm cut off as he pulls at the other side of my dress, taking the lace-trimmed cup of my bra along with it. He doesn't savor me this time; he devours the other breast like I'm something he's been starved for.

With his arms wrapped around my middle, he shifts me closer to him. My ass hangs off the edge of the bar, and for a moment, my skin is cold as he steps back, lowering to the floor and pushing my knees wide. "Been wanting to taste you again. So fucking badly."

His blue eyes watch for a reaction.

I practically pant as I signal for him to keep going, and he grazes his nose along the seam of my pussy.

"Oh god," I breathe out.

"Mmm, I agree, Peach." Pushing my panties aside, he drags his flattened tongue from my slit to my pulsing clit, making me whimper. I'm wound tight with desire as he stands back up, takes a pull from his bottle of bourbon, and smirks at me.

He wraps his hand behind my neck, pulling me toward him. "There's something about kissing this perfect mouth of yours that drives me wild." With his lips slick with my arousal and a bourbon chaser, he kisses me again. *Fuck, I want more.*

I fumble for the buttons on his black dress shirt, eagerly trying to peel away whatever layers remain between us. He pulls back, head resting against mine. His breaths are labored, panting in time with the way my chest rises and falls.

"You've ruined bourbon for me now," he says playfully. "I hope you realize that." Taking over for me, he finishes unbuttoning the last two buttons and peels off his shirt. I shouldn't be surprised that his body is almost laughably perfect. The kind of chest and shoulders a woman of any size and shape would feel eclipsed by when wrapped up in them. The tattoos that run along the right side of his chest and up over his shoulder, down his bulky arms. I'm salivating at how his forearms flex as he works the belt of his pants—*why is that so hot?*

Kicking his pants aside, he peeks his tongue out, licking at his bottom lip as he stands there in black boxer briefs, deciding what he wants to do with me next. As he runs his palm along his very hard, very thick cock, I can't help but lick my lips. "There may never be such a thing as a great bottle of bourbon for me ever again unless I have the taste of your pussy with it."

I smile and breathe out, "Oh my goddesses." Dragging my

teeth along my bottom lip, I lift my legs onto the bar and stand up. Then I'm reaching back, unzipping my dress, and letting it fall. "I don't think I'll enjoy drinking it any other way either, Foxx."

The smile those simple words get me is like a reward—his dimples pressed in and eyes crinkled at the sides.

He crooks his finger at me in a *come hither* motion as I bend at the waist, still hovering above him on the bar. "No standing on my tasting bar."

I stand up straight, fully naked now, letting his eyes roam around my body. The way that he watches me feels like the dirtiest promises are coming, and I can't seem to get enough. "How about fucking on your tasting bar?"

That spurs him on as he reaches up and pulls me down, hoisting me over his shoulder. "I'm too old for that shit. I need a soft place to sit so I can have you every way I want." His teeth graze along my ass cheek as we walk down the hallway.

I scream out with a laugh.

"You're really living up to your nickname, Peach. This ass is so fucking juicy, goddamn."

"My view isn't all that bad either." I snake a hand into the back of his tight shorts.

A door slides open, and from my viewpoint, all I can see are bourbon bottles. Backlit and on display. He lowers me onto a tufted brown leather couch.

"Is this another secret room?" I ask, raising my eyebrows. Between this one and the upstairs space, I'm beginning to think the Foxx brothers have plenty of places to whisk women away to whenever they want.

His eyes rake down the front of my body, hunger flaring that reflects mine. "No more questions."

The demand is one I have no problem giving in to. I want this man so badly that I've forgotten any reason why this is a bad idea.

I shift back and slowly widen my legs while keeping Lincoln's eyes locked on mine.

His eyes follow my fingers as I draw them down the center of my body. I feel every ounce of arousal and appreciation in him as he canvasses my curves, taking note of his favorite parts first and then moving back to my pussy. As my fingers brush against my core, the slick arousal makes it easy to tease myself.

"Let me see you," I whisper.

With his eyes on me, he shoves his boxer briefs to the floor and kicks them aside. Lincoln stands to his full height, cock out, and it's a sight to behold. Thick, hard, weeping at the tip, and pointing at exactly what it wants. He wraps his hand around the base, gripping himself nice and tight before he gives himself a few slow tugs as he says, "Keep looking at me like that, Peach. That's it." He wets his lips with his tongue. "Tell me you want me. I need to hear it."

I trail my fingers along my skin, from my breast to my center at a punishingly slow pace. "Say please."

He smirks as he rocks his wrist back and forth, jerking himself hard and slow. "Please."

I let out a small moan—he did exactly as I asked. It's an entirely new kink I didn't know I had. Two fingers brush my clit as I tell him exactly what he needs from me. "Foxx, I want you." I bring those same fingers, slick with my arousal, up the center of my body. "I want you so badly"—I shake my head with a knowing smile—"that I can't think of anything other than your mouth and cock making a mess all over me."

"Goddamn, Peach." He bites his bottom lip as he moves

closer. "Remind me to say please more often." Dropping to his knees right in front of me, his eyes follow every move my roving fingers make.

"If I forget to tell you later," he says as leans forward and kisses just above my navel, "you're the most beautiful woman I've ever seen. And like this…" He kisses my right breast, then my left, lowering his head to kiss the center of my pussy as I moan for him. "I won't be the same man after it." Reaching up, he wraps his hand around my throat, pulling me forward in the most dominant way. The taste of me on his tongue, our heavy breaths, and the thrum of wanting the other so intimately has the kiss nearly all-consuming.

Before I get too lost in the rhythm of his tongue coaxing mine, he breaks away, yanking my thighs toward him to spread them apart. With my thighs in his grip, he leans down and kisses my pussy like she's being so good for him. My breath catches as he parts my lips with his flattened tongue, lapping every inch of her in one deliciously slow swipe.

"Oh my god," I moan.

He smiles up at me. "Yeah, Peach, I can be that for you too."

I can't help but smile back, eyes closing as I say on an exhale, "Show me."

On a growl, his mouth and lips are everywhere, from my slit to my clit, and I can barely catch my breath as his fingers swipe through me. Teasingly. Edging me until I'm ready to beg for him to fill me. He licks and savors me with moans rumbling from his chest every so often, like he's enjoying every single taste.

He dips one finger in first and quickly changes it to two when I whimper in relief, flipping them up and playing with that perfect spot inside me. When I open my eyes, he's watching me. Studying every reaction I make and cataloging what I like most.

"Touch yourself," I demand on borrowed breath.

He doesn't answer, just does what he's told. *So good.* With his fingers sinking in and out of me, he grips the base of his cock and jerks it twice before he does one long pull. Rubbing his thumb along the tip, he gathers the arousal that's been teased out. His eyes close, as if that specific touch was what he's been waiting for.

But it's the heady moan that escapes him that's the final piece to tip me over. My fingers start to tingle, eyes squeezing shut as my body clenches. That telltale numbness brushes along the backs of my knees and up my thighs until my pussy pulses against his touch, and I moan out my orgasm, shuddering against him. The black behind my lids turns fuzzy and time feels like it's somehow paused to take note. Coming down from the wave of pleasure, I feel his lips brush against my pussy again as my body twitches. I blink my eyes open just as he removes his fingers and dips his tongue in to savor the reward he just made.

"I'm going to need to fuck you now. Please tell me I can." There's an edge of desperation in his tone that has me smiling.

I close my eyes, still slightly dazed. "Such a good boy, Foxx, remembering to say please."

I can hear the laugh that escapes him as he moves. "Fuck, that just made my dick jump."

When I blink my eyes open, he's gone, moving across the room toward the desk, looking for a condom. The view isn't a bad one either. Lincoln Foxx has thick thighs and a round ass that looks so bitable that I'm licking my lips.

When he turns back around, there's a condom on display between two fingers. "The way you're looking at me…" He shakes his head. "Fuck, I'm in so much trouble."

I bite my lip just watching as he rolls it over his length. I'm more than ready for all of him. He cups himself and lifts his chin. "Come here."

Standing up, I wrap my arms around his shoulders as he reaches me, catching his lips with mine as he turns and lowers us to the couch. I straddle his lap the same way I had done on the porch swing, grinding my pussy lips along the length of him.

A hissing breath escapes him. His eyes close as his head tips back onto the leather. "So ready for me," he mumbles, hands gripping my hips.

I play with him again. The same way, letting him part my lips and tease both of us as I rub up and down. "Watch," I whisper as his eyes open to find me.

We both watch as I sink down slowly, my arms braced on his shoulders as I do. His thumb finds my clit instantly and pets her with enough pressure, like she's being praised for taking him so well. The way he touches and watches amplifies everything as he stretches me until I'm impossibly full. I rock my hips forward slowly, feeling every inch of him. A gasping moan steals my breath as he pulls my hips forward, hitting even deeper than I just was. My forehead meets his as I gasp, "This—"

A groan surges from his throat before he finishes my thought. "Feels so fucking good."

As I roll my hips again, it ignites every single sensation along my body. He leans up, wrapping his arms around my waist as he captures my mouth. Our tongues dance at a faster pace, as if there's not a single moment left to waste.

"I can't get enough of you. I want—" he says as he drags his teeth along my shoulder, brushing his lips back to cover the harsh bite with something soft. At this angle, my clit grinds against him with each roll of my hips, but I need more. My whimper is all he needs to hear to deliver.

"Fuck that, I don't just want, I need more. Hold on to me," he says as he sits forward and rises to stand.

I circle my arms around his neck and shift my legs, wrapping them around his hips. He holds beneath my ass as he brings us to the side of the couch.

"I need to fuck you now," he says as he guides my upper body down along the back of the couch. I'm nodding eagerly as he stands at his full height and grabs beneath each thigh before he does exactly as he said. He fucks me. Hard. Deep. And with a punishing rhythm that barely allows me to catch my breath. It doesn't take long before I'm crying out his name.

My orgasm spurs him to hold me tighter. Skin slicked with sweat as his pace quickens, he releases so hard that, even with clenched teeth, he moans so loudly that I get goosebumps. His body jerks just as he collapses forward, slumping as we pant for more air.

He kisses where his lips rest along my chest. "I'll never be the same," he mumbles in between soft kisses that have my heart stuttering. Because I can't help but think how this just changed *everything*.

"These are pretty," he says as he drags his fingers along the lines of my tattoo. "The colors and flowers suit you."

We've been lying here in a quiet daze, wrapped in each other's arms. I hadn't had the urge to move or overthink. Just enjoy the way we just devoured and worshiped the other.

"I had always loved how these vibrant floral tattoos looked on women. I love how it looks on me now." I smile. There's no meaning around the flower or the color, only that I thought it was pretty. I needed something pretty at that time in my life when everything felt so ugly and confusing. "When I left Fiasco, I had a hard time thinking that I deserved much. Let alone pretty things. I walked by a tattoo shop, just after seeing these beautiful dancers on stage at a burlesque show and decided to go in."

I'm draped along his chest, my head resting right over his heart. And it shouldn't be comfortable, someone as solid and built, but I'm moments away from falling asleep. Even with his chest hair tickling at my cheek.

"What does your tattoo…" I shift to trace the lines that wrap along his side and waist. "The Bourbon Boys." His skin is still slick with sweat, but I don't care. I like touching him.

"My brothers have it too." He clears his throat. "Our mom used to call us that—her bourbon boys. If my dad was still here, I know he'd have gotten one too. He'd have done just about anything for her."

I trace the window panes of his tattoo. "Flowers. For the girls?"

He nods and plays with the ends of my blond hair.

"And the glass of bourbon is obvious." I run the pads of my fingers along the blank square. "What about this one?"

"Everything was hard when they were smaller—so much harder than now." He releases a long breath. "I hadn't realized how much parenting I wasn't doing until I was the only one left to do it." A crooked smile quirks his lips as he laughs lightly, like he's glad to not be so overwhelmed like he was a few years ago. "I would never remember to bring things for the girls to do. Liv used to always remember stuff like that—coloring books for restaurants, beads and pipe cleaners for waiting rooms—but I'd always forget. I was lucky if I'd get them places on time, never mind if I remembered activities to keep them occupied once I got there. I didn't always want to hand over my phone for them to zone out on videos of kids playing with toys, so this gave them a space to color. They had to remember the markers, and I'd let them draw." He smiles while talking about the memory. It's too easy to smile in response.

He looks down at me while his fingers move along the outlines of my flowers.

I watch his hands glide along my skin. "It was just the outline for a while, and little by little, I added color," I say with a smile dancing along my lips. "It took time, but eventually, these flowers felt like they were always supposed to be there." My words linger as his fingers trace the lines.

He clears his throat and shifts. His fingers stop moving when he asks, "What were you doing at Blackstone's auction last night?"

I knew I would only be able to go so long without having to explain that.

I pull in a breath for a little courage before I say, "Burlesque dancing isn't the only thing I've been doing since I left."

He turns his body just enough to keep me in his arms, but also to be able to watch me as I tell him more.

"I knew after that night in the cornfield that I couldn't step foot inside that police station in good conscience. That wasn't the kind of officer I wanted to be—starting out already harboring lies. Leaving made it easy to leave that part of myself behind. But then Del…" I smile, thinking about him. "He'd always been a mentor in a lot of ways. Ended up putting the idea of private investigating in my head. It was an easy certification process, and I had no expectations of myself or from anyone else." I swallow and shift to my side, looking up at him. "Looking at the details, asking the right questions, and talking to people has always been my strong suit. Del would send me case information and I'd offer my feedback. It turned into other jobs. And now, one of those jobs has brought me back here."

"Blackstone?" he confirms, brow furrowed.

I give him a nod and add, "I needed to get close to him. Surveillance, digging into his background, looking for things that would be helpful in understanding his clientele. The ones that weren't 'on the books.' The FBI is building a case on someone he's connected to in Fiasco. I needed to get into that auction tonight. I lied," I say, swallowing my nerves at trusting him with this information. "Blackstone is business, not a friend."

"Business that landed you back in your hometown and in bed with one of the people attending that event," he says.

"That it did." I search his face for what this information might trigger.

He pushes my hair behind my shoulder and brushes his thumb along my chin as I sit up from his chest. "I'm not surprised to hear any of this. You're fucking beautiful on that stage, but there were plenty of places you could have gone to dance. And instead, you chose Fiasco."

"I knew it was going to be hard, but I underestimated ..." I shake my head. "I underestimated what seeing you again would do."

With a rough swallow, his Adam's apple bobs. "I didn't like seeing you on another man's lap."

My body warms at his admission, and I can't hold back my smile. "Feeling a little jealous?"

He covers up his smile as his hand runs over his mouth, deciding what he wants to say. "Jealous isn't strong enough of a word. I didn't like Blackstone the first time I met him, but seeing him touching you, I wanted to break his hands first and then slit his throat when I started thinking what else he may have touched."

"I find that oddly sexy." Humming, I rest my chin on his chest and let those words settle around me. "What I do has people looking, sometimes touching, but that's business. And I like what I do, Foxx. Private investigating lets me feel like I can still do what I had always wanted, but tweaked and on my own terms. Just like I love how burlesque makes me feel. That's not something I'm willing to change."

"Good. I don't want you to change." He pulls me closer and kisses the top of my head. "I just wanted some clarity so I didn't end up killing a man for touching someone who's starting to feel like mine."

My eyes widen as my heart stutters. "Yours?"

He looks down his chest at me and lets out a lazy smile. "I can still taste you, Peach. My cock is fucking hard all over again just thinking about how well your pussy treated him. How I know exactly when to roll my hips so I can hit that spot just right… Yeah…" He exhales. "You're starting to feel like mine."

I like how that sounds. How it feels, but I'm not brave enough to agree, so instead, I kiss his chest and let the truths we shared tonight settle around us. There's something about telling him why I'm here that feels freeing. I shared more than Cortez would have wanted, but this is my life, and in Lincoln's arms, I'm not sure I've ever felt this right.

He looks up at the ceiling. With one arm folded behind his head, it's the most mesmerizing view, seeing this part of him for the first time. Vulnerable, content, maybe even comfortable and not so quick to put on a show for the people around him. I knew what that looked like. I did it too.

Kissing his chest, I smile against his warm skin, enjoying this moment with him far more than I should be. "This was fun."

I move to sit up, but he wraps his arms around me too quickly for me to get any further than my chest pressed against his.

"It was more than fun, and you know it." His lips hover in front of mine, teasingly close. And I can't stop myself from leaning into them.

When I pull back, I run my fingers along the scruff on his cheeks and chin. "Have a question for you," he says. And just like last time, I feel nervous about what he could possibly be asking me. "How do you like your bourbon?"

I can't help but bark out a laugh and then nip at his lip. "Any way you want to give it to me, Foxx."

Chapter 24

Faye

Lincoln Foxx should have never been part of the equation. I came back to do a job. To bail out my sister. And now all of it feels like a lie. A half-truth that I told myself because vulnerability makes people weak. I could be a lot of things, but *his* couldn't be one of them. Could it?

It's been a week since the auction—and, coincidentally, the best sex of my life. And that's all I keep replaying—his hands all over me, his mouth, his words. And how this would work. My phone vibrates in my pocket as I'm jamming the poker against the fresh log I just threw onto the fire. We're in the midst of the forgotten part of winter, not cold enough for snow to stick and not warm enough to forget your jacket.

Hadley had asked if I'd stay around long enough for Valentine's Day. I'm starting to feel settled, so I didn't think too long about how to answer. It was an easy yes. I don't have another job lined up, which is also out of character for me, but I suppose I've felt out of sorts since I arrived.

FOXX:

> When exactly am I going to see you again? Replaying you writhing underneath me is only making me want to see you more. And waiting until I run into you isn't the way I like to go after what I want.

FAYE:

> And what is it you want?

FOXX:

> I thought that was obvious...

I stare at the orange and yellow flames dancing around the fireplace before they catch onto the new wood. A smile pulls at my lips, thinking about how to answer his question. It's been a fair amount of texts about random things. My favorites are just the simple, *Hi, Peach*. I can hear him saying it as his lips press against mine, and it does something to me that I can't seem to explain.

Is it eager to tell him that I want to see him *right fucking now?* Our night together hasn't left my mind, for multiple reasons. And it's been long enough without a repeat.

As soon as I came home the morning after the auction, I uploaded all the content I acquired and shared it with Cortez. I had expected some repercussions from my swift departure and run-in with Waz, but I haven't heard so much as a peep from Blackstone.

And then this morning, Cortez confirmed that the private auction was broken up an hour after Lincoln and I left. There was only one arrest made. Brock Blackstone was taken into custody; however, no charges have been filed. It left a nervous feeling in my gut—this isn't going to just fizzle out. Fiasco is going to be the battleground for whatever's coming. Which begs the question: Who's the FBI targeting?

> CORTEZ:
>
> You did great stuff on this case, Faye. Your work on the Blackstone file is complete. Between the surveillance over the last few months that you've shared, in addition to what and whom we were able to identify during his private auction, your contract has officially been fulfilled.

Catching my attention, my sister hurries past the living room, but I call out after her. "Maggie."

She and I need to talk. There're a lot of questions that I'm not okay with her running away from any longer, specifically about Waz. Whatever she's involved in with Waz King is trouble—that much is obvious. But after my run-in with him and the fact that he and Wheeler Finch were at that auction, my sister is in the line of fire. And as much as our relationship is broken, not a single part of me wants her to get any more hurt.

Walking backward, she leans on the archway to the room with a sigh. "Yes, I drank your seltzers. We'll call it part of your rent."

I blink at her first, then crack a smile. "Shut up. I'm not paying rent when I own half this place. But stop taking my things, please."

She raises her eyebrows. "Fine. Stop moving around my gym equipment."

Arguing isn't what I want to do, so I don't counter with the fact that her gym equipment is in *my* old bedroom. Instead, I pivot. "Why are you working for Finch & King?"

She stares at me, her shoulders tensing as she stands up from casually leaning. I'm not sure what she's looking for, or if she's just trying to decide whether the truth might work. But instead of an answer, she throws a question back. "Why are you here?"

The doorbell rings, but she doesn't move to get it until it rings again a second later. Without a word, she moves down the hallway to answer it. I hear her unlock and remove the chain, but other than, "Hey," I don't hear anything else.

"What!?" Maggie whisper-shouts. She never did do quiet very well.

"Nice to see you too, Maggie."

That voice has me standing and moving closer with light footsteps.

"Unless you want an audience, you need to keep your voice down, Cortez."

"You're not answering your phone," he says as I peek around the couch. She's trying to keep the door angled closed.

Maggie's voice raises. "Your buddies at the station took my statement. I have nothing else to add." She opens the door wider now and looks over her shoulder right at me. *She knew she was being too loud, that I would hear.* "He's all yours," Maggie calls out, then walks away and leaves the door open as a signal for him to come in.

When he sees me leaning against the threshold of the farmhouse's living room, he looks surprised and hesitates to come inside. It's interesting body language for someone who came here to see me. It's even more curious that he'd be here at all. After his dismissive work text, I would have thought an in-person visit wasn't necessary. *Unless I'm not why he's here.* There's something about their exchange that isn't sitting right.

"I was hoping you'd still be here, Faye."

Pulling my hair up in a loose knot, I sit back down in the chair I had been zoning out in and glance at the bit of snow that's started falling outside. "What did you want to tell me?"

"Just that the Fiasco Charity Rodeo kicks off tonight. Full weekend of bulls and bronc riders overflowing the town."

"You finished out my case via text, but you wanted to tell me about the rodeo in person?" Brow pinched, I glance at Maggie. "The fuck, Cortez? Why are you really here?"

Maggie's head tilts to the side, watching with an odd mix of irritation and amusement.

My phone buzzes with another text.

> FOXX:
> Hi Faye. Did you know that the caverns in Fiasco have the greatest concentration of geodes and stalagmites in this part of the country?

> FAYE:
> Lily?

> FOXX:
> Yup!

Some people might expect kids to be a deterrent when it comes to dating men. Ninety-nine times out of one hundred, I would have agreed. Except now, this one time, I find a single dad whose kids are just as charming as him.

FAYE:

I'm surprised you went for texting me random facts and not online shopping or something else when the world is at your fingertips.

FOXX:

Nope! Lark and I pushed it with Dottie and Kit. We found Kit, but Dottie was curse purse money, which was still technically Dad's money...

FOXX:

Texting you seemed like the better choice.

FAYE:

Where is your dad?

FOXX:

Currently staring at your house. But don't tell him I told you that.

FOXX:

Would you want to help me find more rocks and gemstones to add to my collection sometime?

> **FOXX:**
> Why does my dad have your name in his phone as Peach?

My cheeks heat at this news, and I smile at the nickname.

"So is that a yes?" Cortez asks, pulling my attention back to what he asked.

I shake my head and focus. "What? Is what a yes?" I glance at Maggie again, trying to understand what's going on here between them.

Cortez smiles at me. "Come with me to the rodeo tonight."

And as much as I really don't want to, I know there's one way to get answers from both him and Maggie.

"Pick me up at six," I say as I move toward the stairs and focus on answering Lily.

> **FAYE:**
> I would love to help you find rocks and gems sometime.

"Are you going to tell me the real reason you showed up at the house today?" I ask Cortez from the passenger seat of his SUV.

"Better question, baby girl: Are you going to stay in Fiasco?"

I know when someone is deflecting. And I'm just about over him calling me a pet name he hasn't earned. "Faye," I correct.

He glances at me, head tilted.

"Not your baby girl, Cortez. You can call me by my first or my last name."

With a nod, he clears his throat.

I've made it uncomfortable, but I'm not interested in making him feel comfortable right now. There's only one person I want to hear call me *baby*…or *Peach*.

I lean my elbow on the car door and watch as he hits a few station buttons until he settles on some classic rock. It's a quiet car ride after that until we're pulling into the packed parking lot, uneasy tension swirling around us.

The arena where the charity rodeo is held is indoors. The typical humid heat that licked everyone's skin during rodeo season is nowhere in sight. Instead, snowflakes dust all the cars lining the entryway.

"I still never found out *why* my sister had bruises all over her face and body. Any guesses?"

"Of course, but you know your sister," he rushes out.

I raise my eyebrows. "I don't, actually. Kind of seems like you might know her better."

I watch his casual body language and try to pay attention to if it changes as we pass more people walking through the front gates and into the main hall. Tables line the edges with local businesses that sell everything from hot toddies to turquoise adorned belts and buckles. Rodeos are an excuse to dust off cowboy hats and pull on your best boots. The talent wears Wranglers and cowhide just about every day, but Kentucky isn't typical cowboy country. They still look damn fine in worn jeans and Henleys, but their accessories include rocks glasses and charm. Present company included. Cortez is in plain clothes, but he and I are similar in that we rarely turn off work mode. He might have asked me here, but he's always on duty.

A group of two women smiles at him as they walk by. Tipping his hat, he gives them an innocent smile, ignoring the way they're blatantly checking him out.

"Are you dating anyone?" I ask him. "This is our second time out and I haven't heard you talk about anybody…"

"You tell me," he says with a smirk. "Like you said, this is our second time out together."

"Oh, please." I laugh. I try not to think about who I ended up with and what we were doing when I went out with Cortez last time. "That isn't why I'm asking."

We stand in line for one of the tents, and it gives me a minute to look around. I'm not sure what I'm looking for, but a small wave of excitement rolls through me when I see Griz Foxx. I scan behind him to see if Lincoln is with him.

"Who are you looking for?" Cortez asks as he follows my line of sight.

I let out an exhale and figure I might as well cut my losses here and just ask him point-blank. "Are you sleeping with Maggie?"

He snorts out a laugh, head rearing back. "What? No." He looks behind him. "Jesus, Faye, why would you think that?"

I shrug my shoulders, trying to decide if his reaction is more of a show than truth. I step up to the long wooden table when it's our turn to order. "What are the chances I can get a hot toddy?"

Marla gives me a tight-lipped smile as I hold out a twenty for the drink. "We're all out."

Cortez laughs to himself.

Romey gives her arm a slap and laughs. "You're such a bitch, Marla." Smiling up at me, she says, "That'll be five dollars, Faye."

Marla makes a show of moving down to the next table that's selling 50/50 raffle tickets.

"Ignore her," Romey says as she hands me back my change. "I know you've got a lot going on, between your sister and just moving back—"

"I'm not moving back, Romey."

She bats away my words. "That's neither here nor there. Marla likes grudges, and you've been gone long enough to be considered a tourist now."

My stomach sinks at not being a part of this place. If they only knew how often I wanted to be here. The way that I planned to never leave this town after coming back from the academy.

"She went ahead and started a whole famous life without us," Cortez says as he slides up next to me. He gives me a wink and that crooked smile that I'm sure gets him plenty of attention around here.

Romey looks between us, smiling. "You two would have the prettiest babies."

Cortez smiles at me, just waiting for my response.

I've never pictured having babies with anyone. Even when my plans included staying in Fiasco, kids felt like a distant decision. I wanted to build a career, get my footing, then decide if that path made sense for me. Now, any path I take seems too shortsighted to even consider it.

"Having babies doesn't exactly fit into my life plans or my career choices," I say jokingly.

She gives me a placating smile as she slices out two small pieces of the fudge she's been selling. "The girls at Teasers were talking about asking you to host a dance class."

"Really?" I'm a bit thrown off by that. It isn't something anyone has asked me before. I just assumed it wasn't the kind of dancing they'd want to see, never mind learn, in a small town.

"Mable can teach ballet with her eyes closed, but she wouldn't know the first thing about swingin' her hips or shimmyin' around."

"Yeah, but Miss Mable is the one who taught me how to move at all," I tell her, thinking about how much I've enjoyed dancing for so long.

"She's teaching an Oldies and Yogies class for a few of us on Saturdays now. You should stop in and see her." She nudges my elbow and wiggles her eyebrows. "And you can show us a few of those moves I keep hearing about while you're at it."

I can't help but smile, imagining what that could look like. "I'll keep it in mind."

She moves her hand to the right of her mouth, like what she's about to say is a secret. "And as far as kids are concerned, to each their own. I just know those Foxx girls can't seem to stop talking about you." She nods behind me. "It's not just your burlesquin' that's caught some attention."

When I look over my shoulder to where she gestured, Lark Foxx leans on the bleachers, watching me. Two rows up, just a few seats from her daddy, Lily is pointing at the massive blue bubble she's blowing, with her eyes wide. They're impossible not to smile at. "I'm going to say hi to Lark and Lily." I give Romey a wave and make my way toward the stadium's bleachers, but Cortez stops as we get closer and then leans his forearms on the paddock.

"You should know that we were able to convince Blackstone to cooperate."

That has my attention. So I mimic his stance and quietly ask, "And what is he cooperating about?"

"I can't share that just yet. But it's exactly what we had hoped would happen. You built out a solid case against him—some shady shit that man has been involved with. Trafficking drugs, exotic animals, orchestrating a disturbing number of encounters with coeds who are just barely above being minors. It's a hefty list."

"And you're telling me that he wasn't who you're after?"

He shakes his head slowly as he looks around the room.

"Bigger fish?"

"Wider wingspan," he says, standing to his full height and waving at one of the bull riders who's making his way toward us.

"Cortez, why are you telling me this now? I've been asking and asking for this." I let out a frustrated exhale. I'm tired of the evasiveness. "Are you going to tell me what you've got my sister involved in or what?"

I follow his line of sight as he looks out across the arena. And sure enough, there's my sister having a chat with Wheeler Finch as she texts away simultaneously on her phone. She looks every bit the Maggie Calloway I knew before I ever left here. Her long blond hair falls down her back in waves. The pair of painted-on jeans and short blue sweater plays off her red lip. She's always been the outgoing Calloway who found pockets of trouble—caught drinking at high school football games, pulled over in a baked-out car—but she would find her way out of getting too much of a consequence. *I guess that caught up with her.*

I wonder, not for the first time, how exactly my sister had folded herself into business with Finch & King. She's a web designer, according to everyone in town. She built out the website for Teasers and Foxx Bourbon. But I also knew she did a helluva lot more for the Foxx family. Maybe that was true for Finch & King as well.

Cortez lets out a breath as Maggie breaks off her conversation and moves in my direction.

A hiccupped laugh echoing next to me draws my attention away. "She's such a slut. Heard she was fucking both of 'em," the buzzed brunette gossips.

Her friend laughs right along with her and says, "She's so money hungry too. I have a feeling she's doing *way* more than just gambling money. Heard she sucked a cop's dick to make bail."

Anger flares in my chest as I turn my head to really look at these two. I can tell Maggie's working something out in her head by the way her posture changes. She heard them. She looked in her element, relaxed, as she talked with one of the bronco riders. I hate that she overheard small-town closed minds. *Fucking bitches.*

My phone buzzes as I watch her storm off

> **BLACKSTONE:**
> You've been keeping some secrets from me, Rosie. I'm not interested in playing along with them anymore.

> **ROSIE GOLD:**
> Seems like you've been keeping secrets for, and from, a lot of people.

> **BLACKSTONE:**
> I enjoyed our time together. Be careful. Plenty of people are observing, Rosie. But you like that, don't you? Being watched?

> **ROSIE GOLD:**
> I would tell you to go fuck yourself, but we both know that's the kind of direction you like.

> **BLACKSTONE:**
> Don't tease me, Rosie.

> ROSIE GOLD:
> ...but that's my job, Brock. Now seems like the right time for this: Goodbye.

I block the number and pocket my phone. He's got plenty of people paying attention to his every move right now. Brock Blackstone is the least of my worries. And as much as he could be a loose cannon still being in Fiasco, I know the FBI has enough to keep him in line.

Cortez shuffles his feet. When I glance back at him, he's looking down and weighing what he's going to say. He starts to say, "We should discuss—"

"Cortez, you son of a bitch," one of the bull riders saunters over to where we're leaning and interrupts.

It works as the perfect distraction to take what I want, plant what I need, and still with enough time to put it back.

But it's the brunette closest to me who grabs my attention as she sucks in a gasp and then rushes out, "Oh my gosh, speaking of sucking someone off—I swear to you, if you want to just get good and fucked, you'll wander into that distillery and find you-know-who."

My stomach lurches as I hear it. These two women went from badmouthing my sister to the man I had just spent an entire night with. I have to laugh to myself, otherwise I'll start feeling like an idiot. Because I was just at that distillery, getting good and fucked. *Jesus.* I shouldn't feel anything hearing this. The logical part of me knows that we're both consenting adults and what he's done before me or chooses to do after me is irrelevant.

"I'll catch up with you in a little bit," I mumble to a distracted Cortez. I look in the direction where my sister went. *Where did she go?*

Chapter 25

Lincoln

"You look like a cowboy with that hat on, Dad," Lily says with her arms full. She sticks out her tongue to pick a piece of popcorn from the souvenir tub I just spent too much money on.

Smiling, I tip the black suede bill of the hat to thank her for the compliment.

Laney leans her shoulder into me as she starts to say, "I know it's horsemen and bourbon boys, but especially with those hats on, and inside this stadium, all three of you are—"

She gets cut off and starts laughing as Grant picks her up by her waist and moves her to the other side of him on the bleachers. "You mind not hitting on my wife for a change?"

"Oh, c'mon," I shout at him with my arms out. "Laney, you better stop telling me I'm the best looking one and that you settled for Grant—" A fist hits me in the shoulder blade. "Ow, dammit. Fuck you too, Ace."

"Dad!" Lily shouts over a mouthful of Pez. "That's twenty in total just today alone."

I rub the back of my shoulder. "Where did you get Pez?"

Rolling her eyes, she shrugs. "Home. My emergency stash for big events. You know I need it when we're in big crowds."

"Yeah kid, I know." I smile. A little something we decided a couple of years ago that would help her feel brave. We said that when you needed it, Pez could give you superpowers. Or, at the very least, a small time-out to figure out where to find the courage you needed to get through whatever felt hard.

I glance at Lark. I know she's not sure what to think about this thing between Faye and me. Quite frankly, I don't know what I should tell her.

Noticing how quiet she is, I study my oldest daughter. She's been quieter like this for the past week. I know my girls better than I know myself. When she's quiet, she's stewing about something. The first year after her mom died, she didn't do much talking. But I didn't do much asking either, and that was on me. I'm not going to fail them the way I had Olivia.

"Lark," I call out.

She turns and gives me a tight-lipped smile. *Yup, something's off.* I wave her over.

Ace asks Lily, "Lily how much has your dad paid you for all the bad words?"

She smiles, and her blue lips from the bite of cotton candy she just had hits me right in the gut. She looks happy today. "Welp, we spent a good portion of the curse purse money on Dottie."

Ace chuckles. "Ah yes, how is Dottie the cow?"

"We're letting her spend a little more time with Hal until we figure out her barn situation," I tell him as Lily moves to the other side of Ace and starts talking about the different type of hay they feed his horses, and if it's the same kind she should be feeding our new cow.

Movement of blond hair and a denim jacket that reads *This Ain't My First Rodeo* on the back pulls my attention away. My pulse kicks up a notch as I think about all the ways I've enjoyed her body.

Lark's Red Hot Chili Peppers T-shirt blocks my line of sight. "What do you want, Dad?" Lark says.

"Wanted to ask you something." I tip my head to the side, signaling her to sit next to me. "Two things, actually."

She lifts her feet onto the bleacher in front of us, her Converse sneakers decorated with swirls and drawings of animated food characters.

"I ordered the decorations for the sleepover party. They should get here any day now. You just need to tell me what kinds of snacks I should get, unless you want to come with me?"

She nods as she says, "Sure, I'll go with you."

Alright, the butter-her-up question didn't hit like I hoped it would.

"You're quiet today." I knock her knee with mine. "Maybe more than just today. Want to talk to me about anything?"

She leans forward, resting her crossed arms on her knees as she looks out to the crowded rodeo.

"You look at her a lot," she says, focused on the woman I was just staring at.

I hadn't planned on Faye being the reason for her being quieter, but I should have considered it. As I glance around our group, everyone is engaged in their own conversations, giving Lark and me a minute to ourselves.

"Does that bother you? Me looking at someone…or liking

someone new?" With sudden nerves, I glance at my daughter to gauge her reaction to that and if I have the backbone to say anything more.

"I don't know," she says, her eyebrows pinching like she's really thinking through it. "I think I got used to it just being the three of us. I hadn't thought about you looking at someone other than Mom before."

I wrap my arm around her shoulders and slide closer to her. "I can understand that."

"I mean, I know the women around town like you…" She casually smiles at me and makes a gagging face, which has me chuckling. "But you never look at them. Not like you do when you see Faye."

Such mature words for someone who can't possibly be growing at the pace she has been. "You're right, sweetheart. I have been looking at her."

"She is very pretty," Lark says as she watches Faye leaning on the paddock.

"She is." I smile, leaning closer to my daughter. "Smart too. And she thinks you guys are pretty cool."

She turns to look at me. "Well, obviously, if you said she was smart." Smiling, I can see so many thoughts passing through her head as her eyes look around my face. "You're the best person I know, Dad. I'm just trying to figure out how all this works."

I pull her in tighter to my side, trying to hold in the emotion of hearing her say that I'm the best person she knows. Jesus, sometimes they really can hit you in the chest. "How all of what works?"

She sighs. "Life."

A laugh pushes past my lips. "If you figure it out, will you give me the details?"

Resting her head against me, we let the joke linger as the rodeo clowns start making their way into the main gates.

"I don't know what's going to happen, Lark. Life has dealt us some shit, hasn't it?"

Lily hops forward in her seat, finger pointed right at me. "Curse purse, Dad."

Lark starts laughing, and I whisper to my oldest, "How did she hear that? Seriously?"

A few girls from Lark's softball team decide to relocate to the section of bleachers near the bull shoot. I squeeze her shoulder when I say, "You and your sister have my whole heart. Always have and always will. And I promise that whoever I look at won't change that."

Her eyes water as she nods in response, and mine do the same.

"I'm going to go with my friends. Is that okay?"

"Course it's okay." I smile as she stands up to weave her way over.

"And Dad," she says before she walks any farther. "She looks at you too. When you're not looking, she smiles when she looks at you."

I glance toward the paddocks again, and I don't know why that surprises me. I know Faye's attracted to me. It's impossible not to see and feel the chemistry between us, but hearing that observation from Lark hits differently.

A slap on my shoulder has me blinking. "What did I miss? Why do you look like that?" Hadley says as she drops down in the open seat. She snaps her fingers in front of me. "What happened? I thought Ace would stroke out before you, Linc."

I smoosh my hand on her cheek, and she starts laughing.

"Hadley Jean," Griz barks out. "You be nice over there."

In a monotone response, Ace says, "Yeah, Hadley, be nice."

"Now you want nice?" She tilts her head to the side. "You feeling soft in your old age, Daddy?"

Ace stands up like his ass is on fire and starts down the metal bleachers. "Quit it with the 'Daddy' shit, Hadley."

She smiles, wiggling her eyebrows. "Why? Does it give you a little poke in the panties?"

Griz is practically cackling into his paper coffee cup.

Ace looks down toward the metal gates, and I can see the moment he decides he's not just going to walk away this time. His gaze flicks to the row of women standing there for a second, ones lovingly referred to as buckle bunnies. Women who want a little fuckery with the rodeo boys. A few of them are watching the exchange as Ace looks back at Hadley.

I shake my head no. He's going to rile her up—something he rarely does, but right now, I think she's pushed him too far.

"Hadley," Ace says. "I'm not feeling much of anything when you say shit like that to me. It's just embarrassing how hard you try." I wince as he takes a step down before he adds, "And I might be older than you, sugar, but there isn't anything soft about me." He tips his head to the row of women he's started walking toward. "You can just ask a few of them tomorrow."

"Ah, fuck," I exhale. Leaning forward, elbows on my knees, I turn to Hadley.

Her face is bright red, and I'm not sure if she's on the verge of tears or about ready to scream her face off. "You need to go for a walk?"

She ignores me, staring at him. "Sugar?"

I snort a laugh. "Maybe he's had enough of your 'Daddy' nickname."

"But *sugar*? I mean, I would've settled for princess, or even darlin'." She leans back against the metal bars behind us, completely bewildered. At the top of the bleachers, there's a view of the entire stadium. "Wasn't that the name of one of his horses?"

Now that I think of it... "Yeah, his horse as a kid was named Sugar. Yep."

"Great, a dead horse. That's what I get, I suppose."

I nudge her knee. "You okay?"

"I'm always okay. It's you I'm worried about."

I look down past the gates and toward the food tents. A curvy blond with a cowboy hat, barely there dress, and purple cowgirl boots has my full attention. That and the built police officer next to her.

Hadley follows my line of sight. "I knew it."

"Knew what?" I ask her, trying to play off that she hasn't figured it out by now. That I'm a fucking goner for a woman who's a walking red flag.

"You and Faye. I thought maybe she was just new and shiny. And well, you're slut-erific. So..." She laughs out as I pinch the skin under her arm. "Ow, you dick!"

"Hadley, that's five bucks," Lily shouts from the far end of the row, having moved to sit with her Uncle Grant and Aunt Laney.

"Put it on my tab, Lily."

I laugh, shaking my head. "You know she does have a tab for you. It's on the fridge. You owe just over three-hundred dollars."

"What are they doing with all this money?"

"Fucking financing a small farm. Did I tell you Lark left me a flyer from Hooch's that was hanging on the bulletin board? Kittens. They want kittens to add to the mix."

"You try telling them no?" She raises her eyebrows, fully aware that's not my strong suit.

I give her a leveling glare. "You try telling them no. It's the one thing aside from the blond curls that they inherited from Olivia. Couldn't tell that woman no either. I swear, I'm raising con artists."

"It tracks."

A voice crackles over the loudspeaker. "LADIES AND GENTLEMEN, WELCOME TO FIASCO'S RODEO PRO-AM NIGHT! ALL PROCEEDS TONIGHT WILL BE DONATED…"

She knocks my knee. "You look like there's a lot working around in that big head of yours. And maybe it has nothing to do with the woman you can't stop looking at down there, but I know what a great sex glow looks like, Linc. And there's definitely some of that billowing off of you."

I glance at her smiling face, not giving anything away. I don't know what the hell I'm thinking right now. After that conversation with Lark, and now this one…

"Okay," Hadley says, lips pursing in thought. "Don't take this the wrong way."

"You realize when you say shit like that, it has the opposite effect."

She pops a piece of popcorn into her mouth. "Lincoln, you're very good at leading people to believe you're happy. But you forget that I know you. I remember what you looked like on your wedding day. I remember what you looked like when your girls were born. The same way I know when you're flirting with someone you're barely interested in. Years from now, I'll remember what you looked like when you were looking at Faye Calloway."

I glance at my best friend, feeling exactly what she means. "I slept with her."

She smacks my arm. "I knew it. Was it hot? I bet it was ridiculously hot."

"Shhh. Can you not be so loud right now," I say through a chuckle. Unable to stop smiling, I wipe my hand over my mouth and give Hadley a side-eye as I answer her question. "Yeah, it was fucking hot. I can't stop thinking about it. About her."

My gaze travels to Faye again. *What is she up to now?* It's like she senses my eyes on her because she turns her head, looking over her shoulder. It takes a second for her to find me in the crowd. When she does, the beautiful smile that kicks up on the side of her mouth makes my chest thump and my dick kick my thigh.

"I mean, just look at her."

Hadley hums, nodding with exaggeration. "Oh, I am. I have a big, fat crush on her. Don't tell Laney." My best friend has always been great at making me feel better while asking the obvious questions. "So is that all it is? A little crush and just a good time?"

I move my thumb against my empty ring finger. My life is complicated. I have kids and a whole world of love and heartbreak from before Faye ever stumbled into my life, but dammit, I like her in it now. I don't need to hide that from her. "Might be the best time I've ever had. I'm not sure I want to let something like that go."

Hadley leans into me and smiles, holding out her fist. I bump it, and then we follow with the finger hooks and elbow tap combination.

My attention wanders back to Faye, who's side-eyeing two women to her right, while Cortez chats with a bull rider. And then Faye snakes her hand toward Cortez's back pocket and plucks out his cell phone. My mouth drops open. "What is she…" I say quietly to myself. What the hell is she doing? She messes around with his phone for just a moment and then slides it back into his pocket. Cortez is none the wiser. This woman gets more interesting by the moment.

Laney calls out from the far end of the bleachers we're sitting on, pulling my attention. "Hey, Lincoln, mind if we take the girls for a sleepover tonight? I think Julep is missing Little Miss Kit."

"You're taking the dog too?"

She looks up at Grant, and he just kisses the top of her head. He calls out, "Yeah, Kit, too."

"You're good with skipping the after-party at the distillery, brother?"

Grant waves the question off like it's obvious. "The second that Lark mentioned something called a candy salad to Laney, I knew our plans were changing tonight." Then a smile pulls at his mouth. "I've got my girl. So yeah, I'm good."

I like how that sounds—*my girl*. Looking down the bleachers, I watch the beautiful woman who's breezed into my life all over again and think…*mine*.

Chapter 26

Faye

"Maggie, wait up," I say, calling after her.

She keeps walking like she doesn't hear me, hustling toward the stables where the horses are being groomed and shined up for their barrel races.

"You know women like that only gossip because their lives are boring as shit, right?"

She spins around on the ball of her foot, the hint of a smile starts to escape the corner of her mouth before she pulls it back. "What women?"

I have to smile at that.

"Maggie!" a woman shouts from the first horse stall. She waves furiously as Maggie starts heading her way. "Please tell me this is Faye."

I smile politely as we get closer. The woman has her hair in a tight French braid draped over her shoulder as she loops the hobble strap of her saddle. It doesn't take much to figure out she's barrel racing tonight. Between her dark blue jeans and a deep orange button-down shirt peppered with brand logos along the shoulder and chest, this woman is a part of the professional, not the amateur, circuit tonight.

"Faye, your sister told me a little bit about her cool older sister." She smiles at her, and the way they exchange glances, I wonder how much more of that was venting about me leaving. I also wonder how well they know each other.

I smile at the compliment. "It's nice to meet you."

Removing her riding glove, she extends a handshake. And instead of pressing for more details about who this woman is to Maggie, I smooth my hand down the side of her Appaloosa's neck. "She's beautiful."

"She sure is." She shifts a glance to Maggie before she says, "I saw Shelby Calloway ride when I was a kid. She leaned into those turns like nobody else. I'm still trying to figure out how she achieved some of the times she had." She shakes her head. "I can see you just dying to tell me what I'm doing wrong, Maggie."

"Shifting too early." Maggie kisses the horse's muzzle just below her noseband. "It's making her drop her shoulders when you're going into the turn."

I raise my eyebrows at the guidance and direction. The way she says it reminds me of our mom. Observation first and then a small rider adjustment that would make a world of difference.

"See, I knew you'd be able to tell me in a second what I was missing," the rider says with a smile to Maggie.

The bell dings from the ring, along with the announcer's voice calling out the names of the professional riders participating tonight.

As the rider hoists herself onto the horse, she says, "Faye, nice to meet you. Hope I see you both at the Foxx Bourbon after-party later."

"Maybe," Maggie says, stuffing her hands into her back pockets. And with a bright smile painted on her face, she watches as the barrel racer trots toward the arena space.

"You like her," I say, watching and studying the way she looks relaxed, maybe even content, for the first time since I've been here.

"I like the way she rides," Maggie says. "She's good. Maybe even better than Mom was." She blows out a breath. "Why did she ever stop riding?"

I answer her based on what I know. "I think she wanted to be more—a mother and a caregiver. It wasn't about breaking records in rodeos." I look at the way the horses move around the stadium, the bull riders swaggering in with their wide gait, and the crowd shouting and hollering for each and every one of them. "I think she was chasing a different kind of happy."

"She sure as shit didn't find it with Tullis," Maggie says as she waves toward another group of riders. "He was the one who said to her that the way she trained horses wasn't professional. Do you believe that shit? That some rich asshole had the audacity to tell her that?"

"I didn't know that." I feel a little lost at the idea of not knowing that detail.

She looks ahead toward the crowd in the main gate, where people hover around tables and wait in lines for food, like she's looking for someone. "Well," she exhales. "There's a lot you don't know."

"Maggie, I know you don't understand why I left."

She barks out a humorless laugh. "Faye, I know exactly why you left."

I search her face as we start walking, trying to pick up on any kind of tell that what she's going to say next isn't the actual truth.

"I wasn't supposed to be there, but I was," she tells me as her eyes meet mine.

"Where?" I ask, stopping in the center of the space. People navigate around us.

"Mom wasn't home when I stopped in to get my fake ID. I was supposed to meet some friends at the bar, and I left my fake at home." She shakes her head, and my stomach swirls with nerves. "I can't believe I'm telling you this in the middle of a packed fucking event." She pulls my arm so we move out of the fray of the crowd.

With one more glance over my shoulder, she says, "Mom came home with Tullis that night, but Waz was with them. It was the three of them in the kitchen."

I lean away to look at her. *How didn't I know this?*

"I sat on the top step and didn't move when I heard Waz shouting at Tullis first, then Mom. I knew she and Tullis were disagreeing about something regarding training, but this sounded different. Mom said that she knew what they were doing and that she couldn't allow it to happen any longer. But then she screamed. I heard something heavy hit the ground. And then it got quiet. So I kept as still and quiet as I could." Maggie's face looks flushed, emotions rising as she takes a deep breath before continuing. "The next thing I heard was Waz threatening her. He said, if she said a single word about any of it, she would end up just like his brother. And that it wouldn't be her choking on her own blood on the kitchen floor, it would be her daughters first. Then her."

My breath catches as I cover my mouth, my eyes watering.

I don't understand any of this—she has to have this wrong. There were no signs that anyone else had been there. And Mom didn't say anything when I showed up...

Maggie wipes the few tears that escaped from her cheek before she says, "I couldn't move. I didn't want to see what had made her scream like that, but I knew it was Tullis. I don't know how much time went by, but then you walked in. And well, you know how the rest of it went."

My head is spinning at hearing this. How could she have never said anything? What had been going on that would have warranted Waz killing his own brother and leaving a witness? "Did you ever talk—?"

But she shakes her head, tears falling before I can even finish the question.

"Mom didn't say a word. And I didn't know how to bring it up. When you left, she shut down for a while. But then she started seeing Griz, and she felt like Mom again. So I let it go. I tried to look ahead and not back." Maggie clears her throat. "She was happy—for a little while, she was happy. And then she was gone."

I blow out a breath, trying to digest what my sister's telling me. This wasn't how I saw any of it back then. There were no signs that anyone else had been there. Or maybe there were, but I could only see my mom. My stomach sinks, and I suddenly feel sick. I think about what this could mean for her, and everything I'm feeling swirls into a protective anger. "You know all of this and somehow you're working for him? For Waz and Wheeler? What kind of shit are you involved in that Waz would have beat you up like that, Maggie?"

She glares at me and crosses her arms across her chest. Sounding frustrated, she spits the angered tone right back at me. "You've been asking the wrong questions, Faye. You've been so dead set on being the savior and protector when you strolled back into town that you didn't stop and think that maybe there was more to all of this."

I rub at my wrist and try not to get defensive, because she's right. So I bite my tongue and give her the room to keep talking.

"I wasn't brought on for web design. They wanted me to apply my skill set for smart coding and numbers. Tweaking the off-track betting systems and manipulating the odds. I've been doing it for a while now." She shifts and crosses her arms, looking around first before she finishes. "It was a way to try to get the jump on Waz. I was funneling extra money into his account. I wanted it to look like he had been skimming off the top. Taking money from Wheeler Finch. But that asshole figured it out. I told him it was an error, but I'm pretty sure he didn't believe a word of it. Made it really clear that my 'mistake' wasn't going to happen again." She lets out a sigh, shaking her head and adds, "Now the rumors about horses being drugged and slaughtered—" Her eyes water at that. "There's a mess brewing, Faye." She wipes under her eyes and shakes off the softness of those emotions.

She's put herself in the middle of something dangerous. He's more than a creep or an asshole. Waz King is a monster. Killed his brother in cold blood. Threatened my mother. Now my sister. Smacking around a woman is easy for someone like that.

Maggie gives me a half smile, and something in that proud look makes me pause to think through the details. She isn't going to let that happen again and she needs help. And then it clicks.

"That's why you're talking to Cortez, isn't it?" I pull her closer to keep her from walking away. "Maggie, answer me."

But instead, she simply shrugs one shoulder. "More than one of us is capable of doing what we believe is the right thing, Faye."

As the air horn sounds, the crowd starts roaring. Maggie's friend waves her over from the side gate. When she turns her back to me, the part I don't understand comes blurting out, needing to know. "Maggie," I call out, and she looks over her shoulder at me. "What were they talking about? In the argument between Mom, Tullis, and Waz?"

She lifts her chin and says, "That's what I'm still trying to figure out."

Chapter 27

Faye

> FOXX:
>
> I see that Lily stole my phone. Thank you for entertaining her. I really need to change my password.

> FOXX:
>
> Where did you run off to, Peach?

> FOXX:
>
> Cortez asked if I saw you too. Ditched him again? Guy must be a lousy date.

> FOXX:
>
> I'll be at Ace's tonight after the rodeo—I want to see you.

I don't know how to respond. My mind has been consumed with what Maggie told me. I've been sitting in the bathroom stall for the entire length of the rodeo, feeling like I'm frozen. Cortez called me twice, but I wasn't sure how to deal with him. There has to be more, but what I do know is that if the FBI has targeted someone, it wouldn't just be Waz King. He's a package deal. And that has me thinking back to what Cortez said, *"A wider wingspan..."*

I've played every detail that I could remember from that night and not a single time has any part of me thought that anyone other than my mom stabbed Tullis. I'm spiraling with this and the fact that I just believed something entirely wrong for the past five years. It has my heart aching and my stomach in knots. So I tell him exactly what I want.

FAYE:

I want to see you too.

It might not be the entire town spread throughout the house and grounds of Ace and Griz Foxx's home, but it damn well feels like it. I smooth my palms over my belted T-shirt, which I've worn plenty of times on stage as a dress, but here it feels a bit short. Shedding my jacket at the door, I hand it off to their very formal coat check. My purple cowgirl boots aren't appropriate for a rodeo, but at an after-party chock-full of masculinity and women just itching for attention, you bet your ass I'm wearing my favorite boots.

Every room I walk past is full of cowboy hats, but I'm looking for very specific eye candy. Specifically one with glasses and a helluva dimple. In the sprawling kitchen, a larger huddle of bronco riders kicks back bourbon as Griz makes them laugh.

His thick white mustache is tilted up, enjoying every minute of entertaining these guys. I can see why my mom would have been attracted to him. He's a good-looking older man, but he's the kind of guy who commands a room. All charm and charisma—Lincoln has the same way about him.

When I push through the next room and toward the outdoor space, it feels like a montage of a party. Only this one is splashed with rodeo cowboys, bourbon, and just the hint of something sexy in the air. Like not a single person is leaving here without drinking something good and a promise to get fucked. Truthfully I want both of those things too.

Looking around, I spot Hadley perched on the outdoor bar, surrounded by a group of men. It makes me smile at the way she's so easily become a friend.

"That's her right now. Faye!" She waves her hand for me to come over. "This is by far the most talented—" Leaning into me, she says, "I'm sorry in advance for embarrassing you." Then she sits higher and finishes her sentence. "AND sexiest burlesque dancer I have ever laid eyes on. If you haven't been to Midnight Proof, this is your sign to see her before she leaves us."

My stomach sinks at the idea of ending my time there.

One of the guys calls out, "She's here now—how about a taste, darlin'?"

I've never understood why having someone's attention while I dance is so empowering, but it is. There are so many ways to paint it ugly if someone wanted to, but truthfully, it just feels good. I smile at the man who tossed out the idea. "I might need a drink first."

Hadley hands me a glass with one rock and at least two fingers of bourbon. The tawny color is a few shades lighter than the bottle I tasted with Lincoln, but I want a sip, nonetheless.

As I move to take it from her, an arm comes from behind me—the smell of oak and tart cherries has me ready to lean into the arms I already know wrap so beautifully around my body, even before he plucks my glass from my hand. Lincoln clears his throat before addressing the small crowd around the dimly lit patio. "Faye actually prefers another way to drink her bourbon."

I tilt my head back to see him, and dammit, I can't help but smile at what he's insinuating. The way his long sleeves are pushed up, revealing the start of his tattoo that dips just below the curve of his elbow, has me holding back a groan of appreciation. I know that tattoo. Where it curves and how it ends. The window panes that are beautiful and still unfinished and that hold so much meaning. Add how his dimples are pinned even as he goes in for a sip from the glass that was just mine, and I'm basically swooning.

I take it back before his lips reach the glass.

Out of the corner of my eye, I see one of the women who had been talking along the gates during the rodeo—the insinuation that if she wanted him, she could have him. *I don't think so. Right now, Lincoln Foxx is mine.*

I do well with an audience and I'm feeling bold—and slightly petty.

I step away from the heat of Lincoln's body, standing so close behind me, and turn to him, raising my glass. "This actually tastes like the 1910, but maybe you can tell me for sure, Foxx."

He smirks at me as I walk toward Hadley, still perched on the bar.

I give her a wink when I say, "I had a private tasting at the distillery..."

When I turn back to look at Lincoln, the way that man is

looking at me...it's like he wants to devour me and taste me all over again. I crook my finger at him in a *come hither* motion as I strut slowly toward the center of the room.

Hadley turns up the music and the girls from earlier shift their weight, leaning to get a better view of what's going on. *Oh, ladies, just you wait...*

When Lincoln follows my direction and comes closer, he leans into my space and, just below my ear, whispers, "You're so fucking sexy right now. Are you about to show all these people that I'm yours, Peach?"

It's a resounding yes from the center of my chest to the tips of my fingers. I peer back and move my head up and down slowly, letting him know that's *exactly* what I'm about to do.

"Do you trust me?" I ask, a little louder.

He chuckles, a sound I feel between my legs, and looks around the space. "Yeah, Peach, I do."

I don't know what I was expecting him to say, but his affirmation urges me on. I tilt my chin up and smirk at him before I say, "Good. On your knees, Foxx."

The hoots and hollers that direction gets from around the space makes me bite my lip to hold back a wide smile. And even then, a small one still escapes.

Hadley whistles and throws a pillow from the bar stool, nailing him right in his face, making him bark out a laugh.

He's so much taller than I am that even as he lowers to one knee and then the other, he's just shy of eye level with me. "If you all want a burlesque show, then you can come to Midnight Proof and be a paying customer. But right now"—I can't help the smile that teases out as I look down at Lincoln; he watches me as I address the little audience we've gathered—"we're at Foxx Bourbon. And I've had the luxury of a master distiller showing me exactly how best to appreciate good bourbon."

His eyes lock with mine, and he huffs out a laugh, knowing exactly what I'm planning.

"Tilt the glass and take note of the color." I tilt my glass into the light from the fire tables surrounding the space. "Then you're going to want to give it a nice little Kentucky chew." Taking a small sip, I swirl it around my mouth. A few whistles sing out from the small crowd as his hands run up the backs of my thighs and settle just beneath the hem of my dress, leaving delicious goosebumps behind.

I erase whatever space is left between us as I nudge the lower half of my body into his chest, his hands dragging up and down the backs of my thighs, pulling me in and encouraging me to get even closer. I take a breath through my nose and swallow. "Let her coat your mouth, maybe even enjoy that burn a little bit before she feels ready to slide down your throat."

The mood shifts from rowdy conversation to the kind of sexy I get off on. I glance at the two women who had no problem talking about all the things they want to do with this man, and I smile at their wide eyes.

I let my eyes flit from them down to him. "Ready for your tasting, Foxx?"

His dimples peek out from his quick smile, but he doesn't say anything. Instead, he tilts his head back just as I slide my hand behind his neck. My fingers graze his hairline, moving them high enough to tangle and find a grip. I tilt the glass against my lips, drain what's left of the bourbon, then tip his head back just how I want it.

His arms hug around my thighs as the spice and heat hit my tongue, and then his mouth opens for me just as I tilt forward.

Erasing the space between our lips, I give him exactly what I promised—a taste of bourbon. But he doesn't stop the momentum. His plush, wet lips meet mine, and it lights every fuse in my body. I ignore the drips that escape down my chin, and the crowd around us that was quiet mere moments before our lips connected erupts in hoots and whistles. I'm lost in the way he didn't shy away from making a scene. And the fact that this will have plenty of people talking about it long after we leave.

He swallows down every drop I give him and then makes sure not a single person misinterprets what we're doing together. His tongue plays with mine as he tilts his head back and pulls me as tightly against his kneeling body as possible.

It's why I don't expect him to stand so quickly and hoist me up and over his shoulder. A screaming laugh escapes my mouth as he says, "If you'll excuse us." Then he's walking us through the house and right out the front door. I barely catch who we walk by, but I don't miss the way Maggie stares at the spectacle. She was talking with Griz and the barrel racer from earlier. I hear Griz call out, "'Bout damn time!"

Lincoln tilts his chin to Griz and mumbles under his breath, "Old man thinks he's a damn matchmaker."

He hustles down the porch stairs, and I can't help but laugh as he slaps my ass when his boots hit the pavement. "You can put me down now."

"Not a fucking chance," he says as he opens the passenger door to his Jeep. Sliding me from his shoulder, down his chest, he kisses my lips, speaking against them. "Do you know how fucking hot it was to be claimed like that?" His fingers dive into my hair, and he devours my mouth in a way that shows me exactly how it made him feel. A way that has my chest fluttering and knees weakening. Pulling back, his forehead rests against mine as he grinds into me, with my legs half wrapped around him as I'm perched on the seat of his truck. "Eight minutes."

"What happens in eight minutes?" I smile against his lips as I take another kiss.

"Until I'll have you in my bed, grinding your pussy on my face and reminding me what my new favorite thing tastes like."

I hum out my approval and sit back in the passenger seat as he closes my door and hustles to his side, throwing the Jeep in reverse and hauling out of the driveway.

He glances at me as he wraps his hand around my thigh, spreading my legs. "I would have thought your favorite thing was bourbon," I say playfully. I've had barely anything to drink, yet I feel dazed by this. The proximity of him, the way he grips me, looks at me, craves me so palpably.

"Then you haven't been paying attention, Peach." His tongue wets his lower lip, one arm draped on the steering wheel, the other holding on to me like he can't not touch right now. "You know I can't stop thinking about you?"

I turn my body slightly so my back is pressing against the passenger door, making my dress ride high as I spread my legs open for him. "And what are you thinking about when you do?"

He does a double take and laughs like he can't believe what's about to happen. "Oh Peach, are you going to give me a private show?"

Without thinking, I let the words fall from my lips. "I'll give you anything you want, Foxx. You just have to ask."

"And if I ask for more?" His eyes flick to me, then the road, and back again.

My stomach swoops. The way I feel when I'm with him isn't something I'm ready to define. I just know he's who I want to be with tonight. Maybe longer than that.

"You're looking at me like that's a complicated question, Peach."

"You know it is. This…is complicated. You have a whole life with kids and…" I look around the cab for a second as a wave of vulnerability washes over me. "You have a dog and a cow, for fuck's sake. I don't even have an apartment that's mine. More sounds—"

I'm cut off as he jerks the wheel and pulls over to the side of the road, unbuckling his seat belt and sliding closer. His hands move over the tops of my legs and then glide under my thighs to yank me toward him as I gasp. "I haven't wanted anyone the way I want you. It's reckless, and I don't have an explanation about why or how. I just know that I like the way you make me feel."

"How do I make you feel?" I cover my eyes as soon as I say it, because I'm suddenly embarrassed for being this woman—overeager for validation and pushy for more than he's ready to give.

But he stops me, pulling my hand away and tilting my chin up to look at him. The blue lights from the dashboard are dim, but he smiles at me. It's sweet, and something about it is different from the other smiles he's given me. "Look at me."

I do as he asks.

"You make me feel like I don't need to pretend when I'm around you. That I can be exactly who I am without being anything other than a man infatuated with a beautiful woman."

"Infatuated?" I say teasingly, biting the inside of my lip to hold back some of my smile.

He nods but doesn't stop there. Moving my hair behind my ear, he cuffs the strands around it gently. "I want a woman who has no agenda other than to help the people she loves. I want to be the kind of man who's good enough for a woman like that."

I lean my head to the side, letting it rest on the leather seat. "You just went there."

"Yeah. I just went there." He smiles confidently. "You scared yet?"

"Since the moment you called me Peach," I answer truthfully. It's really hard not to let butterflies overrun my system when he's looking at me like this—his flirty dimple out and eyes searching mine—to tell him I want him the same way that he wants me.

"I meant what I said. I'm not the same after having you. But if it's too much, I'll understand. I have two amazing kids. And apparently, animals now," he says jokingly. "A wise-ass grandfather. Brothers who I wouldn't have survived without. A town that thinks we're cursed—which is another fucking hurdle that I'm not sure I'm entirely over. And a bourbon business that's draining and so *fucking* hard sometimes…but it defines everything about me."

"Not everything," I whisper. I smile as I make a choice. "You're intensely wonderful with your tongue…"

He leans back with slightly narrowed eyes, knowing that's as far as I'll go right now. I'm not ready to tell him what I want. Truthfully, I don't know. "And?" he teases.

"And your hands." I run my fingers along my neck. "Your fingers, and the way you know exactly what'll make me feel good. Just thinking about all the ways you can play with me…"

He leans forward and wraps his hand behind me, pulling me toward his lips so he can kiss me. It's not sweet or soft. There's nothing hesitant about it. His tongue slides along mine, and I feel it across my skin and straight down to my pussy. But instead of more, he pulls back with a panted breath, then rights himself in the driver's seat. "You better tell me you want me, Peach."

"Yeah, Foxx. I want you."

Pulling into the lane, he floors it. "Good. Now pull your panties aside and let me see how much."

I have to smile at that direction. The man can go from serious to sexy in a blink. In one breath, telling me I've changed him, and in the next, accepting where I'm at with whatever it is we're doing. Maybe it's the fact that he's older, or that he's had an entire life before I ever came into it, but I like it.

The shiver his words create works up my arms, and I do what he asks once more, baring myself to him.

He basically growls, "Give me a taste."

"You're dirty, Foxx," I say, smiling and dragging two fingers through my pussy lips.

"Yeah, but you like getting messy for me, don't you, Peach?"

I move so that I can give him what he's demanded. Kneeling on the seat, I take my wet fingers and bring them to his mouth, but when he goes to open, I pull them away, taunting. I tsk, and instead of letting him lick them clean, I swipe them across his lower lip.

But before I can play anymore, he grabs my wrist and pulls my fingers into his mouth. The way he hums and swipes his tongue across the pads of my skin has my body craving more and winding tighter toward what's coming.

"Fuck," he groans. He pulls the middle seat belt strap and buckles me in before he floors it down the road I grew up on. It's only another minute or so before he's pulling into the driveway and circling around the front of his truck, swinging my door open and holding his hand out for me.

"Where are the girls?" I hadn't thought about the fact that they would be here.

He stops me in the doorway and kisses me—long enough that I feel a little dizzy and short enough that it leaves me wanting more. When he pulls away, he weaves his fingers with mine and says, "Grant and Laney took them and Kit tonight."

We move inside and he guides me past the stairs, through the living room, and down the hall toward a guest suite on the ground floor. Flipping the lights, he dims them just a pinch and hands me his phone. "Tonight, the only thing I get to think about and take care of is you."

He reaches behind his head and pulls at the collar of his shirt, whipping it off and tossing it aside. A shirtless Lincoln Foxx sizing up what he wants from me as he undoes his belt buckle is a sight I'll never forget.

"Whatever I want?" he asks, reiterating what I had promised. Not a single part of me has any interest in taking that back. So I lean against the door as he walks toward the bed, sitting on the edge, legs spread wide.

"Whatever you want."

Chapter 28

Lincoln

"Tease me," I say, widening my legs and leaning back on extended arms. A sexy smile plays across her lips as if she can't wait to do exactly that. She tips her hip to the right and so effortlessly rolls to the left, already drawing me in like the siren she is. As I run my tongue along my lip, I can still taste her there. It's taking all my restraint to wait for her to come to me.

"You look hungry, Foxx," she says while she steps out of her boots.

My eyes roam around her body, from her now bare feet up the length of her toned legs and full thighs as she drags the hem of her dress up to those hips. "Starved, baby."

Her movements stutter for a breath when I call her that.

"Show me," she says as she pulls the dress up and over her breasts and tosses it aside. Looking down at my lap, she tips her chin toward me. "Show me what I'm teasing."

I shift my weight and use one hand to unbuckle my belt,

tugging the leather out of its notch, and then pull open the button to unzip my jeans. My cock has been hard since she put me on my knees at the party. And right now, he's leaking eagerly for her attention. "Look at you—so fucking beautiful. Show me where you want my mouth," I say, fixated on her tits.

She gives me a coy look, biting her lip and trailing her fingers up her center to circle around the sheer pink bra she's wearing. "I want you here." Her nipples are puffy and looking more than ready to be licked and sucked. Reaching behind her back, she flicks open the clasp and lets the garment fall down her arms and to the floor. "Here."

She turns her body so I can see the curvature of her back and draws her fingers over her shoulder, up her neck, and just below her jaw. "I want your mouth and teeth dragging along here."

I'm mesmerized by her, nodding dumbly. My body is tuned in to any small move she makes and every inch she touches, and it feels like I'm strung tight by a live wire.

Looping her fingers into the band of her thong next, she bends at the waist as she rolls it down her thighs and to the floor. Her fingers draw a path up the backs of her thighs, toward the crease of her ass, and along each cheek as she turns her body back to face me. "I want your mouth and your tongue here first." She follows the same lines of where her panties sat along each hip, then to her apex as she moves two fingers down her center, sighing when she slides them past her clit. Knowing how wet she already is has me swallowing a groan. "Then you're going to fuck me slowly. Deeply. Right here."

I sit up as she comes closer. "Your body," I hum as she reaches me and drags her fingers through my hair. "The way you look at me…" I rest my forehead against her as she stands above me. "I can't explain how good it feels. And when you touch me…"

She drags her fingers from the nape of my neck and up to the front of my hair as I tilt my head back to look at her. "When I touch you…"

"It feels like I'm important. To you. In that moment. I've never been so aware of the simplest touch. The way you taste, how you smell, and then the sight of you wanting me." I shake my head and smile.

She lowers to her knees and looks up at me through those pretty dark lashes. Tucking her fingers into the waist of my boxer briefs, she urges me to lift, pulling them down my thighs and off. "I'm going to need you in my mouth when you tell me I'm pretty."

"Oh fuck," I breathe out just as she wraps her hand around my cock to guide it past her lips and along her tongue. I tilt my head back at how fucking wet and warm her mouth feels, how welcoming. Playing with the head of my cock, her tongue draws pathways before her lips wrap around me again and she takes me into her throat.

Moaning, I drag my fingers into her hair and let them tangle. I pull just enough to keep time with the way she moves up and down my length. "You look so fucking pretty. Your lips wrap around me so tight, and that tongue isn't missing a single inch."

She hums at the praise.

One hand follows her mouth, while the other digs her fingers into my thigh. She swallows and moans around me, sucking me so well that I'm lost in the warmth and wetness of her perfect mouth. It's pulling me too quickly to the edge.

"Fuck, this feels too good." I gasp as she flexes her hand

and swallows, her throat constricting around me. When she pulls back, her chest heaves for breath and she looks up at me in a daze, like she's been lost in this moment as much as I have.

"Come here, I need to taste how wet you are from sucking me off," I say as I pull her up and move her to the bed.

She lets out a small laugh as I lay her back and kiss down her body. "Everything, especially my pussy, tingles right now because of y—" She doesn't finish her thought.

A labored sigh and hum of approval escapes as I swipe my tongue along her slit. Fucking soaked. I flatten my tongue and drag it back up, making sure not to leave anything behind. When her hips jolt as I swipe along her clit, I pin them down and suck on that perfect little spot that forces a raspy moan from her throat. I can't help but smile against her as she follows it up with, "Lincoln *fuucckKING* Foxx."

"Let's make sure I don't miss anywhere," I say as I lick up her center, leaving a trail of kisses as my lips follow every line she traced along her skin when she stripped for me. From the center of her chest and around each of her tits, across the swell of each, and then pulling her nipple into my mouth and sucking. She's writhing as I move back up her body and nuzzle into her neck. "This is where you wanted me, right?"

She nods, tilting her chin up to make space for me as she breathes out, "Everywhere…"

I run my teeth along her shoulder, giving her a bite that has her humming, before I move onto my knees so I can flip her to her stomach. She gasps a laugh, looking over her shoulder to watch my fingers ghost along her back as I move farther down the bed. Hovering just off to the side, I lick my way up the back of her thigh, relishing how she trembles. My cock brushes against her skin, and it's almost painful how hard and ready I am for her.

"I've wanted to lick right here since that video you accidentally sent me," I tell her just as I swipe my lips first, and then my tongue, along that perfect crease where her thigh meets her ass. *So fucking good.* She moans as I slap her ass cheek and then grip it nice and tight.

"Foxx," she breathes out. With my guidance, she rolls her body to the side, and I angle mine behind her. Pushing her legs apart, I spread her pussy so I can look at exactly where I want to be. She's dripping, her core shiny with arousal. I rub the head of my cock along her lips and then slide into her slowly, inch by inch. Her back arches to take more of me, whimpering at the stretch when I'm fully seated inside her.

"That's it. Tip your ass back and let me fuck you, baby."

Draping her leg over mine, she opens herself up just enough so I can fuck her deeper. My fingers play along her clit in rhythm with the way our hips meet with every thrust and roll. And in seconds, her body tenses and her chest stops heaving as she holds her breath, readying to fall over the edge and come for me.

"Don't stop," she whispers just as her orgasm flows over her, making her entire body jerk forward and shake as she clenches around me.

"The sounds you make when you come…" I groan, barely hanging on.

She smiles at my words, eyes closed and hair messy. "I'm going to need another one," I tell her as I shift our bodies so I can watch her face this time when she comes. With her beneath me, I nudge her legs wider and slide back into her, kissing her shoulder as I do.

"Oh, holy shit, Foxx," she says on a gasp as I glide in deep and bottom out. I give her a second to adjust to me in this position.

"I'll go slow," I say as she tips her chin up to kiss me. I want to give her another one, so I roll my hips slow, moving deeper with every thrust. It's sweaty and sexy and feels so fucking good that within seconds, her pussy grips me tight and pulses around me, drawing out a guttural moan from my lips. My orgasm builds from the tips of my limbs to the edges of my skin and lingers for the briefest moment before crashing through me until I can't catch my breath.

Wetness and warmth flood her and she moans out the most beautiful sound of pleasure. It's the single most intimate and vulnerable moment of my life with her eyes focused on mine, her hands gripping me so tightly, and the quickened breaths that I can't seem to slow. Tears well in her eyes as she looks at me, leaning up and searching out a kiss that I would never deny her. Our lips and tongues move as if we're sealing whatever this is between us. A confirmation of perfection.

"That was—" she says, and the only thing I can do is kiss her. Answer her in the only possible way, because that wasn't just sex. It shifted everything I've been thinking and instead made it an absolute.

We're a quiet, tangled, and sweaty mess of limbs as we lie wrapped up in each other, coming down from our high, and it isn't until I hear her giggle that I open my eyes.

"You were smiling with your eyes closed," she says as she drags her finger over my nose and along my lips.

I grip her fingers and kiss them before I say, "You've rendered me stupid. Maybe slightly delirious too." On shaky legs, I get up and grab a cloth from the bathroom, a realization hitting me. "We didn't use a condom that time."

She sits up on her elbows, looking down at her body. "I am very much not concerned. Birth control since I turned eighteen, and it's been…" Her eyes meet mine when she confesses, "Aside from you. I have only ever been with one other person."

That has me surprised, but I can't say I'm unhappy about it. "Is it crazy of me to hate the other guy?"

She laughs as I wipe along her thighs. "You definitely hate the other guy."

Closing her eyes, her face pinches. "I didn't have any big plans about my virginity, just that I hadn't rushed to lose it, and then all of a sudden, I was in my twenties. I was in the police academy and my partner was very flirty. And we just did it. A couple times, but I didn't want more."

"Please tell me your partner wasn't Cortez." My eyes narrow on hers.

"My partner wasn't Cortez?" she says, her voice kicking up at the end.

"Yeah, I fucking hate him," I say as she gets up and kisses my lips before moving into the bathroom. I lie back and prop my head along the pillows and think about how I have no right to be jealous of someone in her past—not when I have one too.

She walks back into the room and plucks her dress from the floor, but before she can even think about putting it on, I sit up and pull her toward me. "You're not going anywhere."

"I wasn't paying attention when we got here, obviously, but this isn't your room."

"It's the guest suite. But it is my room. I don't use the primary any longer—" And just as I say it, I realize how much gossip she's heard, but she doesn't truly know what went on the night that Olivia died or the conversation I had been reeling about just before I ran into her on the edge of the cornfield.

Chapter 29

Faye

He searches my face. The most I know is that Olivia died the same night that I kissed and blackmailed him. It was the only thing that Fiasco had talked about those following days after I buried a body—Olivia Foxx collapsing in her kitchen of a brain aneurysm. She was too young, too full of life, and all of it happened without warning. That's what death always felt like to me.

I hate that night for so many reasons, and I hate it even more for how much it hurt him.

"Do you know the first time I saw you, you were demolishing a peach?" he asks as he brushes his fingers across his face to show exactly what he means by demolish.

I bark out a laugh and settle in next to him.

"You either didn't give a shit or it was just that good. And I remember thinking that I wanted to be like that. Messy and not giving a single shit about the cleanup... Don't take that wrong. It was not dirty or sexual in any way. I was just impressed." He reaches out and runs a finger along the knuckles of my hand. A simple touch in a place that shouldn't matter, but the sweetness of it made me want him all over again. "It was the first farmer's market of the summer and a few weeks before I ran into you in that cornfield."

"I remember that farmer's market." I smile fondly. "And those peaches. That was a couple weeks shy from my move back home from Frankfort. I came to celebrate Maggie's twentieth birthday. We demolished the peach cobbler my mom made from those peaches. Then we fell asleep on the porch after far too many shots."

His smile doesn't reach the corners of his eyes or pull out his dimples. "My life back then felt really…" He stares at the path he keeps drawing along my skin. "It wasn't all bad. I just hadn't ever failed at anything the way I failed at the one thing I promised I'd do."

I shift my body closer, but it's not close enough for him, so he grabs under my thighs and drapes me on top of him. We let a little bit of silence settle between us.

"What did you promise?" I ask. As I run my fingers from the front of his hairline and back, his eyes close.

"That I'd love my wife. Through everything. I would love her. And I didn't do that. Not well enough, at least."

My brow furrows at that.

"She slept with someone else," he admits, and my fingers stop their motion. "Maybe more than just one; she wasn't clear about that. Only that she was moving on with her life. And that meant without me."

I hadn't expected him to say that. Anyone who knew Lincoln and Olivia Foxx would have told you they were in love and happy.

His eyes meet my sad ones, and he moves my hand so I keep

doing what I had been. When I see the comfort it gives him, something about it gives me comfort too.

"We had been short with each other. A lot. After Lily was born, it felt like she hated me. Neither of us did anything right, according to the other. There were blips of us being happy, but—" Shaking his head, he draws small lines across the top of my hand and around my wrist. "I thought it was just a bad patch. That we needed to grow through it. But I backed off. Started working longer hours. I didn't make us a priority. I did the things I knew I could do right—making bourbon, being a dad, building out our business. But in hindsight, it was the wrong call. She said, 'This is broken. We're broken. And I have no desire to fix it. I stopped loving you a long time ago.' I'll never forget it, because it was one of the last things she said to me."

I tip his chin up to look at me, my heart in my throat. "Lincoln, I'm so sorry. I didn't know."

"Nobody knows, other than Hadley, and now you." He sucks in a breath. "It felt wrong to air that to the world when she had died so unexpectedly. She was so young, and it tears me up that she left this world unhappy with her life. I *hate* that. But I was so fucking mad at her and at myself for having to pretend I was the loving husband in mourning. I wasn't; I was still angry with her. And I hate that my girls have to miss her."

"If I knew—"

But he cuts me off. "I fucking hated that you pushed me that night, putting me in another impossible situation." His eyes glaze over with tears he blinks back. "Things between us had been over—she wanted a clean break, and then she died. And I've been paralyzed by what that meant for a long time."

I rest my forehead on his and hold him a little tighter. "I'm so sorry."

He leans into me when he says, "I can't lose any more people, Faye. Women do not survive after loving one of us. Grant lost Del's daughter, Fiona, Griz lost my nana, then Shelby. Ace won't go anywhere near a relationship, casual or otherwise…"

"Grant and Laney?" I ask.

"I'm nervous that one day I'll get a call that she's gone too." He drags his hand through his hair, pushing out a harsh breath. "And I feel like a hypocrite because I told my brother to stop holding back, but now that I found…" His eyes lock onto mine, and I know what he's thinking.

"Don't do that to yourself," I say, stopping him. "You are so many things to so many people. A dad, a grandson, brother, friend—and that's just in your personal life. Those are a lot of places where you need to step up and be the strong one. I've been trying to step up and be that my entire life. It's hard every single day. And you do it so effortlessly too." I run my fingers along his hairline and down toward the back of his neck. "There's nothing hypocritical about loving the people in your life. You can worry about what will happen, or you can choose to enjoy people while they're with you."

Nodding subtly, he leans into the way I'm touching him. There are parts of this man that feel so much like me, but the way he can make the people around him feel so good and cared for without it seeming like much effort at all has me not wanting to leave his side. And as we lie together, I let myself do exactly what I just told him and enjoy what I have with Lincoln Foxx while I can.

The thunder turns into a low rumble. A constant hum that never seems to end.

I blink my eyes open, and a wet nose surrounded by black-and-brown fur rests on the edge of the bed, inches from my face. "Good morning, Kit." Growls turn into whines as her tail thwaps on the hardwood floor below her. "Where's Lincoln?" I whisper.

She jumps onto the bed as an answer, which would be more of an issue if Lincoln was sleeping next to me. The drapes have been pulled shut, but they still let in enough light to let me know the day has begun. Our clothes from last night are still thrown around the floor and I am very naked under these sheets. Dropping my head back to the pillow, I pet Kit as I remember last night and how it feels to be wrapped up in Lincoln. I can't stop the smile I have, looking up at the vaulted ceiling and noticing the colors of the wooden beams. I'm relieved to be in here and not in a room he'd shared with his wife. He's already had so many firsts in his life that I haven't had yet—love, marriage, building a family. It's a dangerous thought spiral to run down if I let myself.

Kit lets out another growl. "Yes, I need to get up. How did you get in here anyway?"

I spend a minute combing my fingers through my hair and washing the leftover makeup off my face. After tossing on a white Foxx Bourbon T-shirt, I swish with the mouthwash on the counter and listen at the door for a moment, but the only thing I can hear is a teakettle whistling and the sound of something being fried in a pan.

There's plenty I left unsaid last night, but a part of me feels so good. *Happy.*

I didn't tell him the details that Maggie shared with me. What she saw. I couldn't put him or his girls in any more danger, and if he knew more, I felt like I would be. He's the kind of man to stop at nothing to protect the ones he loves, and selfishly, I'm not ready for him to either push me away, or worse, do something he shouldn't, like confront Waz.

"What does that mean, 'She's your friend'?" Lily asks. I stop short. I hadn't heard anyone. *Shit.* "She's my friend too, right?"

Lark pipes in, "Yeah, but Dad is going to suck face with her too."

I slap my hand over my mouth, trying to hold in my laugh.

"Ew, why? Do you mean kiss her?" Lily says. "Dad, is she a kissing friend like Jordan?"

Lincoln says, "Yes—Wait, who the fuck is Jordan?"

"Curse purse," the girls say in unison.

I inch forward to see if there's an easy path out of here. Nope. Instead, I watch Lincoln in a pair of those thin cotton pants, black this time, hanging low on his hips. He's in a cutoff shirt and a black baseball hat turned backward as he serves out scrambled eggs from a pan. I swallow and feel my cheeks heat instantly at the sight.

"It's been me and you two for a while now. And I'm not saying that's going to change, but I like Faye. I'd like to spend more time with her, and I want to make sure you're both okay with that," he says.

"What if we weren't?" Lark asks.

I lean against the hallway wall and struggle to hear his response. "Then I would have to see if she'd wait for me until you were."

It isn't the answer I was expecting, and part of me wants to throw my fist up in the air, while the other is terrified that he's serious.

"Well, I think she's amazing. And I think you should kiss her as much as you want, Dad," Lily says as she chews on something.

A fork clatters against the plate like someone dropped it, and I quickly try to decide if I should listen to any more. This isn't meant for me to hear. This is for them.

"Lark, you saw the beauty mark. It's not a coincidence," Lily says and then whispers something else I can't make out.

The tapping of nails hitting the hardwood gets louder as Kit turns the corner and is headed right for me, barking like she's tattling on my presence. I raise my finger in front of my lips as if the dog has any idea what that means. Instead, she sits in front of me and starts whining.

"Good morning," Lincoln says with a smile, peering into the hall.

"Hi," I whisper, eyes wide as I gesture to his girls. "Should I crawl out the window or something?"

He holds out his hand and then leans in to grab mine. "Come on. I can't keep this a secret from them."

And just hearing it makes me realize that I'm completely in over my head with a man like this. But instead of holding back and pushing him away, I hold on to him.

"Look who I found creeping in the hallway with Kit," he says.

The dog barks at hearing her name. Lily waves, and Lark says, "Hi, Faye."

It's a better response than I was expecting after listening to that exchange. "Hi, girls. Thanks for letting me crash your breakfast party."

Lincoln kisses the top of my head and ushers me over to the end of the counter. He tosses a dish towel over his shoulder and grabs the pan of eggs. "Alright, I've got scrambled eggs. Those two ate all the bacon, but…" He turns and grabs a bowl. "Avocado. Here's the hot sauce. And we have strawberries and some figs as well."

And while I'm wildly impressed by any kind of breakfast being made for me, it's actually the coffee mug and pint glass in front of me that catches me by surprise.

"And I didn't know how you were feeling this morning, so I did a black coffee, hot—like mine. And an iced coffee with sweetened condensed milk and cinnamon." Grabbing a straw from the drawer in front of him, he puts it in the iced coffee cup. "I had to call my sister-in-law to ask what the hell something iced and sweet was, and we came up with this."

Is he serious?

"Are you okay?" Lily asks from my side. "Dad, is she okay?"

I'm having an internal hip-hop dance party regarding the gesture her father just made. It feels too nice to be surprised by someone like this. I focus on the blue eyes watching me behind his black-rimmed glasses and get distracted by the dimples that peek out as a knowing smile takes over his face. He *knows* he did good.

"Which one are you feeling today?"

"Black would have been just fine, but I'm thinking I could go for something sweet." I take a sip, and he gives me a wink. I eat the breakfast he made for all of us, feeling oddly comfortable, and he chats with Lily about her newest playlist.

"Those blow-up disco balls look like fun. Are you guys having a party?" I ask as I look across the room and see a pile of decorations in their packages, from confetti poppers to glitter streamers.

"My birthday is this weekend, but tonight is my sleepover party," Lark answers. "It's my first one and Dad went all out. He even said yes to individual tents for all of us."

It's impossible not to smile at her excitement. And the fact that she's telling me about it.

"I got special pajamas for it too," Lily shares, but Lark shuts that down.

"Dad, does Lily really have to be here for the whole thing? It's not fair. I just want to have my friends and not her."

Lily pushes her plate forward and crosses her arms. "You're my big sister, why can't I be excited about your birthday?" Hopping off her chair with a huff, she storms upstairs.

Lincoln looks at his oldest with the definition of a "dad glare," and then glances at me as I'm taking a bite of sliced fig.

"Lark," he grits out. "That really was mean. I told you I was going to keep her busy for most of the party so you had time with your friends, but you can't say that to her. She thinks you're the coolest person to ever exist."

Lark tilts her head back and lets out a dramatic sigh. "Fine."

"I wouldn't mind some company later today. If Lily's free, I was thinking it might be nice to have a tour around Fiasco from a local."

Before Lincoln can even answer whether that's a good idea, Lily comes charging down the stairs, practically running Lark over in the process. "Yes, I'll do it. Can I go with Faye, Dad? Please. Please."

He points at Lily, eyes narrowed with suspicion. "We're going to talk about Jordan."

She gives him a wide-eyed look and shakes her head. "Faye, please tell my dad that I'm nine. I do not have kissing friends… yet."

I laugh out, "I am just an observer here." Then when he turns around, still listening, I stage-whisper to her, "But I'm not against hearing all about it."

Chapter 30

Lincoln

"Have you figured out what you're doing with your specialty bourbon yet?" Griz asks with his arms crossed, preparing to give me his opinion on what I should consider.

"Not yet," I tell him. "Ace shot down my idea."

Kit scratches at my leg with her two front paws. Boosting her onto my lap, I scratch under her neck. "Lark, I think Kit needs to go for a walk."

Griz watches on and adds, "You realize that is not a lapdog?" And he's right. The dog has paws the size of my palm and she's nowhere near the end of growing.

"Kit, tell your great-grandpa that you can be whatever you want to be. And to get off my back about the bourbon blend," I repeat in a low, mocking voice. The dog looks up at me, her tongue hanging from her mouth as if she's smiling. She barks out as if to answer.

"Kit, tell your dad that it's my job to be overly judgmental and pushy," Griz says as he scribbles away at his crossword puzzle.

Ignoring my suggestion to take Kit for a walk, Lark interjects from the living room, "Dad, we're missing a tent." I lean back in my chair and look out into the sea of single-person tents draped in white Christmas lights that line the entirety of our open living room.

Griz joins me in surveying the sea of blankets, twinkling lights, and tents that have thrown up all over my house. "This looks like a good time."

"It took three trips to the hardware store to get enough lights for the drill sergeant over there to approve." I nod to Lark, and she rolls her eyes like I'm being dramatic.

"Dad, I'm turning twelve, and I've never had a sleepover with friends. I want it to be perfect."

Griz looks around the room, his hands on his hips. "I still don't understand why there are tents inside."

Lark takes a breath from blowing up a plastic disco ball, but I answer for her. "Aesthetic, Griz. It's all about the aesthetic." She lets out a relieved exhale before she goes back to blowing up the disco ball.

I toe off my boots and wade through the sleeping bag pile and the new fluffy blankets Lark begged and pleaded to order. Sitting next to her, I help tie off the white tent flap on the tenth assembled tent. "You know, I think the aesthetic you're making is pretty amazing," I tell Lark, but she still looks unsure.

"You're not a twelve-year-old girl with unrealistic expectations for a Foxx birthday party."

"What can I do to make this better?"

She doesn't say anything at first. Her fingers loop into the twinkling fairy lights around the post of the tent she's been working on. It's not until I notice that she's holding back tears that are welled up in her eyes that I realize something is wrong. *Shit.*

"Mom would have made it really pretty. She was good at making things pretty." Her voice breaks. She sits down, her legs crisscrossed as she stares at her fingernails.

I push down my emotions in this moment—the way hearing that makes me feel like I've messed up. Like I'm not enough for my girls. And they'd be right. Enough would be their mother still alive. But I can't change that simple, awful reality. Just like I know her feelings aren't about me. It's about my daughter missing her mother on her birthday.

I pull in a deep breath, rubbing at the back of my neck, and try to search for the right words. Therapy has helped all of us figure out different ways we've each experienced loss, but it doesn't stop the feelings from surfacing and what we do with them.

Wrapping my hand around her shoulder, I give it a squeeze. "Your friends are getting here around five." I lean back, looking at the clock on the mantel "That's about six hours to play around with. Maybe we can look through some pictures together. I can tell you about your fourth birthday party and how your mom was convinced she could make a six-layer rainbow birthday cake." I look around the room. "And if you give me a few minutes, I can figure out how to get another tent here."

"Okay." She smiles.

I shoot a glance over my shoulder at Griz and Lily wrapped up in their own discussion. When I turn back to Lark, she's wiping her tears. Maybe I need to make her feel like she has more than just me to figure all of this out. "Do you want me to have Auntie Hadley or Aunt Laney on standby for later, just in case?"

Shaking her head, she wraps her arms around my neck and says, "Nah, I think we got this, Dad."

PEACH:
> We're on our way back. Is that okay?

LINCOLN:
> Right now, it's a mix of chaos with a side of drama about who can sleep next to Lark. But yes, Lily can hang out with me. I was actually feeling very left out.

PEACH:
> I can stick around to keep you company too if you'd like.

LINCOLN:
> I would very much like.

About thirty minutes later, I ignore the cold and the fact that I can see my breath so vividly when I breathe out. But right now, the porch is a quiet sanctuary from fifteen twelve-year-old girls.

Faye climbs the porch stairs with a smiling Lily in tow. "Well, you look like you didn't have any fun," I tease Lily.

My daughter holds up both wrists. "I have so many crystal bracelets now. And Faye told me all about how the moon can affect people's moods, so we stopped into that crazy psychic lady's shop. The one you always tell me doesn't know what she's talking about, but DAD…SHE DOES! She is *not* crazy, by the way. I think she's very cool. Her name is Pearl and she's a Scorpio, but she was born when Mercury was in retrograde, so she said she can be a lot to unpack sometimes. Maybe that's why you were so turned off by her without even knowing her. She said it happens more often than you'd think."

Faye covers her mouth, trying to keep from laughing. She looks beautiful in her chunky knit sweater hanging from one shoulder and a pair of leggings that look like they're painted on. "Yeah, definitely no fun at all."

Lily smiles at Faye and looks back to me as she asks, "Can I see Lark and her friends now?"

I tilt my head toward the door. "Go for it."

I look back at Faye's amused face and leave my filter off. "You're beautiful," I say to her without reservation.

I glance at my youngest, who's already inside. "She's a big personality. Thank you for indulging her today."

"The psychic was a last-minute addition. I hope that's okay."

I link my pinky with hers and bring her wrist to my lips. "You're new around here. I know what it's like to take that kid out. You're not the one in charge, despite what you might think."

"Oh, I knew that the minute I met her," she laughs out.

We wade through a mess of bags, a bundled sea of blankets, and tents that have somehow shifted into more than just the living room. A huge rumble that sounds like a herd of elephants upstairs drowns out everything else.

"There's one girl locked in the bathroom because she was pissed off about something another girl said to her. Then Lark got upset because nobody could agree on what they wanted to do. I think maybe I need to feed them? Honestly, I'm stuck on how they're all still supposed to coexist until sunrise tomorrow."

Lily yells out from the kitchen island, "I don't know why everyone is upset. I mean, look at all this candy?!" She's sitting with her legs folded on the counter and a mountain of candy bags surrounding her.

"What do you think they would have fun doing?" Faye asks her.

"You're asking me?" Lily says in surprise.

Faye shrugs her shoulders. "You're her sister. What would she think is the absolute coolest and most fun thing to do?"

"Hmmm...candy salad and get all fancy like you."

Faye smiles at me and then raises her eyebrows, wordlessly asking if it's okay.

Seconds later, Lark comes downstairs with about eight girls on her heels. "Dad, can we—Faye! Hi." She waves.

"I heard you were having a party." Faye gives her a small, gray-folded cloth wrapped in a bow. "I know you were looking for a particular one, but this was the one I had gotten when I saw Dave Matthews Band in Seattle. It might be a little big, but—"

Lark's mouth drops open, eyes widening. She isn't my screaming kid, that's Lily, but she's damn excited right now. "Oh my gosh, Faye. This is so cool." Lark looks at me as she turns the shirt around.

"Very cool, kiddo," I say, mirroring her smile.

Over a mouthful of Skittles, Lily says from the counter, "Lark, Faye said she would do everyone's makeup if we wanted."

Lark raises her eyebrows as two of her friends squeal and start saying how fun that would be. "Can you?" She glances at me before she corrects herself and asks, "You wouldn't mind doing that?"

"I would love to do that," Faye says as she looks over toward

Lily. "Your sister is whipping up a candy salad—not really sure what that entails, but there's no way it won't be good."

I stack a bunch of board games from the mudroom. "I found Twister and Clue."

Before the girls grumble, Faye says, "I love Clue."

And because the pretty stranger said it, everyone is all about it. Not a single "that's so lame" or rolled eye. Two of her friends start screeching and jumping up and down, and I swear I might have lost my hearing in my right ear when Lark excitedly says, "Please tell me you have more of those rhinestones too for our eyes?!"

"I do. Let me run next door and grab my makeup kits. I just bought some new gems too, so this is perfect timing. Lily, want to be my assistant?"

Lily's eyes brighten and she hops down from the counter. "Really? Yes, please!"

"I feel like we need some good music." Faye looks at Lark. "I saw the mirror balls and friendship bracelets, so I'm assuming you have a playlist in mind?"

Lark nods, and they all start shouting song titles. Lily rolls her eyes, like she doesn't listen to the exact same music as her older sister. "Soooo overplayed."

It takes just under two hours and there's glitter everywhere. Hair and arms, counters and pillowcases. All fifteen girls have some variation of sparkles on their eyelids. Half are having a dance party in the center of the living room, while the other group is trying to figure out if it was Mrs. Peacock with the wrench or Professor Plum with the dagger. But somehow, the entire party shifted. The bits of drama have fizzled, and both of my girls are smiling about something.

I lean against the kitchen counter as Faye puts the last of

her makeup tools away. "You looked like a natural assistant, Lil," I tell my youngest as she finishes the remaining Pez from her holder.

She blows out a breath. "Thanks, Dad. That was hard work."

Faye looks over my shoulder from her makeshift workstation at the time on the microwave. "I need to get going."

Lark's head whips up from the game. "Thanks for helping, Faye."

The rest of the room rings out in thank-yous and praise for how awesome and cool she is.

"Thanks for the invite, Lark. You have really fun friends." She smiles, glancing at me as she shoulders her oversized bag filled with all of her makeup. She looks for Lily. "Catch you later, Lily!"

My youngest has a cupcake stuffed in her mouth as she mumbles a goodbye and waves.

It's like a slap in the face how much I want Faye to stay. I hate the idea of her leaving and not being here with me to entertain this crew in the morning. "See you later, Foxx."

Raising my hand, I give her a wave as she heads out the door because, truthfully, I have a room full of preteens who are the epitome of gossiping little monsters. I scrub my hand over my face and mouth. *What the fuck am I doing?*

"Hey!" I rush outside, closing the door behind me and stalking down the steps without stopping until I reach the middle of the street. I wrap my arms around her and my lips crash into hers. Her fingers rake up the back of my neck and into my hair, sending that Faye-inducing feeling down my spine and across every inch of my skin. I hold her tighter and let my tongue have its way with hers before pulling away. Smiling against her lips, I give her one last kiss. "Come back over later."

She's smiling right back, narrowing her eyes playfully before nipping at my bottom lip. "You have a house full of kids."

"Semantics."

She snorts a laugh.

"Have any plans for Valentine's Day?"

She sighs, looking around my face. "I have a show at Midnight Proof."

"Good. I'll come watch. Then afterwards, you're mine for the night."

"I don't—" She shakes her head with a smile still lingering on her lips. "What are we doing, Foxx?" she asks softly. The vulnerable tone of voice isn't something I'm used to hearing from her, but I like that she's showing that part of herself to me.

I wrap my arms around her tighter and tell her the most honest thing I can muster. "I want to be around you. I like me more when I'm around *you*. So let me be around you, Peach. And we figure it out as we go along. Lean into what feels right."

She lets me run my nose along her cheek, and I can feel her smile when she whispers, "I like me when I'm around you too." Kissing my cheek, she moves to pull away. But I'm not ready to let her go.

"Come back here. Let me kiss you like I'm going to miss you."

"You're going to miss me?" she teases.

I cuff a piece of hair behind her ear. "You're making it really hard for me not to."

She frames my face with her hands and kisses my lips one last time before she pulls away and starts walking toward her house. When she looks over her shoulder back at me and smiles, I know without a doubt that I'm falling hard for her.

I close my eyes before I face my kids. The porch swing morning under the blankets I lied my way out of and played off, but this isn't something I can walk back from if they just watched it happen.

And when I turn, both of my girls have their dog on a leash and are watching me try to figure out how to explain what I was just doing. "Shit." I run my hands through my hair. I didn't think this through. How do I handle this conversation? I puff out my cheeks and blow out a breath. "Okay, sometimes grown-ups kiss each other. It doesn't—"

"We know why grown-ups kiss, Mr. Foxx," one of Lark's friends says matter-of-factly.

Great, I'm never going to hear the end of this.

More of the girls from the party have filtered out here now, the porch quickly lining with glitter-infused preteens. And then it gets loud again with a succession of questions aimed directly at me.

"Are you going to marry her?"

"Is Faye your girlfriend?"

"My mom said Faye Calloway was going to teach her how to dance."

"Why does your hair look so crazy?"

"Is she staying in Fiasco?"

I clap my hands and take the porch steps two at a time. "You're turning into the gossiping old ladies from the book club." I smile at them. Holding open the front door, I nod toward inside. "Let's fire up a movie and those fairy lights."

"You doing alright, sweetheart?" I ask Lark, who was the last in the line.

"It's a great party, Dad. Thanks." Lark tips her head back as she walks under my arm. "I'm glad Faye was here too."

Chapter 31

Lincoln

It might just be a day, but there are plenty of people in the town of Fiasco who prepare for Valentine's Day as if it's the most over-the-top important day of the year. Even more so when it falls on a weekend. Our town green is splashed in pink-and-red lights, while the shops along Main Street stay open late for their annual Galentine's Day Sip & Stroll. The girls in Crescent de Lune are working late tonight, and I hold up my hand and wave at the sisters who run the place as they fold their hands around pink dough. As I walk down the flight of stairs and through the double oak doors of Midnight Proof, it's as if the place has been dipped in the colors of romance.

Crystal chandeliers bathe the room in warm light. The usual black velvet and deep emerald-green drapes and decor have been swapped out for velvet reds and a deep burgundy. Sheer pink material billows out from every chandelier to each corner of the room. All of it frames the circular stage at the center spotlighted in pinks, just waiting for my girl to take it and wow every person in the room.

"Lincoln Foxx, out on Valentine's?" Hadley says as I slide into the only empty bar chair.

"I didn't think how packed this place would be tonight." I smile as she pulls out a rocks glass and starts to pour my favorite bottle she carries. "I like your wings."

She smiles big, spreading her arms wide, and spins, showing off the red heart-shaped wings fixed to her back. "I decided to lean in this year. I may not have a Valentine, but I plan to make a lot of people tipsy and horny tonight! Naughty Cupid, at your service," she says with a salute.

I bark out a laugh as she holds out her fist.

I meet it with a bump and we follow with the finger hooks and elbow tap combination that makes up our handshake. It's ridiculous, but it makes both of us laugh. There have been plenty of times in our lives where a laugh was needed, and being ridiculous helped.

"Lark and Lily told me all about the kissing in the middle of the street thing." My best friend gives me that look of hers that screams *"I could have called it."*

"How did they seem when they said it?" I ask, holding up the glass for a cheers with whatever she's pouring for herself tonight.

"They told me you want Faye to be your girlfriend, and I quote, 'Our dad deserves to smile the way he's been smilin' at Faye.'"

"Are you fucking serious?" I ask, sitting back as warmth fills my chest. I don't think I could love my girls much more than I already do, but then they go ahead and say shit like that…

"Lily was over the moon about it. She told me we need

to go see Pearl, her psychic, to find out if there's going to be a happily ever after."

I bark out a laugh as she holds up her finger to pause our conversation and moves down the bar to pour a drink for the couple at the far end. When she comes back, she leans against the bar and asks, "This is serious then? You're falling for her?"

The jazz band starts to kick up the volume, which means my girl is just about ready to take the stage. I've always told Hadley everything—she knew about Olivia wanting to end things before she passed. My best friend knows how I've gotten lost for a while in faceless women to move on from the layers of loss, but she's never known about my history with Faye. I never told her about the blackmail and the night in the cornfield. And now I'm happy I never did; I like having that just between Faye and me. I rub my thumb along my lip as I think about waking up next to her. The way she fits there so easily. The way I don't overthink or get lost in my own head while I'm with her.

"It feels serious," I tell her. "I wouldn't have let her get close enough to my girls if I thought it wouldn't be." And that is what should have me concerned. It isn't logical or levelheaded, but that fucking curse always lingers beneath the surface. The idea of wanting her and caring for her doesn't make me want to back away, though; it makes me want to hold on and protect her. Spend moments and embrace all the uncertainty because it's worth it for how good I've felt with her around.

But then Hadley asks the one question I don't have an answer to. "Does that mean she's planning to stay?"

Before I can think of a way to answer, the trumpet starts in a low hum and then kicks in a high note, signaling the crowd to start paying attention. I take a taste of my bourbon—one with a smokier oak and hints of caramel. It has me remembering how much more I enjoy the taste when I'm drinking it with the beautiful woman standing beneath a pink spotlight. I let out an exhale and with it the lingering question. *Is she planning to stay?* "We haven't talked about it...but I want her to."

Hadley gives the bar top a little tap. "Sounds like something worth talking about then. Work that Foxx charm so we can keep her, Linc."

The strings tip in and the mood shifts as the singer starts crooning the words, "At last." The slower-than-usual song flips the room's lighting into a warmer pink as Faye comes into view with an oversized red satin bow tied perfectly over her chest, while the rest of the ribbon is wrapped around her body nice and tight. My body lights up for her. A full shiver that settles right into my cock. Fucking hell, I want her. The ribbon ends at the tops of her thighs, where just a sliver of skin peeks through before her red fishnet stockings wrap around her legs. I can't help but smile and watch as she flirts with the couple at the table in front of her.

Her red fishnet gloves match what's pulled up her legs, and she puts the tip of her middle finger between her teeth, pulling slowly and teasing the crowd just by removing something as simple as a glove. Fucking hell, she's stunning, but the way she can work a room is more than impressive. It's a talent that can't be learned or practiced. Her blond hair sparkles in the lights—plenty of that same glitter had been all over my house after her makeover fun for Lark's party. Leaning my elbow on the bar, I fix my glasses and sit back as she sways her way through the audience.

"Damn, Linc. She's got everyone here practically salivating, and she's only removed her gloves," Hadley says in awe.

"Beautiful," I whisper, my eyes fixed on Faye's lips as they tip up into a seductive smile as she continues to work the room.

I rub my thumb along my lower lip and smile when I think about how I'm going to enjoy every inch of her later. My pulse races as I catch her eye, and it's like she was looking because her lips, painted in red to match the tiny hearts along the edges of her eyes, tip up in a smile just for me. Her path changes, and she works her way in my direction, her steps a sensual strut that keeps my gaze glued to her.

The song rises to its finale just as she reaches me at the end of the bar. She steps close and turns around, facing the crowd before she hops up beside me.

Once her ass is firmly planted on the bar top, Hadley hands her a coupe glass filled halfway with champagne. Faye holds it up as the audience hoots and hollers, "To love!" And with that, she's taking a sip and focusing on me. Her legs kick up high, extending one after the other as she slides smoothly off the bar to stand right next to me. She tips at her waist, ass out to the crowd while her top half leans into mine, and it's taking everything in me to not interfere with her performance and kiss her already. Holding the ribbon end of her bow toward me, she sweetly says, "Unwrap me, please?"

I can't help but smile at the request and…her. I'm not sure how it's possible to be this enchantingly sexy and also cute as fuck. But she pulls it off somehow.

And I do exactly as she requests. The band drags out the end of the song as I pull the ribbon. She spins away from me, unwrapping the red satin from her chest, all the way down to the tops of her thighs, leaving her in nothing more than red heart tassels perfectly placed over each nipple and the tiniest pair of panties—a red heart covering her pussy connected by two tiny strings leading to another heart that barely covers her ass. My adrenaline spikes as I watch on.

When she puts her hands on her hips and bounces just right to make those tassels spin, the crowd goes wild—every single person claps and hoots and whistles.

Hundreds of eyes on my girl, but that's all they get. A show. The fantasy. It's nowhere near as fulfilling as the real thing—worshiping this woman, tasting the way I turn her on, and rewarding her mouth and body with everything they demand.

She smiles against my lips. "You weren't supposed to be like this."

"Like what? Great in bed?" I laugh, trying to make a joke. "My reputation is failing me then."

She runs her fingertips along my chin. "What was it I heard in the bathroom at Bottom of the Barrel or at the rodeo…the slutty single dad?"

"Very to the point." I wince, dragging my fingers lazily across her skin. "Fiasco is going to talk about something. Might as well make it something juicy, like sex and strangers. It's better than the sad and lonely widower."

Tilting her head up, she leans on one elbow. "Slutty, I can handle. But this…" She looks around my face and down to my chest. "You weren't supposed to be fun and sweet. And you definitely weren't supposed to be sexier than you already look. And this wasn't supposed to feel…"

My neck warms, and the weight on my chest comes out of nowhere. "Feel like what, Peach?" I want her to say more. I need her to be the one to do it, because if I'm wrong and this is only a good time for her…

But she kills my nerves when she says, "It was never supposed to feel so right with you. We shouldn't feel this right."

Relief runs through me. Hearing that admission from her makes me feel like we have a new secret—one that I want to keep because it's special and just for us. "Mmmm," I hum as I let those words seep in and ease my worry. It finally feels like I'm right next to who I'm supposed to be. "But we do. Maybe we shouldn't because of how we started, but I don't think that needs to have anything to do with how we let the rest of this play out." As I graze my fingertips along the under curve of her breast, she smiles and exhales a light, satisfied moan.

"You're dangerous, Foxx," she says with a lazy smile. I like how it feels when she says it. As if I'm the one who's setting the tone in all of this when, really, it's her. She talks to me like she has nothing to be intimidated by or fear. I know what my daughters meant when they said they liked how she talked to them. It feels honest and real. There's care and warmth in everything she does. "You smile and these"—she circles her finger around the dip of my dimple—"they're your secret weapon, because they make you seem cute."

"I am cute."

She ignores my remark, but it tips up her smile a fraction. I turn my head and grab her finger with my teeth, which makes her giggle. "See? dangerous."

I close my eyes as she runs her fingers along my hairline, and it feels so good that all I can think about is, *I want more of this.*

With a sigh, she looks around the apartment above Midnight Proof. Hadley passed me the key and told me to have fun tonight. It's a great studio space. High-end everything with no expense spared, because that's Hadley. She left us both a note with a tube of lube that said, *Just in case… Have a sexy time, lovers!*

"Thank goodness for Hadley and this place," I tell her.

"I don't think I would have been able to wait to get home after your performance tonight."

She ghosts her fingers over my chest, looking up at me curiously. "You two were always just friends?"

I'm surprised it didn't take her longer to ask. "Just friends—there's no attraction there. She became a part of our family, and somewhere along the way, she turned into my best friend. We love one another, but it's the same love I have for my brothers. I know that's true for her too." There's more to Hadley's story, but I'll let her tell that to Faye someday if she wants.

She nods against me, smiling. "She's been a good friend to me while I've been here. I get why you would consider her family."

Lifting slightly, Faye trails her fingers down my neck and over my chest.

"That feels good. Keep going," I say, peeking my eyes open to watch her. Her mouth tilts up, hinting at a smile as she moves her fingers farther down the length of my stomach, and she sees that I'm already hard again. "I thought you were pushing forty, Foxx?"

"Not yet, Peach." I tilt my head to the side, chuckling darkly. "With a comment like that, it's like you want me to spank you."

That seductive smile shines my way again as she turns her body over, chest rubbing against the arm of the couch and her perfect ass tilted up just enough. Her tits dragging across the leather, those thickly toned thighs and that curvy dip to her waist, is a path I want to claim. She looks at me like she's equally turned on and ready for whatever I tell her to do.

Sitting up, I graze my teeth along her ass cheek, and she yelps before wiggling her ass for another.

I give the same spot a slap and then grab. Gritting my teeth,

I tell her, "Your body is so fucking sexy. But this mouth…" I move to stand in front of where she's perched, rubbing the pad of my thumb along her bottom lip. "I've had fantasies about this mouth. Open. Tongue out."

And fuck me, she does it without hesitation.

I tap the head of my cock along the length of her tongue. One. Two. Three times, before I push it farther. I drag it back as she looks up at me, eyes telling me she's ready for it all. Again, one, two, three times, making me slippery wet. "Now wrap those pretty lips around me," I barely breathe out, because she's already doing it before I finish saying the words. Pulling my cock back, I tease myself along her lips, a shiver rippling through me. "Keep that ass tipped up for me, baby."

She makes a muffled mewl around me. "You like me calling you that?" *Baby.* But instead of letting her answer, I push into her mouth as I move my hand down the center of her back. She takes me down her throat so fucking far that she gags around it. But when I move to pull back this time, her hand wraps around my leg and she pulls me deeper. *Fuck.*

Relaxing her throat, she holds me there, and with a hum—like she's turned on by all of this—swallows. My head drops back, eyes slamming shut as I thank every higher power right now. When she does it again, I practically see stars as the movement of her throat sucks the head of my cock. I hiss out air between my teeth and try to keep it together, but fucking hell, that might have just ruined me.

As I pull back slowly, feeling how wet and juicy her mouth made me, I hold my fingers under her chin.

She watches me through her thick lashes and watery eyes.

"You're a fucking goddess," I tell her as I rub my thumb across her lips now smudged from her leftover red lipstick.

"That was perfection…" I lean down, kissing her, and then shift my body around her to get to what I want. "Ass up, baby."

As she arches herself more for me, I kneel behind her and let a finger drag down the crack of her ass and through her soaked pussy right to her swollen clit. I let my fingers play in that spot as she moans, fluttering along the crease of her ass cheek, and as I move it higher, I rub a small circle right in the spot I'm planning to slap. With one fast move, I spank her ass cheek and then spread her open without another second wasted. I need a taste. I drag my tongue along the entire dripping length of her, relishing her whimpers and how she pushes back into me. I don't miss any part from her pretty puckered asshole down to a pussy that I need to fuck.

She pleads for more, the sound of my name muffled by her mouth meeting the cushion.

"This isn't going to be soft, baby," I tell her as I roll another condom down my length. Her thighs are wet from how turned on she is by this, and she rubs them together in anticipation.

"Good," she groans out. "Show me."

I sink into her wet, swollen pussy in one fast move and give her a nice slap on the ass with my first thrust. *Goddamn.*

She moans with a laugh. "That's all you've got?"

I watch as my cock pulls out of her. It's a filthy sight—the deep pink color of her pussy and the way she rewards me, coating my cock with a sheen of arousal. Wrapping my arm around her front, I bring her back flush against my chest. I nuzzle my nose along the crook of her neck and breathe her in. "Tell me what you want. I'll do anything you beg me for right now."

She hums and leans into the kisses I pepper along her skin. Gliding her fingers over mine, she moves my hand down to her clit as I rock into her. "Play with me. And I'll come all over that thick and delicious cock of yours."

It's all the encouragement I need. I roll my hips into her hard, pulling back just enough to do it again, little slips of breath escaping her lips each time my hips punch forward. I move my fingers in circles along her clit until she's shaking in my arms.

"I'm going to…" she cries out, just before her pussy pulses and squeezes around me.

I fuck into her as deep as I can, and it still doesn't feel like enough. Not even when she moans my name, coaxing me closer. Turning and lying in front of me, she pushes her tits together.

"Everywhere, Foxx."

I rip off the condom and do exactly what she asks. I paint her tits and stomach with my cum as my orgasm rips through my body, leaving someone I barely recognize in its wake. I rest on my heels as I watch her rub it into her flushed skin. It releases some kind of primal need I never knew existed within me. It feels like I've claimed her as mine—it's dirty and so *fucking* hot.

She smiles as I help her rub my mess across her chest. "I like that."

I blow out a breath and pull her up and into my arms. She laughs, not caring about the sweat or the cum.

"Yeah, Peach." I rub my lips along her shoulder and up the side of her neck. "I more than liked that too."

Chapter 32

Faye

"You realize you're staring, right?" I ask my sister as I come down the front stairs and catch a glimpse of her standing and staring out the front, fixated on our very shirtless neighbor throwing hay bales from the back of a trailer.

"Yeah, I'm aware," she says, and a twinge of pride has me smirking, knowing that I've had my hands all over that very delicious looking chest. "I know what he's doing, but what's with the hay? They have a dog, not horses."

"A cow," I tell her, watching on with embarrassingly full attention. "Where's his shirt? It was just above freezing this morning."

She glances at me with a baffled look. "Where are they going to house a cow? There's not a barn on their property for that."

I sip my black coffee. "He's one-fourth owner of the largest bourbon brand in the world; I have a feeling if he wants to build a barn, he will."

Nodding, she chuckles. "I can't believe you're sleeping with him."

It feels like so much more than just sleeping with him. Sighing, I give her a side-eye glance. "We don't do much sleeping. And why is that so hard to believe?"

Maggie barks out a laugh and then shifts to fully look at me. "Faye, you're this independent badass. And he's a…dad."

Okay, that's not what I was expecting her to say.

"He's old. Like, a decade older than you," she says and squints like that's the grossest thing in the world.

"He's thirty-eight. I'm thirty. That's not gross."

As her gaze travels back to the front window, she says, "I mean, he's good looking, that's very obvious. It's like a thick-fit dad bod he's working with." She tilts her head to the side. "He does have that I'll-take-care-of-you vibe about him, though, too. And you're…"

I wrap my hands around my mug, shifting my stance, and try not to be instantly triggered that she's going to say something offensive. "And I'm what?"

Focused on our neighbor just beyond the screened-in porch and yard, she says, "You always take care of everyone else. You were the one who always stepped up, especially when Mom couldn't when we were little."

My chest warms, and I feel a sense of relief that I can't figure out how to process. But she keeps going. "I could see why you'd want to take a break from having to be that way and feel what it's like to be on the receiving end of it."

Eyes blurry and throat thickening with emotion, I turn my head slowly to look at her. It feels like the simplest observation, but when someone sees you and says it out loud, it's validating. And hearing it from Maggie feels like we owe each other more than what we've been giving and receiving for a long time now.

"We could probably offer the barn to them since it's barely used," Maggie suggests. "Mom left this place to both of us, so if you think it's a good idea, then so do I."

I blink, not knowing how to process this, because this feels like a version of how we used to be. Sisters and friends in a way that wasn't wholesome like an after-school special, but love and care in the small moments. Friendship that lingered in the familiarity of each other's favorites—cake for dinner, impromptu dance parties, and an over-appreciation for *Practical Magic*. Our relationship was one of the most important things in the world to me when I was younger. I just had never stopped to recognize it or call it out. It was something that I felt lucky to have, and then I felt punished when I didn't. I welcomed the punishment—for my choices, for what I helped bury and the lines I allowed to blur. And all of it had been for the wrong person—all of it was wrong.

My voice sounds raspy when I say, "Maggie?"

She stares out the window, eyes glassy, almost afraid to look at me. "Yeah?" she says as her chin wobbles.

"I'm sorry I stopped," I tell her.

Her eyebrows pinched, she turns to me, questioning what I'm saying.

"I stopped taking care of you. I left you and Mom." I swallow the lump that's rising—a tide of apologetic emotion that needs to surface and crash. I had my reasons at the time, but I should have found a better way.

A tear escapes, and she immediately bats it away as she shakes her head.

Before she can argue with me, I make her a promise. "I'm

not leaving now. I can't change the past, but I promise you, I won't leave you again."

She looks at me in a way that feels like she's holding something back. It's like she wants to say more, but instead she tilts her head forward, resting her forehead on my shoulder. She hadn't done it in a long time. Maggie never loved getting hugs—physical touch wasn't her favorite unless it was on her terms. And when she needed comfort, she opted for a shoulder to rest her head on while she rummaged through her thoughts. She loops her pointer finger with mine and whispers, "I missed this. Missed you."

I look up, trying to keep more tears from streaking down my face. "Me too," I whisper. We stay like that for another minute, letting this moment sink in as we watch Lincoln toss hay bales from behind the front porch windows.

Taking a deep breath, she wipes her face and smiles before moving through the front door and heading up the stairs. "I'm borrowing that showgirl fan with the pink fluffy feathers," she says.

"Wait, what?" I ask, processing what she just said.

"I have a date later," she calls out.

I hold up my finger and turn toward the stairs. "First of all, fuck no, you're not!" I shout on a clipped laugh.

She ignores me and keeps walking. When she almost hits the top landing, she stops to look back at me. "I'd like to come to one of your shows. At Midnight Proof. If that's okay?"

My stomach swoops with excitement, abandoning the request for my feather fan prop. It might even be nerves rooting around at the idea she'll finally see something I'm proud of doing. It's a part of me that feels equally vulnerable and empowered.

I swallow roughly, smiling up at her. "Yeah, that would be more than okay."

She takes the rest of the steps two at a time and disappears from sight. The door to the bathroom shuts, and the shower turns on. When I move back out onto the porch, I feel relieved—the weight of losing her was something I didn't even realize I carried.

Looking out the window, I watch Lincoln laugh as the owner of the trailer says something to him, and I can't help but smile at the sight. His gloved hands grip around the bale string as it's hoisted across the trailer hooked to his truck, forearms flexing and biceps straining as he lifts it. *He's been the perfect distraction.*

As the trailer pulls out of his driveway and down our road, I open the screened-in door of the porch. The air is a pinch cooler than I was expecting, the earthy smell of hay mixed with the sweetness in the Fiasco air acting as a nice late morning pick-me-up.

My phone buzzes in my hand.

FOXX:
You enjoying the show?

I look up and, sure enough, he's looking right at me with his phone in hand. Jesus, this man is delicious. Like he's trying to tempt me even more, he takes his glasses off and wipes his forehead before he puts them back on.

FAYE:
You showing off?

FOXX:
There's this girl I'm trying to impress. You think it's working?

FAYE:

Maybe a little. Where's Lark and Lily?

FOXX:

Inside, traumatizing Kit with a sweater. Why?

Pushing my phone into my back pocket, I step a little closer to the porch stairs, angling my body so he can see me a bit better from his angle. This isn't the usual attire I'd wear for a show, but the effect will still be the same. I unzip the hoodie I had thrown on after my shower and give him a perfect view, just like he's been giving me. He's far enough away that I can't make out his facial expression, but I can see him hold his phone up to his ear just as mine vibrates in my pocket.

His voice on the other end is so low and deep that I swear I can feel the rumble through the line. "You're entirely too comfortable showing me those perfect tits whenever I'm thinking about them."

"I show plenty of people my tits. But you showed me yours, so…"

"Yeah, well, none of those people get to taste those beautiful things," he hums out, and my body heats in response. "They don't get to see your nipples go from delicate soft pink to hard and flushed darker with the simple flick of my tongue." Moving his free arm above his head, he rests it on top of his backward hat. "I'm going to need those for dessert later."

Before I can say anything else, the roar of an old muscle car engine comes flying up the road. The speed at which it turns into Lincoln's driveway almost makes the color less noticeable.

"Hadley," he says, and I can see him shaking his head. "She's not allowed to drive my kids anywhere. Now you know why."

Chuckling at that, I don't rush to cover myself up, the two sides of the hoodie moving over enough to cover what's needed.

"I'll see you later?" he asks, just as she throws her door open.

I can hear her voice through the phone. "You're hauling hay? What is this? Some kind of fantasy farmer draft I didn't know about?" She follows his line of sight right toward me. I only hear the next few words before he hangs up. "Oh my gosh, you two are obsessed—"

I bark out a laugh. She's not wrong. I've quickly become obsessed with the way I feel when I'm around him. And Hadley has no problem calling him out on it.

Music from inside echoes out here. Biggie Smalls lays down his reality—it might have been all a dream, but the lyrics are too good to forget. And it has me smiling.

When I head back in, Maggie is wearing the same nostalgic smile as she struts down the stairs. A towel wrapped tightly around her hair, she smiles, and it's wordless communication about what comes next. The music plays loudly over the speakers installed throughout the house and I meet her rhythm in the center of the hall. *Save the Last Dance*-style moves roll into the middle of the street "Top That" dance-off from *Teen Witch*. We're both laughing as she says, "Mom could not handle your rap phase. She never understood how Biggie or Tupac were just as iconic as Stevie or Carly."

I laugh harder at the memory. "Oh, I remember. I don't think she ever got as riled up about anything as much as she would when she talked about music or horses."

Maggie smiles, lowering the volume as we both catch our

breath. "Did you catch any good concerts while you traveled the world?"

"It wasn't the world by any stretch."

"It was away from here. Places I've never been, never seen—anywhere outside Fiasco feels kind of like the world to me."

She moves into the kitchen and fills two glasses of water. Passing one to me as I follow, she says, "Then tell me about some of the places you've been."

"You've been to Nashville, right?" I ask, already knowing the answer.

She nods. "Spring break right before graduation. A few of us drove down for a week."

Maggie kept school local, since university had an equine program and computer programming. She was talented and had an eye for both. Mom had been adamant that she wasn't going into the horse training business for Finch & King. It was a point of contention between them.

"I also did some private investigating work that took me all over. Louisiana for a little while, and then up to the Pacific Northwest around Bend, and then Seattle. I spent a good part of a year in New York doing work on a case where the woman had been murdered, but the client was adamant she hadn't."

She smiles, looking down first when she says, "Like I said, badass." And the compliment pulls a sense of pride forward. She stares back out the window, changing the subject when she says, "What's New York like?"

"Loud. Busy. Different from how it is in stories and the movies. The lights of Times Square are overwhelming, just like the crowds there. The tree at Christmas time in Rockefeller Center is just a tree. But for some reason, surrounded by buildings and an ice rink, it feels more like Christmas than anywhere else."

"Mom missed you at Christmas. I think not seeing you that time of year really was the hardest for her."

My chest aches, making me want to break down and cry, because it was one of the hardest parts for me too.

The chiming ringtone of her phone interrupts the conversation. "Shit," she says with an exhale as she types furiously away at the screen and then pockets it. "I've gotta go."

"Everything okay?" I hope that she'll tell me, but I don't expect her to.

Grabbing her bag, she opens the front door and says, "It will be."

As I watch her pull out of the driveway—in my truck—I know that something needs to break here. I hate that she was forced to carry the truth of what happened that night. And that the only option she had was to stay quiet. I left her with that instead of talking to her and leaning on her the way she needed the same from me. The lashing out, gambling, all of it makes more sense to me now.

What choices exist when the end never changes?

Maggie's endings have been people leaving her. Not anymore. There's no way I'm going anywhere knowing there are still loose ends. And knowing that Waz King isn't just a creep, but a murderer, a manipulator, and the source of what broke my family apart? That isn't going to be the end of our story. The thing that I did best is find out little secrets that have the power to fuck people over—and Waz has plenty.

Chapter 33

Faye

There are a few things in private investigations that always work well for me: asking the right questions, giving people the space to insert their foot in their mouth, and a great distraction. And Cortez was distracted at the rodeo, which is how I lifted his phone and added the screen mirroring app. I knew he didn't come to the house to see me that day—that had been obvious. But I read the exchange between him and my sister all wrong. It wasn't personal or sexual. It's business.

MAGGIE:
Go fuck yourself, Cortez.

CORTEZ:
Maggie, you fucked up. You've been fucking up. And now I need you to do the right thing. Get me what I need.

MAGGIE:
And if I don't?

CORTEZ:
We've already gone over this. Then we forget about our agreement. We've got plenty of evidence around your "web design" business. What you've been doing is called grand larceny, btw.

CORTEZ:
But you and I both know that's not what we're after.

She told everyone she was a web designer, but Maggie isn't building landing pages or rebranding websites. She's been manipulating the coding that ran off-track betting in Kentucky for Finch & King, siphoning off funds in a way that I will probably never comprehend. She was hired by them to do "web design." It had been the same story as Foxx Bourbon, but neither company was rebranding their website—they were cover jobs. Foxx had her selling specialty bourbon on the secondary market, but Finch & King had her manipulating the off-track betting systems to increase their winnings. And she did all of it without even having to step foot inside of the racetrack. I knew this from what Maggie had shared. But if that was what Cortez was investigating, the case would be with the district attorney, and their arrest warrants would have been issued. But that wasn't what was happening, which meant whatever they were after was bigger than that. She was an FBI asset.

That's what Blackstone brought to the table. They needed

someone involved in Finch & King's business who was dirty enough to threaten and turn him into a source.

I shove the doors to the precinct open and scan the space behind the front desk.

Del's huddled around a small group on the other side of the glass, and I give him a wave. He raises his hand, but it's not the usual happy-to-see-me greeting.

"I'm here to see Agent Cortez," I say to the front desk clerk.

He buzzes me on through, pointing to the corner office on the left. "I'll let him know you're coming."

"You would think after all the shit that went down with the Foxx fire that we'd catch a break," an officer to my right says.

I angle my body to listen.

"I got FBI breathing down my neck about these horses that are being fucking slaughtered. Money showing up in transfers anonymously to Fiasco Savings Bank from offshore accounts too. The FBI catches wind of it, and here we are, taking direction from Cortez. Fucking hate that guy," he grumbles. "Don't even get me started on the U.S. Marshall bullshit too. I hear she's coming through in a week or so."

"Faye, what are you doing here?" Del asks as he comes over from where he'd been huddled. "There's a lot going on today, so if it's to grab a coffee—"

I cut him off and offer a tight-lipped smile. "I have something for Cortez."

He glances at Cortez's office and then back to me before he asks, "Everything okay? I thought things with your support had closed?"

Instead of answering him, I say, "I'll bring coffee next time, Del."

Del gives me a nod, just as someone calls out, "Delaney," and Cortez waves me over.

"Hey, ba—" Stopping himself, he says, "Faye, I mean. I was actually just going to call you."

"What are you doing with Maggie?" I ask point-blank, not in the mood to fuck around. And without giving him a chance to respond, I hold up my hand. "Don't give me some bullshit line. I know you're using her, have proof of it, but what I haven't figured out is for what?"

He sits back in his chair and folds his hands. "Shut the door," he says. When I do and take a seat, he admits, "She's been working with me as a source." Releasing a heavy breath, he leans forward and takes a sip from the coffee mug on his desk. "There had been complaints filed about inconsistencies in winnings and odds versus attendees. Payouts were unbalanced." He starts ticking off locations where some of the most attended races take place: "Saratoga, Belmont, Louisville, Lexington. All of them had the same pattern of winnings, but your sister's smart. She shuffled money around, and that's what took us so long to find her. She made it look like she just had a helluva gambling problem, not that she was the one running this. She was smart about the optics. When people started seeing her with Finch and King, and the fact that she hadn't been taking on any new web design clients..." He shakes his head. "It's not something that would have been noticed if we hadn't lived in such a small town. But that was just the beginning of it."

Cortez leans on his desk and runs his hand through his hair. His posture is all off, like he's trying to work through something.

So I fill in the blanks. The details that hadn't been obvious before now. "Finch and King have been raising flags here for a while. So Maggie being involved, you just assumed it was bad news? Is that why you're using her?"

He tilts his head to the side, weighing his response. "There's a ticker tape of things happening with horses, jockeys, trainers—and even owners. If we're going to pursue anything, we have the burden of proof. Maggie was the start."

"That's why Blackstone is pivotal. He's another source? Like Maggie?" Cortez needed to work Blackstone the same way he had worked Maggie—get enough dirt and evidence to threaten them to either cooperate or serve jail time for their own criminal actions.

But Cortez looks past my shoulder, through the glass on the door, and toward the bullpen of officers before his eyes lock onto mine. "Was. He *was* pivotal. Blackstone is dead."

I freeze, blinking my eyes to really register what he just said. *Dead*. That can't be right. My chest tightens. "What?" I pinch the bridge of my nose. "How?"

"This morning. A call came in from housekeeping at the estate he'd been renting. His throat had been sliced on either side of his neck. Strung up in the ballroom. Bled out."

My stomach sinks and bile rises in my throat as a flash of the murder scene I walked into five years ago flashes through my mind. There's no such thing as coincidences. *The devil was in the details.* I know who's responsible immediately.

I grit my teeth, stand, and point at him, making it crystal clear that this wasn't okay. "Get my sister away from this, Cortez."

"We're on the same page here. I don't want her getting hurt, Faye. We knew this went beyond fixing horse races. This is an entire industry being manipulated. Blackstone was who Finch & King had been using to acquire massive amounts of drugs. We're talking performance enhancers, cocaine, snake venom. All traces found in the bloodstream of horses that had been tested post-race and those that had been found dead."

The shipment documents for his private auction had each of these line items.

"We've had two jockeys, a veterinarian, and a trainer go missing. I have boxes filled with suspicious incidents from injuries to personnel deaths." His hand runs along his five-o'clock shadow just before he adds, "The coroner's report never flagged anything in your mother's death, but with her being a trainer for them for so long, and then her sudden heart attack, that had concerned a few in the department at one point as well."

The room feels like it tips just enough to throw me off balance, both lightheaded and weighed down all at once. I step back, the backs of my knees grazing the chair, guiding me to sit. This was too close. What they were after would take down an entire industry. And now, my sister was at the center of it. "Dammit, Maggie."

Cortez leans back in his chair, clearing his throat. "Maggie cornered me that night, before she was drunk or arrested. She showed me a series of exchanges between a trainer, a jockey, and Wheeler Finch about last season's Triple Crown winner having to be put down. She said it was the eleventh one this past year. And it didn't feel right. She had no idea that we had been building a case already. And all of a sudden, I had an asset with direct access to everything. And you were already lined up to deliver me Blackstone." He pauses, regret laced in his tone, and says, "The Calloway sisters were my secret weapon in taking down an empire."

"We're not—" But he cuts me off before I can tell him that he has no fucking right.

"Four hours later, Maggie was picked up on a 'drunk and disorderly.' She had been beaten up, bruises along every inch of her, and she wouldn't talk. She refused to be checked out. Del tried talking to her, even getting her involved with the U.S. Marshall, but she wasn't having any of it. I haven't gotten a piece of intel from her since—that's why I've been leaning on her. She backed off."

I know it's because of Waz King. She wanted to see him pay for what he had done. What my mother and I had shouldered the blame for. It's the one thing that none of them understood. The piece that seemed to never be digested very well: Nobody, especially women, wanted to be used for someone else's agenda.

I sit forward, stabbing my finger into his desk. "Only you kept me in the dark about all of it, Cortez." I shake my head. "And now your other source is dead. So what's the plan?"

He crosses his arms. "The plan is the same, Faye. Build the case. You and I both know that the only way things stick is if it's done the right way. We need sources."

"You need *proof*," I say with a bite. "And I have plenty of ways I can get that for you. Let me do what I do better than any other person in this place. If I can get access to Finch & King property, the training center, and possibly their staff lounge, there is no way I won't get exactly what you need. And if I can figure out a way into Wheeler Finch's private residence, there's no reason why I couldn't plant—"

"Are you out of your fucking mind, Faye?" Cortez cuts in. He looks over my shoulder and out into the bullpen of the police station. More quietly this time, he says, "You do realize that none of that would be admissible in any court proceedings."

And as I say it, I know right away why it would never work.

"Then get warrants. Loop in the district attorney. There are ways to make this work here, Cortez."

"You haven't been gone *that* long, Faye." He levels with me, pushing out a breath. "You think the Foxx brothers have connections? That's nothing compared to what Wheeler Finch and Waz King have. The friends they've made are very wealthy, powerful people. We're talking judges, attorneys, clerks, and I wouldn't be surprised if there were local PD out there on some sort of payroll too."

I think about the people Wheeler rubs elbows with—business owners, judges, just about everyone in this town. He's not wrong. I know everything he's saying makes sense. More criminals got out on technicalities and the mishandling of evidence than for any other reason.

There's too much history. Too many awful things that my family and I have had to go through at the expense of Waz King and Wheeler Finch. I'm not interested in waiting, the same way I'm not interested in seeing when the FBI is going to make a move.

When I stand up and move for the door, Cortez says, "Faye, I'm serious. I do not want you involved in this."

Filled with resolve, I smile and turn to look over my shoulder. "Involved in what?" I say, feigning an innocence that we both know doesn't exist.

There's no way in hell I'm going to sit back and wait for Cortez to fix this or for something to happen to the only source they have left.

Chapter 34

Lincoln

I GUIDE THE NEWEST MEMBER of the Foxx family into her new home. Lark and Lily are going to freak out when they get back from school and see her over here. "You're sure Maggie doesn't mind that we board Dottie here?"

Faye slips her hands inside the back pocket of her tight blue jeans. She looks around the renovated barn and smiles as she says, "It was her idea, and I technically own half this place, so it's as much her decision as it is mine." She looks around the stalls and beams overhead. "I don't understand why she would pour money into it and not have at least a few animals to enjoy it."

When we leased the cornfields for Foxx, she had gotten a nice bonus. There needed storage built for harvesting to be stored.

Dottie moos as I brush along her body. "I'm going to have a schedule for all of us to make sure she's taken care of properly. Just because she's here doesn't mean she's your obligation. I have

YouTube videos queued up to figure out how the heck to have a pet cow."

Faye nods. "Oh I know." She tries to bite back a smile, and I give her a double take.

"Why is that funny?" I ask, eyebrow quirking at the somewhat guilty look on her face.

"This can go either way here…" She closes her eyes and says, "I know you've been watching a decent amount of videos about grooming and raising a highland cow because I may have put a hidden mirroring app on yours and Ace's phones."

Out of all the things she could have said, I wasn't expecting that. With a small laugh, I ask, "And did you find anything interesting?"

She opens one eye and apprehensively admits, "Ace is very organized."

"That's not news. I was hoping you'd tell me he sends nudes regularly to someone or belongs to a knitting circle that meets on Saturday nights."

She barks out a laugh. "That's specific." Seeming a bit nervous, she pets along Dottie's shaggy coat. "Are you mad?"

I toss the brush and move closer to her. "Look at me, Peach."

She moves her focus from the cow to me, eyes locking right onto mine.

"I've got nothing to hide from you," I tell her. "And I'm not mad. I do want to know exactly what you found on my brother's phone, though."

She shifts closer. "I needed more details about what you and Ace were doing and if your ties to Blackstone—"

I cut her off, wrapping my hand around her forearm and pulling her against me. "I still have nothing to hide." I swallow down the emotion surfacing for what I'm going to say next. "You can trust me."

Her nod against my chest is enough of a confirmation for now. Truthfully, I'm not surprised—the woman is an investigator.

She grows quiet for a few minutes as she holds me right back. Any time my girls get quiet, I know something isn't right. Before I can ask, she looks up and says, "Blackstone is dead."

That isn't what I was expecting. I put down the brush and move closer to her. "What happened to him?" I ask.

She cuffs a piece of hair behind her ear, taking a deep breath. "That's the problem. It was exactly what killed him that has me…" Looking up at me, she shakes her head. "His neck was sliced in two places. He bled out and—" She clears her throat. "It was the same wounds that Tullis had."

I search her face for what she's trying to tell me. Because, according to her, it was her mother who had killed Tullis and left Faye to clean up her mess. "But your mom—" I start to say, but she cuts me off.

"Maggie was there. She heard everything before I walked into that kitchen. It was never my mother." A tear escapes the edge of her eye, but she bats it away, trying not to let herself crack.

"When did she tell you this?" I ask, trying to make sense of how she would just be finding this out.

"At the rodeo." She shifts a glance around the barn, giving herself a second to elaborate. "My mother didn't kill him." When she meets my gaze this time, she looks so dejected it makes my chest ache. "Waz did."

Are you fucking kidding me?

"He threatened her. Told her to keep her mouth shut about

what Finch & King had been doing, which is still unclear the extent of what that meant. And then he told her he'd come back for me and Maggie if she said anything. I suppose killing Tullis was his insurance policy. Kept her looking like the guilty party if he needed one and made room for him to take on a bigger part of Finch & Kings."

A sob breaks from her chest as she punches the side of the horse stall. She's pissed off and upset. I don't blame her.

My adrenaline pumps just thinking about the level of danger she's been thrust into. And now Blackstone ends up dead the same way as Tullis? It's too specific to be any type of coincidence.

"Maggie never said anything. My mother couldn't. And I went ahead and assumed the worst and buried it," she says, blowing out a breath.

I wrap my arms around her. Her shoulders shake, and I let her stain my shirt with tears.

Once her breathing calms, I move my hand to her face, tilting her chin up to look at me. "Listen to me," I tell her softly. She keeps herself wrapped around me like she can't bear to move away right now. "None of that is something you could have known or stopped. You protected your family based on what you knew back then. It's as simple as that."

Like she's physically pained, she closes her eyes. "I should have paid attention. Noticed the details better, and then maybe—"

"Don't," I cut her off. "What-ifs and maybes aren't reality. They're ideas. And if we're not careful and focus too heavily on them, they'll make us spiral." I lean down and kiss her forehead before I wrap my arms around her again. "I did it for too long and it got me nowhere. Except therapy."

She steps away just enough to wipe her tears and let out a small laugh at my lame attempt to lighten this. "I promise you that I won't let any of this any closer to your family than it already is."

I cross my arms and pick up what she's not saying. "Then you have a plan?"

"The FBI has to play by the rules. There are layers here that are much deeper than I realized, but while they build a case…" She closes her eyes, steadying herself. "Maggie is their only source. And she's fed them all she can without Finch or King realizing it. At least, I hope. I know Waz is suspicious, and then you throw me into the mix, and what's happened with Blackstone."

I don't like any part of it. She's important to me in ways I never expected or planned. And I damn well won't let anything happen to her.

"It puts a lot of people in danger, Foxx. I can't just sit and wait for something bad to happen."

I feel exactly the same way. But what I've come to know about this woman is that she's not going to ride this out.

"You're smart and capable. And I know the worst possible thing I can do is to tell you to let them handle it." I run my hand along my jaw and choose my words carefully. "Tell me what you need from me."

Speechless for a moment, she only blinks at me. "Just like that?"

I give a nod when I answer, "Just like that."

"I need to talk to Maggie first."

Same. I hold out my hand and she takes it so I can wrap my arms around her. "Just don't expect me to leave your side."

"Okay," she says, nodding as she gives Dottie a few more pets.

"How would you feel about coming over for kitchen-sink dinner tonight?" I ask. I like the idea of her being at my table and being a part of something that the girls and I do a couple of times a month together.

She smiles curiously. "What's kitchen-sink dinner?"

I turn on the hose and make sure the trough is filled. "You'll have to come over to find out."

"This is my favorite mix right now—it's a bunch of mashups from these DJs on TikTok. They pull together classics from the 70s, like ABBA or Hall & Oates, and then pair it with a solo diva artist like Celine or Mariah," Lark says as she and Faye share the EarPods and hover over her iPad.

"My mom used to play this Mariah Carey album every Saturday morning. It was our cleaning day. And that meant two things: Nobody was sleeping in and the music was going to be loud. Maggie and I grumbled the entire time."

Lark adds, "I would have too."

I turn around, grabbing the pot to boil water. Most of what we have in the refrigerator will go best over rice or pasta. "Girls, are we doing a rice, pasta, or a salad base tonight?"

Faye listens to the split vote between all three options. "Do we get to know what else is going with it?"

Lily opens the refrigerator doors and starts rattling off the half-used items and leftovers. "Two tomato halves, diced onion, some leftover chicken, and dad's shrimp scampi leftovers. There's half of a container of strawberries." She turns toward me. "Dad, is that parsley or cilantro?"

"Cilantro," I answer.

"Rice," Faye calls out. "I have an idea. Am I allowed to help?"

I shift a glance to Lark and then to Lily. "Can she help?"

They both give their happy yeses in unison, and I hold my arm out, ushering Faye to take the reins. "Kitchen-sink dinner is all yours, Peach."

Just under an hour later, I rinse off the last dish and add it to the dishwasher. "This one definitely means vivid energy," Faye says as she points to the gemstone bracelet on Lily's arm. "Here, let's figure out if you wear that during a new moon phase, if it will have healing capabilities that morph into something else."

Lily laughs out, "Do you think that's how it works? Like, everything is connected like that?"

Faye shrugs her shoulders. "Everything is connected in some way or another—gems and stalagmites seem like they might take some charge from the moon, don't you think?"

"Or the sun," Lily says with interest.

"Dad," Lark whispers next to me. When I look at her, she keeps her eyes trained on Lily and Faye.

"Yeah, sweetheart, what's up?"

She keeps whispering, "That was, like, really good. It was better than the usual kitchen-sink dinner. I've never had strawberries in a taco bowl, but it worked. And I kind of want it again another night."

I lean into her space and ask something I'm hoping she'll be on board with. "Should we ask her to come to dinner again then?"

She's watching what I am: Lily and Faye getting excited about the fact that it's a waxing gibbous moon and Lily has a natural cluster of citrine.

"Yeah, I think it would be nice to have her here," she says with a smile as she grabs her iPad and moves to the living room.

"Lark, you're not allowed to watch an episode without me," Lily calls out, storming into the living room after her sister.

Faye looks at the glass I slid in front of her after she takes a sip. "Why do I love this? What is this?"

It's not hard to feel pride at hearing her say that. "It's the bourbon I'm testing out."

"I like it," she hums with a relaxed grin.

"You're looking a little more carefree than earlier today," I tell her as she moves into the kitchen. Coming up behind me, she cages me in, wrapping her arms around my waist as I finish rinsing the last pan. She rests her head on my back, and I can't move fast enough to dry my hands and turn around to hold her. I don't know when it started feeling comfortable—this sense of ease when I'm around her, but on a night like tonight, I feel it. I feel how easy it would be to have more nights just like it.

As I settle into the weight of her leaning into me and my arms wrapped tight, my nerves kick in. In my gut, I know this could fall apart in a minute, and I plan to do everything in my power to make sure that doesn't happen.

Chapter 35

Lincoln

"You got a minute?" I ask as I plow through Ace's kitchen.

Both he and Grant have their coffee cups halfway to their lips, not expecting me this early. Julep greets Kit on her leash at my side. "Sit."

She listens and looks up for her reward. I dig into my pocket for a dime-sized cookie. "You saw the article, I'm guessing?" Ace asks, leaning against the counter.

I look at Grant, who passes me the phone. On the screen is a picture of the three of us as school-aged boys. I remember this from the 75th Anniversary of Foxx Bourbon. It was one of the biggest celebrations we'd ever seen in Fiasco at the time. The headline of the article reads, "100 years of Bourbon & the Secret to it All."

I look up at my oldest brother and he looks pleased. When I scroll down, in italics is exactly what I said to Murray that day, and right at this moment it feels especially true: *...what* *ends up in those barrels is called 'the heart' for a reason. It might be the Kentucky water, the thriving culture of bourbon, but I believe what makes Foxx Bourbon the best bourbon is the pride poured into those barrels and the respect the Foxx family has for it. As they celebrate 100 years of bourbon, one of the most distinguished brands keeps the heart while evolving as palates and audiences change.*

The timing of those words couldn't be more perfect. I put the unmarked bottle on the counter. "Grant, grab three glasses." But he's already sliding them across the marble. I take note of the viscosity of this batch—deeper browns this time has it looking more like a double barrel bourbon than the single barrel it initially had been. We've been making specific blends for important moments in our life ever since I can remember. It was one of the things that helped us keep track of what years we liked more than others.

"There was nothing significant about this batch. It was a typical mash bill: 71% corn, 16% rye, and 12% barley. Aged her in barrels in our rickhouse for four years." I look between the two of them before I confess what I've been doing. "Then infused with thyme and peaches for two and a half weeks."

Grant smiles to himself as he noses it.

Ace holds up the glass in the light to see the color before he smells it, tossing a glance my way. "Peach?"

I give him a stiff nod as my younger brother smiles around his sip.

Ace shakes his head. "I'll give it to you and Grant, you assholes both really take shit literally, don't you?"

Grant says, "It has a great palate."

I chime in with my thoughts. "You can drink it on the rocks, chilled neat, mix it, whatever. But it opens up potential for a new audience." I nod to my glass. "You want to see Foxx brand in more glasses, then we need to appeal to the crowd that doesn't typically like bourbon. This doesn't need to take away from our roots or stifle the true bourbon market, but it has potential."

Ace takes another sip. "I don't hate it. Might want to try it with a higher percentage of rye instead of corn. The rye could add that layer of spice to balance the sweet." He shrugs one shoulder before he says, "See what keeps the flavor profile best."

Most of our blends were higher percentages of corn. It made our mash sweeter. The sugars ate into the oak from the barrels and the temperatures that fluctuated during the aging process is what Ace always said was what made our tasting profiles the most robust. We didn't agree on everything, or even that logic, but this feedback from him feels like a win; one of the biggest of my career to hear the approval of my older brother.

"Don't look so pleased with yourself. You're the one who's going to have to tell Griz that you want to put fruit in his bourbon. And I want a front-row seat to that shit show."

"Did someone say shit show?" Hadley says, waltzing in.

Ace barks out a laugh. "I forgot that was your calling card."

She hisses at him like a damn cat.

Grant and I share an amused look as Ace says, "Your maturity level never ceases to amaze me, Hadley."

She tips her head back and looks at the ceiling, laughing to herself. "Too easy." Then she focuses on Ace. "But I'm not here for you." Shifting her attention to me, she says, "I stopped by your house to give you that architect's information and Maggie was sitting on your porch. She said she needed to talk with you. Figured you'd be here." Looking down at the bottle on the table, she raises her eyebrows, wordlessly asking how it went. She knew I was going to pitch this today.

I give her a half smile and a wink of success.

"Good. When you're ready, I'll take a case. I think it's an instant kitty winner."

Ace exhales, "Fucking hell."

"Anyway," Hadley says, striding out the way she came. "She's out in the stables with Griz."

"Thanks, Hads," I call out.

I shift a glance at Grant, curious for his two cents. I want to ensure I'm making the right call here before I put anything into motion. "Grant." I nod toward the hall. "I need a second."

His brow furrows, but he doesn't question it. Once we have some privacy, I say, "A hypothetical for you."

Grant crosses his arms. "Alright," he grunts out. The grumpy bastard. "Hypothetical," he says on an exhale.

I mimic his stance, crossing my arms. "If someone was trying to build a criminal case, but obtaining search or surveillance warrants could alert the person of interest and jeopardize it, what would you do?"

That crease between his eyebrows only deepens. "Do I want to know—"

I shake my head.

He takes in a deep breath. "Alright, I'll play. Following the rules is what keeps a case airtight. But I'm assuming gaining access to warrants isn't possible because maybe a judge or higher-ups might be too close to the situation?" *Ding, ding, ding.* He keeps talking without my answer. "Sources and witnesses would be the best option to build out a case like that."

That's what Cortez had been doing. It's what puts Maggie at the center of whatever Finch and King are up to.

I nod and grasp his shoulder as I move past. "Thanks."

Grant calls out just as I reach the door, "If there was a public outcry."

I turn back to listen.

He looks down for a minute weighing his words before he says, "If there was enough social media attention or if the person of interest was mentioned in the news being in anyway associated with that crime, it could push things forward. It's hard to ignore a situation when it's staring you in the face. Building pressure could be an option."

That's what I needed to hear. I knock my fingers along the door frame and nod. "Thanks." He gives me a tight-lipped nod and adds, "Careful here."

I don't add anything else even though a part of me wants to. When I make my way down to the stables, Griz and Maggie are leaning over the stall to one of the foals that was born late last autumn. I overhear Griz tell her, "Making this right is not going to bring her back. Whatever you're doing, it needs to stop before someone gets hurt."

"He's got good advice most of the time," I say, pulling their attention. "Griz, you mind if I talk to Maggie?"

He gives her a kiss on the side of her head and then wraps his hand on my shoulder as he leaves. "Go easy, yeah?"

I don't know how Griz knows some of the shit he does sometimes. Maybe it's my body language or how I'm glaring at someone who is kicking up a lot of dust and I'm worried it's going to hit the people I'm supposed to protect.

As soon as Griz is out of earshot, I'm saying what I need to, my tone one of warning. "I know you're playing in some deep water. Don't bullshit me here, Maggie. What are you doing with Finch & King?"

She hums a laugh. "Why do you care, Linc? I'm still doing

what you and Ace hired me to do. I just sold out most of what you guys have on reserve. Your bourbon is in some serious circulation, and you have the profit to prove it."

"I'm aware, and we both know it's got nothing to do with that."

"Faye?" she asks as she passes the horse a carrot.

"If anything happens to you, she gets hurt. If you end up on the wrong side of whatever it is you're planning, then she becomes leverage. I become leverage. My family. My girls. And I won't let that happen."

"Linc," she says, resting her head on her folded arms along the stable door. "She told you everything, didn't she?"

I give her a nod. "She's not going to just let this linger and hope for the best." When I look at her pointedly, I can see in her eyes, she knows I'm right. She's nervous, not that she'll admit it.

Pulling out my phone, I filter through my contacts and make a call. "Hey, Murray." I smile into the phone when he picks up on the second ring.

"Lincoln Foxx, I wondered when I might hear from you," he says in an upbeat tone. "What did you think of the piece?"

Maggie watches me curiously as I say, "It was a great article. I wanted to personally thank you."

"Nothing to thank me for," he says kindly. "I visited a number of distilleries and not a single one left me feeling the way yours had after our interview. You do have something special there."

I take the compliment. "I think so too." I glance at Maggie, hoping this is going to go how I want it to. "Listen, Murray, there's someone here who might be able to answer your questions about what's happening in horse racing down here. Thought you might want to hear what she has to say."

That's got her attention, but not in a good way. Straightening, she's shaking her head to shut me up.

Murray shuffles something in the background, likely a recorder or something to take down anything else I'm going to say. "Any chance you have a name for me so I can follow up?"

But I don't give him much else. "I'm going to leave that in her court. Just wanted you to know I hadn't forgotten you asked."

We exchange a few more niceties before I hang up.

Maggie crosses her arms, nearly shouting, "What the fuck, Linc?"

I lean against the chair to her right and level with her. "You've put all your faith into the FBI figuring this out and making sure the people who hurt you and your family will end up getting justice. I don't like those odds." She understands racing and gambling, and I see when what I'm saying clicks in her mind. "If all of this doesn't end how you want it"—I hand her Murray's card—"now you have another option."

She looks down at it, not convinced. "This isn't going to fix anything. This would create a mess."

"Sometimes you need to make a mess in order to make things right."

"I've already made bad calls here, Linc," she says, tilting her head and turning over the reporter's business card, her tone shifting. "I kept things from my sister, from my mom. And Cortez. The fucking FBI is leaning on me. I don't care about anything more than making Waz pay for what he's done." She chokes back a sob. "And it's gotten—"

I give her a Foxx shoulder squeeze and cut her off. "I know what it feels like to be stuck. To feel like you don't have any other choices in doing what someone else wants. Doing the right thing sometimes is as simple as protecting the people we love." I look at the card she's holding, tapping it once. "That's another way."

She searches my face for what I'm really saying. And then she lets out a breathy laugh. "You love her," she says, like it isn't something she had considered.

My chest warms as I smile. "I protect what's mine, Maggie. And that includes Faye now."

She looks down at her nails, reminding me of Lark when she gets into her head.

"You had to keep a secret for a long time. I know how that can feel like you're drowning in it. But you're strong, Maggie. Just like your sister. And now you're in a position where you hold all the cards. If it gets too dangerous for you. For her." I look at the business card in her hand once more before I step away. "That right there is your fail-safe

Chapter 36

Faye

Clive hits the bass at the same time that Marshall on trumpet digs in and throws the best solo I've heard in a really long time. For as much as Griz wanted to bad-mouth these guys, they're some of the best jazz players I've ever had the pleasure of performing with. The kick of the piano riff is the perfect spot in the song to finish the number.

With soft pink ostrich feather fans outstretched above and below me, I move around the room as the spotlight follows. The red satin slip dress scoops low enough that if I tip my hips forward and bend, the audience is teased with glitter-brushed cleavage and the very tops of my rhinestone tassels. I was going for an old-Hollywood look, as usual, but tonight deserved a little extra glam. In the velvet love seats tucked into the corner, Prue and Romey shimmy their shoulders in time with the music as Marla sips her draft beer. Marla isn't smiling, but she's been dropping in a few loud whistles between lulls in the music.

I pop my hips toward the bar, raising my arms gracefully while the feathered fans rotate in each hand. Tonight's song is the bluesy rendition of Nina Simone's "Feeling Good," which is exactly how I'm feeling, knowing there is a plan in play.

When I hop up onto the bar as directed, a shot of bourbon waits for me. After the chatter about mine and Lincoln's little show at the rodeo after-party, Hadley thought it would be a good idea to add in bourbon at the end of the night.

So tonight, with the band readying the final few notes, I hold up my shot of bourbon as the jazz singer says, "Ladies and gentlemen, you've been a wonderful audience. Cheers to Foxx Bourbon for the last round, always on them." She tips her glass toward the door, and there he is. Lincoln Foxx, looking like a fantasy, perfectly assembled in black, with a smirk painted across his lips and dimples pinched, doing maximum damage to every pair of panties watching. His ocean eyes are focused on the only thing he sees: me.

As I wait for the audience to tip theirs back before I follow, another familiar face in the crowd catches my attention. With his attention fixed on me, Wheeler Finch sips a glass of port, relaxed back in his seat. Alone. Hadley has been very clear that Waz isn't allowed at Midnight Proof. He'd gotten himself in enough trouble, and she'd asked her father to keep him away. But I hadn't expected Wheeler to be here either for some reason. I haven't seen him at a single one of my shows since I started here.

Tonight, of all nights, seems like a bad coincidence. A cool shiver rushes up my back, and I keep my smile from faltering, actively trying to avoid looking back his way again.

Keeping up with the finale, I stand on the bar and pour my shot of bourbon with flair. As soon as the long pour goes down my throat, Hadley knows to pull the string on the back of my dress, and it falls away as I give my hips an exaggerated twerk. My hiked-high satin shorts are cut so my ass cheeks get the proper attention, while the rhinestone covers accentuate each breast, giving the crowd the finale they've been panting for. I move my shoulders and hips so that my entire body shimmies in time with the drummer hitting the cymbals, the trumpet carrying out the last note. It's the kind of show that people don't forget.

When I hop down from the bar, I move with quick steps down the hallway toward the small dressing room that Hadley converted from a storage closet. Before I can even start to unbuckle my heels, there's a tap at the door as it opens. "Hey, Peach."

I release a silent sigh of relief that it's him. As he walks in, I'm smiling wide, and he doesn't stop until his arms wrap around me and his lips press just below my ear. "Mmm, you smell like my bourbon."

Taking a deep breath of him, I love the way it feels to be in his arms—the warm scent of toasted oak and tartness like a bourbon-soaked cherry consuming my senses. It's delicious.

"I didn't think you would be here tonight." I glance at the clock that reads just after midnight. "Who's with the girls?"

"They opted for an evening with Griz to learn the harmonica. Lily told him she wanted to try to read his palm for him." He smiles, moving his hands to my hips as he looks at me. "And I don't like missing you out there—"

I cut him off with a kiss, too worked up about what's happening next tonight. Moaning against my mouth, he holds on to me tighter, kissing me thoroughly—just what I needed.

The clearing of someone's throat and a knock on the open door interrupts, and we break apart.

"Faye, just wanted to see if we were still going to have that drink," Maggie says confidently, leaning against the door frame

There's no plan for drinks, but she's figuring out a way to get Lincoln out of the fray. He isn't supposed to be here, and since I'm trying to keep him away from the plan, he probably thinks he'll be taking me home now that my performance is over.

But Maggie and I have an important task to complete tonight, one that he'll find out about later if everything goes smoothly.

Within the next hour, we'll be at Finch & King stables, planting the rest of the surveillance cameras before the staff arrives for the 5 a.m. training. I had already gone on a Finch & King stables tour, which, as I had assumed, was a well-oiled machine. Tours run frequently, even in the winter months, taking groups through the stables, feeding horses, and observing the vast landscape peppered with horses on their paddocks tours. It's the mask for what happens behind the curtain. The mistreatment and criminal-level manipulation of an industry that my sister and I are determined to expose.

I had set up a few small cameras along the exterior, but places that would garner the most activity would be inside the facility and offices.

Cortez used Maggie as leverage and me as bait. The Calloway girls were done playing by someone else's rules. It isn't just about doing the right thing. For Maggie, this is retribution, and for me, it's about protecting who I love.

The horse racing season will be starting soon, and if we have anything to say about it, Finch & King will no longer be allowed anywhere near the winner's circle. With enough evidence, they will find themselves behind bars. At the very least, visuals and recordings of what is happening behind closed doors could push the case forward.

Lincoln kisses my neck, and as he pulls back, he says, "I'm going to check in and make sure the girls are asleep. Come find me when you're done."

I smile as he kisses my wrist and then turns to leave. He gives Maggie a squeeze on the shoulder and a tight-lipped smile as he heads down the hall toward the bar.

When he's out of sight, she gives me a look of concern. "I noticed a particular face in the audience tonight." I know exactly who she's talking about. "What the fuck is Wheeler Finch doing here?"

I button up my cardigan and slip my joggers over my tights and satin shorts. "This is his daughter's place. Maybe he wanted to check in on Hadley?"

Maggie bites her thumbnail and shakes her head. "They're not close. Hadley smiles and gives him a kiss on the cheek when she sees him, but that's as far as it lands. It could be a random stop by, but I don't trust it."

I slip Lily's good luck amethyst rock into my pocket and pin my hair up out of my face. I'm overheated and anxious about what we were heading out to do.

Maggie's hair is slicked back into a ponytail and dark shadow smudges along her lash line. Her long-sleeved black shirt works with the wide-leg jeans to hug her figure. "You look good. Wait, are you meeting someone later?"

She rolls her eyes. "Oh, please, that sounds far too planned. I swiped on Tinder just in case tonight was a bust."

I blink at my sister. "We're going to break into multiple properties owned by Finch & King, and then, depending on what time we wrap it up, you're going to embark on an unattached hookup?"

"I like having options," she says, wiggling her eyebrows as

we make our way down the hall of Midnight Proof toward the back entrance. "Don't judge me about unattached hookups just because you're a regular on the dad bang train now. We both know you'll end up over at his house later."

"Clever and disturbing," I say on a clipped laugh. "But don't say 'dad bang train' ever again."

"Speaking of. You're going to have to run defense with Lincoln when he realizes you left him here," she says as she follows me up the stairs and out the back exit.

"I know." I'll let him know what I'm doing once it's done. I don't like leaving out details, but I need to do this with Maggie without anyone else involved.

The metal door to the back lot clamors open, and I appreciate the chill as soon as it hits me. But it isn't the smell of croissants in the air or the evergreens across the street on the town green that wafts over me; it's the thick cologne and a twinge of cigarettes instead. As soon as the door behind me clicks shut, I realize I left my bag back in my makeshift dressing room. Without my keys, I can't get back inside this way.

A subdued whispering whistle makes me stop mid-step as goosebumps pluck along my skin. Maggie hears it too because her fingers brush along my hand, urging me to stay quiet and listen.

Our heads jerk to the left when a voice says, "You think I don't know what you've been doing, little Maggie Calloway?" Waz laughs to himself as he eases off the wall that had been bathed in darkness along the alleyway. *Shit.*

Maggie stays quiet and shifts closer to me. *What the hell is he doing here?*

"Thought you would've learned your lesson the first time not to creep up on a woman, Waz." I tilt my head, looking at him as I draw a circle in front of my nose. "That didn't heal very nicely."

"Faye. You should have stayed in your own slutty world. Why'd you start poking around here? I can't figure out if Blackstone was a coincidence or if you're as sneaky as your sister." He circles closer, blocking the path down the alley. Tsking, he tilts his head to the side as he watches us try to create distance between us and him. "Maggie, Maggie, Maggie, you didn't learn your lesson the first time? You think I wasn't serious when I told you if you tried to double-cross me again, I'd slice you up nice and pretty?"

Maggie doesn't say a word, seeming almost too calm, but my adrenaline rushes through my veins in a way that makes me desperate to defuse this.

Waz licks at his lower lip, the tobacco dip that was shoved along his cheek dribbling out just after he spits. Maggie and I both tense at the sound of a switchblade opening, pulling our attention to the knife at his side.

"You try to make it look like I was stealing from Wheeler." He moves his head back and forth slowly. "You don't think that made me keep a closer eye on you? That beating was just for fun, girlie. We just wanted to see how far you were willing to go. Do you think Wheeler is in charge just because he shakes hands and is from this fucking town?"

"That's exactly what I think," Maggie bites back, her fierceness rising to the surface as she stares him down.

"That's fine by me, Maggie. The truth is, nobody in this town thinks much of you anyway." Eyes wide and bloodshot, he chuckles, like something wonderful just came to him. "This town likes to talk, don't they? And they love to chatter about people who're fuckin'. Is that what you're doing with that Officer

Cortez? You fuckin' him?" He smiles a creepy, slow smile that shows off his crooked teeth. "Or are you just as much a rat like that fucker Blackstone? He bled out faster than my brother. Who knew all you needed to do was let gravity work in your favor. Could've saved a lot of time with the horses we need to cancel too."

"You're a fucking psychopath," Maggie grits out.

"You say that like that isn't already common knowledge. I don't try to pretend to be something I'm not." His eyes shift to me. "Like you've been doing, Faye." He says it like he's just working all of this out. That, until this moment, it hadn't dawned on him that I'm not only here for entertainment. "Wheeler isn't going to be happy to find out any of this. Extinguishing what's left of the Calloways wasn't my plan tonight, but I do love surprises."

Another shiver rolls up my back as Waz smiles at me, but his calm demeanor is just a decoy, as a second later, he darts for my sister. I suck in a sharp breath as he grabs her ponytail and yanks her toward him when she sees him coming and tries to turn away.

Holding her against his chest, he whispers something in her ear as she screams out. Her face squints up as if whatever he said to her is causing her physical pain.

That's when I see his wrist flick forward.

"No!" I shout as he twists that knife slowly into her side. It's thrust all the way to the handle, right where a kidney would be.

She groans out, "Fuck. You."

"Maggie, why would you want to bite the hands feeding you?" he croons and looks down the side of her face. "Unless you were you there that night…" he snivels into her ear, and my stomach clenches. "Did you see something you weren't supposed to, girlie?"

I feel helpless. Her face is crunched up and streaked in tears. I know she's fighting like hell not to give in to it. She heaves in audible breaths, and on each inhale, she winces.

"That hurts, doesn't it? Someone toying with you? Your mama and my brother just needed to fall in line. Tullis couldn't keep Shelby under control, so I had to step in." Sneering, he licks up the side of her face. "I have no problem doing the hard things. Just like you, Maggie. We do the hard things."

He rubs his groin against her, pulling a sob from her chest, just before she says, "Let go of me, you sick fuck."

I rack my mind about what the hell I can do to stop this. I try to think of what I have on me. I didn't have my karambit knife. My stun gun was charging. *Goddamnit.* I look around the space and nothing that could be used as a weapon is within an arm's reach.

He pulls her tighter, his forearm against her chest, and runs his nose along her cheek as her chest heaves up and down. "There's a little spot…" He pulls out the knife from her back slowly.

The guttural scream that tears from her throat has anger overpowering the fear of him hurting her any more than he already has.

Waz uses the tip of the now blood-painted knife to point just below her ear. "This is the sweet spot right around here that if you catch it just right, with something nice and sharp, a horse, a human, anyone who might not be doing as they're told, will bleed so beautifully. It comes out fast at first, like drinking water from a garden hose, and then it runs steady with the beat of your heart." He lets out a low whistle, just before he says, "It makes for a nice show."

"That's enough," I seethe, blood boiling as my heart pounds in my ears.

He hums in response. "Is that so? You think I'll listen to you just because you dance that tight little cunt around?"

She squints as he rubs his cheek against hers, her eyes searching mine for a way out of this. When I look down, I notice her jeans are turning darker, wetter as they saturate with her blood as he holds her. It has my heart sinking to my feet.

So I make a quick decision and say, "You jealous, Waz?"

His eyes flick over to mine. But I don't let him answer. "Want something you can't have?"

He shifts Maggie forward so fast, his boot meeting the center of her back, shoving her off of him and to the ground just a few feet away. In the commotion of it, I try to reach her, but he gets to me before I can make up the distance.

I hear a voice calling my name, but I don't get a chance to listen for it again, because pain explodes in my stomach and vibrates throughout my back.

Waz punches me again before I can recover, harder this time, knocking the wind out of me. He shouts in my face, but I can't make out the words as I try to catch my breath. He grabs my jaw, pinching it so hard that pain radiates across my face. With a second of clarity and desperation, I feel behind me, trying to reach for my pocket. My fingers brush over the rock I'd put there before we left. One side smooth, while the other is craggy and purple. Its jagged edges won't do much, but if I hit him right, it'll startle him enough to let me go.

He spits in my face as he says, "Shoulda killed your mama that night too. Had my way with her like I kept promising. Then woulda come for Maggie next. Saving you for last. I think you'll be the most fun to watch bleed."

I try to move with all my strength, but his hold grows tighter every time I push against it, shouting and panting.

He glances at my sister, but I can't see her from where he's holding me. "Maggie," he calls out. "I'm going to have fun with you fir—" But his words die off as I swing my arm out wide and with as much strength as I can find. I slam my fist against the side of his head, using the rock as weight and leverage.

And everything that happens next happens so fast that I can barely register it.

Lincoln screams my name.

Waz's hands release me.

My body stutters away, barely staying on my feet as Waz laughs. "This isn't going to matter," Waz says as he holds the side of his head and spits out the wad of chew. "I've got a lot of friends in far higher places. I'm not going to just go awa—"

Finally, that's where his words die off. If I had blinked, I would have missed the quickness of Lincoln's moves. Fast and precise, he swipes Waz's knife from the ground, and with no hesitation, grips it tight and slashes the blade across Waz's neck. My breath catches as his skin flays open as if a zipper had been pulled. Blood pours down his neck, his hand flying to the wound, just as Lincoln turns and rushes to me.

Maggie grits into her phone, mumbling her words. "Cortez. Get here now," she says, just as Waz drops to both knees and then face-plants onto the pavement.

My hand covers my mouth on a sob, tears streaking down my cheeks.

"Look at me," Lincoln pleads, eyes wild and full of panic. His hands cupping my face, he pulls my body toward him, and I collapse against him in a momentary state of shock. "Look at me, baby. Are you hurt?" He looks around my body, but it's not me that's—

Oh god.

"Maggie!"

Chapter 37

Lincoln

"Maggie!" Faye shouts frantically. "Lincoln—Oh fuck. There's so much blood."

I pull off my jacket and shove it along Maggie's back. Faye does the same with her shirt, pressing it along her side. Sirens blare and the red-and-blue lights swing in chaotic patterns along every inch of the back-alley entrance of Midnight Proof in the next few seconds.

Cortez rushes over, taking inventory of the shit show that's just transpired: Maggie unconscious, being hoisted onto a gurney and put into the back of an ambulance. Faye doing her best to hold herself together right now. My right hand and forearm blanketed in red.

Faye grips onto the front of my shirt, full-fisted and wordlessly begging to feel safe, grounded, anything other than what seeing her sister being rushed away is doing to her right now.

Cortez scans her quickly from top to bottom. "Faye, are you hurt?"

"Yeah, she's fucking hurt. She's leaning to the side because that fucking animal punched her. That's just the physical shit, Cortez," I bark back. "This should have never gotten this out of hand, and you know it."

He looks at me and then down at Waz slumped over, his own blood pooled around him. "Who did it?"

Faye's hand squeezes my shirt tighter, her hold and breaths trembling and so unlike her. But we both keep our mouths closed without so much as a look at the other. "Maggie should have had backup. Or some kind of surveillance, Cortez. You're walking into a crime scene because it was self-defense against a fucking lunatic who has been loose in this town for far too long. Everyone knows it."

The cop in full uniform comes over with crime tape and speaks to Cortez. "We have a DOA and a weapon." He looks at both Faye and me pointedly before he says, "Are we—"

Cortez canvasses Faye and then focuses on her hand holding on to me. I don't know what he's trying to understand here, but he eventually clears his throat and says, "No arrests are necessary. I'll need you to come down and give your statements. Go make sure Maggie will be okay."

Faye nods, already stepping forward without letting me go.

With another look at the body, he adds, "The way it looks to me is that this was self-defense. You're going to need to corroborate that, but based on what I heard on the phone call from Maggie, and what I see here, it'll be written up as such."

I give him a nod and fire off a text to Grant. He'll be able to understand what comes next here. What, if any, repercussions I'll see after all is said and done. Every muscle in my body is still wound tight, adrenaline coursing through me. The moment I saw Waz holding my girl's face like that, I knew I would do whatever was necessary. *I won't lose anyone else.*

"Faye," Del calls out from his dark Crown Vic and waves us over. "Get in. I'll take you to the hospital."

We shift into the back of the car, and as soon as the door closes, he floors it, practically catching up with the ambulance on the main road riding its siren.

"Faye, honey, I never wanted you in this position. I knew shit wasn't stacking up right. Had a gut feeling that Maggie wasn't just going to take a beating like that and keep working for them. When I saw you meeting with Cortez, and then the way Blackstone had been murdered… I know this wasn't what you signed up for."

She leans forward and holds his shoulder. He pats her hand. "Del, if you hadn't called me, I don't know what would have happened here."

When we arrive at the hospital, it's a whirlwind trying to find out anything right away. But now we sit and wait for Maggie to come out of this, detecting the faintest smell of cloves in the hallway near Maggie's room as the doctors assess the state she's in.

Faye's arms wrap around my shoulders, and I've never wanted to hold on to anything so tightly in my life. We sit quietly together for what feels like hours. Dried blood on my shoes and flecks of it on my forearm are the only lingering hints that I just killed a man. It would guarantee me more rounds of therapy, but there's no remorse in any part of me for having done what I did. What matters is that Faye's safe.

"Thank you," she says in a quiet voice. This isn't how anyone expected this to go. She nuzzles into me and brushes her lips against my neck. "I've been trying to save other people for so long—" Her voice cracks, and she sits back. "I didn't know what it felt like to have someone look out for me. Not like this. Lincoln, I'm so sorry I involved you in all of this. This was never your mess—"

I wipe the tears pouring down her cheeks with my thumbs. "Look at me."

She lets out an exhale as her eyes flit to mine. *So beautiful.*

"Hi," I tell her softly with a smile.

It does what I want. She smiles back, and her body relaxes. "Hi."

"Listen to me. I'm *not*…going to say I love you while you're covered in blood and in a hospital."

Her hands find the hem of my shirt again as she plays with the material.

"I'm *not* going to tell you how I want your mess. And I won't tell you how you are exactly the kind of chaos I want mixed with mine."

She tries biting that favorite lip of mine.

"You didn't involve me in anything I didn't want to be a part of, Peach." Her pretty green eyes pool with more tears as she listens and searches for every truth I'm giving her.

"There's so much more here than I ever planned." I give her lips the kiss that they've been begging for, just tender enough to let her know that I'm not going anywhere. "So I'm *not* telling you how much I want you to stay and be with me. And my girls."

She smiles, letting out a small laugh, one filled with relief. "Alright."

I don't want this to be lost in all of the emotions swirling around tonight. "When we're past this, when you're ready to hear those things from me, you tell me, okay?"

But the clearing of the doctor's throat pulls her attention from me. "Miss Calloway, your sister has lost a lot of blood, but I'm confident she's going to be okay. We will need to get her into surgery. The wound along her back was deep enough that I want to make sure there isn't more damage. I'll be able to answer questions once we've taken a better look. For now, she's comfortable, but I'd like to get in there sooner rather than later."

My phone keeps vibrating in my back pocket, and when I pull it out, I see Hadley's name lit up on the screen. There has been a succession of missed calls from her and texts from Grant.

I kiss Faye's forehead and swipe my phone to answer. Hadley's voice comes rushing out. "You better be alright."

Faye squeezes my arm and walks toward the lobby of the hospital as my brothers and Griz bypass the front desk and head straight for us.

"I'm okay. We're okay," I tell her.

"And Faye, is she?"

Grant tilts his head and kneels to look Faye over. I can see them making sure she's alright, and the sight of her folded into my family makes my chest ache. This is how it's supposed to be.

"She's okay," I tell Hadley as I turn and stare at my forearm in the reflection of the window. I zone out, studying the outlines of my tattoo and the things that are most important to me—my girls, my bourbon, and the one that's empty. "If I hadn't gotten there when I had—"

Hadley cuts me off. "But you did."

I clear my throat as my brothers and grandfather stand in front of me. "But I did."

"Listen, Laney and I are at your house. Grant wanted to come to you so if you needed him, he'd be there. My guess is Ace and Griz aren't far behind."

"I'm staring at all three of them right now," I tell her as Griz grips my shoulder with a squeeze. His eyes close for a moment, his face squinting, the worry falling away as I lean into his hold.

"Both of the girls are asleep and in their pajamas. Kit too, which is a whole level of cute, by the way."

"And Dottie?" I ask.

"Your cow is tucked into the barn across the street. She was there when I came over and hadn't left. I think it's too chilly for her—seems like a summer kind of gal. Doesn't matter," she says with a laugh. "We're good here. You take care of your girl, and we'll be here, okay?"

"Thanks, Hads. You're the greatest, you know that?"

She exhales dramatically. "No shit, bestie. Love you, bye."

When I hang up with her, Ace grips my other shoulder as Griz says, "Del called Grant. Said there had been an accident." He lets out a stuttered exhale. "You boys are the most important thing in the world to me—" His mustache tips up to the side as he tries to bite back the emotions. "Need you to stick around long after I'm gone. Not the other way around. You hear me?"

I look at Grant, who understands as well as I do how quickly things can be taken away. We might not hug it out with each other, but a heavy hand and tight grip on a shoulder carry more weight between us than anything else. It's always been that way. I squeeze Grant's shoulder, and he grips Ace's. The four of us take a moment together—a touchpoint to make sure each of us is accounted for and okay.

The double doors to the hospital wing swing open as the doctor passes through. She stops short when she sees all of us. Faye leans against the wall with a smile, watching our exchange. "I've been asked to bring Faye and Griz back with me to see Maggie."

Faye looks at me for a moment, but before she does anything else, she walks right into my arms and kisses me. I can't help but smile against her lips. Just as she pulls away, she whispers quietly, just for me, "I love you."

I don't have a chance to wrap my arms around her tighter. She turns away and loops her arm with Griz's. I watch her walk away and move toward the double doors.

"Peach," I call out. "You're going to need to be a little louder with that later."

She looks over her shoulder with a smile that I burn into memory.

I started falling in love with Faye Calloway on the edge of a cornfield, on a stage, over a bottle of bourbon, and every time she's been in my arms since.

Chapter 38

Faye

Griz and I follow the doctor until she stops us right outside of a closed door. A man stands just to the right of it, wearing plain clothes with a gun holstered to his belt on one side and, on the other, a silver U.S. Marshall badge. Griz holds my arm as he mumbles, "Goddamnit."

But it's not until the door opens and we're escorted inside that I understand exactly what's happening. My sister is sitting up, fully clothed in what looks like fresh clothes, hair wet and slicked back, and ice packs bandaged to her side.

My eyes water as I rush out, "Maggie, you're okay."

Her chin quivers as she nods and says, "I'm okay."

And to her right, there's a woman who looks familiar, but I can't place. And Del.

"Bea." Griz addresses the woman. "You've got to be fucking kidding me right now."

I try to figure out what the dynamic is here. It dawns on me that Del was married to Bea a long time ago and that she traded up her Fiasco PD badge for the shiny star that sits on her right hip, reading, *U.S. Marshall.*

"Del, what are you doing here? What's going on?" I ask, nerves taking over as I scan everyone's face.

"Faye," Bea says as she leans against the farthest wall. "I've heard a great deal about you over the years from Del. Your mom too." She looks at me, then at Maggie when she says, "Listen, I'm going to make this short and sweet. I'm pissed off that I'm already back in Fiasco, folded into more drama with your damn family, Griz."

He grits his teeth, his thick 'stache barely moving when he says, "Stop grumbling and tell me exactly what's going to happen here."

But it's Maggie who responds. "I've shared information with the FBI that might put me in danger. And because of that, until that information can be used properly—"

Griz cuts her off and looks at Del. "You knew about this?"

"I knew Maggie was in over her head, but I didn't realize how much. You know Bea's the last person on earth I want to call for help."

She pulls out a clove cigarette, whispering, "Fuck you, Delaney…"

Del gives her the side-eye. "So me calling in a favor with my ex-wife—again, I might add—should say a lot about the severity of this, Griz."

Griz tips his chin toward Bea. "You seem to be collecting and owing a lot of those lately." He settles his attention on me, asking, "Are you going with her?"

Brow furrowed, I glance at Maggie. I wasn't planning on going anywhere.

"Before you answer that, Faye. The entire reason I'm even looping you both into this is because there's some overlap here. And"—she tilts her head to the side—"I think you should all be aware of it beforehand."

Griz exchanges a nod with Bea first before he says, "I vowed to never break this promise. Betray her trust. But you've both gone through enough of this life without knowing."

Confused, I lean against the wall and listen, paying attention to the way Bea types away at her burner phone. She says, "Del, that's your cue to leave."

Del gives me a tight-lipped smile as he walks in front of me. "Whatever you decide here, I'm proud of you."

I bite the corner of my lip, trying to keep from sobbing like a baby at hearing him say that. "Appreciate that, Del," I choke out. After wrapping me up in a big hug, he waltzes out the side door without looking back. I blow out a shaky breath.

Griz looks at me and gives me a smile, but his hand runs along the back of his neck. It's the most anxious I've seen him. Reaching into the inside pocket of his jacket, he pulls out a folded-up postcard and hands it to me.

I glance at Maggie before I take it from him. The softened paper is worn along the edges like it's been open and folded far too many times. On its front are faded, blue-tinted mountains surrounded by wildflowers in the foreground. And in bold, block letters it reads, *WELCOME TO HIDEAWAY, MONTANA.* When I flip to the back, there's a coffee ring stain in the upper left corner and is addressed to Griswald Foxx in a looping cursive handwriting that I'd recognize anywhere. It has my heart stuttering.

Mom.

In the note section, it reads, *A lifetime wouldn't have been enough.*

"What is this, Griz?"

He clears his throat. "I suppose it might be worth seeing for yourself." Then he nods to my sister. "Both of you."

I pass it to Maggie as tears fall down my cheeks and run down my neck. I don't understand and look toward my sister, whose eyes are glassy too. "Maggie? Did you know?"

She covers her mouth. "No," she says with a curt shake of her head.

"I made a promise to someone I fell in love with and couldn't keep safe," Griz says, looking down at his empty ring finger. "I never planned to fall in love again. I'd had a great love and lost her. I had made peace with that." Shaking his head, he blinks away the sheen in his eyes. "But your mother. There was just something about the way that woman would talk and smile. It was like a magnet. I couldn't stay away from her. I had no business with a woman so much younger, but she told me I made her feel safe. And those words from any woman are powerful. Even more than hearing 'I love you.'" He smiles fondly, and it has another tear trailing down my cheek. "And she said that eventually too."

He sits on the open chair, clearing his throat and leaning forward, elbows braced on his knees. "Wheeler Finch is not a good man. It's why we always opened our door to Hadley. He has never been a good father to her. And she didn't want to be around her dad, especially when he was conducting business." He looks at me when he says, "Your mama got wrapped up with Finch & King because she was a damn good horse trainer. Tullis sunk his teeth into her, and I sure as hell don't know what she ever saw in him, but he convinced her he was in love with her and that she needed him. Made her believe he could help her thrive in that business."

Pausing, he swallows roughly before continuing. "We all knew something wasn't right. I didn't know your mother very well back then, but anyone who paid attention had thought so—Marla, Romey, Prue. All of them shared with her later that they knew Tullis was trouble. In hindsight, what would they have said?"

I answer him, "It wouldn't have mattered. She was stubborn and he manipulated her, gaslit her, for far too long."

"Tullis might have had a reputation as one of the best horse trainers, but that was where the good ended. Both of the King brothers and Wheeler Finch turned Kentucky horse racing into a billion-dollar empire, which made them untouchable." He looks over at Maggie. "You can imagine that Wheeler was *not* happy to discover when Tullis left. Cops called it a missing persons case after random credit cards being used at motels throughout the Southeast stopped happening after about a year and a half—"

"Two years," I correct him. With all eyes on me now, a little bit of truth wouldn't hurt to slip through.

Griz thinks for a moment about what I've said, but instead of asking questions, he carries on. "Two years, and then he had been presumed dead. But his brother, Waz, was always adamant that your mother had something to do with it. Kept that rumor going for a long while. And that eventually he'd find proof of it too."

Waz is a psychopath, plain and simple.

"She told me what happened, what Waz had done to Tullis. How he threatened your mama and you girls." He runs his hand over his mustache and down his chin. "When he caught wind that something had been going on with us, he tried to blackmail her in other unsavory ways. That was what tipped things over for me and for her. I knew I couldn't protect her. Not back then. I had to look out for my boys. Lincoln had just lost his wife. He was trying to navigate that with two small girls. And Grant was still spiraling after Fiona's death." He glances at Bea in a quiet exchange. When he looks back at me, he says, "So I made a choice and called in a favor. A really big fucking favor."

Feeling overwhelmed, I shake my head, because truthfully, this was too much. I need it spelled out. "Griz, what are you telling us here?"

"That your mother is alive and well," Bea answers.

Maggie leans back, hand covering her mouth as she mumbles, "Oh my god." My eyes connect with Maggie's, and all I can manage to do is shake my head. That can't be right. My throat is dry, and it feels like someone shoved me, knocking the wind right from my chest.

"The only thing I have ever known how to do well is make bourbon," Griz adds. "I didn't know how to keep her safe." He looks up, trying to keep himself from letting any tears escape. "Girls, not a single day goes by when I don't wonder if I'd made the right choice to stay behind. Without her."

Bea cuts in. "And now you have an opportunity to see her. If you both want to, I'll take you to her."

My stomach sinks, warring with my chest that feels light and my head that feels dizzy at everything that's just transpired.

Harper glances at Griz and then back at me. "This is not protocol, and truthfully, I've bent so many rules at this point I'm skating legal lines." She gives Griz a tight-lipped smile before she moves toward the door at the far side of the room. "Maggie can't come out of this room if she wants to be folded into WITSEC." She looks at Maggie. "You have a lot of shit piled high right now, kid. It'll make it a lot harder to get you out of here and a good cover story if you decide not to do it now."

Maggie nods and looks at me, her eyes rimmed red. "Okay."

"Faye, we have a small window of time to pull this off," Bea tells me.

"I can't just leave," I say, raising my hands to my side as I start to follow. "Lincoln—"

"Will understand," Griz assures me. "Go and see her. Tell her there isn't a day that doesn't pass by when I don't think of her."

Chapter 39

Lincoln

Still groggy from nodding off in the hospital waiting room chair, it takes me a minute to register what Griz is saying. I clear my throat, sitting up. "What's wrong?"

Griz crosses his arms and stands in front of the three of us, the same way he used to do when one of us was in trouble. But it's the look on his face that has my chest tight. Sad and nervous about something.

"Griz, the fuck is going on?" Grant asks, standing beside me.

Ace leans forward, elbows on his knees, and looks down as if he already knows what's coming.

With his focus on me, Griz says, "What happened tonight is going to cause a chain reaction of events. There're things that I can't share with you boys." He looks down and rubs at the back of his neck. "Linc, you know what Maggie had been doing—digging into Finch & King, but her reason why—"

He cuts himself off, and I instantly know it's because of

what she witnessed the night that Tullis died. The fact that it was Waz King who killed him.

Glancing at Ace, he says, "There's more going on than I even know about, only that Maggie isn't safe staying here. Waz King might be dead, but…"

Ace finishes his sentence. "But Wheeler isn't."

"The Calloway girls need some time." Griz continues while watching my reaction, but I feel frozen in place. "To visit their past and get right with it. I don't know what story will come out of tonight. That's going to be up to them. For now, the cover story is that Maggie is in the ICU."

Griz grips my shoulder, sitting on the chair next to me. I'm trying to work through all the things he's said. And all the things he may not be saying.

"Tell me she's coming back, Griz," I say quietly to him. "She wouldn't just leave."

Instead of answering me, he says, "If she's fallen for you the way I think she has…"

I pull off my glasses, smiling to myself as I think about what she whispered to me. Words I hadn't realized I was so eager to hear.

Griz gives me a smile. "Then she'll come back and be a part of this family," he says assuredly. "My great-granddaughters think she's their soulmate—women, let alone Foxx women, are never wrong."

I look down at my hands, my left ring finger bare, and it's freeing. This morning I decided to keep it off. It's the first time I've gone out without my gold band knowing I wasn't going to put it back on. The girls hadn't noticed, but I was okay if they had. I hadn't worn it for any other reason than for them.

"People always think that you get one great love of your

life, but I think whatever asshat said that never considered all the different kinds of love that could show up over the course of a lifetime."

My eyes water. I don't want to fall apart here, but I killed a man tonight. And while I should feel some sort of way about it, the only thing I can think about is I won't be okay if *she* doesn't come walking back out here.

Griz wipes his hand along his thick mustache. "I've been lucky enough to raise you and your brothers. Your father before that. I've had two exceptional women come into my life and love me in ways I never deserved, but I had it anyway. And then you went ahead and had two beautiful girls who ended up being two more loves of my life."

I lean forward, elbows on my knees as I take a grounding breath. "Loving someone just for them to leave—"

He squeezes the back of my neck, cutting me off. "When someone feels right, you lean into it. Loving someone again doesn't mean one has to be better or stronger. If you're smart, you'll fall in love as many times as the world will allow; sometimes, it's with the same person and all the new versions of each other that grow over the years. And for others who experience loss or goodbyes, it's when someone new shows up, shakes you up, and all of a sudden, things feel a whole lotta right. Don't think for one second that loving Faye isn't the bravest thing you've ever done. Don't give up on her yet."

Chapter 40

Faye

"You and Lincoln Foxx?" Bea says with a side glance.

"That's what I said," Maggie adds from the front seat.

"Not surprised. They have that way about them, those Foxx boys."

"I came back for a job and for Maggie. Lincoln ended up being…a bonus," I tell them with a shrug, not able to hide my smile.

They both sniff out a laugh. And then Harper adds, "All of my bonuses ended up being Jelly of the Month clubs, if you catch my drift."

"The last bonus I had, I faked," Maggie sighs. But before I can even get a laugh out, Harper cuts the wheel into a private airfield and pulls right up to a small plane that looks like it's fueled and ready to start taxiing.

"I understand the appeal. Really, I do." Harper hops out of the truck and adds, "Griz wasn't too rough on the eyes back in the day." She blows out a plume of smoke as I help my sister out of the truck, and we hustle toward the private plane.

A bulky pilot stands at the end of the two boarding stairs with his arms crossed. "Harper, you realize I'm not your personal pilot, right? They have services for that. Your branch of government, in fact, has a fleet of airplanes and pilots for this kind of thing."

"And yet, here you are, Riggs," she claps back as she moves up the stairs. Over her shoulder, she says, "Henry, this is Faye and Maggie. You never saw them. This is off the books." She flicks her clove. "You know how that goes, right?"

Whatever history exists between them has him grunting to himself and giving Maggie and me nothing more than a quick nod.

Five hours later, after a fairly long flight and a short drive, we pull off the stretch of road. With nothing more than flat lands on either side and mountains in front of us, we park along the front of a small square diner with a sign that reads, Hideaway. At just past 7:30 in the morning local time, it looks closed. Except for the one car parked in the front and a tawny-colored horse tied up on a pole.

Bea shifts the truck into park and opens her door. "Maybe you girls want to grab a coffee. And then, Faye, you can decide what you'd like to do." She stretches her arms above her head and pulls out another clove. "You've got twenty minutes, and then decide if you're feeling like heading back, or if you'd like to stay and explore what Montana has to offer."

Maggie clears her throat and whispers, "This is real, right? I'm not in some post-life haze where I think it's real and I'm dead?"

I pinch the skin above her elbow.

"Ow," she yells out. "Fuck a duck, Faye."

I shrug a shoulder. "Feels real to me." I take a grounding breath and hold the door handle. Before I pull, I ask, "Ready?"

She nods. And when we walk into the small shop, the bell on the door that clamors against the glass reminds me of Hooch's. The snow that dusted the path we took from the car to the door is stuck to my shoes, but I stomp them off quickly. The woman behind the counter gives us both a kind smile. "You can sit anywhere you'd like, ladies."

But as I look down the length of the room, my eyes stop on the only other person in the place. A woman at the end of the bar with a cup of tea and a pastry, who's looking right back at us like the world just paused and somehow her eyes are seeing something she can't believe. My chest hollows out and then expands as if someone just passed air into my lungs.

She stands, and with watery eyes, says, "When Bea texted, I didn't think—" Her hand flies over her mouth as her eyes pinch closed. But it's Maggie who doesn't waste any more seconds and limps over to her faster than I thought she would be able to move right now.

Their arms fly around the other, and the only sounds are whimpering cries mixed with my mother's calm voice that I hadn't realized how much I missed hearing. "My darling girls." Her eyes close as she whispers, "What are you doing here?"

She leans back and holds Maggie's arms out. "Just look at you, Maggie." Worrying her lips, she looks past my sister to me. My mother is still so beautiful. Small signs that time hasn't stood still—her wavy, wheat-colored hair is streaked with more silver than blond and cropped into a short bob now. She wears a pair of worn jeans, cowgirl boots, and a tied off Carly Simon tour T-shirt. Her long cardigan sweater looks hand-knitted and warm enough for what's left of winter.

"Mom..." is the only thing I can get out before I wrap my arms around her. She smells just like I remember: lavender and sugar. *She smells like home.*

"Oh, Faye, honey." Her voice breaks when she says, "My beautiful girl. My protector." She pulls back to look at me. "I'm so sorry. Oh, I messed up so horribly." Pausing, she bites back the sob I know she's holding in. "I just let you clean up a mess that you had no business being near. I'm so sorry."

I shake my head. "I know," I tell her through my own tears.

She looks around us toward the waitress. "Annie, can you bring these girls some coffee?"

We move into a booth, and she smiles at the waitress, waiting for her to leave before we say anything more. "Thanks, Annie." Reaching for a hand from both Maggie and me, she then says, "Tell me everything."

Maggie takes the lead on telling her about the night that Tullis died. How Maggie saw everything. How she watched Waz murder his own brother, threaten her, and how I assumed Mom had killed him.

"There was never a time to tell you. And what good would it have done? There was no way I could have known what was coming," Maggie says. She glances at me before she continues with what Griz told us. "That Waz continued to threaten you." I squeeze Maggie's hand.

"I thought if I took myself out of the equation, then you both would be safe. I didn't want to leave," Mom says, looking up.

Maggie wipes under each eye. "We had a memorial for you."

I chime in, "The whole town celebrated you, Mom. All the girls from your book club. Everyone who knew you missed you."

"And then I found my own brand of coping," Maggie says. "A lot of drinking and gambling. But it served two purposes." She glances at me. "My vices turned into exactly what I needed to get onto Finch & King's radar."

Our mother looks at me quizzically and then back to Maggie. "Please tell me you didn't get involved."

"She did more than just get involved, Mom." We spend the next handful of minutes talking about exactly what brought Maggie and me here. But that, of course, led to even more questions.

So we sit together in the middle-of-nowhere diner for most of the morning while Maggie and I share every detail, from my involvement with Blackstone to the carefully orchestrated system that Maggie had been able to deliver to the FBI. Between the surveillance I'd pulled, the delivery of drugs via private auction, the long money trail, fixed off-track betting, and the suspicious deaths of horses, trainers, and jockeys, all of it building a case pointing directly at Finch & King.

Our mom's eyes close when she asks, "Are they looking for you? Those men have reach. Waz is the psychopath. He will keep coming after you. But just because Wheeler doesn't get his hands dirty doesn't mean he forgets anything. He hires people—"

But I cut her off. "Mom, Waz is dead."

She searches our faces, eyes wide when she asks, "How?"

"Last night. Lincoln was there," I answer. "He got there just in time."

"Lincoln Foxx? Griz's grandson? What was he doing…"

Maggie props her elbows on the table and her chin on her palms. "Oh yeah, Mom. That's the best part. Faye went ahead and fell in love with him while all of this was happening."

With a watery laugh, she says, "Something about those Foxx boys." Her eyebrows raise. "I get it. I fell for one too."

I look out the window at the quietness of the town she's set up in. "Griz didn't come with you."

She shakes her head and takes a sip of her tea. "He had a life and family he needed to be there for. They needed him more than I did."

"He told me to tell you that he thinks about you every day," I say.

Her eyes water all over again. She dabs at the corners with her napkin. "Bea picked Montana. Middle of nowhere, but she picked a place where I can ride a horse instead of drive a car if I want." She laughs lightly, smiling. "She comes off harsh, but she knew it would be a good place for me. When I got here, I was in bad shape. I had a lot of healing to do." She bites back the emotion as she says, "Guilt for leaving. And never having the chance to tell you both how much I loved you."

I swipe away the tears and take a steadying breath.

"The horse sanctuary I've opened has become a place of healing. For me and for a number of women who need to find their footing again. I was here for about a month, and when I went to the bank to open an account, there had already been one opened there under my new name. It had just over a quarter of a million dollars in it."

Maggie guesses what I'm thinking. "Griz."

Mom smiles and nods. "That was my guess. He's the best man I've ever known. We had six months together, and it was the most I ever felt love from a partner before. That feeling, once you have it, you feel lucky for it." Quiet for a moment, she sits back and looks out the window. "And Bea has been a good friend when I need a familiar face. It's simple and calm, but I have a good life here. As good as it can be without my beautiful daughters. I'll never forgive myself for allowing my mess to bleed into your lives."

I swipe away the tears that just keep coming. "I never thought I'd have this with you—another minute to tell you I love you and that I've missed you." I look over at the clock, recognizing that we've more than exceeded the time Bea Harper had laid out for us.

"I saw you once," my mom says, drawing my attention back. "On stage in a club in Louisiana."

"Mom…" I never thought she would have seen me dance like that. And I'm not embarrassed, more proud than anything.

"The one thing you never knew, Faye. That I never had the chance to tell you." She holds my hand and the lull of her voice makes me want to savor every moment of this. "I'm so proud of the woman you've become. The way you look dancing is the way I feel about training horses. It makes up a part of you. Not defines, but molds and makes us stronger. Finding things that make you feel like the best version of yourself is the kind of life I always hoped for you. And private investigating…" She smiles to herself. "You're a protector, a fixer, and that was bound to shine through somewhere."

The affirmation isn't something I thought I needed, but it hits my chest like a freight train.

A clank on the window has the three of us jumping. Bea stands there as she points at her watch. She calls out loud enough to hear through the glass and quiet of the outside. "Time to go."

Chapter 41

Lincoln

I suck in a deep breath as I push open the barn doors and walk through to where I've made myself a makeshift workspace. I've been distracted and half listening to just about everyone that stepped in my path. Somehow, I volunteered to run a PTA event I have no business participating in. I fucked up a mash bill so badly that the entire distillery smelled like burnt hair for three days. And all of it is because of the one thing I had decided I'd never do again: fall in love with a woman. *Fuck, I miss her.* How could I miss someone so much that I've only known for a short time?

And then when Lark asked, *"I thought Faye was going to come over for dinner this week."* I damn near lost it trying to explain that she had to go away for a little while and I wasn't sure when she would be back. *If* she would be back. I've sent text messages and left voicemails, telling her I miss her, but nothing has been read or returned. I don't know where she is or if she's safe, and that chews away at me every night when my arms feel empty without her in them.

"Dad," Lily laughs out. "I think she likes the bows in her hair. She's smiling." The cow is definitely not smiling, but she's well-tempered and lets Lily put bows in her hair while Lark brushes her hide.

I walk over to the stall with Dottie's name over the top and smile at what I'm witnessing.

I look between them—Lily and Lark, and then the two newest Foxx girls, Kit and Dottie. A cow and a dog. I can't help the smile the sight pulls from me. Fixing my glasses, I say, "I didn't know what you two were thinking when you decided to bring home these two furry creatures. But I get it—you both have big hearts. You make everyone in this family smile and feel so loved."

Lark looks around the barn space, toward the empty stalls and then back to me. Her eyes water when she says, "We wanted you to be happy. You said that the happiest you've ever been was when we were happy, Dad."

I smile. "And are you?"

Lily smiles wide. "Dad. If this is about you telling us that you love Faye, then we already know that."

I hadn't thought through the idea of them just being okay with me loving someone new already. If it's been fast for me, then it's bound to feel the same for them.

I shift and look at Lark, and she smiles. "You'd have to be blind not to see it, Dad. You love her, right?"

I look up at the rafters and suck in a breath. "Yeah, Lark, I do. I love her a whole lot."

Lily points at me and says, "I knew it. The moment I saw our soulmate marks and those diamonds near her eyes, I knew it. Dad, did you know her middle name was Rose?"

Actually, I didn't.

"Hello?" Lily says, throwing her arms up. "Her middle name is a flower. Soulmate!"

I bark out a laugh. "So wise, Lil." I don't try to keep the welled tears from falling. "I've

been worried about how you'd feel. She's not Mom—"

But Lark cuts me off. "We were lucky to have Mommy for as long as we did." She wipes away the tears as she lets her sister rest her chin on her shoulder.

Lily hands her one of her gemstone rocks. "Here, Lark. An onyx rubbing stone for courage."

Olivia and I were broken before she died—our relationship had lost so much of what made us happy as a couple, but she was an amazing mother. She was the kind of mom a man hopes his kids luck out having. I would always be grateful to her for that. For them. I'm so proud as I watch them work through this—creating space for someone new.

"She loved you very much. More than anything."

Lark sniffs and then smiles at me. "I think Mom would want us to have more of that feeling—of someone else loving us and wanting to spend time with us."

"You two are pretty great," I say, rubbing my hand along Lily's back.

"Obviously," Lily whispers.

Lark smiles at her sister and rubs her thumb along the smooth black surface of the stone. "Dad, you're my best friend in the whole world." Pausing, her brow pinches as she says, "I liked Faye from the first minute we met her. I was nervous she'd take all your time. But I know that won't happen now. I just don't want to be sad again—love someone, just to have them taken away."

My stomach sinks at hearing that, because I feel that too. I swallow the lump in my throat and look up, trying to stop more tears from falling. "We have a great life, just the three of us. I didn't want to find someone else to add to this. We've been figuring things out pretty okay on our own, yeah?"

Lily wipes at her eyes as she nods.

Lark chuckles, looking at me knowingly. "But then Faye showed up."

"Knocked me right on my butt," I say with a smile.

"Dad, is that why you hated her at first?" Lily asks, always so curious.

They don't need to know the details of how we started, but I can be honest enough here. "I didn't know her. I had an idea about her that ended up being wrong." I suck in a deep breath. "I'm scared too. Loving someone and them leaving. Or not coming back. But if she does—"

Lark chimes in to finish the rest. "Then you're going to make sure she knows how much we want her here."

"Yeah, kiddo, then I'll make sure she knows how much we want her to stay. And how much I plan on loving her."

"We," Lily corrects. "How much *we* plan on loving her."

Chapter 42

Faye

There are sixty-four horses living on Hideaway's rescue ranch. Four dogs, a couple of barn cats, and two dozen chickens. A highland cow would round it out nicely. I smile at the thought of Dottie—the way Lark and Lily are probably enjoying having her so close to their house. It's beautiful and quiet here, just like Mom said. It's been just over two weeks, and I still haven't seen the entirety of the property. The snow that flurried in this morning was normal here in late February, according to Mom. The cold mornings transitioned into brisk days that were always accompanied by deceivingly bright sunshine.

"The silverback over to the left likes to be in charge; she's been here the longest. She was pretty thin when she arrived, but somehow, she ended up being the one to heal me. I think watching her get stronger helped me do the same," Mom says as we sit and swing on her porch.

"It's beautiful here," I say as I close my eyes and let the sun warm my face.

"You miss him," Maggie says. It's not a question, it's an observation.

"I love him," I tell her on a sigh.

"He's a good man, Faye," Mom says, searching for my hand. With a squeeze, she says, "If there was anyone I could have picked for you, it would have been Lincoln Foxx."

I smile, looking down at our hands when I ask, "Why is that?"

"He always leans in—to hugs, to his family. It's something that I thought set him apart from his brothers most. He was a lot like Griz in that way—a natural storyteller, could captivate a room full of people without even trying, and he's very good looking."

"She's right," Maggie agrees with an eyebrow wiggle that has me laughing.

I lean my head on my mom's shoulder, knowing that I won't be able to do this whenever I want or maybe even ever again. She may not have the threat of Waz King any longer, but Wheeler Finch is too connected, whether he's behind bars or not. The same is true for Maggie. I'm the wild card—I'm not a threat to him, as far as he knows. Anything regarding his case is tied to Maggie. Del, along with Bea and Cortez, will all make sure of that.

Mom clears her throat, cutting into my thoughts. "A man like Lincoln isn't one you love and leave. He's the kind you let hold you and then make sure you never let go."

My eyes water as the three of us watch the horses run the length of the closest paddock. "I'll miss you forever," I say with a shaky voice.

"And I'll never stop missing you, my beautiful girl," she says, squeezing my hand tight.

Maggie stands up a minute later and claps her hands in front of her. "Alright, if this is our very last meal together as the Calloway girls, then I vote cake for dinner."

"Cake for dinner," I agree with a laugh, even as a tear slips down my cheek.

My mom smiles and stands. "Let me go find the ingredients."

I stand up and move over to Maggie. She leans her elbows on the porch railing, looking out over the landscape. The afternoon blue skies are peppered with wisps of white clouds—it feels like a perfect kind of day.

"If I forget to tell you later, Faye," she says and then pauses. "You're my favorite person. Always have been. Probably always will be too."

My chin wobbles as I try to bite back the sob that her words bring. "You know I love you?"

She nods, her lips tucked into her mouth as she tries to hold back the same emotions. As she rests her forehead on my shoulder, I absorb all of it, banking it to memory so I can call on it when I might need to.

A few minutes pass before I whisper, "Promise me you'll be okay?"

She tips her chin back and takes a deep breath. "It's going to be boring as fuck out here without you."

I chuckle. "I'm sure you'll find some trouble to get into."

"Obviously," she says, looping her pointer finger along with mine. "Feels good to do the right thing."

I smile wide. "What do you mean?"

She turns on her heel and heads inside as she says, "You'll see."

Chapter 43

Lincoln

It's felt like the longest two weeks of my life. Lifting my glasses off, I use my forearm to swipe the sweat from my brow. The winter has finally let go and spring is doing a damn good job of reminding us it's coming. A few daffodils and tulips have started popping up around the mailbox and the sun warms the barn roof just enough that by midday, I need to turn on the massive fans I installed.

The Calloway girls will more than likely appreciate the few upgrades out here. I needed a break from some of the planning I've been doing with Laney. Our release of Foxx & Peach is approaching and the hype my sister-in-law built up for it meant prepping for events and expanding tours. It's nice to have my own space here, a breather from the distillery and a spot that makes me feel closer to her.

"Lincoln Foxx," a sweet voice from behind me says.

I suck in a breath and close my eyes in relief. Every muscle in my body relaxes. I drop the rake as soon as I turn and see her beautiful face in the barn doorway. She looks down at my body, my T-shirt off and hanging from my back pocket. I can feel her eyes move down the length of me, and goddamn, I love it when she does it.

"You came back," I say as I rush to her, wrapping my arms around her tightly.

Any words that she was going to let out die off as my lips meet hers. Kissing this woman is like getting lost and finding where I'm meant to be all at once.

She pulls back, just enough to say, "There's so much I need to tell you." She shakes her head, trying to stop the tears from falling. "But I was always coming back, Foxx. This time, I wouldn't have been able to stay away."

Her fingers run along my jaw and the overgrown scruff that I've been too lazy to worry about. I nuzzle my nose along hers, the smell of mint and vanilla along her lips. "I couldn't figure it out. When I couldn't look away from you and craved being near you, I couldn't figure out what it was that made me feel it."

She searches my face, her fingers gripping onto my shirt. "Obviously my brilliant personality," she teases.

And though she's not wrong, that isn't exactly it. "I realized what it was about you that made you so fucking perfect for me." I brush her hair from her face as she looks up at me. "You show up for your family and the people you care about, and that's always been what love looks like to me. You are what love looks like to me."

A smile dances across her lips as her arms wrap around my shoulders. She threads the tips of her fingers along the hair at the nape of my neck. "How am I supposed to not melt for a confession like that, Foxx?"

"Just flexing my charm. Making sure you're locked in."

I can't hold on to her tight enough, and she must feel the same because, without thought, I lift her up and her legs wrap around my waist. She runs her nose along my neck and nips, firing off every need and desire to claim her as mine.

"Too many layers on, Peach," I say, mumbling over her lips.

She starts laughing, and it's easily one of my favorite sounds. Dragging her lips along my jaw and down my throat, she says, "You know it's winter outside and you're topless in here?"

"I wasn't sure when you were going to show up, so I've been like this for days."

She barks out a laugh as I pull her sweater up and over her head.

With her in just a tank and her hair wild, I cup her face with both hands. "You didn't let me tell you. You said I love you and then left. Like the ultimate mic drop."

She smiles against my lips, brushing her tongue against the seam of mine—so eager to get to what she wants. I move us off the wall and down toward the far end of the stables. We move past where Dottie grazes on hay. As Faye licks up the side of my neck, it sends a rush straight down my spine and to my cock. "Where are you taking me right now, Foxx?"

When we reach the farthest room, I put her down on the counter that runs the length of the space. "You realize this is a barn and not a rickhouse?"

"Just a small storage space for a little while. I've been trying something new with my specialty batch." When she looks around the space, she spots one of the label mock-ups that Laney had dropped off earlier.

Holding it up, she smiles, her eyes brightening as they flick between mine. She reads the label aloud, "*Foxx & Peach*. You named a bourbon after us?"

I move away from her and pluck an open bottle from the rack that had been used for tasting earlier today. I could have kept this at the distillery, but I didn't want to be far from here. "I needed to know the minute you were back. So I took over the space. I could keep an eye on Kit and Dottie, get some work done while the girls are at school, and wait patiently for you."

I take a sip from the bottle, tasting the peach immediately as the bourbon hits my tongue. It's almost as delicious as the one in front of me.

She smiles as I swallow, watching my throat work the bourbon down. The way she looks at me, like she wants me so fucking badly, is something I'll never get over. "You're obsessed with me," she teases as her hands drag down my chest and move toward my belt.

"Yeah, baby. I'm obsessed with you." I nip at her lips. "That okay with you?"

"Mm-hmm," she hums. "I want some of that."

She unbuckles my belt as I pull down the front of her tank, her tits spilling over the pink bra she has on. But I'm not feeling patient right now as I yank the bra down so I can see exactly what I want to wrap my mouth around.

"You can have some when I say you can."

Her eyes widen at hearing the way we're going to play. She pushes her chest forward, waiting for what I'm going to ask of her. "Push those pretty tits together for me."

She does exactly as I ask, palming the sides of both and gripping them tightly together.

I suck in a breath, groaning. "Fuck, look at you." Leaning forward, I grip her waist and run my tongue right through the deep cleavage she's making. "There's only one way you're allowed to drink bourbon when you're with me, Peach."

She smiles, and then like the good fucking girl she is, she opens her mouth, tongue out, as I take a pull from the bottle and give her exactly what she's asked for—a shot of our Foxx & Peach bourbon.

Her eyes open and lock onto mine as she smiles. "I love this."

"Good." I smile back. "I love you."

She lets the bit that's escaped her mouth dribble down her chin and right onto her tits. Licking along its path, I moan against her skin. I pull her hips closer to the edge of the counter she's perched on and roll her leggings down.

"Hold on to me."

As I lift her ass to work them off the rest of the way, she loops her arms around me. I kneel and toss them across the room, pushing her knees wider so I can smell what's mine. Whipping off my glasses, I graze my nose up the center of her pussy, and she shivers. "You're so wet, baby."

She lets out a tinkling laugh. "I get wet just thinking about you, Foxx."

I stand and flip my jeans open, ripping the zipper down with it. Shoving my boxer briefs down, I grip my cock. "As much as I want to drink every drop you've made for me, I need that pretty pussy wrapped around my cock right this fucking minute."

"Foxx?"

Spitting on my hand, I jerk my cock twice before I drag it along her slit. "Yeah, baby?"

She sucks a breath through her teeth as I tease her lips. And I know what she's going to ask me. Which is why I don't let her get the words out when I fuck her deep and hard on the first thrust. It knocks the air from her, and her mouth falls open before she smiles at me. "If I forget to tell you later, I love you."

I kiss her plush lips in response. The words travel along my skin like a caress and seep into me, all the way to my soul. Her tongue swipes along mine, and with my cock buried inside of her, I pull out of her slowly and lift her higher. "Wrap those legs around me nice and tight, Peach."

Doing as I ask, she rests her forehead on mine, whispering, "I missed you."

My lips nip at hers as I lift her off the counter just enough to pull out of her and tease myself back inside.

She moans against me as I rock back and forth, her hips rolling to meet my thrusts. "That's it, grind that pussy on me," I say on a groan, feeling her clenching around me.

"That's it, Foxx. Eyes on me while I fuck you," she says between breaths, edging me closer. I can tell with the way her mouth parts and her body tenses that she's already so close. A sheen of sweat highlights her chest as she keeps the pace of grinding into me, her body bouncing in the most beautiful ways. My dancer. My fantasy.

"My turn now, baby." I shuffle us to the flat wall, and with her legs still wrapped around me, I use the wall as leverage to glide my hips into her, making sure I rub against her clit with each roll forward.

Her breathing speeds up, and I'm barely holding on when she wraps her arms tighter and quivers in my arms. A drawn-out moan starts soft, but it quickly becomes my unraveling as her pussy pulses around me. "Don't you fucking stop, Foxx. I want to hear you moan like a man."

And *that's* the woman I'm in love with. Quick to make me

fucking kneel for her, see every part of her, and not get lost in the fall. I do exactly as she tells me. On the cusp of her orgasm ending, mine ripples through my body, from the top of my head and down my back, right through my cock as I spill into her.

I moan out so loud that it doesn't register that the sound came from me, but she smothers the end of it as she kisses me with every last bit of energy we've got. I rest my head against her shoulder, my breathing heavy and a delirious smile against her skin.

"You're going to need to do that again," she mumbles. She's still jacked up against the wall with my hips pinning her in place as I drip out of her. "Think you can keep up?"

I chuckle darkly. "Peach, you keep squeezing that pussy, and I'll be hard again in a minute." And it's true, but it's the sound of squeaking brakes from the school bus that has me pulling out of her as I kiss her forehead. I pull my pants up enough so I don't trip and move to find her leggings.

She smiles at me, leaning against the wall in a daze, looking like a satisfied goddess. "Are you in a rush?"

I shove my semihard cock back into my briefs as I button and work the buckle closed on my jeans. Leaning forward, I press a quick kiss to her lips as I tell her, "Yeah, a bit. And you should be too, unless you want my girls to see your tits and bare ass."

Jolting to awareness, she stands tall and gets moving. "Oh my gosh," she says through a laugh.

"A hazard of falling in love with a single dad."

She shrugs her bra back into place and pulls the Led Zeppelin T-shirt on, and then works her legs back into her leggings with a shimmy. As I tug my shirt over my head and shrug it on, she pouts, making me laugh. She helps pull the hem down and kisses me. "Perks," she says against my lips. "Perks of falling for a Foxx."

I hear the double doors slide open, and both the girls start talking to our cow. "Dottie, you're looking awfully sweet today," and "Hi, Dottie, I think we're going to need to trim your bangs soon."

Kit barks out repeatedly, announcing her presence, and barrels down the main drag of the space. I pull Faye's arm toward me and wrap myself around her.

I didn't plan much past seeing her and holding her. I couldn't let myself get too far ahead without knowing for certain she would want this. But right now, I can't help but ask, "You're sure this is what you want?"

She tilts her head back to look at me. The noise around us is muted as she drags her fingers along the nape of my neck.

Lark yells out, "Faye! You're back."

And Lily follows with a squeal that blends in with Kit's barking.

She smiles so big that her green eyes squint and that beauty mark gets lost in the creases. "You're exactly what I want, Foxx." Her eyes shift to Lark and Lily, who both stand in the archway with goofy smiles on their faces. "You and your girls," Faye adds, then kisses me one more time before she turns and opens her arms for my girls. "Oh wow, I missed you guys. Tell me everything I missed."

They start rattling off a roster of things I didn't even realize happened in the past few days. Apparently, Laney and Hadley are planning a girls-only welcome back party. "There's a new mix I made for you, Faye. I think it's the perfect mash-up for when we're making dinner." Lark rattles off the songs that made the cut.

Lily talks over her sister. "You timed this perfectly. Tonight is a full moon, and it's supposed to be pink. And then we can look at all the pink gemstones... Lark, I'm talking."

Faye looks over at me, and I feel it—that sense of calm. That exhale of contentment that comes when you've made enough of the wrong decisions but somehow find your way to one that feels right.

Chapter 44

Faye

"Faye," Cortez says, coming in from the garage. "This came for you." He tosses an envelope at me. "Hey, I've got a domestic case. I could use a little assistance in working the neighborhood. They're not interested in talking with Fiasco PD right now, but they might talk with you."

I give him a nod and wrap my jacket around me. "I'll send you an invoice for my hours."

He taps the desk as he walks back toward his team. "You make better money than me. You do realize that?"

"And imagine that, it's a side hustle," I shout back, chuckling to myself.

The desk officer gives me a half smile this time. His mutton chops look as thick as the coiffed hair on top of his head. "Faye, you let me know when you want an assistant, if that's true about pay."

I give him a wink.

My phone dings, and within a few seconds, the rest of the

station's phones start dinging. Before I can even slide the news alert open, I hear one of the officers say, "You've got to be shitting me."

The headline stems from *The New York Times* in national news: "The Men Behind the Largest Scandal in Horse Racing's History" by Murray Ackroyd.

I read through the article about the history of winnings and the long lineage of horses that had been iconic race winners over the past decade and a half. The amount of money that is being estimated to have been won and earned throughout—and how misappropriated funds, the drugging of horses pre-race, the web of trainers, jockeys, and staff who all fell beneath one name: Finch & King. All of it had been brought to light by an unnamed, protected source.

Maggie.

When I step out into the cold air, I pull the tie on my jacket tighter. I start down the sidewalk toward my new favorite place to go on Saturdays now. My phone buzzes in my hand that I just buried in my pocket.

> **FOXX:**
> Urgent matter. You are being volunteered to pick up all the proper candy for tonight's candy salad bar. According to Lark, I've gotten the wrong kind of sour straws.

I can't stop smiling as I answer his very serious request.

> **FAYE:**
> I'll stop on my way home.

FOXX:

You're calling my place home now?

FAYE:

Minor slip. I'm still very much enjoying a big house all to myself.

FOXX:

I still very much enjoy it too. Should we ditch the kids and meet there instead? Father of the Year is asking hypothetically of course.

FAYE:

But now I'm craving candy salad.

FOXX:

You said salad, Peach. You make my dirty thoughts soar with shit like that.

FAYE:

Love you, see you in a while.

FOXX:

Hurry up, I miss you.

I open my bag to toss my phone in, and the letter that Cortez gave me catches my eye. The manila envelope is stamped with no return address and sent to Cortez, but attention to Faye Calloway. When I open it, I swallow, my throat suddenly dry. It has been right around six months since I left her and my mom behind. And this time, it felt so much more final. Saying goodbye was more than most had, but I still felt like I wish I had more. Maggie chose to stay with Mom, and I needed to forget where that was—there was still a chance that connections and associates of Wheeler Finch would go looking for the woman who brought down an empire. But right now, with the looping cursive handwriting, my chest feels lighter.

Dear Faye,

Hopefully by the time this reaches you, you'll have seen the news. As it turns out, I'm the hero now. If there's ever a time when I get to rub that in your face, don't think I won't.

I heard that the tree at Christmas time in Rockefeller Center is just a tree. But for some reason, surrounded by buildings and an ice rink, it feels more like Christmas than anything else.

I'd like to see that sometime. Maybe you would too.

Love ya, Bye!

—M

I bat away the tears that stream down my face. I'm so fucking proud of her. There had been plenty of things wrong with what Maggie had been forced to navigate on her own. But everyone's biggest mistake was that they had underestimated her. She had her crutches and faults—gambling had never done her any favors—but my sister managed to dismantle an empire and decided not to let anyone get away with using her as a pawn.

She'd stayed in Witness Protection to make sure Wheeler Finch couldn't find her. This article guaranteed that every single person who had any affiliation to horse racing in Kentucky knew what Finch & King had done. And while most would never know what my mother had to sacrifice for it, or what each of us had been forced to sacrifice for it, we came out on the other side alive and knowing what it felt like to be loved.

It's warm tonight, but for the first time all summer, the breeze cuts through the humidity and it finally feels enjoyable to be outside. The air has the perfect sweet smell of cinnamon and sugar as I walk around the back of the house. The blown-up movie screen is set up along the edge of the patio. Lark's talking to Lincoln about something, and Lily's trying to throw popcorn into the air and catch it on her tongue.

Lincoln sits between his girls, arms spread behind the back of the outdoor couch, head tilted back and looking up at the sky. I always like catching him in moments like this, observing and cataloging the details of a new life that I continue to fall more in love with each day.

Kit lets out a bark as soon as she sees me and jumps down, greeting me with a slow gallop. And at the same time, all three of them turn to look at me with matching smiles.

"Faye! Okay, we're trying to decide what movie tonight. Lily wants to watch *Field of Dreams* or *Princess Diaries* again," Lark says, rolling her eyes. "But I'm thinking it should be *A League of Their Own* since we have softball this weekend."

"Maybe we can do something new?" Lincoln suggests. "How about the new *Transformers* or the *Ghostbusters* movie?"

Lark gives him a grimace, like it was the most awful idea.

Lily chimes in, "Bad call, Dad. Do you remember how long I had bad dreams about Slimer when I turned seven?"

He points at her. "Your Uncle Ace should not have let you watch that movie when you were seven," he laughs out.

I hold up the bags of candy. "I got the good sour straws and extra-butter popcorn," I tell them with an eyebrow wiggle.

"I'll make the popcorn!" Lark grabs the bags and heads inside as Lily trails behind her, singsonging that she's on candy salad duty.

Lincoln smiles at me from a few feet away. "I saw the article," he says.

"Have you talked to Hadley?" I ask, concerned about her and the fallout that will undoubtedly start bleeding into her life from all the chaos that her father has brought to Fiasco.

He nods, pulling my hand into his and kissing it. "She's dealing with it. She might need a minute, but she's not there yet. When I told her she should come over for movie night, she was planning on a night with her firemen." Shrugging, he shakes his head. "She'll be okay."

He wraps his arms around me and nuzzles his nose along my chin before kissing me. His lips meet mine, and he pours all of himself into it. Our tongues meet in a slow swipe that has my belly flipping as he holds me tighter. My fingers move along his neck and rake into his hair, keeping him close as he hums against me.

"You keep rubbing up on me like this and this movie is going to be painful to watch," I tell him through a giggle.

"Peach, it's too hot out to get naughty under a blanket," he says, dragging his lips along my neck. The low hum of the cicadas and the random ticking of crickets fill the silence.

Seconds later, Lark and Lily come rushing outside with two big bowls—one with popcorn and the other with a massive mix of sweet and sour candy. They perch on the couch, while Lincoln and I cozy up together on the chair. Summer outdoor movies have become our newest thing. Since summer began,

I've been spending even more time folded into their lives. It's felt easy and natural to be here with them.

Lark starts the movie, and the music echoes through the surrounding speakers. It's a random night that I'll try desperately to remember. With my back to Lincoln's front, I nudge into him, and I hear a gasp leave his lips before he whispers against my neck.

"Planning to drink some bourbon later, Peach?"

I smile and nod as I sink into his hold. Both of us know exactly what happens when we mention drinking bourbon together—it always ends deliciously messy. And while I'm wildly turned on while wrapped in his arms, it's only a fraction of how I feel when I'm with him. Protected, worshiped, and so cared for.

With Lincoln Foxx, it feels bigger than a simple word like love. When I'm with him, it feels like home.

Epilogue

Lincoln

A little later...

Chemistry isn't just about the composition of substance structure and properties; it's about how those substances interact and change to make something new. It's what I've always found fascinating, what I thrived off when it came to making bourbon. But there was more. It's complex and emotional. My chemistry with Faye Calloway defies reason, because it didn't make things more complex. It turned out to be very simple: She was my catalyst. My entire life had become about my two girls and Faye. There's also a dog, a cow, as well as six baby chicks. And the chicks, surprisingly, I actually knew about this time. A lot of women who made my life feel always slightly out of control, but undoubtedly complete.

"Dad, do you want to practice?" Lily asks, perched on the counter.

"No, I don't want to practice," I say to her in the mirror as I button up my black shirt.

"You do look kind of nervous—" Lark says as she leans against the ledge of the tub. She holds up the newest bath bombs I bought, and her eyes widen. "Dad, these smell like vanilla and cherries. Lily, smell this one."

Lily holds my glasses for me and says, "Are you worried she won't say yes?"

But instead of being able to answer, Faye pops her head into the bathroom, catching all of us off guard. Out of breath, she says, "Worried about who not saying yes to what?"

Her eyes move from both the girls and then back to me, all of us having an *oh shit* moment because she's not supposed to be here. Hadley and Laney were supposed to keep her out for at least another hour until I had set everything up.

Lark's wide eyes meet mine as she glances to the counter and toward the small red velvet pouch.

"I told Hadley and Laney I needed to change quickly after class. You'd think teaching the book club ladies how to dance with feather fans would be less intense, but it's not." She laughs and shakes her head, walking into our bathroom off the primary suite.

With the growing roster of animals, we decided to move into the Calloway farmhouse and completed some renovations that made it feel like ours instead of Maggie's. I was more than happy to sell our home—there were too many harsh memories that lingered there. I wanted my girls to remember their mother, but that didn't have to mean staying in a place that didn't feel good anymore.

Faye smiles, giving both the girls a high-five combination that they've decided is much cooler than mine and Hadley's.

She wraps her arms around my shoulders. "Hi," she says sweetly against my lips. I run my hands down her back, but the wrap on my arm catches her attention, making her brow pinch. "What happened?"

I smile to myself, because it really doesn't matter how we do this. There isn't a single thing about the two of us that ever went according to any plans—why would that be different now?

"Dad, should we…?" Lark, catching on, asks, gesturing to the door.

I give her a shake of my head. "Stay. It's okay."

Faye looks between all of us as I peel off the wrap that covered the tattoo I had just gotten finished. It didn't take much thought to decide how I wanted to fill the blank space of that third windowpane. Faye's gaze drops from mine to my arm, and her breath catches as she takes it in. The splash of color and shape of a perfect peach. "Everything that makes my life feel good is there now."

She wipes beneath each eye as she looks up at me. "Are you kidding me? I don't know what to say—"

"Alright." I move back slightly, giving myself space to do this right. My knee moves to the floor, and I palm the little velvet bag. "Then just say yes."

She searches my face, jaw dropping slightly and eyes widening. "Foxx…" she exhales.

"It's a great last name, Peach. I'd very much like it if you'd make it yours. But no pressure." With a wink, I give her an easy smile. I glance at my girls, who are holding each other in a hug, tears brimming as I ask the woman I love if she'll marry me.

I reach for her to pull her closer, but she doesn't need coaxing. She props her ass right on my bent knee.

"I had a whole big idea for this—planned to wear a tux,

bought you a dress." I pull out the rose gold band with an oval diamond in the center. Around it are smaller diamonds that look like they've been dusted pink. The moment I saw it, it felt like something she would love. "The dress matched this."

She covers her mouth, muffling my name as more tears trail down her flushed cheeks. "Lincoln—"

"I want to do this life with you. You're everything I could ever ask for in a partner, friend, lover. I'm obsessed with every part of you, from your perfect lips to your big, protective heart." My eyes water, but only because I can't contain how much this moment means to me. To be here with her and feeling so ready to make her mine. "You are so many things, Faye, but the only thing I'm really hoping that you never want to stop being is ours."

Her breath hitches as my daughters sniff from just a few feet away. She glances at the girls and asks, "Are you both okay with this?"

They both smile at her. "More than okay, Faye," Lily says. Lark just nods, trying to keep her tears from turning into an all-out cry.

Faye smiles and focuses back on me. "I couldn't remember what home felt like. I missed the idea of it, but I couldn't remember how it felt. The warmth of it and care. That fierce protectiveness of it. You're my home, Lincoln Foxx. You're the love of the life I'm choosing, and I'm so fucking lucky to have all of you. Yes. Absolutely, yes," she says as she wraps her arms around my neck.

I hold on to her so tightly and try to never forget this moment—the way she feels in my arms during one of the happiest moments of my life. When she pulls back, we both look at Lark and Lily, giving them the nod to get over here.

Lily whispers, "See, Dad, we were right. And Faye, don't worry, curse purse doesn't apply today."

We both laugh through our happy tears, looking at each other and then the girls as they hustle out of the bathroom. She stands, and I follow, holding her left hand out and sliding on the ring.

"So beautiful," she says, looking up at me. The smile that she has is one that I'll do everything I can to keep there.

I lean forward, and just before her lips find mine, I tell her one last secret. "I never planned on loving you, Peach. But now, I never plan on stopping."

THE END

Extended Epilogue

Faye

A year later...

A TAXI CAB NEARLY SIDE-SWIPES me in the crosswalk, and a nervous laugh rolls out of me. It has Christmas tree garland wrapped around its lit-up cab number along its top and colorful Christmas lights woven along the back window. Two tourists gasp behind me and I get a stink-face glare from the dog walker who's clearly a professional at navigating the congested streets of New York City. It was a rookie move, one that I'm certain I'd never made before, but here I was a little while living in Kentucky and couldn't navigate a busy crosswalk like I had once learned.

Rockefeller Center is even more crowded than Times Square this time of year, but it wouldn't keep me from seeing her. It had been too long this time. This year, the massive tree was brought in from a small town outside Burlington, Vermont.

An English teacher, her husband, and two young sons were interviewed about the tree's journey from their backyard to 45 Rockefeller Plaza and it is only a fraction of why I am anxious to get there. The 75-foot spruce is flanked by skyscrapers on three of its four sides, with a charming ice rink at its base and frosted with thousands of white lights that looked even more beautiful in person than it had ever in the past.

The white food truck that sells hot chocolate with toasted fluff along the rim of the paper cups is easily more than thirty people deep. *Wow, that looks good.* But as I scan the crowd and try to decide if it is worth the wait, I see her. Just off to the left in a black leather jacket, jeans, and cowgirl boots, is Maggie. Her blonde hair is tinted red this time. A deep auburn that reminds me of Laney's hair. I swallow the lump in my throat and look up at the skyscrapers that fill my periphery and try not to let the tears fall. At least not just yet. We still have to be careful. There is still too much uncertainty from the fallout of the country's largest horse racing scandal. The reach of Finch & King is still unclear, which made it impossible for her to be Maggie Calloway. I don't know what name she is using or if there are many, and I can only see her at least once yearly in this spot. Our relationship has become a series of postcards with song lyrics scribbled in the empty spaces and the occasional sunset photo message of somewhere I don't recognize from a number that is never the same.

This day, once per year, we have an entire afternoon to talk about what the last year brought and the excitement of what is coming up.

"Excuse me, ma'am?" a woman with a thick Brooklyn accent says to my right. "The truck is all set for whenever you'd like."

I smile at her. "Thank you. And the other guest?" I ask.

She clears her throat. "She told me to fuck off," she says as her cheeks tint pinker than they already had been from the cold. "But I think she made her way inside."

The truth is that, for the hot cocoa this establishment serves, while it is more than just hot water and chocolate powder, the mixologist and confectioner hadn't needed a truck as big as the one that is parked there. It was Lincoln's gift to me, to us really, the first time we came here. The one-way mirror that took up the entire side of the truck, facing the Christmas Tree, looked like a pretty mural of cocoa, cookies, hot toddies, and bourbon, of course. But inside it is a cozy little space with plenty of snacks, blankets, and an oversized swing that looks just like the one on our porch back in Kentucky. I expect to see that when I open the door and sneak inside. What I wasn't expecting was my sister sitting there with a swollen belly and her feet kicked up.

"Holy shit, Maggie—"

She smiles and holds out her arms. "I know, I put on some weight."

My eyes water, "You know I'm going to say it, right?"

She wipes the tear that escapes the corner of her eye and she squeezes her arms around me. "That I'm glowing and you've never seen a more beautiful pregnant woman?"

I bark out a laugh before I tell her, "I miss you."

Her eyes water and blur her vision. "Are we done with the sappy stuff now? We only have—" she pulls out a flip phone. "Six hours and a year's worth of catching up to do."

Less than twenty-four hours in Manhattan and even less time with Maggie, but my heart feels full. I miss her and Mom terribly, but my life is in Fiasco. I know they're safe. For now. And that's the best that I can ask for. I could have stayed in Montana. I could have trained horses with Mom or traveled with Maggie, but I have my own family now. One that I missed very much. I glance at my phone, noting the time as I walk into his office. Ace wants to have a chat ASAP. And in Foxx time, that meant he wanted me here yesterday. I wasn't a big fan of jumping whenever the oldest Foxx brother demanded, but I knew he wouldn't be asking if it wasn't urgent.

I watch as Ace pours two fingers of bourbon into my glass. Normally I'd balk at bourbon neat, but he threw a large ice cube in it and poured Foxx & Peach.

"The mirroring software you put on my phone," Ace says as he sits back in his chair, his fingers intertwined in front of him.

Shit.

"There's a lot you don't know about me, Faye. But one thing I am not is careless. I knew you had done it, but I had nothing to hide from you regarding Blackstone. So I let it play out."

I scrunch my eyes closed before I say, "So you're telling me you're not angry then?"

When I open my eyes, his stoic gaze is studying me. Ace can really play up the intimidation card when he wants. "I want you to get it onto Hadley's phone for me. I don't need you to monitor it. I'll handle that part."

I can't help the knowing smile that takes over my face. I knew something was up with the two of them.

"It's not like that," he says, cutting off the thousands of questions that I'm sure are running in a ticker tape across my face.

I widen my eyes and bite back my smirk. " I didn't say anything," I say, leaning back in the leather chair.

"She's a pain in the ass, but somehow we got stuck with her as a part of this family." He lets out a sigh before continuing in his gruff tone. "And someone, or maybe many someones, want to see her hurt. Or worse."

That had my attention. Hadley had become one of my closest friends next to Laney. The three of us had grown close since I'd moved back to Fiasco. And while she's had a rough year, I hadn't thought it crossed over into dangerous territory.

"There isn't anyone I can trust to look into this for me, Faye."

"You can trust me, you know that. Linc and I have boundaries when it comes to my clients and cases. He won't be privy to any information you don't want him to have." I wait a beat before I say the caveat to that. "Unless it affects him in some way. Or our girls. They'll always be my priority."

He smiles. "Understood," he says.

I give him a nod. "Then I'll make it happen."

He opens his mouth readying to say what I'm already expecting.

I cut him off and hold up my hand. "I'll be discreet about this. You have my word."

He leans forward, grabs the rocks glass from his desk, and takes a sip of his bourbon.

I do the same. I hadn't expected Ace to ask a favor, but I'll always help out anyone in the Foxx family—my family.

My phone buzzes in my back pocket. When I pull it out, I can't keep the smile from cracking and spreading.

FOXX:
> For your eyes only, Peach. A little something to wet your panties...

"My brother?" Ace asks with a smirk.

I smile back and pocket the phone. "Am I that obvious?"

Ace moves to stand from behind his desk. I had noticed the split knuckles when I walked in, but until now, I hadn't seen the way he was favoring his side. My brother-in-law is nothing if not mysterious. He is the only one in this crew that I had more questions than answers about. And this request for my help just added about a dozen more.

I note the way he favors his knee also when he cuts in. "Don't ask," he says as he limps to the office door.

"I won't." I stop in the doorway before I ask, "You'll tell me if she needs help, right? If Hadley needs help of any kind, you won't hesitate to ask me." I said it as a statement. There were more people now that I needed to make sure would be okay. Hadley fell into that group.

He gives me a nod before he says, "I will." He clears his throat as I move my way out of the room. "You just missed Griz," he calls out behind me.

"Book club?" I ask with a smile as I look over my shoulder.

Following me he says, "Probably, but you never know with him."

"You don't need to walk me out," I say glancing back and down at his knee. "I know my way. Give Griz my love. I'll see you on Friday for dinner."

I make my way down the hall, through the main foyer across the Foxx logo that's prominently painted on the hardwood floor. When I get into my car, I open the video message from my husband. It looks like his phone is propped up. The image opens at waist height with his new tasting room in the background. The renovations of the farmhouse hadn't stopped at a pretty new ensuite bathroom or suped-up barn for our animals. Nope, my husband wanted a private tasting room, just off of his office.

When I click play, a zoomed-in image of Lincoln's worn-in wranglers takes over the screen until he steps back a couple of feet, just enough to keep from his neck down to his upper thighs on screen. He unbuttons his black shirt and then shrugs it off. Something jazzy plays out in the background that I can't make out, but it's likely one of my mixes from my burlesque routines. He's been a big fan of those. The sound of his belt buckle clangs as he unbuckles it and then his fingers undo the top button before he slides the zipper down. He takes a step back and leans forward putting his face on screen.

"Get your ass home right now, Peach. Both the girls were dropped off at their sleepovers. I'm already hard thinking about what I want to eat."

Before I throw the car in reverse, I type out my obvious response.

FAYE:
Show me.

I can hear the phone buzz as a message pops up on my car's display screen. I shift in my seat, already anticipating the video message that's waiting for me. It takes barely any time to get home. That's the beauty of living in a small town where family lives not too far from each other. I snatch my phone and move out of the car. I swipe the screen open as I move up the porch stairs. The video continues with Lincoln moving his hand into his pants, pulling out one of my favorite things.

"Whatcha watching, Peach?"

I let out a gasping yelp and slap a hand over my chest.

"Fuck, you scared me," I laugh out. But the laughter dies on my lips as I walk closer and finally focus on the fact that my beautiful husband is sitting on the porch swing, ass-naked, working his hand up and down his hard dick. "Are you warming yourself up for me?" I ask as I lick my lips.

I drop my bag and then shrug off my coat. The screened-in porch had been a part of our upgrades, which included air vents to keep us warm in the winters and cooler in the summers.

"I'm always warmed up for you," he says with a smirk. "I was getting impatient."

"Busy day?" I ask as I unzip my left boot and then my right.

"Laney booked us out for New Year's Eve so yeah, it was busy. I hear you're the entertainment. Something about an oversized martini glass and balloons?"

I smile thinking about how over-the-top it's going to be. "Wait until you see the costume I have for it," I say as I lift the hem of my sweater up and over my head leaving me in my baby blue satin bra.

Lincoln growls out and tugs harder.

"Do you like?" I ask as I untie the drawstring of my flowy pants.

"Show me the rest," he demands. The cadence of his voice has a shiver working its way across my skin. His eyes move up from my body to meet mine. He licks his lips, wrist rocking up and down. "Tell me you want me, Peach."

"How about I show you, instead?" I say as I shimmy out of my pants and walk over to him, placing one knee on the outside of his thighs. I don't sit or grind against him just yet, his hand still pumping languidly along the length of his dick. His eyes are hooded as he looks down my body. I move my panties aside and swipe along my slit gathering exactly what he wants. I run my finger along his bottom lip and then glide it into my mouth. The salt and heat bursts along my tongue as I lean in and kiss his lips. His tongue meets mine as a moan escapes from his throat, urging me to take more. He wraps his free arm around my back, guiding me forward and onto his lap. I lean away enough to break our kiss and tell him exactly what he wants to hear, "I want my husband so badly. Please," I reach between us and swipe my thumb along the crown of his leaking cock. Then I lick my thumb.

"Fucking hell," he mumbles out.

I raise myself up just enough so he can line himself up. I sink onto him—both of us moaning as if we've forgotten how good that feels every fucking time.

"Fuck, I missed you," he says as I roll my hips forward. He knows to tip back just enough so that when I do it again, my clit will rub against him just right.

I smile as I run my thumb along his lower lip, the same way he does to me. "Foxx?"

"Yeah, Peach?" he says as he kisses my thumb.

I lean in, nip at his lip and say, "Then be a good husband and fuck me like you missed me."

He growls out, wraps his hands under my thighs, and stands, moving us towards the house. "There's my bossy wife." My back hits the wood from the front door and he angles his body just right. "Hold on, baby," he says as I wrap my arms around his neck. "Give me that pretty mouth," he demands as he pulls out. And just as my lips meet his, he pushes back into me, stretching me exactly how I've asked for it. I let out a sigh thinking how good he feels. His arms, anchored around me. I let myself enjoy every inch of him—his body against mine. Damn, it feels good to be a Foxx.

CAN'T GET ENOUGH OF
THE FOXX BROTHERS?
TURN THE PAGE FOR A SNEAK PEAK
OF THE NEXT INSTALLMENT IN
THE BOURBON BOYS SERIES

Chapter 1

Ace

THE SCREEN DOOR SLAMS SHUT behind me as I drag my fingers through my hair slicked in sweat and river water. Unbuttoning my shirt, I toss it into the trash. I can burn it later. The caked dirt and blood along the collar and cuffs are hard to see on a black shirt, but they won't go unnoticed at the dry cleaners. I wear a suit to the distillery every day, but killing someone is few and far between. If it had been planned, I would have changed and called in the necessary support. I don't fucking like surprises.

All I have going in my favor is that it's the Fourth of July, and in Fiasco, that's the perfect time for someone to disappear. Everyone is in town celebrating and enjoying the distractions of dancing and fireworks. I prefer to avoid both. And truthfully, tonight, that worked out for the best.

I pull on a pair of Wranglers I typically wear to the stables and tuck my wallet in my back pocket. Not wanting to go upstairs, I dig out a pair of socks from the dryer. My black undershirt is still damp, but I need to get out of here. Right now, I want to disappear for a while, take one of the horses out for a long ride, and clear my head.

"Where are you goin'?" Griz asks when I turn the corner into the kitchen.

Swallowing down my frustration, I pour a heavy-handed splash of bourbon into the first glass I see sitting on the counter, ignoring the question that I don't have an answer to.

"Things get out of hand?" he presses as he gives me a once-over. I'm good at masking emotions, but I just put a man down, and I'm still pissed about it.

I drain what's left in my glass. "Why aren't you in town?" As I pull on my boots, I add under my breath, "Usually can't drag you off that stage."

"Atticus," he says in a more biting tone, eyeing the way I'm trying to get the hell out of here. "Not gonna ask for the details…"

He never does. My grandfather knows there are things that need to be handled sometimes, and asking questions only makes those things linger when they'd be better off forgotten.

When I still don't respond, then push out of the screen door, his voice carries through it. "Find something that'll ground you, Atticus. If it's those horses or a woman, I don't care. But the only way I'll stop hovering is if you can figure out a way to balance all of this without letting it consume you. You'll only be able to do it if you have something more—something to care about."

I love him, but sometimes I could do without him telling me what's best. I've taken on enough of the family legacy. I like the ease of being on my own, caring for the family I already have, and getting lost in the details of making good bourbon. He just needs to let me do life my own way.

Picking up my pace, I move past the garage and toward the stables. I grab a saddle, pads, bit, bridle, and reins to suit up my fastest horse. An old black stallion that's pretty as hell, but he's an asshole of a horse when he's not running, and he's always trying to bite me. I don't care. He's fast. And that's all I want. To feel the wind on my face and my heart pounding so loud the beat drowns out everything else.

The sticky air hits my skin, and I tilt my head up toward the purple-tinted sky—a storm's coming. When the road bends and forks, I slow down and realize something's off. It should smell like damp earth and the sugared air that Fiasco inherits from our distillery, but instead, exhaust and burning rubber have my instincts flaring. *Fuck this day.* Every part of me urges me to ignore it and keep riding. There are no headlights in sight, but as I move to the left of the fork, I hear music. An angry anthem jacked up loudly but muffled through speakers. Pulling on the reins to bring my stallion to a stop, I squint to make sure I'm seeing what I think I am. The outline of a classic muscle car. It's too dark to be sure, but I have a gut feeling that it's a 1969 Ford Mustang. And it's idling too close to the riverbank for my liking. There shouldn't be any cars this far out, not to mention perched along a muddy edge on the side of the river that's running angrier from the heavy rainfall this summer.

Nearly blinding me, headlights flip on, the music cresting louder and clearer as the driver's door swings open. A riff of an electric guitar and aggressive bass has my horse stepping back, just as AC/DC screams out about being back in black.

What the hell is she doing out here?

I try to see if there's someone in the passenger seat. Maybe she was fucking around with someone. It isn't uncommon for people to park on the trails. But the dim interior light only proves that there isn't anyone else in the car.

"What are you doing out here?" I shout over the music, trying to keep the horse at a distance, but despite pulling the reins, he moves us closer.

She mumbles something to herself and looks up at the night sky. "Playing with myself," she yells back sarcastically. And then follows it with a raspy and unconvincing, "I'm fine."

I know she isn't fine. She wouldn't have said that if she truly was.

My horse skirts to the side of the car to be out of the glare of the headlights, allowing me to see her better. It's dark outside, but the reflection of the dashboard light catches her just right. I give her a once-over. She isn't drunk; she's smarter than that to drive out here wasted. That isn't it. But the way her dark, wild curls are messier than usual, how her tank top hangs too loose around the neckline, and smears of blood color her eyebrow and collarbone have me down and off the horse before I even notice her feet. No shoes.

It's like an alarm has been set off.

Bloodshot eyes find mine as I rush toward her. She holds her hands up, warding me back from touching her or coming any closer. My gut sinks at thinking about what the fuck happened. Who would have done something to make her hands shake and voice sound like she's been screaming.

"Where are they?" The words come out gruffer than I want, but it's taking a helluva lot of willpower to tamp down my rage.

Her blue eyes snap to mine, knowing what I'm asking. *You're not dealing with this on your own.* I've witnessed Hadley Finch in a lot of moods over the years—pissed off, playful, prim and proper—but not shaken or on edge like this. This is panic and anger, and those two things never go well together.

It's clear someone was pawing at her and got rough. As much as I've found her annoyingly optimistic, gradually appealing in the past handful of years, and slightly unhinged beneath her surface, she's as close to family as one can get without having our last name. Hurting her will never be acceptable or even remotely tolerated. This isn't going to end well for anyone involved.

Blinking back tears, she lifts her chin. "I took care of it. Knocked him out with a cinderblock." *Good girl.* Her face breaks for just a moment, squinting to cry, but she composes herself almost as fast. "I don't know… He may be more than knocked out."

I stay quiet, studying how she's working really fucking hard to keep it together. When she finally meets my eyes, I tilt my head to the side and say, "Don't make me ask again, Hadley. Tell me where."

She exhales, swallowing roughly. "The stables. At my father's stables."

A part of me wants to hold her and tell her I'll fix this, but it's clear she doesn't want a hand anywhere near her. *Fuck.* "Do you need to see a doctor?" I bite out.

Tears finally fall as her eyebrows knit together, but she shakes her head. "Didn't get that far," she mumbles.

I can feel my adrenaline spiking as I watch her let out another trembling breath. This will *not* happen again. Clenching my fist, I twitch my jaw at the thought of her being hurt in a place where she should be safe. Without another word, I'm striding back to my horse and turning us back the way we came.

"Where are you going? Ace, I don't need you—"

"Don't finish that sentence, Hadley. You go to the main house, and you stay there, shower, do what you need to do. But do not come looking for me. I'll come find you."

She slams her foot against the side of her car. "I've had enough of men telling me what to do tonight!" she seethes through gritted teeth. Eyes watering and fists clenched, she shoots daggers my way.

I've always told myself that I tolerate her in my life because she loves my brother the same way I do—without an ulterior motive. Just because. I've never needed to ask Griz what he thought of her; he considered her one of us the first time she smiled as she destroyed him in a chess game. It's a long list of moments that would be categorized as mundane and unimportant, but they mean something to my family—to me. Hurting her isn't going to go unpunished.

"Then I'm asking," I say back in a calmer tone. I mount my horse and wait for her to acknowledge what I've asked.

She's so goddamn stubborn that she stares at me, battling with herself. Her chin wobbles and watery eyes start spilling again, but she doesn't say anything. On an exhale, she simply nods.

I ride fast, head down, and pray that nobody sees me. I don't slow until I reach the stables at Finch Stables, passing her father's estate on the way. I ignore the logic that keeps ringing through me to stay out of it. To call my brother Grant instead and have him come out with a patrol car. But I'm not going to be satisfied until my knuckles are bloody from giving someone a reason to never touch her again. It's a part of me that's been cracking for a long time: morals that linger on the edge of acceptable, sanity that's been waning—hell, even a twinge of sadism teetering along my skin. I'm expecting to find a douchebag knocked out or, at the worst, nursing a bruised ego and maybe a broken dick, but instead, I find a man smiling with a handkerchief pressed against his lip.

"Who the fuck are you?" he asks with a careless glance.

Shit. This isn't just any fucking guy who works for Wheeler. The youngest Switcher brother is a real son of a bitch. Coming from one of the largest cattle ranch families in the west, that tends to have money and pull, means this isn't going to be a simple fix. This can't be the last place he's been before he goes missing. Rumor is, his father's on death's doorstep. Switcher's set up to take over the business, and if I had to guess, that's what led him to Fiasco in the first place. A calculating Wheeler Finch. A man who makes deals with shitty people as long as it pads pockets or gains him some kind of clout.

I move my right hand to my belt buckle. I'm not going to bust open my hand on this one. My knuckles are already bruised from earlier. Glancing around him, I can't see a holster of any kind, so he's not carrying, but I wouldn't put it past him if he has some kind of weapon nearby. He's a cattle rancher, and they're rarely unarmed.

He takes me in, smirking as he stands. "You're Ace Foxx."

"And you're in some trouble," I toss back.

"How's that?" His eyes narrow as he sizes me up.

"You put your hands on someone who doesn't belong to you," I say, walking closer as my blood heats. I wrap my belt around my fist and, without stopping, throw two quick jabs to his nose before he even knows what's coming. The second one cracks and busts open the bridge on contact.

One hand flies to the streaming blood, and the other moves to his back, pulling out a small pocket knife. *Pathetic.* "You're misinformed. She very much belongs to me—just made a nice little deal for her."

Her fucking father. I knock his wrist with my fist, and the knife goes flying. As I rush forward this time, my forearm meets the front of his neck just as his back hits the wooden pillar in the center of the space. "We don't put our hands on women here unless they ask."

His voice comes out strained as he seethes, "This ain't your business."

The fuck it isn't. Any other night and this might be different, but my nerves are already shot. And seeing her like that… I swallow the smart choices and good sense and instead give in to the anger that's climbing. As I throw my weight against him, he yells out the second the metal pierces his skin. The nails that had been protruding from the center wood beam are there to hang reins and rope, but right now, they dig into this piece of shit. They hold him up perfectly, like a partner in a fight, and I rear back for a left hook to make sure he feels it. Three more, and the weight of his body is too much for the rusted nails nestled deep into his skin. His body hits the cement and hay with a nauseating thud. Blood slowly pools around the crown of his head like he hit something hard and sharp the moment he hit the floor. *That was too easy.* I would have preferred a little more of a fight with this fucker.

Chest heaving, I focus on the blood and hair caked along the protruding nails. My throat burns as I try to calm myself.

I pull out my phone and fire off a text like I've done countless times before when I need an assist.

ACE:
Need to schedule a cleaning.

The bubbles beneath the text pulse immediately.

THE JEWELER:
A specific piece?

I drop a pin with my location.

> **ACE:**
> Full set. Brand new.

THE JEWELER:
Timeline?

> **ACE:**
> By sunrise. Between us only.
> I'll owe you a favor.

THE JEWELER:
My favorite form of payment.

It's just past midnight, but my colleague will work fast. I know the travel distance and exactly what needs to be done to erase this.

I don't check for a pulse. If he isn't dead yet, he will be shortly. There's too much blood for it to coagulate and clot. One of those nails nicked an artery, pulsing red out in time with his heartbeat that looks like it's already slowing.

Fuck him for dying so quickly.

I send another text to make sure all loose ends will be tied up if worse comes to worst with witnesses.

> **ACE:**
> I'm going to need a list of everyone
> who was at this house tonight.

I pin the address to the Finch estate.

THE ARCHITECT:
Easy enough. Any trash to sort?

ACE:
Already handled.

As I glance at his slumped-over body, the silver glint of an obnoxious, oversized belt buckle catches my eye. I bend down, flip it open, and take it off him in one quick pull. He doesn't look like any kind of bull or bronc rider. His lanky body barely looks like he's worked a day at the ranch, never mind riding pissed-off animals for a living.

I step outside, needing to breathe and think through the kind of repercussions this might bring my way. The ripple effect of someone's life coming to an end. Someone who has people who'll look for him. It isn't regret I'm feeling, but rather the weight of inconvenience. I have people for this. But tonight turned into a clusterfuck I wasn't prepared for.

Small flashes of lightning illuminate my surroundings, but not a single light shines anywhere amongst the property. The trainers, farrier, and whoever else Finch employs are in their housing on the far side of the property, likely sleeping or still out for the night. I'm pissed that not a soul was here to help Hadley when she needed it. Lincoln mentioned she had her father's obligatory Independence Day dinner party, and yet nobody's here.

Just as I pocket my phone, I take a step out onto the dirt road and glance down the main drag, catching on the lights still on at Finch's estate. I shouldn't provoke this situation, but there's a part of me that knows, even with Switcher dead, this won't be the end of Wheeler Finch pimping his daughter out to the highest bidder. The thought of her being used as a bargaining piece makes my stomach sour.

Bourbon is in my blood—how to make it, age it, sell it, drink it. A Foxx knows bourbon better than anything else. An art form and business that began in backyards and basements. It survived being outlawed, oversold, and under delivered. The point is, it survived. It came back stronger. Better. For just about anyone, it should have been enough. Luck and hard work aren't the forces that allow our brand to succeed. It's that we're willing to color outside of the lines that built its longevity. There's more to being a Foxx that lingers under the surface. Gray lines and moral compasses that never really pointed due north. Hadley lives among the gray as Wheeler Finch's daughter. The most important difference is that my family doesn't use each other. We support, fight for, and protect each other. No matter the cost. Hadley's been treated as if she's an expendable commodity. And that makes me want to hurt someone.

The businessman persona is levelheaded and strategic. But I have a wicked temper if provoked. And I am fucking provoked.

I turn over the silver buckle in my hands as my cleaner pulls up and gives me a nod. He takes in the situation in front of him and starts to process what will wipe this clean.

"Ace, does that need to disappear?" he asks, looking at what I'm holding.

I give my friend a tight-lipped smile. "Probably." But I'm walking away before I can think any better of it. I ignore the last bit of cleanup that needs to happen in order to erase James Switcher's existence from ever being in this stable.

"You look like you're about to make a bad choice, Foxx," Julian calls out.

I ignore him. He knows me as well as, if not better than,

my brothers sometimes. My brother Lincoln had an inkling, but not the level at which I'm willing to cross lines. And right now, I'm fueled by more than anger or even adrenaline—it's the need to protect someone who means something to my family. To me. Too many people would ignore this and chalk it up to it somehow being Hadley's fault—saying the wrong thing, wearing the wrong thing, being in the wrong place at the wrong time. No fucking way is this going to be a preamble to what lies ahead for her. It'll be easier to plant this mess on Hadley's father, to create a situation that looks like he killed a man in cold blood, but even more than that, I want his daughter out of his business dealings.

Reading Group Guide

1. Several new characters enter the Bourbon Boys universe in this book—some allies, some threats. Which of these newcomers did you trust most? Least? How did they change your understanding of the Foxx family dynamic?
2. Secrets—both those kept and those revealed—drive much of the tension in the book. How do the characters navigate the balance between honesty and self-protection? Which secret had the greatest emotional impact on you as a reader?
3. After the events of Bourbon & Lies, Laney and Grant appear stronger than ever—but what new challenges test their bond in this story? How has their relationship evolved since we last saw them?
4. The Foxx family's legacy continues to shape every character's choices. How do notions of reputation, family loyalty, and redemption manifest in this installment? Do you think the "Foxx curse" still lingers?
5. Wilder again grounds her story in the bourbon country of Kentucky. In what ways does the setting influence the novel's tone and atmosphere? How

does the landscape reflect the characters' internal conflicts?

6. Bourbon-making once again serves as both backdrop and metaphor. What parallels do you see between the craft of bourbon and the process of healing or rebuilding a life? How does Wilder use sensory detail—taste, scent, texture—to deepen emotional resonance?

7. Both Faye and Lincoln confront the lingering ghosts of their pasts. How do they process grief differently? In what ways do their coping mechanisms complement or clash with one another?

8. Throughout the book, several characters make sacrifices in the name of protecting others. Do you agree with their choices? Were there moments when protection crossed the line into control?

9. The balance between love and fear—trust and suspicion—plays out across many relationships. How does Wilder sustain romantic tension amid danger and betrayal? Were you ever uncertain whether love would win out?

10. Gossip, forgiveness, and reputation remain central in the small-town setting. How do the people of Foxx Hollow embody or resist these forces?

11. Which secondary character do you think deserves their own story next?

12. Faye continues her journey toward self-definition. Do you think she has fully reconciled her past with her present self by the novel's end? What does "freedom" look like for her now?

13. Aside from bourbon, what recurring images or

motifs stood out to you (fire, water, music, etc.)? How do these symbols reinforce the novel's major emotional themes?

14. How does the dual-POV storytelling affect your reading experience? Does it change your sympathies or understanding of each character to experience the story through their eyes?
15. By the conclusion, nearly every major secret has surfaced. How does the truth change the characters—and do you think they're better for it?
16. Wilder leaves some threads open for future stories. What do you predict—or hope—comes next for the Foxx family?

Acknowledgments

There are so many pieces of this story that I loved writing, but one of my favorites was the sister relationships between Faye and Maggie as well as Lark and Lily. I have two sisters who turned out to be pretty amazing women. Brianna and Blair, thank you for growing with me well beyond our childhood. You're both the best kind of inspiration.

Blair, I can't help it. I have to say it. With a hand enthusiastically raised, "We stole a car!" Thank you for letting my chaotic ideas run wild and helping me rein them in with snorting laughs and exaggerated hand gestures.

To my editor, Mackenzie, this book would not be what it is if it wasn't for you. You are an incredible editor and a brilliant friend. Your insight, creative thoughts, and the way you push me are things that I will NEVER take for granted. I am forever grateful to have you in my corner.

To the incredible artist who brought Lincoln and Faye to life for me: The covers you've created for me are beautiful and captivating. Loni, your talent is inspiring. You're an amazing colleague and friend. I said it with *Bourbon & Lies*, but I'll say it again, you are the creative soul that I didn't know I needed to find. Thank you for saying yes. I can't wait for what we're going to create next!

To Amy, my PA, beta reader, proofreader, and the most incredible support person: Thank you for being a part of this story with me. Your insight and feedback truly impacted how these characters were brought to life between the pages. Thank you for always seeing the small things that pack the biggest punches. I'm so lucky to have you in my corner.

To my Wilder beta team: You are so important to me, and I cannot thank you enough.

Jill, thank you for always pouring a couple fingers of bourbon before reading these stories. I am so happy to work with you. Thank you for making sure I'm being mindful in descriptions and calling out the necessary triggers. But also for the way you went feral over Lincoln and his dirty mouth!

Kate, thank you for diving in and reading this story. You bring such a great perspective and your feedback is absolutely invaluable to me.

Sierra, it looks like you're stuck with me now! Thank you for all of your feedback and for helping me see the quotes and hooks throughout the story that I hadn't even realized were there!

Kelsey, thank you for reading and asking the right questions. I'm thrilled to have met you and to have you on my team.

To my sprinting crew: Ashley James, Jenn McMahon, and Julia Connors. Thank you ladies for being such an incredible support crew and cheer squad. I am so grateful to have you in my universe. SHANIA & good luck!

Esmé, thank you for answering all of my questions and sharing your insight as well as your stunning talent in dancing burlesque.

To my ARC Team: GIRLS, you are THE most amazing people. Thank you for reading and taking the time to not just hype this story, but to add your creativity to all of your social posts. I will never forget that it is all of you who help my stories find new readers. Thank you for loving these bourbon boys! I love you all so much.

To my mom who is enjoying retirement by reading even more books than usual: I know you will devour this book in one sitting. And thank you to my dad who will only crack it for the dedication and acknowledgments (keep it that way, Charlie). Thank you both for being my biggest fans and the kind of cheerleaders every kid, no matter how old they are, deserves.

To Mr. Wilder: There are always bits of you in every story. You are the best thing.

About the Author

Forever a hopeful romantic, author Victoria Wilder writes contemporary romance with deliciously witty and wild characters. Her stories range from small-town to romantic suspense with swoon-worthy men and fierce women who aren't afraid to ask for what they want.

She's an East Coast girl living in southern Connecticut with her husband, two kids, and Yorkie, Linus. She's always chasing the next season and believes in romanticizing whatever you can along the way. You'll always find her either reading, writing, or ready to dish about movies and books.

> instagram.com/authorvictoriawilder
> tiktok.com/@authorvictoriawilder
> facebook.com/victoriawilderauthor
> bookbub.com/authors/victoria-wilder
> threads.net/@authorvictoriawilder